# BRUCE BLAND

# Phobos VII

While you live, while it is in your power,
be good.

MARCUS AURELIUS

# Contents

# Prologue

The monk found the boy perched on the spire of the garden's dead fountain, gazing upon the smoldering city. That strange, blue mask clung to the boy's face. It's single, painted eye was oddly pristine under the light of the moon, contrasted to the opening that revealed the boy's own tired eye.

The monk made no effort to hide his approach. The boy caught sight of him. With a grace proving his background as a performer, the boy descended from his perch, tumbling cleanly through the air and teleporting to the ground with his queer magic.

The boy's short stay in the city had not been kind to him. The monk could see the wounds peak through the boy's bandages, could hear the pain in every rasped breath. It was a wonder he had survived so long.

"Hm," The boy grunted, "it seems you managed to survive."

"Indeed, I am known to do such. Your own survival is more noteworthy. I would never have been so bold as to challenge the Dominus."

To the monk's knowledge, the boy might have been the only one with both the audacity to attempt and the capacity to survive such a direct confrontation. It had generally been more prudent to challenge the Dominus in other fields.

"I'm surprised you know about that."

"I try to keep abreast of important matters, regardless of circumstances. Especially when said matters led to circumstances like this."

The state of the city was obvious enough to not require direct address.

"This was not my fault," The masked boy hissed.

"No, it was not. Far too many hands were at play in this tragedy for any one individual to claim responsibility. But your actions did contribute. Regardless of anything else, the Dominus was a stabilizing influence for the city."

The boy bristled. "The Dominus was a monster."

"Physically? Perhaps. Living on a dead world is not good for the body. I would expect, if you too live for a few centuries, your own arcanum would mutate in a similar manner." In better circumstances, the monk would have loved to study the boy, to better understand the degradation these natural arcanum users experienced without the protection of a living world. It was a fascinating topic, lacking in surviving subjects. Sadly the matter could not be prioritized "Morally? I've had a great many disagreements with the Dominus in my tenure, but it is not my place to make judgments. I simply work with what I have towards what I view as best."

"And how is that working out for you?" the boy scoffed. "The city dead and its remnants fighting over the scraps?"

It was an adorably short-sighted sentiment. But the monk would not admonish the boy for such a shallow assessment. Governance of the city was a matter of palliative care, not treatment. Degradation was to be expected. "The situation is far from optimal, I would agree, but I do not consider this a failure case. Some level of suffering was, perhaps, inevitable. It is a simple matter of energy: life is not sustainable in a dead world. We can only scavenge for as long as we can. And perhaps, as a result of this cataclysm, we may yet be able to scavenge for much longer. A stronger and better society with less risk of starvation is still a possibility, I would say."

"Didn't you object to the Senate's planned slaughter? Or was that just an act?"

"I did not fundamentally object to the culling of the population if it would properly address the problem. But the senators were more concerned with maintaining their wealth than with effective policy. It would not have been my preferred solution, but I can see the reason for it."

"Maybe you are also a monster. Maybe I should kill you too."

A part of the monk's mind stirred, considering how he might combat the boy should the matter become necessary. The boy's feats were well known from his time in the arena, and it made for an amusing thought exercise. But it was a fruitless diversion; the boy would not strike him. "Perhaps. Though I don't believe it would be of any aid to anyone. If you wish to slay monsters, one of the late Lord Macro's chimeras has taken residence in the former southern slums. The residents that remain would be grateful for its removal."

The boy did not rush to volunteer. The monk did not expect him to. Instead, the boy sat down one of the garden's crumbling, marble benches. The monk took his seat across from him.

He waited for the boy to gather his thoughts.

"What was your preferred solution?" The boy asked. "What did you want to happen?"

"'Want' is a strange term," the monk mused. "Every possible policy was a matter of mitigating fundamental facts. Food production is unsustainable. The cyclical nature of the famines makes matters worse. That human sacrifice can be employed to draw out the process leads to perverse incentives. The whole situation is undesirable." It was a captivating puzzle, one he had dedicated most of his life to considering. Given such limitations, how could one structure a functioning society? How long could one push back the inevitable tide? What feats were achievable in these limitations? What outcomes were impossible?

He continued. "Lady Hirtius had a novel goal of incentivized sterilization and suicide. In the ideal case, it could have allowed for a slow, gentle euthanasia of the city. Of the options, I found this the most agreeable." He adopted a small, wry grin. "It is amusing that such a simple solution had not occurred to me, but Lady Hirtius was an exemplar in many ways, may she rest in peace."

The boy closed his eyes and exhaled. "If that's what you wanted, why did you support Libertas? Or was somebody else Enjolras's mysterious contact?"

The monk smiled. He enjoyed this, seeing the realization in another's eyes as they solved their own puzzles. The boy was refreshingly more curious than the Dominus had been. "Did you just figure that out now?" The boy seemed annoyed in spite of the confirmation. Even so, the monk would continue to reward the boy for his curiosity."As I said, it is a matter of mitigation. There were a number of outcomes I would have found acceptable, and I worked towards all of them. Lady Hirtius's plan was just one of them. A more impartial decimation of the city was another. Allowing a revolutionary group to seize control of the government was a third. In the initial days of a new government, it would have been simple enough to ensure that enough enemies of the new state died to stave off the current famine, and the resulting government could be better placed to deal with the next." His lips turned to a frown. "I must admit I am disappointed Enjolras was unsuccessful in seizing power. I had thought him more competent than this." It was, perhaps, the most aggravating part of this whole affair. By all accounts, this transition should not have been so turbulent, with Enjolras and Libertas so well placed. The devastation was within acceptable parameters, yes, but it was also beyond the expectations of his models.

The boy gave a sardonic laugh. "If that was your plan, it never would have worked. Libertas is the perfect revolution. It can never die, never be quashed, never end. No different from the magic tools you described to me. And what is a victory but another type of ending?"

The monk blinked. "A soul-crafted movement? Fascinating. I did not think such a thing was possible. But it would explain a great deal." He bowed his head. This realization, if nothing else, proved the entire conversation worthwhile. He would have to conduct his own experiments to validate the hypothesis, of course, but the implications were fascinating. What would it mean for the city government if an antagonistic element could never be eliminated, nor ever succeed? What would happen to a 'perfect revolution' when all of its members inevitably starved to death in the generations to come? He would need to speak with his counterpart on this matter. "I must thank you, Stas. Your insight will save me a lot of wasted effort in the challenges ahead."

"Challenges ahead?" the boy scoffed. "The city is dead. The Gate is destroyed. People are killing each other over the last stockpiles. There is nothing to do but die."

"Quite a morbid assessment, but I disagree. With the reduced population from this ... civil war, shall we call it, the restraining factor on food is no longer production, but distribution." The puzzle was still at hand. There were more knots to untangle, different levers to manipulate. "The labor force remaining is large enough to grow and process a new batch of crops, if the blood of the deceased can be harvested in time. If one of the current factions emerges victorious and properly puts the city to work, I imagine society will resume in as little as a year. A reborn city to last another few centuries, lacking the flaws of the old." Perhaps he would not be forced to interact with so obstinate and banal a Senate. It would be a refreshing change of pace.

"No wonder they call you mad." The boy huffed. "In this fantasy of yours, do you imagine yourself ruling this decrepit husk?"

Direct rule? How deplorable a concept. It was far more interesting to handle matters without such a crutch. "Traditionally, that honor would go to the one who defeated the prior ruler."

"What?" The boy seemed to be as inimical to the idea as he himself was. "No. Absolutely not. I refuse."

He made a show of sighing. "A pity. A strong, unifying individual with a semblance of legitimacy would have made this upcoming matter much simpler. And since Libertas is not an option as you have explained, I must select the best among the former senatorial factions to lead. Far from ideal ... Are you sure I cannot convince you otherwise?"

The boy glared with his one visible eye.

"Well, I have no desire to force you. Perhaps it is for the best. I suspect the Dominus is not as lost as you might hope. Should they return in the coming years or decades, discovering someone else has taken their title would certainly enrage them."

The boy shook his head. "No. Impossible. Those reflections ... they're not a good place, not something anyone can survive."

"Hm. The Dominus has survived many lethal afflictions over the years. But I will accept your expertise on this matter," he said. The Dominus was a master of survival, beyond anything else. But the monk revised his estimates accordingly. Perhaps it would take them thirty years to return instead of three. "If you will not accede to becoming the new ruler, I would request something else of you, if you would allow it."

The boy said nothing.

He continued. "Even in a situation as chaotic as this, rumors manage to flow. It is a human point of excellence, the seeking of information. When one asks what happened to the Dominus, many names surface: the Man in the Blue Mask. The Devil Himself. Libertas Incarnate. The Champion of the People. Some even acknowledge Stas the Gladiator." He watched in amusement as the boy seemed to flinch from the name. "Though it is a less known and less popular explanation, for obvious reasons. That you have been absent this past month only exacerbates the rumors. People do love a good mystery."

"Get to the point," the boy, Stas, said.

"The uncertainty is useful for me in crafting the narrative that would be most beneficial to the city. As you are not interested in stepping into the title, I would ask that you instead step away from it entirely: disappear from the story so that it may best be molded unhindered."

The monk let the implication hang. He was curious as to how Stas would react.

"No," the boy said after too long a pause. "I will not die for your convenience."

"I would not ask you to," the monk said. "Rather, I would ask you to leave this world."

"The Gate is destroyed."

"Indeed, for good and ill. But it is not the only method of travel. The Dominus came before it existed. A select few have been pulled before, when it was important to escape notice. Returning you to the world of your birth is possible, with aid from the other side. I am willing to arrange it for you, should you accept." His counterpart would be more than willing to see the boy safely returned to the world of his birth. His counterpart had been greatly amused by the Dominus's misfortune, and would be willing to reward that, if nothing else.

Stas seemed to be hesitant, so the monk continued. "You should know that your birth world is much bigger than the tiny corner the Dominus commanded. Many would happily welcome you with open arms, knowing what you have done. Alternatively, my previous offer is still open. If you wish to join me in making the best of this dying world, I would be more than happy to have you." The monk could use the boy just as well as any on the other world. He would not lack for patronage, if he did not desire to be a free agent.

The monk watched Stas come to a decision. The choice was entirely in the boy's hands.

"Send me away, then. There is nothing for me in this miserable world."

# One

*Eighteen months before*

The view from Stas's box seat was astounding. The whole of the amphitheater lay before him, a marvel of architecture that left the simple dwellings of his former home in shame. It was a sculpture of marble and gold, a work of art for all who made use of it. Even the sands of the arena seemed to shimmer with gold.

Stas had been informed that nearly one hundred thousand people could cram into the gilded stands of this, the largest of the city's four stadiums. And, from the sheer mass of people currently occupying them, he had no trouble believing it.

"The arena is always the most crowded for the Kalends fights," Alain explained from the seat beside him. The broad-shouldered man fit in his seat easily, despite his size. "The first of the month is when the most anticipated matches are scheduled. Everyone who cares to attend tries to make it on the first."

"And that's nothing compared to the spectacle at New Year," Geoffrey, on Stas's other side, continued. "It's said that the competition for each New Year's ticket is fiercer than the match itself. But we don't have to worry about that." He chuckled, hair fluttering. The man had opted to let his braid down for this excursion.

Stas laughed lightly at the easy joke. "Ah, yes. These seats are

1

excellent." And they were – box seats, the likes of which were generally reserved for nobility. Far from the crowds that crammed together, he and his fellows were afforded a level of anonymity. With cushions over the otherwise harsh stone seating and space galore, they stood far beyond those afforded to the general public.

"Ah, but the seats hardly compare to the sands below," Geoffrey retorted with a grin. "It is too bad Ludo did not schedule me for today. Sitting on my ass is enjoyable, but I would rather allow you all to bask in my glory."

"Who is competing today? Anyone from our school?" Stas asked.

"No, sadly." Alain shook his head. "Ludo is a newer lanista, in the scope of things. He does not have the sway for festivities such as this."

"It will not be so long yet, my friend," Zola proclaimed from Alain's other side. The woman was hard to see behind the much larger man. "We are hardly sitting on our laurels. Soon enough the people will be demanding our presence."

"Quite," Alain said. "As for today's matches, the lots were drawn before the intermission. There are three matches of note: Radek Twinblade against Daxton of the Sand, Esmae of Rubies against Lafayette the Hunter, and Lance Victorious against Ostynn the Unconquered. They will be interspersed by a chimera hunt and a show of acrobatics."

"And then the closing ceremonies at the end," Geoffrey said. "I'll probably be heading back during the acrobatics. With how stuffy it's been here, I'll want some time in the baths before the day ends."

"Not much point in staying for the closing ceremonies," Zola agreed. "But I do want to see all three matches."

"Of course. There's little better preparation than seeing our competition in action," Geoffrey replied. "Which is why I'm staying as late as Lafayette's match. He's got a similar style to mine."

"The first fight interests me more," Alain said. "Stas, you are a provincial, correct? Did you know Radek before you both came to the city?"

Stas shook his head. "No. The country is spread out. Lots of towns, villages, farmsteads. We don't all know one another. I knew a couple of people named Radek, but neither had left for the city before me."

"Right, you aren't from the city," Zola said. "You traveled through the Gate, then? How was it? I have always been curious."

Stas thought back to the experience of a week ago. Truth be told, it had been a miserable journey. He had felt his stomach churn from the trip; the sights and sensations were unpleasant, to say the least. And the accommodations of the grain cart that served as his transportation were not very comfortable.

"It was unique," he said. "But the view on the other side was far more interesting to me. The forum was a marvel to behold." The marble streets and gilded market stalls had left quite an impression on him, as had the throngs of people with their colored fabrics and their shining adornments. He had spent far too long gawking at the teeming crowd—the rich, beautiful people shining happily, escorted by those strange, stone-faced automata that manned their stalls, minded their children, carried their bags.

And above it all were the omnipresent eyes of the city: the bird-masked watchers. They oversaw the whole of the forum and its Gate from their numerous watchposts, never letting a single person slip their notice.

Zola nodded. "Indeed, I remember the first time I ever got to visit the forum. I wanted nothing more than to come back again and again. And now look at me! I can visit whenever I want!"

"It is a bit less interesting when one lacks for money, but I understand your point," Alain said. "I believe intermission is due to end soon."

From the looks of things, the arena staff had finished setting out a fresh layer of sand and removing the props from the previous act. The band had returned to their pit and were readying their instruments.

Zola nodded, leaning out of the box's window. "I believe I see the Dominus back in their box now. That is a good sign they are about to restart as any."

"Hah, you think this is a good seat, Stas, just imagine sitting with the Dominus," Geoffrey declared. "I heard the air is kept cool and the noise from the crowd is muted, but you can hear everything on the sands just fine. And there is no better view in any arena than from there. I dream of being invited, one day."

"Who would not?" Zola agreed. "I believe the honor belongs to Horatio Undaunted today, but I am not certain."

"Yes, the Undaunted has been favored lately," Geoffrey said. "I imagine Horatio will be unseated when I ruin his record."

"You would have to be able to beat Alain first, my friend," Zola told him. "And there are many more steps one must embark upon before fighting the champion."

"Don't drag me into things, Zola," Alain mumbled. "Now shush. I believe the match is starting."

Indeed, from the orchestral pit a sharp clang arose as the arena band announced the continuation of festivities. Stas watched eagerly as two men emerged from the far entrance, holding a gold engraved litter. And, standing upon that litter, arms raised to accept the roaring cheers of the stadium, was a man in splendid attire, draped silks concealing fine armor with cuts designed to flatter the figure. His helmet did little to conceal his handsome face, but managed to guard more than not. Dozens of intricate glass bottles filled his bandoleer. A small, circular shield, and a long, sinuous whip were strapped to his back.

The announcer was shouting an introduction, but Stas could not hear it over the roar of the crowds.

"That's Daxton," Alain explained as the man leaped from his raised platform to the sand below, basking in the cheers of the crowd. "A crowd favorite. Well, everyone fighting today is a crowd favorite, so that doesn't say much."

The music of the band shifted in tone, slowing and steadying at another arrival.

"Radek," Alain said as the muscular bare-chested man made himself known. The bulking provincial looked even larger than Alain. He had two swords strapped upon his back and lacked even the understated armor of his opponent, only possessing a pair of arm guards. He wore a simple red sash for a belt and had a single ruby earring. A number of glass vials were attached to his sash, though far fewer in number than on Daxton.

The cheers he received more than rivaled those of his opponent.

"He's quite bold, isn't he?" Stas's eyes locked onto the unprotected muscles of the gladiator's back.

"Indeed. Radek has made a point to avoid wearing armor or helmets throughout his career. I don't know if it's the most intelligent move, but it has endeared him to certain demographics."

"It's annoying, that's what it is." Geoffrey snorted. "Armor can be uncomfortable and doesn't always work with what you want to do, but now if you take it off, people just assume you are copying Radek Twinblade. Feh."

"I assume you are rooting for Daxton, then?" Zola said.

"Well, I know you like Radek—at least one of us has to. What about you, Stas? Rooting for your fellow provincial?"

"I just want to see an interesting fight," he replied neutrally.

"Hah. Well, these're some of the best, so it's sure to be that if nothing else."

Both competitors walked forward to the center of the sandy arena. As one, they turned to face the Dominus's box, and the music came to a quiet halt. Both fighters bowed to the lord of the city.

They then turned to face each other. Daxton retrieved his whip and Radek unsheathed his two blades.

And, at the signal of the announcer, they both moved. The music resumed.

Daxton's whip cracked forth, snaking across the distance in an instant. Radek wasted no time in dodging the wild swing.

"Bit of an obvious opening," Stas said.

"That's Daxton." Alain shrugged. "He always begins the same. He'd be more surprised than anyone else if it connected, but it serves its purpose."

Indeed, taking advantage of the space gained from the opening, Daxton reached for a glass vial on his bandoleer and quickly gulped down the contents in a highly practiced motion.

He then chucked the finished vial at Radek, who caught the projectile between his two blades.

The sand around Daxton's feet whirled and the crowd's cheers grew.

Alain gestured vaguely. "Hence the 'of the Sands', if you hadn't caught on."

"I gathered," Stas said dryly.

The sand rose into a tornado, a spinning wall of desert all around Daxton. Stas could barely make out the man's figure through it all.

Radek launched the vial back in retaliation, chucking with far greater force than Daxton had managed. But the moment it reached the barrier, it shattered under the force of the sand.

"Bad luck for Radek, eh?" Geoffrey said. "Didn't get a hit in on Daxton before he got his magic going. And see how many elixirs Daxton brought? I bet Radek is going to run out of steam long before Daxton. If it were Lafayette out there, we'd actually have a fight to watch."

"Don't underestimate Radek," Zola declared. "He'll not need to endure. He'll simply win outright."

In the ground below, the sand beneath Radek's feet was rumbling. The muscular swordsman leaped to the side in time to avoid a grasping maw of sand that threatened to devour him.

Even as he moved, a solid clump of sand the size of his head was ready to meet him. Radek twisted around it, avoiding the projectile by the thinnest of margins.

The crowd roared.

"So, confident, are you? Well, we'll just have to see."

Stas let the bickering fade, opting to drink in the fight. He pictured himself as Radek, and wondered how he would handle Daxton.

Maddeningly, there did not seem to be much in his arsenal. Not with the defense and the constant supply of sand available to Daxton. But that was the point of learning and training.

Radek remained unperturbed, even as he twisted out of the way of further projectiles. He kept light on his feet to avoid the occasional rumbles of the sand below him. The music matched his movements: frantic yet steady; urgent yet purposeful. The swordsman occasionally swung at the projectiles or blocked them with his vambrace.

Stas tried to imagine what the gladiator was seeing, what he was thinking, as he dodged around with no progress made. The dodging was spectacular, to be sure, a display of masterful awareness and acrobatics, but it was hardly any good for reversing the pressure. A man's stamina, unlike the sand of an arena, was not limitless.

In a particularly showy move, Radek tossed one of his swords into the air as he dodged another maw from below. The sword spun freely in the air to the awe of the crowd.

In that same motion, Radek grabbed one of his own glass vials and consumed the elixir within. He caught the spinning blade upon its descent, earning further cheers. Zola's shouts nearly deafened Stas.

Color drained from the swordsman's skin, leaving a metallic sheen in its place. And, with a dash, he made a beeline for his opponent, the musicians marking it with a climactic beat.

Radek batted his now empty vial at the whirlwind. This one failed to shatter, only cracking against the force of the sand. Following the glass, Radek charged through, twin swords readied.

The wall of sand fell to the ground, revealing Daxton in the midst of reaching for another elixir. He had been knocked to the arena floor by Radek's charge and had a pair of swords against his neck.

The crowd exploded at the sight.

"Damn it, Daxton!" Geoffrey cursed. "Why'd you have to be so frugal? Don't you dare get smug about this, Zola! This was Daxton's match to lose and he went and lost it. If he'd just drunk more elixir …"

Zola smirked. "Victory is victory, no matter the reason. But I don't know why you care so greatly. To my knowledge, you are not a fan of either of them."

"It's easy to get invested in this sort of thing," Geoffrey mumbled.

"Honestly, Geoffrey," Alain said. "I think you are still underestimating Rodek too much. Even through all that, he didn't even use his sword."

"His sword?" Stas asked. The man had used both of his blades to defend against the sand onslaught, so he imagined he meant something special.

Zola answered in Alain's stead. "One of Radek's swords is supposed to be magical. His … left one, I believe."

Stas scrutinized the two blades in the provincial's hands, trying to discern their supposed magic. From the distance it was hard to make anything out. "What does it do?"

Alain shrugged. "It can cut through anything, I think. Not sure what else a magic sword would be good for."

"And what would that be good for against sand?" Geoffrey scoffed. "'Oh, I can cut each grain in half with a swing.' All you'd do is double the amount of it."

"Would it be doubling if each grain is half the size?" Alain said.

The box, and the crowd at large, hushed as the two fighters, swords still in threatening position, turned once more to the Dominus's box. The music mellowed to silence.

Two feather-clad officials, one in pure white, the other in pitch black, slowly trotted forward to the center of the arena. Both wore intricate beaked masks, faces fully obscured.

"I have heard it can cut the air over a distance." Zola spoke softly. "But he never uses it like that unless he has to, for fear of hitting the crowd."

"That's just a rumor," Geoffrey said. "If I had a sword that could do that, I'd just learn to aim the damn thing."

"How would one even get a magic sword?" Stas wondered aloud. The thought of a marvelous weapon like that appealed to him greatly.

Alain shrugged. "I don't know. Have a fan that is insanely rich and get them to gift one to you? That's probably how Radek got one."

"One would need fans before they can be milked for riches, my friend." Zola smirked and then quietened down, along with the rest of the box.

Stas refrained from voicing his response.

The officials reached the field's center and completed their short examination. The white one then raised a hand, signaling Daxton's health.

The officials and Radek turned towards the Dominus's box.

A large cloaked figure made a gesture that Stas could not see. Radek nodded and his swords fell to the sand.

Radek helped Daxton to his feet and both gladiators turned to face the cheering crowds. The music played a jaunty tune, matching the grins on both gladiators' faces.

"That'll be me, someday soon," Geoffrey proclaimed.

Stas was of a similar mind.

# Two

"Seems we're facing each other in three days," Geoffrey said suddenly.

"Hm?" Stas set down his weights to acknowledge the other gymnasium occupant.

"Ludo managed to schedule us a match this Friday. In the Lunar Arena," Geoffrey explained. "That's the third largest one, furthest from the forum."

"I see." Stas had managed to tour two of the arenas in his short time in the city, each a grand construction. To say one was only the third largest was hardly a complaint. "Is there anything special about the Lunar Arena?"

"No. Not particularly. The field's the same, but there's less seating. It can be flooded when they need to host naval battles. But that hardly matters to us. Unless you plan on sailing at me?" He spoke with mock seriousness.

Stas chuckled. "I had not planned on such, no."

"Hah. Honestly, I'm surprised Ludo managed to find something at such short notice. These things tend to take longer. The New Year's game is scheduled half a year in advance. So, if you're going to win fame and acclaim, it would be best to do so before midsummer, otherwise you have to wait even longer." Geoffrey gave him an easy grin.

"I'll keep that in mind." Stas returned it.

11

"Make sure you do. This is prime advice from your doting senior, after all."

"Indeed, so senior you must be retiring any minute now."

"Ach!" Geoffrey slapped his heart in fake dismay. "If my joints didn't ache so much, I'd bend you over the knee and teach you a lesson for your cheek, young man." He shook his head. "In all seriousness, Ludo probably managed to snag the slot because it coincides with a big race. I'd not expect much of an audience, sadly."

"Because they will all be at the tracks?" Stas frowned. "Why would anyone want to watch some charioteers when they could watch the arena?"

Geoffrey shrugged. "You'll find no disagreement from me. There's a reason I chose to be a gladiator, not a racer. And it is not just because the perfume of horse shit does not agree with my pallet."

Stas chuckled lightly.

"So, I haven't managed to catch you training in the training yard yet. What can you do?"

Stas quirked a brow. "Hm? Worried already? Have more confidence in yourself. I'm sure, as my senior, you won't have too much of a problem acquitting yourself."

"Haha. Very funny. But seriously, what is your style? How do you fight? This is important information."

"I am sure it is," Stas said. "Which is why I will save it for the arena. Don't worry, Geoffrey. I have as little an idea of your style as you do of mine, so neither of us has an advantage in this."

"Stas," Geoffrey said slowly, as if speaking to a child. "If we do not know each other's style, we will be unable to prepare."

"Exactly. It will be a truly natural fight. It's an opportunity we'll never have again. So let's keep this one a surprise." There was skill in preparing for one's opponent. But there was a visceral joy in fighting blind, too.

12

Geoffrey inhaled deeply. "Stas, if we are not prepared, we will not be able to play off one another well. It would be far too easy to trip up, make a mistake before the crowd. Surely you understand this?"

"Play off one another?"

"For the crowd, Stas. For the audience. They come to see a show. We go to be remembered. It's in everyone's interest for the match to be as spectacular as possible. As glorious as possible."

Stas frowned as he considered the logic.

"The best shows require preparation. We both want to come out of this looking good, and that isn't something you can ensure happens blind. Is there a gimmick you wanted to try out? I could help you come up with one. Always good to establish your first real fans early."

"You are making this sound like a dance recital," Stas said, eyes narrowing.

"Hah. I'd love to take the chance to stage the whole thing out, but I don't think either of us are good actors. No, we just need to establish the general highs and lows, the rhythms. Something with a good pace before I end it."

"Excuse me?" Stas stilled completely. "I thought I heard something very arrogant coming from your mouth, but I may have been mistaken. Care to repeat yourself?"

"It's the obvious outcome." Geoffrey shrugged. "Upsets have their time and place, but this isn't one of them."

"You want me to throw the match!"

"Can you just think for a second, Stas? I've been establishing myself for over a year now, climbing my way up. This is literally your first match. If I lose? To a provincial? On his first match? My career is in the toilet." Geoffrey spat. "It's the only sane outcome."

"And it just so happens that you benefit from it."

"This is about what's best for both of us," Geoffrey growled. "The goal is for both of us come out of this looking good. And that can't happen for me if I lose." He took a deep breath. "Look, if this bothers you so much, then once you've established yourself, we'll have another match and I'll lose, all right? Tit for tat. Does that work for you?"

"I don't want you to throw a match for me. I don't need it," Stas responded coldly.

Any calm Geoffrey had projected was lost in that instant. "You're insane! I'm trying my best to be helpful here and you just throw it back in my face. I didn't even need to offer! Either we work on this together so both of us win, or I crush you into the dirt on my own. Understand, you piece of shit?"

Stas spat in his face. "See you in the arena." And he marched out of the gymnasium, leaving Geoffrey sputtering.

Furious, he marched directly to Ludo's office, stomping past servants and fellow students with no care for their presence.

Once there, he rapped on the door with two slamming knocks.

"What? What?" a startled voice squawked from within. "You don't have to knock so loud. I'm in and can hear you just fine."

Stas opened the door, stepping inside the office. Ludo was sitting at his desk, looking over papers. "Lanista, I need to report an altercation with a fellow student."

"I didn't say you could come in …" Ludo muttered under his breath. He shook his head and set his papers aside. "An altercation, you said. Is anyone injured?"

"No. I removed myself before I was too tempted."

"Thank the Dominus for that at least. What is it then? What happened?"

"Geoffrey came to speak with me about our upcoming match. He wished to stage it in advance."

Ludo raised an eyebrow. "And?"

Stas bristled. "He wants to make a mockery of the arena!"

Ludo took a deep breath. "Stas. People come to the arena to see a show. The job of a gladiator is to provide the show. If two gladiators decide they can put on a better show by coordinating, that is between them."

"I refuse to throw a fight just to make for a better 'show,'" Stas growled. "Sir," he added after a moment.

Ludo held up a hand in a placating gesture. "And nobody is forcing you to. If you want to fight for real, then fight. Geoffrey can hardly stage the fight on his own."

"He shouldn't have tried to do it."

Ludo's voice turned stern. "Geoffrey is well within his rights to make an offer, just as you are within your rights to refuse it. I understand you have a high opinion of the sanctity of the arena, and in an ideal world, everyone might agree with you. But this is not that world, and you have to acknowledge that not everyone sees it the same way."

"It's disgusting."

"It is what it is. You can't change that. You can only control your own fights." Ludo sighed. "If I were in your place, I would consider taking Geoffrey up on the offer. Even the friendliest fight can result in injury. A staged fight minimizes the risk, and you aren't always going to have the opportunity."

"I am not afraid of injury."

Ludo waved his hands. "Yes, yes. I know. You wouldn't be a gladiator if you were. As I said, it is entirely your choice. That said ..." His voice turned stern once again. "Your conflict with Geoffrey. You will limit it to the arena. You will not fight with him before your match, and, once your match is over, you will consider the matter settled. Geoffrey is your colleague, and you will treat each other as such. Am I understood?"

Forcing a retort down his throat, Stas nodded. "Understood, sir."

"Good." Ludo nodded to himself. "Now get back to training, or whatever you were doing before. I have work to get back to. And next time, wait for me to give you permission to enter."

"Yes, sir." He trudged out of the office.

# Three

The cells below the Lunar Arena lacked the opulence Stas had come to appreciate. Where the arena above invoked awe and beauty, the hidden staging ground was built with simple utility in mind.

A great part of this underground space was devoted to the operation of the stadium: storage for various prop pieces, mechanisms to raise and lower beast cages, pipes to flood the stands. Between the currently empty chimera cells and the relatively full ones for human prisoners, almost half of the working space was devoted to confinement. Gladiators like himself had to contend with simple benches and tiny lockers. The many bird-masked prison guards did not look any more comfortable.

Supposedly, the Grand Arena had dedicated gladiator suites, but Stas was not in a position to enjoy that privilege. His lot was to wait impatiently on a hard stone bench with seven other competitors while the first set of executions were carried out. He kept his back to Geoffrey lest he be tempted.

An arena worker marched into the room and gestured for them to come. Stas dutifully secured his scabbard, strapped his shield to his arm, and donned his helmet. Around him, his fellow gladiators followed suit.

Stas shielded himself from the brightness of the sun as he emerged from the arena's entrance. Once his eyes had adjusted from the abrupt shift, he took his first view of the scene. The stands all around him seemed to stretch on and on and on, mountains of elegantly constructed stone scraping against the sky.

They were also depressingly empty. By a quick estimate, there were only a few thousand people spread across the multitude of seats. He could only blame that damnable chariot race.

The audience was somewhat of a blur at this distance. To his dismay, he saw a few of them leaving. Leaving! The gall of it struck him. What sort of degenerates would come for the executions and leave before the main events?

Stas forced himself to calm down. There was no reason to care about those measly few. Thousands of people were here ready to see his rise to glory. They only looked so sparse because the arena was so massive. Objectively, it was a great crowd.

After the workers finished dragging away the corpses, the two feathered officials stepped forth. Stas listened as the announcer, a fair-voiced youth, declared them, one name at a time. Each gladiator marched forth into the sun when called.

Stas reveled in the cheers that came with his own name. He knew, intellectually, that nobody here actually knew of him. He was simply an unknown fighter. They had no reason to laud him, no reason to know why he deserved their admiration. But he allowed himself to imagine that they did, that a great number of people watching craved for his victory, and his victory alone.

It was a pleasing sound.

After the last name had been announced, the eight of them reached for the box of lots the white-feathered official held out.

On his turn, Stas allowed the official to guide his hand onto the proper marble and, like everyone before him, held it aloft for the crowd to see. Or pretend to see. He doubted anyone in the audience could make out the small marble at the distance.

Once the process had completed, the announcer declared the matches. He was to be in the final bout. Stas felt irritation at the delay as he walked back to the cells below with the five others not immediately competing.

The bout in the sun had been far too short. Back in the dreary cells, Stas sat on an uncomfortable bench. He closed his eyes and meditated.

The first match ended with little fanfare. Any reactions from the crowd were muted in the underground cells. The two competitors re-entered the staging area in good health and two more went to the arena above.

The second match took longer, far longer. The second pair of gladiators came down, battered and exhausted.

There was a break after that match for another round of executions. The prisoners around Stas cried in fear and sorrow as they were led to their punishment by the bird-masked watchers. Stas could not blot out the weeping; there was no getting back to his meditation.

After far too long a time, an arena worker came down to fetch the third pair.

The third match took nearly as long as the second. Stas felt his irritation growing with each passing minute. Then finally, finally, they returned, one far worse for wear than the other.

"Geoffrey, Stas," one of the arena workers called. "You're up. Don't dawdle. We're running far behind schedule."

"And whose fault is that?" Stas spat, his voice dry. "I didn't make the schedule too tight."

The worker adopted an unamused expression. "Right ... just get up there and try not to take too long."

For a moment, Stas considered drawing the match long out of spite. Calm, he reminded himself. Calm.

There was no personalized music upon his entrance, nor any spectacle as he had seen before. Instead he and Geoffrey walked side by side to the center of the arena, accompanied by a standard procession tune. They both turned towards the aedile's box.

The old man acting as the patron for this minor event was certainly not the Dominus. Stas imagined that the lack of pomp reflected the man's lack of actual rank. Even so, he bowed as was the custom, and received the old man's raspy greetings with full respect, as did Geoffrey beside him.

Then they took their paces and faced one another.

Stas observed his opponent with a keen eye. Geoffrey had equipped himself with two throwing spears, both strapped across his back, along with a sword matching his own. He did not have a shield, instead opting for heavy arm braces. His legs were armored more heavily than his torso, which Stas believed prioritized ease of movement over full protection.

Geoffrey had a single elixir vial on his bandoleer. Stas himself went without.

Geoffrey looked calm, composed. He was at ease with the crowd and the hot sun.

Stas grit his teeth at the sight. A coward who feared an honest fight should not pretend to be so carefree.

Fast, he decided. He would crush the arrogant jerk immediately.

Stas unsheathed his sword, keeping his grip loose but firm. Geoffrey went for one of his spears.

Stas suppressed a smirk. Between the sword, the elixir, and the throwing spear, Geoffrey had chosen the easiest one to deal with.

The aedile gave his signal, the music resumed, and the match began.

Geoffrey pulled his arm back, in perfect form to throw.

Stas *reflected*.

In an instant, Stas was behind his opponent, leg sweeping out, while his free hand held the man's shoulder tight.

Caught completely off guard, Geoffrey could not brace himself and was easily tripped to the ground. The spear clattered out of his hand.

With his opponent stunned flat on his back, Stas held his foot upon Geoffrey's throat.

He slid his sword back into its sheath, closed his eyes and waited. The whole endeavor had taken less than a second.

It took a few moments for the crowd to process the fight. The audience quieted quickly at the scene. The band, barely a measure in, halted. The feather-clad officials hesitated.

Geoffrey might have said something, but Stas kept the pressure on his throat to prevent him from doing anything.

The officials seemed to come to a consensus and moved to make their judgment. Stas shifted his foot to allow them to do their examination.

They quickly noted Geoffrey's breathing, and the white-feathered official gave his signal.

The crowd, back in familiar territory, cheered.

The aedile, in turn, signaled mercy for the defeated, as expected.

Confirming the match's end, Stas removed the pressure from Geoffrey's neck and raised his arms for the cheering crowd. Geoffrey stumbled up behind him slowly.

In the corner, he could see a worker gesturing wildly, pointing at the stairs. Stas scowled. Not even a minute and they were already starting the next series of executions. Was he not allowed the time to bask? It rankled at him.

Spitefully, he pretended to not see the worker for a few more seconds, letting his victory wash over him. Only then did he "notice" the worker and move for the exit.

On the steps leading back down, he was forced to the side by the number of prisoners and guards waiting in the wings.

At the bottom, he found the worker from before. "Was that fast enough for you?" he questioned with a glare.

The worker averted his gaze.

Stas, with no reason to remain, headed back to his school.

# Four

"What in the Dominus's name were you trying to accomplish?" Ludo snarled the moment Stas arrived in his office.

"I won my match."

"Won your match? Won your match? You didn't just win a match, you debased your opponent, humiliated him! You went out of your way to make him look like a fool."

Stas held firmly. "I only acted to ensure I would win."

"Do you think I am blind, you vainglorious child? An idiot? You forced Geoffrey to the ground, you stepped on his neck, you sheathed your sword before the fight was called! You even drank an elixir before the start!"

"I didn't drink—" Stas began to defend himself, but Ludo interrupted.

"You went out of your way to disrespect your opponent. You risked his life with that hold! What if you had broken his neck? There are proper, safe ways to end fights, and I know you know them!"

Stas held his tongue.

"Any one of those things I might forgive. Ending a fight quickly? Fine. Wasting a trump card on a petty match? Horrendously shortsighted, but fine. Using a nonstandard hold? I'd send you to remedial lessons, but forgivable. No, what appalls me is your blatant disrespect for your fellow gladiator, your intentional, selfish maleficence. You wanted to crush Geoffrey, your coworker, for what? A miserable match for only a few thousand people? What in the Dominus's name made you think that was a good idea?"

"I—"

"No. Not to me. I don't want to hear that idiocy. If you wish to remain in my school, you will apologize to Geoffrey. I don't care if he wants you to grovel at his feet. You will do it, and you will not complain."

"But …"

Ludo glared. "This little feud ends today. It will not escalate any further. Do you understand?"

Stas swallowed his complaints. Ludo held all the power here. If he were to be dismissed from his school, Stas would be left adrift. He lacked the fame to dictate terms. "I understand, sir."

Ludo nodded, closing his eyes. "Good. Remember, Stas. Magnanimity is one of a gladiator's core virtues. It is not enough to be the better fighter. You must also be the better person."

"Yes, sir."

Ludo sighed, body relaxing. "You are young. You feel victory is all that matters. But in time you will realize that methods matter more than the results. I acquired you because I believed you had the nature to succeed as a gladiator. I expect you will take the steps to prove me correct. Now, go. You have an apology to make. Shoo."

Stas exited the office, walking past the servant who attended Ludo. It irked him to know that somebody else had heard his chastisement. At least none of his fellows had been present for the private scolding.

Stas knew he should just get the apology out of the way immediately. When it failed to have any results, he would have a defense against Ludo's ire.

But he dallied, opting to instead head for the gymnasium to work off some frustration. Ludo had commanded him to apologize today, but he never required that it be done immediately.

After a long enough period that Stas was forced to acknowledge that today might be ending in short order, he approached a servant about Geoffrey's whereabouts.

"In the baths," was the reply, "entertaining guests."

Stas thanked her curtly and made his way to the baths.

He found Geoffrey lounging in the atrium of the baths, accompanied by two women he did not recognize. Geoffrey seemed to be regaling them with some story or another as they picked at a selection of fruit. A half-empty bottle of wine sat in the fruit basket, and each of them held a goblet at varying states of fullness. An empty bottle lay on the floor.

The injustice of the scene grated fiercely. Why did Geoffrey, the loser, get to bask in simple luxury, while he, who had won handily, had been scolded and forced to grovel?

Where was the fairness in that?

Mindful of Ludo's potential wrath, Stas forced the thoughts from his mind and cleared his throat awkwardly.

Geoffrey turned to face him, and, for a mere moment, his expression turned vile. In the next instant, it was replaced by a serene smile. The transition was quick enough that Stas doubted his own eyes.

"Stas, what brings you to the baths?" Geoffrey rose slightly from his couch. "Ah, I can imagine it is for the obvious reason. Allow me to introduce my lovely companions. This wondrous dark-haired beauty is Julia, and the fiery redhead is Augusta."

The fiery redhead waved shyly. Julia grinned. "Oh, so you are Stas, then? Geoffrey was just talking about your fight."

It would have been more accurate to say he had been lying about the fight because there was no way he would have told the truth. Stas bit back the urge to announce such. What did he care about how two vapid fans were misled?

25

"Yes," he said instead. "I am he. We fought earlier today."

"We're sorry we didn't have the chance to attend," Julia declared. "We've been trying hard to attend Geoffrey's matches, but this one was such short notice. Thankfully, we have an opportunity to hear about it straight from the source."

Only the task at hand prevented Stas from rolling his eyes. "Yes ... about that match, Geoffrey. I wish to ..." The words were slow to come, but Stas forced them out. "I wish to apologize for my unbecoming conduct. It was ... unprofessional of me."

The confusion on the girls' faces was proof enough that Geoffrey had been lying.

Geoffrey seemed to note it as well. "Hm? Oh, there is nothing to apologize for. It is a shame to lose my victory streak, but I will recover it soon enough. I can do nothing less for my fans." One of his arms reached around for Augusta's shoulder, and she pressed herself into it with a smile.

"To be clear, then," Stas reiterated. "You forgive me?" Ludo wanted an accepted apology, and Stas was happy to take advantage of the situation to get it.

Geoffrey waved it off with a smile. "It's all water under the bridge. Come, eat with us. Share some wine."

Julia nodded. "Yes, please join us." She fluttered her eyelashes. Stas blamed the drunkenness.

"No, thank you. I have already eaten." Stas paused. "Where did you get the wine? Ludo does not provide any alcohol."

"I bought it, of course." Geoffrey shrugged.

"With what money?" Stas demanded.

"There are many ways a resourceful gladiator can make some coin in the city. There are more fights to be had than what our master doles out."

"You freelance? Is that permitted?"

"We have our free time to use as we see fit. So long as you are in good shape for the official matches, there is no issue. If we find matches for ourselves, who can complain? In fact," Geoffrey's smile grew, "I know of one opportunity this evening, within an establishment known as the Bell, right on the street south and west of the forum. It would be easy enough to find for anyone who looked. You could easily win some spending money there."

"In the evening? Past curfew?"

Geoffrey raised a hand in a placating gesture. "I am, of course, not suggesting that anyone break curfew. That would be quite foolish." He shook his head. "But enough of that. Julia, Augusta, I believe I have had my fill of fruits. Shall we proceed to the hot bath for a little swim?"

Augusta nodded. "That sounds wonderful."

Julia grabbed Stas by the hand. "Won't you join us? I'm certain we can have a good deal of fun."

Stas blanched. "No ... I am not really up for a swim right now. Still tired from the match," he lied.

"Oh? No need for anything vigorous. We can relax in the water."

"No." Stas shook his head. He left the baths before it could get more awkward.

"Goodbye, Stas," Geoffrey called out, heading towards the changing room. "Have fun."

Stas did not acknowledge the parting call.

# Five

Stas found himself in the forum without any problem.

Late in the day, fewer shops were open. The denizens of the city seemed to love to complete all their work in the morning, should they have any, and keep the afternoon for recreation. The grand mass of people had departed, leaving a more manageable crowd, which better showcased the sublime beauty of the architecture that surrounded him: the marble of the grand buildings, the golden mosaic of the street below, the fountains that sparkled in the sun.

The Gate stood high in the center, a wondrous arch of blackened granite, covered in arcane symbols inlaid with gold. A pair of workhorses, hauling a cart full of grains, trotted slowly out of the portal. The bird-masked watchers observed from their perches, their fine garb decorating the roofs of the buildings.

Soon enough night would fall and curfew would be upon this district. Only the watchers would remain of this throng.

Stas made his way south and west, to the edge of the forum. He deftly avoided a curio store owner hawking his wares. He had no money to allow temptation.

Stas couldn't help but feel that somebody would notice him at this point. He had no real excuse to leave the forum, for all that Geoffrey might pretend otherwise. And yet, nobody seemed to care that he, among the throng of people, happened to be leaving the district.

He found the street, a simple cobblestone path away that contrasted with the mosaic he was just upon. Stas averted his gaze from the bird-masked watcher who guarded the egress. The man appraised him, searching for anything of note. But Stas had left his weapons back at the school so there wouldn't be anything to attract the guard's attention.

The guard let him pass. He walked unaccosted.

The city outside the forum was ... different. Modest houses, simple storefronts. One of the houses had a minor crack in its facade, a strange imperfection next to the pristine marketplace.

The buildings in the forum were designed to impress, art unto themselves. Here though, they were simple, efficient.

The people too lacked elegance. Sleepy-eyed individuals were slumped up against the brick exteriors, or standing, pacing, or sitting in some measure. They wore simple garb, not ostentatious displays.

People, idle, doing nothing. No urgency or purpose. Not like the forum where everyone happily moved from here and there, from store to amusement.

The path had narrowed at some point. Cobblestone gave way to gravel and dirt. Refuse lined the edges in ways that would have been unthinkable on the forum. And the people themselves were more tattered.

A raspy voice called towards Stas. "Oi." You just came from the forum, didn't you? Have any grub to spare? Any tasty treats?"

"Oh, come off it, you lazy bastard," a woman's voice responded, shoving aside the older man who had called. "You should have waited in line today like everyone else. Skipping on food just to gamble on races, honestly." She shook her head before turning to Stas. "But do you happen to have any change? A quarter would be enough—just want to get in the baths today."

Stas quickened his pace, pretending to not hear. He felt somewhat naked without his sword.

"No?" the woman called after him. "That's a no, then? Then just say no, you mute bastard." The woman scoffed but didn't pursue.

The street continued in that vein. The buildings were outright ramshackle by now. And the people, while they did not beg like the man and woman had, were certainly attired for the occupation. Some wore cleaner clothes, some had clean-shaven faces. But most of the street's occupants would look out of place in the forum.

Stas halted. To the side of the road was a child, young, perhaps nine years if not younger. His clothes were tattered and dirty as was the blanket he clung to, but his face …

Distorted, lopsided, one eye horrifically big, the other swollen shut. His skin seemed scaled in places, and near absent in others. It was hard to see from the boy's sitting posture, but it seemed that the child's arms were radically extended, as if there was a second elbow near the first. His breathing looked troubled, as if the weight of the world were pressing down on his chest.

The boy noticed Stas's gaze and, with a mute expression on his mangled face, held his hands out towards him, cupped together, palms up. On the ground next to him were some scattered coins.

Everyone else was studiously ignoring the boy, who waved his hands up and down slowly, looking directly at him.

Stas averted his gaze. "Sorry," he mumbled. "I don't have anything. Sorry."

Stas kept marching past. He avoided looking at any of the people, studiously focusing on the buildings for some sign of "The Bell."

It was not a long walk. Stas had no trouble finding the large building with a simple etching of a bell on its sign.

Outside the large wooden double doors stood a gruff man with broad shoulders and a patchy beard.

"Is this the Bell?" Stas asked.

FIVE

The doorman rolled his eyes. "Obviously." He held out his hand. "It's fight night, so entry is a half assarius. If you just want cheap swill, you'll want to go somewhere else."

"Actually, I want to compete."

"Hm?" The doorman appraised him. He seemed to come to a positive conclusion "Fine, then. Head off to the left when you enter, through the doors. Talk to Odon, he'll get you sorted out. But if I find out you're only trying to skip out on the entry fee, I'll take it out of your hide, got it?"

Stas rolled his own eyes in response. If he wanted to watch matches, he had far better opportunities than whatever this stage could provide.

The doorman opened the door and Stas walked in.

It was ... grungy was perhaps the best word for it. The place was primarily a bar, from what he could tell. Customers dotted the seats and tables consuming various beverages while two wenches skittered between them. One carried some sort of fish dish with an awful smell to a bald man. He could smell it all the way from the entrance.

He was not alone in that opinion. A dark-haired woman who had the misfortune of sitting near said customer curled her face up in disgust. She swapped seats for one further away, abandoning her drink.

The center of the building was dominated by an elevated wooden stage: simple and exposed on all sides for the audience. There were no barriers or rails on the platform, only the short fall to the floor below marked its edge. No sand coated the construction.

He could make out a bit of blood staining the wood. Sand would have prevented that.

In the back, men were smoking simple pipes. Bloodshot men loudly inhaled powders from small boxes. Two obviously drunk patrons were arguing loudly with one another.

To the right, a man behind a bar was writing up some numbers on a slate as other customers lined up in wait.

A man pushed out from behind him, and Stas realized he had been standing and watching for too long. He made his way to the unmarked door on the left.

He emerged to a room filled with a number of men waiting on benches. Some were clearly nervous. Others exuded calm. One seemed to be polishing a small blade. Another solemn-faced man was fiddling with a snuff box.

Standing off to the side, tallying something up on a piece of slate, was a man who greatly resembled the doorman outside. Odon, Stas presumed.

"Excuse me."

The man looked up and blinked. "Hm? You here to fight?"

Stas nodded. "Yes. I was told to speak with Odon."

"That's me." He shrugged. "Coming a bit late, aren't you? You're a first timer, right? Don't recognize you. But whatever. You wait in here, and I'll let you know when to go. Winner of each match gets three assarii. You want more than that, place a bet at the counter on yourself. Try to bet on your opponent, we'll toss you out. Do anything that could hit a customer, we'll toss you out. Wreck our stage, we'll toss you out. Match goes till surrender, or death, or whatever."

Stas nodded.

"Right. We have some weapons back here." He gestured to a locked chest by his feet. "You can use them if you like. But if you try to steal them—"

"You'll toss me out."

Odon gave an unamused glare. "We'll skin you alive with them first, then toss your sorry ass out." He took out a key from his pocket and removed the lock from the chest.

Stas grimaced. The contents were abysmal. Rusty blades, chipped knives. A single studded glove. One of the "weapons" was just a wooden slab with a metal spike jutting through it, something that almost certainly came from one of the chairs in the establishment.

Far from a treasure trove or an armory, this chest was more of a garbage dump. And a mostly empty one at that.

Stas selected a single dented shield from among the refuse and stepped back.

Odon quirked a brow. "You sure you don't want something sharp, too?"

Stas shook his head. The knives looked like they would fall apart in his hands. He'd be far more at risk from lockjaw than from his opponents. Better to rely on his fists.

The other men were watching as he made his selection. All but the boldest turned away when he turned his eyes towards them.

Odon shrugged and let the chest fall shut. He locked it closed, as if anyone would actually want to steal the garbage.

"Right. We're starting soon." Odon closed his eyes and swirled his fingers in the air. "Right, you ..." He pointed randomly at the man sharpening his sword. "And you." He pointed at a particularly nervous man clutching a knife. "You two are up. Go out and let the bettors see what they have to work with. You know the drill."

He opened the door, and the two designated men wandered out.

"After them will be ... you—" he pointed to Stas "—and you." He pointed at the man with the snuff box. "When they get back in, go to the bookie's table and let them see you all. When he tells you, you'll come back here to wait for your match. Or wait out there, for all I care. Third up will be ..."

Shortly afterwards, Stas stood at the bookie's table with his opponent by his side.

The man gestured for them to come over. "Name?" he inquired of Stas as he appraised him, eyes focused on his choice of weapon.

Stas considered for a moment. "Brutus." He wasn't exactly supposed to be here, after all.

"Brutus," the bookie repeated, marking it on his slate. "And you?" His attention seemed locked on the snuff box.

"Tristan." The man replied.

"Uh huh." The bookie pursed his lips and marked it down on his slate. He called out towards the crowd. "Right. Second match for the night is Brutus—" he gestured at Stas "—versus Tristan." He gestured at the other man. "Odds are evens for Brutus, and two to three for Tristan."

The crowd immediately made their own appraisals before clamoring for the table.

Stas parsed through that statement slowly. He scowled when he realized the bookkeeper seemed to think Tristan was favored.

Tristan also seemed annoyed, for a reason Stas could not determine.

"You can go now," the bookkeeper said. "Odon will let you know when you're up. Sit down, or head back and wait."

Stas did so, returning to the room with the benches. He tried to meditate, but the smell of fish made it difficult.

# Six

There was something disorienting about being on a stage. In the sands of the arena, the audience was above and a good distance away. Here the crowd was very close; the nearest seats were breaths away from the edge of the platform. The Bell felt louder, uglier, smellier. He could see the dirty faces of the people watching him.

Stas very much preferred the grander venue. But he was a professional. He wouldn't let the suboptimal conditions affect him.

He focused his attention on his opponent.

Tristan was a large man with a powerful build. He had the body of one of the farmers he had known, a man who worked hard in the fields every day. The man's eyes were sallow and tired, but his body stood firm and vigilant. He lacked any armor or shield but gripped a simple, sharp knife in his dominant hand. His snuff box bulged out of his pocket.

Stas took a moment to ensure his shield was secure. He would be relying on it against the man's knife. He took a deep breath. His opponent did the same.

The bookkeeper rang a large bell. The fight was on.

There was no music in the Bell, no band to mark the flow of the fight. The din of the drunken patrons served in their place. The torchlight was a poor substitute for the noonday sun. The wood beneath Stas's feet lacked the give of the sands. But the fight was the same.

They circled around one another, getting a feel of each other on the minuscule stage. Stas did not plan on running head first into his opponent's blade.

The audience's cheers turned to jeers, but Stas held firm. He batted his hand against his shield, demanding action.

Tristan broke first, charging forth, knife brandished. It was an attack so obvious it had to be a feint.

Stas met the knife with his shield, letting it slide off the surface. He pivoted his body to catch the follow-up attack.

It never came.

Stas narrowed his eyes as Tristan slowly edged backwards. He banged his shield again and took a step forward.

Once more, Tristan dashed forth, knife flailing. Again, the motion was easily caught and deflected. Once more, his opponent failed to follow through.

It was pitiful. Infuriating. "Take this seriously," Stas growled.

But the man refused to. He made a mocking attempt at aiming for Stas's unshielded side as if that would make a difference.

Stas knocked the knife arm out of the way and slammed his elbow against his opponent's ribs. The crowd shouted in satisfaction.

Tristan reeled back, hacking. The opening was so blatant it had to be a feint. "Stop playing around," Stas hissed. "Take me seriously."

Tristan narrowed his eyes, widened his stance. He held the knife out in a pitiful mockery of a guard.

Stas banged his shield again, but Tristan would not rise to the taunt again. So Stas acted instead. He glided across the stage, arm cocked back in a telegraphed motion.

Tristan, as expected, swung his weapon. Stas pivoted, catching the knife with his shield. He slammed his foot against the man's torso.

He tumbled towards the edge of the stage, heaving sickly.

"I told you to take me seriously! Fight me!" Stas roared.

Tristan fumbled in his pocket and retrieved the snuff box.

Stas exhaled, satisfied to be taken seriously. He didn't know what sort of weapon this was supposed to be, but he would be ready for it. If he had to defend with magic, so be it.

Stas increased the distance, keeping light on his feet. He watched Tristan open the box, revealing a dirty brown powder within. In a jittery motion, the man snorted the powder. The veins in his forehead bulged, his face flushed deep red, and blood dripped from his nostril.

The snuffbox was an elixir, then: some strange, powdered version of one. Stas grinned in anticipation.

Tristan stumbled to his feet, inhaled deeply, and exhaled a stream of fire. It was no thicker than an arm.

Stas's grin fell away.

Slow moving. Small. Pathetic. Even a fool could dodge this arcanum, but Stas didn't have to. The pitiful dented shield he wielded was enough for this worthless flame.

The fire washed around his arm. He could barely even feel the heat.

The stream ended quickly. Too quickly, as Tristan hacked out a cough. Stas waited for the real attack, the actual magic. But nothing came. Just his opponent standing there, heaving over, with his tired, mocking eyes.

Something snapped.

"Why won't you take this seriously?" Stas raged, charging forth faster than the piddling fire had managed.

Tristan didn't even pretend to block. Stas's fist crushed into the man's ribs. They cracked with a sickening squelch. He punched again, and again. The man didn't try to dodge or block. And with each punch, Stas felt his rage growing at the lack of respect.

The man fell to his knees, heaving. Blood, vomit, bile of all sorts stained the wooden stage. Sand wouldn't stain. It would have been cleaner.

Stas stood to the side, waiting for the medic to take the fool away. Tristan's body stopped quivering before he realized no one was coming.

"Hah! He fucking punched him to death!" a drunken man bellowed. "Told you you should have bet on him," he smacked his companion on the shoulder, "but you never trust my gut."

"It's not fair," another patron complained. "It's cheating! Giving the weakling a knife just so we bet on him and leaving the strong one with a shield! This shithole just wants to steal our money."

Two men came from the sides to examine the body. Heedless of the bile and blood, they hefted the body over their shoulders and dragged it down the steps. A third man came with a broom.

"Cheers to Brutus!" a patron called out. "For winning me a good bit of money!"

Stas wordlessly walked down the steps.

He did not feel guilty. There was nothing wrong with what he had done. The man had chosen to fight, same as he. Everyone knew the risks. For riches and glory, they were worth it.

He did feel … disappointed in himself. Killing by accident meant he lacked skill. It was fine to be upset at that because he could fix it. But there was nothing else to be upset about.

Nothing at all.

Odon waited by the stage. "Your winnings, Brutus."

Stas opened his palm and let Odon pour them. He counted them out. Six copper coins: simple metal discs with ornate eyes etched on their front, marked as half assarii.

Three measly assarii. Worth less than that stupid knife Tristan had wielded. Enough for a handful of treats in the forum.

Stas pocketed the pittance.

"If you want to fight again, head back to the waiting room for another round." Odon walked away without further word, leaving

Stas alone.

"Hey there, Brutus," a woman's voice called, shaking him out of his thoughts. It was the black-haired one he had seen before. "Or is it Stas?"

Stas stared at the woman. Her hair was her most prominent feature, long and well cared for. Her clothing stood out similarly; the quality was closer to that found in the forum than what people around the Bell wore. She was almost as tall as him, though far thinner. Her clothing concealed most of her figure.

Stas wondered why she hadn't stood out more before. It was obvious she differed from the other patrons.

"I saw your match in the Lunar Arena this morning. Who would have thought I'd get to see you fight twice in a single day?" She shook her head with a smile. "It's funny how things work out."

"What do you want?"

"Hm? Oh, you have me all wrong. I just want to thank you. After all, you won me quite a bit of money tonight. I don't think the bookkeeper knew you were an actual gladiator when he made his odds. So I came out ahead easily, money burning a hole in my pocket. Let me buy you a drink with some of it."

"That was hardly a fight worth a drink."

"Upset about that bit of unpleasantness at the end?"

"I am not upset," Stas growled.

The woman nodded. "Good, because you shouldn't be. Tristan back there had been racking up debt and had gotten pretty desperate. He took out another loan and bet it all on himself to try to get out from under it. Losing meant they would come to collect his corpse in repayment. You probably made it cleaner than it would have been." She shrugged. "And he wasn't going to win as much as he needed to."

Stas clenched his teeth. "I said I wasn't upset. You don't need to explain things."

She smiled. "Great. So you're good to get a drink. Not here, the swill is terrible. If there were no fights, there would be no point in coming here. But I know a good place. I'm Eponine, by the way."

"No," Stas simply stated.

"Please." She stepped in front of him and looked up into his eyes. "I insist."

The interest this girl had in him was off-putting. "Not interested." He headed for the exit, stepping around her without consideration.

Eponine huffed, but did not pester him further.

Stas had no desire to stick around. Worthless fights and pitiful rewards weren't worth his time. He would be happy to leave the dirty, raucous patrons, the smell of blood, vomit, and rotten fish.

So he headed out.

"Oy!" the doorkeeper called. "That shield isn't yours."

Stas ripped the dented piece of rubbish off his arm and tossed it at the man.

# Seven

Stas's mood did not improve as he walked back up the street. The setting sun cast a pale glow over the ugly buildings. The layabouts that had dotted the throughway were still present. Some of them seemed to be settling down for the night, outside as if they had nowhere better to be.

The insipid coins in his pocket seemed to weigh more. His fingers traced against the etched symbols upon them and the piercing eyes seemed to burn through the fabric.

He passed by the hideous beggar boy. The child had curled up in an alleyway like the other layabouts. It was as if he, too, had nowhere better to be.

Stas bit out a curse and tossed the damnable coins at the child. They clanged and clattered at the child's feet.

Stas did not wait for the child to react. He kept walking. The coins would no longer weigh him down. Their etched eyes would no longer follow him. He had no more reason to feel guilty.

The money was worthless to him. He simply wanted to get back to his bed and to sleep.

The street gradually widened, and its cobblestones became more regular and cleaner. It was easy to tell that he was nearing the forum.

A watcher guarding the forum stepped forward, arms crossed.

"The forum is closed at night," the bird-masked man stated. The masked eyes perfectly mirrored those etched on the coins.

Stas kept his breath steady. "I have business. In the forum." He didn't want to explain himself. He did not want word getting back to Ludo.

The watcher laughed. "Hah. Business? At this hour? Coming from the south?"

"Yes," Stas said simply. He stepped to move around the man, but the watcher moved to block. The elixirs on the guard's bandoleer jangled.

"Go back to your shithole, pleb. Come back in the morning like everyone else."

Stas grit his teeth and sucked in a breath. "Look. I just need …"

The guard's punch took him completely by surprise. Stas staggered back.

"I said, get out of here, you piece of shit," the watcher spat. Stas could practically see the man grinning under his mask. Mocking him.

Stas reached up for his face. It stung.

"Are you deaf and stupid? Get the fuck out of here!"

Stas smashed the watcher's face in.

The bird mask cracked, the guard's nose with it. The sound was music to his ears.

This time it was the guard who staggered.

Another jab came, but Stas was ready this time. Stas caught the brunt of the blow with his guard and followed up with a jab to the stomach. Though less powerful than his opener, it was still enough to force the watcher back.

Stas moved to capitalize, returning to proper distance. He raised his fist to strike.

A baton smashed against the back of his head and Stas stumbled in confusion.

A second watcher stood behind him, weapon raised. Stas had failed to notice. Ignoring the pain and the spinning world, he got back into a proper stance, fists raised to meet his new foe.

The second watcher lashed out with his baton, but Stas was again prepared. Light on his feet, he jumped out of the way, using the momentum to strike up at the watcher's chin. Knuckles scraped against exposed skin, brushing against the mask. Stas went to follow up but abandoned it just as quickly as the first watcher laid out another punch. Stas twisted to the side in a failed attempt to block. The blow connected with his ribs.

Rolling with the hit, Stas pivoted, taking a step back to gain some space. He placed himself so that both watchers were in view, appraising them.

The second watcher fingered his baton. The first grabbed a knife from his belt. He spat out a glob of blood. "You're going to die now, fucker."

Being outnumbered was a bad enough prospect. Being out-armed made matters dire.

Stas needed a weapon; reach was paramount. The second guard's baton was the best option, he determined.

Stas held his stance fast, making sure to keep both guards in view. He kept his back to the wall to prevent another unfortunate surprise.

The two watchers moved simultaneously. The coordination was too natural to be anything but trained.

Stas darted towards the baton-wielder, placing himself within the weapon's range and out of the knife's. Twisting, he knocked the baton's swing off course into his partner's knife strike. In the moment Stas had earned for himself, he elbowed the baton-wielder with as much force as he could muster.

Stas's target heaved over, grasping his stomach. The knife-wielder lunged forth, blade extended. Stas caught the attack with the crook of his arm and squeezed the limb in place. His other hand came down violently. Bones cracked. The knife fell to the ground.

Stas kicked the weapon as far away as he could manage. He released his injured foe just in time to evade another baton swing from his target. Stas stepped backwards to regain his distance.

The former knife-wielder scampered after his weapon rather than face him unarmed. Stas smirked. It might be for only a short moment, but he had achieved a one-on-one fight with his target.

He rolled his shoulders in a taunting motion, meeting the baton-wielder's masked gaze with his own. Then he charged.

A quick jab served as a feint, drawing the guard to lash out in a predictable manner. Stas delivered the blow and shoulder-checked his opponent. Within the baton's reach once again, the weapon no longer provided any advantage. And yet his target did not relinquish it.

Stas felt the familiar thrill of combat surge through him. The battle followed his rhythm now. Every motion followed his will. The guard's training did not hold a candle to his own, and the difference in skill showed brilliantly.

The watcher's attacks were ineffectual, his attempts to block feeble. Stas dominated the man, body and mind. Only now did he attempt to disarm his target.

His fingers clasped the solid wood and ...

The street beneath Stas's foot gave way and he stumbled, only barely managing to catch himself. On the rooftop, a third bird-masked watcher stood, an elixir vial pressed to his lips. The cobblestone rose like a stream of water, snaking around his caught leg, threatening to crush it. The knife-wielder, back and reequipped, went for a lunge at his unprotected back.

Stas *reflected*.

The knife stabbed thin air. The cobblestone caught nothing. Stas slammed his elbow into the back of the baton-wielder's head.

The man fell to the ground, his baton falling from his grip. Stas deftly caught it before it could reach the ground.

The first watcher growled, gripping his knife tight. Stas brandished his baton, smacking his other hand against it.

He made for a charge and *reflected* partway through.

The knife-wielder was canny. He immediately spun in place to face Stas's new position, knife ready and waiting for him. Stas was forced to abandon the attack to avoid being cut. The cobblestone from beneath his initial position erupted.

Stas *reflected* behind the arcanum user, his baton extended for a debilitating blow.

A lash of water intercepted him, smacking against his torso. It took all he could manage to keep a hold of his stolen weapon.

From another rooftop, a fourth watcher had emerged. The bird mask gleamed dangerously and a whip of water extended from the guard's hand.

Back at the street's entrance, he saw the knife-wielder reach for his own elixir.

Stas *reflected*.

The fight became a blur, a constant struggle of weapons, magic, and reflection. Every time one of the watchers offered an opening, one of the others would prevent him from capitalizing. Stas was forced to teleport constantly. To stay in one place would be the end of him. To arrive where he was expected would be the end of him.

His attacks were becoming less and less effective. The number of bird-masked men increased minute by minute.

A stream of fire, a proper mockery of Tristan's weak showing, blazed towards him. Stas snarled and *reflected* it, sending the full attack back at the surprised watcher who had summoned it.

The flames engulfed the man. He screamed in pain, clothes and flesh burning quickly. The water user moved to douse it, but Stas was on him quickly. The baton cracked against the man's skull, but his weapon broke along with the bone.

Stas cursed. Another watcher leaped down from the rooftop.

Exhaustion was dawning. His *reflections* were taking more and more out of him. Stas needed to gasp, but he couldn't waste the moment. The onslaught continued.

A loud bang ripped through the air. Thick black smoke enveloped the street.

Stas felt a hand grab his own and drag him towards an alley.

"Come on," a woman's voice hissed.

Stas exhaled, trusted his gut, and allowed himself to be pulled away.

Away from the smoke and the shouting guards, Stas could make out his companion. The woman from the Bell had followed him, it seemed. Eponine.

She dragged him to and fro, up and down different alleys and streets with seemingly no rhyme or reason, never slowing or looking back. After long, exhausting minutes, the shouting behind them faded into a quiet din.

Eponine stopped, gasping for breath. Stas was no better.

"Hah!" She grinned, panting. "Looks like we got, hah, away."

Stas waited for his breathing to calm and leaned against the wall for support. It took a few moments to compose himself. He sighed deeply.

Eponine directed her satisfied smirk at him. "Lucky for you I was there. Hah. Got you away clean."

"I didn't need your help. I could have run away any time." He rubbed his forehead. "They'll know who I am now. They'll know my arcanum." If only he had had a mask like all the watchers.

Eponine waved her hand dismissively. "As I said, lucky for you. I handled it." She grinned. "Arcanum. They aren't going to remember you, or me, or how you fought. None of that."

Stas blinked. "Really?"

Eponine nodded. "Yup. Don't worry. Helping other people go unnoticed is my thing."

Stas paused, looking her in the eye. "Thank you." He meant it, truly. He had thought his life was over, that he would be forced into hiding by a bastard of a guard. "I should get going." He would have to take care sneaking back to the school. But he believed it would be manageable with some well-timed *reflections*.

Eponine held up a hand. "Ah, ah, not so fast. I might have managed to muddle them about you, but I can't hide the fact that there was a fight. Not when there is actual evidence about it. The bird eyes are going to be on full alert."

Stas halted. "Of course ..."

"You aren't going to be able to sneak through the forum for a couple of hours yet, until they all calm down. So ..." Her grin turned almost predatory. "Looks like you don't have an excuse to get out of that drink, then."

# Eight

"So, I take it you're from the provinces, Stas?" Eponine inquired from behind her mug of beer.

Stas examined his own mug with suspicion. The bar she had dragged him to was far cleaner than the Bell had been. It sported a simple musician of passable skill and soft, understated decor. As near empty as it was, the bar seemed hospitable. But alcohol ruined the mind and the body, or so he had been repeatedly warned.

"Hm." He gave the beverage a quick sip and cringed at the bitter taste. It seemed there would be no risk of becoming a fat wastrel.

"I'll take that as a yes," Eponine continued. "Did you come through the Gate? Or did you take the long way around?"

Stas sighed. "I don't know anyone who takes any long way around. It was a long enough trip already."

"What was it like?"

"Unpleasant."

"Just unpleasant? I'd imagine that something as wondrous as the Gate would leave a grander impression."

Stas huffed. "It was dizzying, nauseating, like being dropped in all directions at once. My skin started crawling as soon as I went in, and it has yet to settle almost a week later. It was an absolutely miserable experience."

Eponine smirked lightly. "So it did leave an impression." She sighed.

"Even with that sterling recommendation, I still want to go. Not much chance of that, unfortunately."

Stas rolled his eyes. "There's not much to see on the other side. Just acres and acres of farmland. And between the farms there are a few miserable little villages where nothing ever happens."

"I take it you're from one of those little villages, then?"

"Hm." Stas took another sip of his beverage. It was no better the second time.

"Hm, indeed." Eponine looked over Stas's shoulder for a moment, tilting her head to the side. "I've had the pleasure to see a few of your fights so far, but I don't think I've seen you drink an elixir. I'm quite curious how you managed it."

"I didn't see you use an elixir when you stopped the guards from pursuing," Stas noted in turn.

Eponine tapped on her cheek. "I keep some elixir capsules behind my teeth. It helps if I need to make any sudden escapes or daring rescues. Or if I otherwise need to keep it hidden. But that's only good for quick and small bits of arcanum. The feats I saw you pulling off would have taken a full keg of the stuff, I'd imagine."

Stas shrugged. "It's not exactly a secret. I've just never needed elixirs for my magic. Not for as long as I can remember."

"Really? Elixirless magic? Like the Legendary Hermit?"

"Who?"

"There's some old stories about an immortal old man who lives outside the city. They say he's been around since before the city was even founded. Some say he's older than the world itself. He used to visit the city, years and years ago. He'd wander the streets and the markets without ever saying a word. But if a child asked to see a trick, he'd humor them. There's stories of him making fire dance, making sculptures of water, summoning honey from thin air as a treat ... He is said to have turned an entire house into gold to pay for a loaf of bread."

That sounded very strange to Stas's ears. He mentioned as much.

"Well, it is something of a children's fable," Eponine admitted with a shrug.

"The absurdity of such magic is unusual, but to my knowledge all of that is possible with elixirs."

"That's the thing. The tales say he visited the city to do his tricks even before elixirs were discovered. Back when nobody had magic. Nobody but the Hermit and the Dominus, at least."

"It still sounds like elixir magic to me. What I can do is ... different."

"Different?" The woman once more looked past him. "How so?"

Stas frowned. It was hard to explain the obvious. "Elixir magic is an action. Making things, changing things, moving things, destroying things ... A practitioner might move sand or harden their body or turn a house into gold. All of it is doing something, anything. My arcanum doesn't, because there's nothing to do."

"I don't believe I follow."

"It's like ..." Putting it to words was annoyingly difficult. "The world itself has a side to it that's always there, but nobody but me ever seems to notice. There's a whole part of the world that mirrors everything—that is mirrors, reflections. It's right there. In front of you. But you all are somehow ignoring it. I just can't ignore it."

From the confusion on Eponine's face, she clearly didn't understand.

Frustrated, Stas tried to continue. "Look. Everything casts a reflection, right? The reflection is there, even if you take away the mirror, because the reflection comes from the object, not the mirror."

Eponine frowned. "I don't think it works like that. A reflection is light bouncing. It's an image, not a thing."

Stas grit his teeth. "No. It's ... Look, that part doesn't matter. When a mirror is gone, the reflection is still there, because the object is still there." It was like trying to explain how water was wet. "Except, the mirror is never gone, even if you take it away, because the mirror is always there. Everywhere is a mirror, everything is a mirror. That's all there is to my magic: I can see what's there."

"And how does this enable you to teleport without elixirs?"

"There's nothing special about teleporting. It's just like sprinting or jumping. I look for a proper mirror that points to where I want to go. Meaning my reflection is already where I want to go. But my reflection is me because everything is a reflection, so I just have to take its place. If you could see it, you'd be able to do the same."

But Eponine could not see, Stas knew. It had taken him years to realize that nobody else saw the mirrors. They did not see the reflections of the world around them when they closed their eyes to sleep. They did not see the unnerving mirrors that reflected the oblique sides of the world, behind its comforting facade. They did not see the strange reflections of space twisted and bent, where the reflections of horrors slinked in the corner of his eyes.

But Stas had long since learned to ignore the unnerving mirrors. They were easy enough to avoid.

"Interesting," the woman murmured, but Stas didn't think she believed him.

"What about your arcanum?" he volleyed back.

"Oh, it's as you said. Making things, changing things, destroying things…" Eponine ran her fingers through her hair as she looked over her shoulder. "The things in question happen to be memories."

That did not sound very useful to Stas. He tried to imagine how such abilities would fare in the arena. What would she do under arrow fire or against a beast? It was not a pretty picture.

A mug slammed down on the table next to Stas, spilling some of its contents. He turned to see a large pox-scarred man behind him. He was bulky, both from fat and from the muscle beneath. His head was a patchwork of gray with a prominent bald spot in the center.

"Well, well, if it isn't little Eponine." The man swaggered, sporting an ugly grin. "What brings you to this nice place so late at night?"

Eponine huffed, looking away. "Sanson."

"It's been lonely here tonight. I think I'll sit down here with you," Sanson declared. He plopped himself down on the seat next to Stas. From his stench alone, this man could have easily been a patron of the Bell.

Eponine grimaced but did not argue.

"So," Sanson rumbled, "who's this here, then? Some boy toy of yours?" He jabbed his elbow into Stas.

Stas grit his teeth.

Eponine rolled her eyes, clearly unamused by the suggestion. "You can ask him yourself."

"Maybe I will," Sanson said proudly. "So, mister boy toy? Who are you? You some rich, hoity-toity patrician slumming it for the evening? Your teeth sure sparkle like one."

Stas exhaled sharply. "No. I am a gladiator."

"Oh?" Sanson's eyes sparkled in amusement. "A high and mighty gladiator, are you? I never would have guessed, seeing how scrawny you are. I suppose it goes to show that they're scouting for looks and not prowess." He laughed, grabbed a mug, and chugged it back. Stas's mug.

Sanson looked down at the table and his own mug on the right, blinking. "Huh. Guess that was yours, then." He shrugged. "Well, it's mine now!" He smiled widely, yellow teeth chattering, beady eyes gleaming, pockmarks shadowed in the light.

It was repulsive. Infuriating.

"Have you ever killed a man in those big fancy arenas of yours?" the disgusting man said. "Have you ever watched a man's life slip away at your hands? Can you even hear them beg for mercy with the crowd roaring behind you?" Sanson grinned cruelly, pressing himself closer to Stas's face.

Stas refused to avert his gaze before this disgusting wastrel. But the image of the Bell's wooden stage forced itself forward once again. If anything, that infuriated him more. What did this lout know of anything?

"Sanson," Eponine hissed. "What do you think you are doing?"

Sanson's wretched grin was turned away from Stas for a moment. "I'm just needling him, you know. Seeing what makes him mad. It's all good fun."

"And what if you did make him mad, asshole? Have you considered that?"

Sanson shrugged. "Well, then I'd handle it. Pansy boy like him wouldn't be much trouble for me."

Stas's fist slammed into the table, cracking the wood. He put the full weight of his frustration into his glare and attempted to cow the annoyance into submission.

Sanson, if anything, seemed amused.

"So that's what it takes then." Sanson nodded with a grin. "You're a prideful little shit, aren't you? Are you hoping I'll piss myself now? I'm not drunk enough yet for that." He pursed his lips. "Seems like I need to fix that! Barkeep, get me another!"

And he got up, wandering off for the bartender.

Stas leveled a glare at Eponine.

She glared back defensively. "Don't blame me for that idiot. I'll get you another drink."

"Don't bother," Stas grumbled. "How long until I can head back?"

"The longer you wait, the safer it will be." Stas grunted at the non-answer. Eponine sighed. "The bird-faces have a protocol for when you kick the hornet's nest. They won't settle down for a few hours more."

Stas rubbed his forehead. Being up this late was already an issue.

He was going to have trouble waking up in the morning.

Really, the situation was just exhausting in general. He didn't even really feel angry any more. He had no energy to maintain that state.

"Eponine?" a man's voice called. "I didn't expect to see you here."

Eponine looked towards the entrance. "Enjolras?" She seemed more surprised now than she had been with the lout.

Stas examined the new arrival. Enjolras was a striking man, sharp faced, tall in stature. His hair was a silvery-blond, ruffled slightly out of a pristine arrangement. But his posture was proper and his clothing impeccable—fine yet tasteful.

This man would fit in well with the forum denizens; an ugly pocked wastrel this was not.

"I was taking an evening stroll, enjoying the city. It can be quite calm at this time of night."

"If you ignore all the delivery vehicles and the drunkards," Eponine retorted.

"If you ignore those, yes." He offered an easy smile. "I wandered around a bit, ended up in this neighborhood and decided to stop in. Ah." He stopped, eyes settling on Stas. "Am I interrupting? Terribly sorry for intruding like that."

His eyes were a deep, piercing silver. It took Stas a moment to realize he was staring.

Stas shook his head. "No. No. It's fine." He stood up quickly. "You can have my seat if you wish."

Enjolras waved his hand. "No need. There are plenty of seats. Ah, but allow me to introduce myself. I am Enjolras Gracchus Julianus, a humble man of the city." He held out his hand. "Might I know your name?"

Stas clasped it easily. The man's grip was firm and steady, but his skin was smooth.

"Stas," he said simply, making sure to not clench too hard. "I am a gladiator from the provinces."

"An up and coming one at that," Eponine added. "I caught a few of his matches today. He was quite the dominating presence."

Enjolras's eyes twinkled. "Indeed?" He released his grip and Stas let his own hand fall to the side. "If I might join you?"

"Please do." Stas spoke quickly. His words were met with a soft smile.

Enjolras sat next to Eponine and across from himself. "From the provinces, you said? How has this fair city been treating you?"

"I've only arrived a week back," Stas admitted. "And I suppose it has been ... overwhelming?" The city was a constant deluge of action and sensation, far from the dreary countryside he had known. There were so many people, so many places, so many spectacles. "It's a very busy place."

Enjolras chuckled. "Busy. Yes, I'd quite agree. I've been here my whole life, but it is an apt descriptor."

A telling smell returned and Stas's nose wrinkled in disgust. Sanson trudged back to the table, three mugs precariously held in the crook of his meaty arms. "Enjolras?" Sanson grimaced. "The fuck are you doing here?"

Enjolras met the accusation with his smile. "Just keeping a personal eye on matters. I find it enjoyable."

"Feh." Sanson sat his mugs down on the table, settling himself a few chairs down off to the side. He grabbed one and started sloshing it down.

It was disgusting how much the man was drinking. But Stas found he preferred the annoying, consistent gulps to the man's grating voice.

Enjolras eyed the scene with some distaste. He glanced at the state of the table, and Stas's empty mug. "I see that you are dry. Why don't I treat you to a drink to make up for barging in?"

Stas blinked. "There's no need for that. You aren't intruding."

"Well then, please allow me to treat you because I enjoy treating new friends."

Stas looked down. "I would appreciate it."

"I can grab it for you," Eponine said, getting up from her seat.

Enjolras handed her a few coins. "Thank you. Something for all three of us, if you would, please. I believe a sweet wine would be more to our new friend's tastes."

Eponine nodded and set for the bar.

"How do you feel about the people here?" Enjolras asked.

"I haven't really had the chance to speak with people much yet, outside of my colleagues. Not much chance to talk to other people when they aren't permitted on the palace grounds."

Enjolras nodded sagely. "Indeed. You gladiators are kept somewhat isolated. It is good that you tried to come out and see the city proper."

"Ah, yes," Stas replied awkwardly. "Today was my first real time out of the school. I haven't even explored much of the estate yet, never been to the palace itself. Supposedly we'll have a chance to attend some parties or something in the palace proper." *Hobnobbing*, Zola had called it.

"A fine opportunity, to be sure. I've had the chance to visit the palace a few times. A great wonder of architecture, a true beauty to behold. But I think there is some charm to be had from the parts of the city where people actually live as well."

"Looked to be falling apart in places from what I saw," Stas muttered.

Enjolras chuckled. "Sadly. But those sorts of things could be fixed. I like to see things as they could be before I judge them for their current, unfortunate state. I feel that every building in the city could be made as marvelous as the palace with some effort."

"A whole lot of effort," Stas said, thinking of the ramshackle buildings and haphazard streets.

"Of course, of course. But the results ..."

"Are you an architect or something?"

"Of a sort." Enjolras smiled. "Perhaps a patron of the arts might be more accurate." He paused as if in thought. "An aedile, in a sense, one always in need of participants for my works. Or so I hope to be one day."

"How you could be, not your current, unfortunate state?"

Enjolras laughed. The sound was exuberant, but not truly wild, quite like the man's hair. "Yes, that. But if we strive earnestly, will we not one day be what we seek? Ah, it looks like Eponine is back."

Eponine returned with the drinks. She set them out, one by one, taking care to place Stas's far from Sanson. "Let's make sure he doesn't take this one too."

Enjolras raised his glass. "A toast then?"

"For what?" Stas inquired.

Enjolras smiled. "For anything you wish for it to be. You should have something worth toasting every day if you're living life properly."

"So what are you toasting?"

"I'm not sure yet. After all, the evening isn't over yet."

Eponine smacked him on the back of the head lightly, but the silver-eyed man took it in his stride. He turned his gaze to Eponine.

She sighed, lifted her glass and turned to Stas.

Stas shrugged and raised his own. The three glasses clinked together.

Stas took a sip. It was, as Enjolras proclaimed, quite sweet. The fruit complemented the alcohol far better than the ale had. He could find himself quite liking this.

# Nine

Time passed in the bar. Stas forgot his anxiety and was no longer counting down the minutes until he was free.

The music was pleasant, the drink amicable to his palate, and the company enjoyable. The hour or so flew by without care, filled with unimportant conversation and sweet wine.

Enjolras, after wrapping up an anecdote about some childhood mischief or other, sighed and pushed back his chair. "I apologize, but it seems the hour has turned far later than I had intended. I must be going."

"It is late," Eponine agreed. "The watchers have most likely calmed down by now." She directed her words to Stas.

"How convenient." Enjolras nodded. "I wish you the best of luck with that, Stas. It was good to meet you." He held out a hand and Stas grabbed it for a quick shake. "If you are amenable, I would like to meet again. There is an exclusive locale that I believe you are a good fit for."

The words seemed to shake Sanson from his quiet stupor the table over. The pockmarked drunk rose to his feet and glared. "I didn't take you for such a fucking fool, Enjolras."

Eponine shot a glare straight back. "Oh, shut your gab, Sanson. Enjolras has the right to decide these things."

"Feh!" Sanson spat. He kept his attention fully on Enjolras. "You've already made a mess of things, trudging in here, interrupting my process. Now you plan on inducting someone after one fucking meeting? You are out of your damn mind!"

"Of course he's going to treat this differently. Enjolras recognizes the opportunity," Eponine retorted. "A fresh gladiator, one without ties, proven and strong. You're the moron trying to treat him like any random plebeian."

Stas knew he lacked the context to understand what was happening.

"An 'opportunity' you say? More like 'bait,'" Sanson spat. "Anyone with half a brain could see it's too damn perfect. But you've always been one to let greed cloud your senses." Sanson turned back to Enjolras. "Trust me, Enjolras. Just let this one go. Let's wipe this last bit from his mind and move on. Everybody should forget about this."

The words put Stas on edge. His gaze darted from Sanson to Eponine. He knew she could manipulate memories, or so she claimed, but ...

Eponine wasn't even looking at him, glaring instead at Sanson. She moved to speak but Enjolras held up his hand and looked Sanson in the eye. "I applaud you for your caution and recognize your earnest advice." He turned to Stas. Silver eyes locked on to his own. "But I know when a good man stands before me."

Stas swallowed. He felt small under the weight of the man's words.

He did not know if he was a good man. But in that moment, he knew he wanted to be. He averted his eyes, no longer able to stand Enjolras's trusting conviction.

"Feh!" Sanson groused, turning back to his drink.

Enjolras smiled. "We are having a meeting in one week's time. Since the two of you seem to get along, I believe Eponine would be the best one to show you to the location."

"We can meet up here," Eponine declared. "Sometime before sunset. I'll take you where you need to go from there."

"If, of course, you wish to attend," Enjolras said.

"I think I'd like to." He was met by twin smiles.

"I look forward to seeing you again," Enjolras declared. "Have a pleasant evening, Stas, Eponine." And so he left.

"Do you remember the way back to the forum?" Eponine inquired. "If not, I can take you back."

Stas drained the last few drops from his cup. "I remember it fine."

"Stay safe, then. And see you again in a week."

Stas waved and, humming along to the musician, exited the bar. He made his way back to the forum, light on his feet. The night air felt cool on his face, and a pleasant wind ruffled through his hair.

He felt good. Uplifted. The stress of the day had drained away with company and drink. There was a spring in his stride now.

In fact, why was he walking at all? Teleportation would make for faster travel.

He could see no reason not to.

So he *reflected* down the street, *reflected* up the alley, *reflected* to the rooftop, *reflected* across the city. He made a game of it, *reflecting* into the shadows and around the backs of the wagons, staying out of view of those still out at night. He *reflected* himself at any distance he desired, to any height, traversing the city in sharp staccato, with little care for his destination, humming that simple tune all the while.

He hadn't used his magic so intensely since he had first discovered it, when in those months he had explored just what he could reflect and by how much.

A roof tile he had *reflected* to failed to hold his weight. He slipped, stumbling off the rooftop. Another quick *reflection* brought him to near ground level. His back crashed against the cobblestone.

His stomach churned. He had never teleported while falling before; it was a sickening task when he wasn't still. Vertigo overwhelmed him; the world swam in place.

He rolled to the side, in time for a bit of vomit to spew from his mouth. It smelled sweet, like the wine.

Stas pushed himself back up to his feet and wiped his mouth of the stray spittle. His headache pulsed from the sudden blow.

Perhaps *reflecting* to and fro was not the best idea.

Stas paused to settle his stomach and head. His body ached, back especially. He had thought he had caught himself before the fall could do any real damage, but the soreness was pervasive. His whole body was off, his concentration sapped.

He decided to walk the rest of the way back.

Or rather … he would if he knew the way. He had a general sense of where the forum was, and Ludo's school with it. But he wasn't perfectly sure.

If he were back on the rooftop, he'd likely be able to spot his destination. He would need to risk his stomach once more.

He found a target (ensuring it was made from a properly sturdy material this time), steeled himself, and *reflected*.

He ducked behind a chimney immediately, having caught sight of a watcher on an adjacent rooftop. According to Eponine, he would not be recognized, but Stas had no desire to test that. The bird-masked guards would not care for anyone intruding into their domain, or sneaking into the forums after curfew.

Thankfully, the guard did not seem to have noticed him, focused as he was on the street below. Even better, he could see the forum from his vantage point.

He could also see patrolling guards and watch-nests. He would need to be careful.

Well aware of the watcher on the neighboring building, Stas snuck out from behind the chimney and started plotting a path.

He paused. On the roof across from him were two men, not one. Both wore masks but only one was beaked like a bird. The other mask was a smooth, deep blue, and covered the whole face. It had some pattern on it that Stas could not fully make out, like a single painted eye.

The blue-masked man crept silently behind the watcher, staying in his blind spot, knife gripped in hand.

When he was close enough, he grabbed the guard by his mouth and slit the man's throat.

Stas watched the guard slump silently, blood seeping from his neck.

He wasn't the only one to notice. Another watcher across the way ran to a bell by his post and rang it loudly.

The blue-masked assassin watched the development impassively. He held himself in place, adopting a fighting task. He tossed his knife to his left hand and uncoiled a length of chain from his back, which he slowly twirled. Stas could make out a glint of metal at the end: some small hook attached to the length.

A guard across the way imbibed an elixir. He pulled his cloak out like a pair of wings and leaped forth, gliding past the chasm between the buildings.

The assassin swung his chain. The gliding guard shot upwards to dodge, carried by a strong updraft. But the chain changed course just as unnaturally. It flew towards the man unerringly.

Like a cruel parody of a fisherman, the assassin retracted his line.

The guard was pulled in violently. Stas saw the winds blow furiously at the man's direction, but they were impotent. The bird-masked man could not fight the chain's swift pull. In but another instant, the guard was within the assassin's reach. And in that same moment the assassin's dagger was in his heart and he slumped dead.

The assassin placed his boot on the fresh corpse and pulled upon the chain. The hook released its prey, ripping out bits of armor, leather, cloth, and flesh with it.

Weapon freed, the assassin spun in place to catch the assault of a third watcher. His fist buried into the bulky guard's chest, releasing a resounding crack. Something had broken, either a fist or rib, but both men stood strong, so Stas could not tell.

A metallic coat oozed out of the guard, painting his skin and clothing. He held himself tightly and pressed forward.

The assassin jumped to the side, avoiding a bolt of fire a fourth guard, over three roofs away, had launched. It smashed harmlessly into the metallic guard's clothing. The fire-wielder ran closer, launching another volley of fire.

The assassin swung his chain behind him, allowing it to block the flame. In the same motion he rushed the metallic watcher. The guard planted his feet in preparation, but at the very last moment the assassin juked and rushed past.

He made his way to the building's edge. A fifth watcher, who had been climbing the scaffolding, found the assassin's foot waiting for him at the top. He was unceremoniously thrown to the street below.

Stunned by the fall, he offered no defense when a thrown dagger flew into his throat.

The metallic guard made his own charge, shoulder extended into a tackle. The assassin crouched low.

Stas stood, transfixed.

Temptation churned in the back of his mind. The fight before him called out to him in ways he couldn't fully explain. For one, he did not even know which side he wished to join.

The assassin was a scoundrel, a murderer, a criminal, striking out from ambush to kill men who were only trying to do their Dominus-bound duty. Stas could think of no justification for the blue-masked man's rampage.

Other parts of him, raging at the injustice these same guards had dealt him but hours before, yearned for the chance for retribution. The guards outnumbered the criminal greatly. What sort of coward would he himself be if he added to that number?

Stas was a gladiator, not some common thug. In a battle between supreme skill and sheer masses, why would he ever wish to side with the mass?

Stas's heart pumped wildly. His blood demanded he involve himself, to not let such a skillful fight pass without his participation. His choler raged against the criminal for his dishonor, against the guards for his earlier treatment.

But the calmer humors prevailed. He swallowed the desire. All the desires. His tempers were rash and his patience was thin, but Stas did not let them control him.

The metallic watcher extended his arms, attempting to grapple. But the assassin was too spry. Like a gymnast, he vaulted over the guard's extended limb. And, with the force of the motion, unbalanced his hapless footstool. The guard teetered on his feet.

Simultaneously, the criminal lashed his chain whip out towards another guard who had been climbing to the rooftop. As with the glider before, the hook effortlessly dug into his target's chest, ignoring armor and flesh both.

The impaled guard gasped but held strong. He grasped the bloody chain protruding from him. The metal sizzled and melted beneath hands that dripped with a vile green liquid.

The assassin cursed loudly. It was the first sound Stas had heard from the criminal. But he did not abate.

The assassin took his remaining length of chain and wrapped it tightly around the neck of the metallic guard. Using the makeshift garrote as a hinge, he pivoted around his newest victim, leaving the choking man between himself and the impaled one.

He seemed to be wielding his enemy like some mockery of a tower shield, but it was an effective tactic. The impaled guard hesitated; the green mass of liquid he had been accumulating fell away. He did not appear to be willing to fire on his own ally.

Judging by how quickly the liquid had eaten through the chain, it was an understandable choice.

The human shield was not idle. The bulking man struggled valiantly. His thick metallic hands clenched at the chain around his neck. He thrashed violently, throwing the assassin out of cover and into the line of fire.

The assassin abandoned his attack, focused on avoiding the flame. With an audible grunt, the metallic watcher tore the chain asunder, leaving his foe with the bare remnants of his weapon. He gasped for a deep heaving breath. His moment of weakness went unpunished as fire and acid rained upon his foe.

It was an eerie reflection of Stas's own fight with the watchers—the superior combatant outmaneuvered by superior numbers. The assassin could not capitalize on any openings because another foe would always provide cover.

The starkest difference, however, was the mask. Unlike Stas, this criminal could simply melt into the night, so long as he could retreat.

Surrounded as he was, that did not look likely.

The assassin raised his fists in a defiant stance; it did not look like he was even trying to flee.

The fire-spewing watcher moved first. He dashed in for the assassin's blind spot. His hands were alight with a heat that distorted the air around them. Any glancing blow would have surely melted flesh.

The assassin twirled in place to meet him. A quick swing caught the fire-wielder by the elbow and forced the deadly appendages away. The assassin continued his motion into a full body kick.

The metallic watcher struck with a heavy fist.

The assassin immediately aborted his own attack, retracting his leg in an instant. The burning watcher, bracing for the blow, was unprepared when it turned into a grapple instead. Once again the assassin used his foes as human shields, bringing the fire-wielder to intercept the metallic guard's blow.

The guard hesitated, hastily redirecting his blow out of the way of his ally, only for it to get in the way of the acid watcher's own attack.

Stas could barely parse the confusing mess of limbs and bodies, but the assassin had no such issues. He dove between the bodies with as much ease as one might swim through water. He was ready for every attack. Where his fist could not divert an attempted blow, he forced one of his foes to do so instead. In this perilous dance, his opponent's numbers acted against them: their most deadly arcanum could not be used without fear.

The fire watcher cursed and his flames sputtered out. He retreated to grab an elixir, while the metallic watcher guarded him.

The assassin made the first mistake of the night. He slammed his open palm forward into the metallic watcher with the full force of his body. It was a wasted movement with no visible result. As the metallic watcher capitalized with an attempted grapple, the unbalanced assassin was forced back blindly.

The acid-wielder was waiting. His hands, dripping with the caustic substance, were well positioned to melt open the assassin's throat in but an instant. Unbalanced and clearly panicking, the lone fighter was doomed.

Except ... the scene changed. The panic evaporated from the assassin's body as he twisted in space. With speed even beyond the prodigious ability he had displayed as yet, he avoided the lethal blow and swung for his opponent's throat.

A knife sprang out of the man's sleeve into his surprised foe's neck.

The sudden turnabout shocked everyone, Stas included. Only the assassin was prepared to capitalize. He grabbed the dangling bit of chain still connected to his newest victim and jerked his hook free.

He swung the strange weapon and let it fly. As before, it curved unnaturally through the air, lodging itself in the metallic watcher's unprotected eye.

The man's screams grew as his orb was fished from its socket. The brutal attack left the man on his knees, heaving. The fire-wielder, too, was stunned by the grotesque display. When the assassin swung his hook once more, the man covered his eyes as best he was able.

Another dagger found its way into his unprotected throat.

And then, with a cold apathy, the assassin pressed his foot against the retching metallic guard's neck. When shining skin returned to pale flesh, his dagger came down. And that was the end of it.

The victorious assassin looked up to the moon and sighed deeply. For the first time in the tumultuous fight, Stas could make out the man's mask clearly. It was a plain thing under the light of the moon: a smooth wash of blue with a simple nazar of white, black, and lighter blue painted upon its left. Opposite was a single hole for the man to see through.

The masked man kneeled down and carefully removed the bandoleer of elixirs from the corpse. Then he moved to the next.

A whir of thoughts and emotions stormed through Stas's mind. He stepped out of his hiding spot, fists readied.

"Hey!" he called. But before he could even figure out what he wanted to say, the blue-masked man was dashing for him.

Stas *reflected* out of the way, swinging his fist down at the assassin's skull. But the man avoided it, unfazed by the arcanum.

Stas blocked an elbow to his gut, catching it with a sweep of his arm. His own kick was caught by the man's blind grab. He found himself flipped through the air. There was far more strength in the awkward motion than he had expected.

Turning the free fall into a more controlled exercise, Stas managed to land on his feet a good distance away.

The assassin turned to face him. He dropped his knife and chain, raising his fists in their place.

Stas grinned. A proper match, on equal terms. And the masked man wasn't holding back like he had with the watchers. His headache pounded in time with his pulse; his body felt far too warm in the night, and the nausea had not fully escaped from his stomach, but Stas felt the best he had all day.

The assassin was light on his feet and ready for an attack from behind. Stas would not oblige him.

He took a deep breath and *reflected* and *reflected* again. It was a difficult trick that required a good bit of advanced planning, but with two *reflections* he could appear wherever he wished without facing the wrong way.

He appeared in front of the assassin, who would no doubt be guarding the wrong side, and ...

A jab to his stomach disrupted its uneasy state. Vomit spewed from Stas's mouth to the assassin's mask.

It was a shameful, and worse, unintended attack, but it served its purpose. The assassin aborted his follow-up in favor of avoiding the sweet-smelling bile.

Not that Stas could really capitalize in his disoriented state. He opted to regain his distance to give his stomach and head time to recover.

He was more tired than he cared to admit, and the alcohol wasn't doing any favors. But his stomach was clear now, and his mind was focused.

Stas had gotten that assassin's measure now. He was fast and strong, but Stas was just as fast, and even stronger. With magic on his side, there was no question about it. This would be a good fight, and he would win.

The punch had done nothing but clear his nausea.

Stas clenched his fists, charged forth, and met his opponent with a proper exchange of blows. The masked man weaved out of the way of his attacks, but Stas had the man in his rhythm. As the assassin's tempo set him to dodge, Stas *reflected* and aimed a decisive punch for the man's shoulder blades when he surely wouldn't be ready.

And yet, the assassin leaned to the side in a sudden jerk, clamped Stas's arm with his own, and pulled him forward. The man threw his head back, crashing the back of his skull into Stas's face twice. Then he threw Stas over his shoulder.

Stas crashed hard into the roof, face down. The masked men kept his arm in a submission grip, his knee pressed into Stas's back with ruthless force.

The pressure on his arm was immense, an implicit threat to break it. But he didn't.

Instead a tired voice spoke out from behind the blue mask. "You done, brat?"

Stas twisted his head to see as far back as he could manage. The blank, painted eye bored into him.

Held in place as he was, Stas couldn't *reflect* out of this position. The pressure on his arm increased, and the pain jolted Stas back to a proper mindset.

"I'm done." He spoke quietly, the words a curse on his breath.

"Don't do anything foolish," came the threat.

The pressure abated. Stas's arm fell to his side, and the knee was removed from his back.

Stas pushed himself to his feet, rubbing his sore muscles. It would be easy to resume the fight, but that would make him no better than the assassin. "You're not going to kill me?"

The assassin grunted. "I don't make a habit of it." He retrieved his weapons, examining the damage to the chain before coiling the small length with the hook on it onto his back. He moved to another watcher's corpse, collecting its bandoleer of elixirs.

"It looks like you made a habit of it with those guys."

"Difference is, I don't have a quarrel with you."

Stas quirked a brow. "So you have a quarrel with the Dominus's watchers?"

The assassin did not respond, continuing his task. When he had finished, he moved to the edge of the building.

Stas followed. "How did you know where I was going to be?"

Again, the assassin said nothing, opting to climb down the building's wall.

Stas reflected to the road below and called up to the man climbing down. "Hey, answer me. How did you know?"

The masked man sighed. "You kept making the obvious move. Easy enough to predict."

Stas scoffed. "I saw where you thought I would be and went somewhere else instead, but you still caught me."

The assassin jumped down the last bit of the wall. He grunted from the exertion. "As I said, you kept making the obvious move."

Stas grit his teeth.

The assassin rifled through the corpse on the ground, retrieving the two full elixir vials it concealed.

"Aren't you concerned more of them will come?" Stas said. "Why aren't more watchers coming?"

Again, the assassin ignored the question.

Annoyed, Stas *reflected* towards the masked man. He found a knife waiting against his throat.

"Why are you still bothering me, brat?" the assassin growled, removing the knife. "Go home."

"I saw your fight against the watchers."

"I noticed."

Stas blinked. "You were skilled. Even with such lopsided odds, you prevailed. Then, when you fought me ..."

"I swatted aside your drunken stumbling. What of it?"

Stas clenched his fists but held steady. "I'm not the best at unarmed combat. I'm far better with a sword and shield in hand." If he had had a sword or even just a shield, Stas knew he would have presented himself far more skillfully. "But I am trained in the art. And you are better than me in this discipline. And I saw your skill with your other weapons. You are a versatile fighter."

Again ignored, Stas realized he needed to get to the point. "I want you to train me."

The assassin stopped. "What?"

"I want you to train me," Stas repeated. "You have a lot of skills, and I can see them fitting well into my style. Really, I'm impressed by pretty much everything you demonstrated. Anything you could teach me would be helpful."

The assassin remained still, hanging to the wall like a spider. Eventually, he spoke. "Why in god's name would I teach you anything?"

God? Stas ignored that bit, continuing. "Why not? I'm sure I can get Ludo to pay you for your time." Ludo had mentioned being willing to employ trainers from the city. If the assassin showed up without his mask, he'd just be one of many.

"I don't need money." He hauled himself up to the roof.

Stas realized he was not in much of a bargaining position. He *reflected* up to meet the man. "Well, what do you want then?"

The assassin scoffed. "You don't have anything I want."

"Nothing? Really? I'm sure there is something ..."

The masked man whirled in place, knife extended. He glared at Stas directly in the eye, anger pouring through the solitary hole. "Go away, brat. I'm starting to reconsider my habits."

Stas faltered. If the man truly wasn't interested, what could he do?

It wasn't like he needed the man when there were ample trainers at the school.

He sighed. It really was far too late.

"Fine," he grumbled, leaving the corpse looter to his task.

# Ten

Stas did not have much difficulty making his way back through the forum. The assassin's actions had, perhaps, cut a hole in the watcher's patrols. With careful movement and a few well-timed *reflections*, Stas had been able to return to the palatial gates and reflect back to the other side. From there, he stealthily made his way back to the school.

Outside his room, with great care, he climbed up to the window. He hefted open the shutter and threw himself through onto the bed below.

The bed shuddered under the fall, and a servant sitting in his chair startled up, eyes wide.

Stas's own eyes matched. "Ah ..." He spoke quietly. "I don't suppose you could forget me climbing through the window? I would really appreciate it you didn't mention this to Ludo ..." He tried to recall the servant's name, but came up blank, so he just trailed off awkwardly.

The servant shook her head. "The lanista is already aware of your breaking curfew, Master Stas. Master Ludo posted me here to inform you to speak with him at once, when you arrived."

Stas bit back a curse.

The servant bowed deferentially. "If you would follow me, Master Stas?"

Stas debated ignoring the request, just lying in his bed and heading to sleep.

No. Stas knew Ludo would only be more infuriated if he tarried. So he meekly followed the girl towards Ludo's personal quarters.

Once there, the girl spoke quietly to the servant at the door, who nodded before entering the room, closing the door behind him.

Stas waited awkwardly. The sounds of thumping furniture and ruffled clothing escaped the room. Finally, after a good long moment, the servant opened the door again, revealing the balding master of the school.

Ludo glared at him through his disheveled spectacles. He had clearly been awoken.

"Well, boy?" The man huffed. "We both know what this is about. How are you going to try to defend yourself? Don't you dare pretend you weren't breaking curfew."

"I ... went for a walk. Through the estate," Stas said slowly. "Just a night walk to clear my head. The curfew slipped my mind."

Ludo's scowl deepened. "Don't lie to me, boy. Your breath reeks. You went out drinking in the city. Have the decency to admit it."

Stas said nothing.

"By the Dominus! What were you thinking, you fool boy? Were you so enamored with your time in the arena that you wanted a stint among the executions too? What a way to entertain the crowds that would be, hanging by your entrails or drowning in the sands. I'm sure your status would get you some memorable method of death, because it is hardly enough to save you from it. You aren't invincible!"

"Nobody caught me," Stas mustered in his defense.

Ludo pulled at his thin hair. "I caught you, you imbecile. If a single watcher saw you in the forum after hours, if a single watcher saw you climbing the gate, you would be dead, do you understand? You don't have the status to protect you from that. I don't have the status to protect you from that," he hissed.

"But it didn't happen," Stas retorted. The situation had been treacherous, but it had worked out.

"It's not about the results," Ludo snarled. "It's about the actions themselves, and the person doing the actions."

"What is so wrong with breaking curfew? It's a worthless law."

"It doesn't matter what you think of it. We suffer the laws as they are, not the laws as we want them to be. There is virtue in avoiding needless conflict, in proper capitulation. In rightful obedience. Bullheaded stubbornness, arrogance, excess pride, those are what are immoral. You don't get to write the laws, you can only follow them."

Stas kept his head down.

"Cavorting about in the city after sundown. And don't you think I forgot about your stunt earlier today. Or should I say yesterday, given the unreasonable hour … Did you even apologize yet, or do the words coming from my mouth mean nothing to you?"

"I already did," he said softly, to avoid letting his anger be heard.

"Then you went off to get drunk to celebrate. I have half a mind to confine you to your room for the next month, but I'm not going to waste any servant's time babysitting you, and I'd be a fool to assume you wouldn't just sneak out if you weren't constantly supervised."

Stas grit his teeth.

"Since you are clearly far too idle in the evenings, you will spend them in the laundry with Cassandra, doing whatever she commands of you."

Stas sucked in his breath. Servant work and drudgery were as painful a punishment as he might expect. "For how long?"

"A month," Ludo declared. "Or longer if I determine you still lack in virtue. And for that duration, you will not be permitted to employ the services of any of my instructors."

"What?" Stas could not hold back his outrage. "This is unacceptable."

Ludo glared back. "The instructors of this institution are reserved for its students. Its students obey its rules. Your own actions place your status in doubt."

"You can't let me fall behind like that!" Stas growled.

"It would be your own failing if you did. Use this time to shore up on your basics. Let the posts be your instructor, for no one else will be."

Stas scowled. "The damn posts are no substitute! Are you trying to sabotage my career?"

"Are you trying to sabotage your own?" Ludo retorted. "My decision is final. You are lucky I don't rescind your next match as well." Ludo rubbed his forehead. "Now, it is far, far too late at night. Cassandra will gather you tomorrow evening. If you do not cooperate, she will inform me. Do not make me call you to me again. Am I understood?"

Vile phrases begged to be released from his lips. Stas nodded, not trusting his voice.

"Good. Now go." Ludo removed himself from the doorway and the servant closed it.

Stas seethed. The laundry was bad enough, but being denied instruction … It was maddening. How was he to improve without teachers? How was he to keep up with his fellows when they were given opportunities he was not? Merely practice his swings against the wooden posts, endlessly? It was laughable. Ludo had to have known that.

He needed instruction, somehow. His failure with the assassin stung all the more now. Had he known the man might have been his only option, he would have tried to recruit him all the more.

But all of this was a problem for the morning.

The servant girl was leading him back to his room, completely unnecessarily.

He realized he still didn't know her name. "Are you Cassandra?" he asked.

"No, Master Stas," she replied demurely.
Stas turned his head to the side, embarrassed.

# Eleven

The hot sun beat down and the damnable post stood mockingly. Stas swung his training sword as hard as he could. Simple, long-perfected motions. Mind-numbing, repetitive exercise. The iron-cored wood threatened to fall from his grip. Out of spite, he had selected the heftiest one, far heavier than any true blade.

Anything else would be preferable, and yet this was all he was permitted. High, low, switch hands, repeat. Perfect form, as hard and as fast as he could manage.

He channeled his anger into his strikes, daring the wooden posts to shatter with each blow.

He didn't notice the man behind him until he called out. "Hey, Stas."

Stas whipped around, letting the sword fall from his exhausted limb. "What do you want, Alain?" he managed between panting breaths.

"Ah, Zola and I were heading to the races. Would you like to join us?"

"Bah." Stas spat, turned back to the post. "I need to train."

"You've been training pretty hard," Alain said. "Maybe you should take a break?"

"No." An hour at the post was worth maybe a minute of instruction. He could not fall further behind.

Alain hummed. "Are you certain? You might find it beneficial. We'd go to the baths afterward. Exercise, relax, bathe, massage. In that order. That's the best way for your body to improve, I've found."

"No." Alain didn't understand. He wasn't being deprived. Stas paused as the thought churned. "Alain. You've been working with Rosa learning new sword forms, correct?"

"Yes?" He squinted. "I've been spending the last few mornings with her."

"Do you think you can pass on what you learned?"

Alain blanched. "Ah, I'm not really the best, and I was just planning on heading out, so ..."

"Anything is better than nothing. And tomorrow if not today."

"Look, Stas." Alain put his hand on the back of his neck. "To be truthful, I am concerned about upsetting Ludo. He would not appreciate me helping you skirt around your punishment."

Stas growled and went back to the post.

Alain continued. "I would be happy to aid you after your punishment ends, you know that, right? Helping you catch up on what you missed out on, it would only be fair. But doing it now ... Stas, I don't think this is that healthy for you. You really should take a break. Please."

Stas ignored him, just as he ignored the burning pain of exertion.

"Alain, what's taking so long?" Zola asked as she walked into the yard.

"I wished to see if Stas wanted to come, but he's not interested."

"So I see. But, hey, you'll never guess who I saw walking past."

"Only so many people are permitted near here, Zola. It would hardly take me forever to guess them all."

Zola rolled her eyes. "It's an expression, and you know it. Anyway, I saw Lord Galbrio walking by with the Dominus's monk."

Stas paused, letting the heavy sword fall to his side.

"Lord Galbrio? Here?" Alain said.

"Walking past, yes. We may be able to catch up to him if we move quickly."

Stas set the sword on the ground. One did not need to be a native of the city to know of Lord Galbrio. The acclaimed lord was said to be a man with a great love of sport, a discerning eye, who delighted in taking gladiators under his influential wing. To be a gladiator under Lord Galbrio was to be on the forefront of the arena, and to enjoy the finest the city could offer.

He was the most prominent lanista any could name.

"What do you mean by 'the Dominus's monk?'" Stas asked.

"Hm? You haven't met him, my friend?" Zola replied. "He comes to watch us practice sometimes. Quiet man. Very creepy."

"He's a mystic. The Mad Monk, they sometimes call him," Alain explained. "They say he traveled to the east and discovered the secrets of arcanum. He claims to be able to use magic without elixirs, but it rings dubious to most. Regardless, he amuses the Dominus, so he enjoys life in the court as an advisor."

Stas himself did not find the claim so outrageous, seeing as he himself did not require elixirs. He wondered if the monk might make for an appropriate instructor.

"I wonder what Lord Galbrio is doing with him," Zola pondered.

Alain shrugged. "He is part of the Dominus's court. And both of them are interested in the games. Perhaps they're friends?"

"Well, I just so happen to be going in the same direction as them, so I'm going to rush out and listen to what they are talking about. Maybe introduce myself," Zola declared, dashing out.

"I don't know if that last part is the best idea, but I'm going the same way as well, so ..." Alain also dashed out.

It was fine to take a quick break, Stas decided. He quickly wiped his sweat away and followed.

The three of them walked along on the estate's gentle path and, as one, adopted a more casual pace just within earshot.

The two men were easy to make out, distinctive in such a way that Zola could not have been referring to anyone else.

The first was an unexpectedly short man, garbed in a level of casual finery. It looked well in place for the gardens they strolled within: elegant, though unsuited for combat. The man sported a long, dazzling mane of blond. The neatly combed hair flowed past the man's broad shoulders. He grasped a jeweled walking stick in his hand, though he did not seem to require it.

The man was Lord Galbrio, clearly.

The other man was far less spectacular. He looked flimsy, with ashen hair. His clothes were a strange flowing robe in pristine white. Perhaps it was the garb of a monk. He was unremarkable: a far cry from the title of *mad*. Stas's gaze drifted from the man to his better-dressed companion.

The boisterous voice of Lord Galbrio resounded. "But that is what he says, at least. And I suppose his golems lend credence to his claims. Fine quality, to be sure, for the ones he let us see. But I feel that Patruinus is too insistent about the matter. Mentioned his production levels repeatedly, you see. No doubt hiding some weakness. I am concerned about some poison pill. Makes me hesitate to purchase."

The monk nodded. "I understand your meaning. He has been acting strangely." The monk's voice was soft, but it carried all the same. "But you may be reading this too directly. Perhaps it is not a matter of concern for his product, but his reputation. He may anticipate some scandal coming to light. His daughter has been the subject of some rumors recently."

"Bah." Lord Galbrio scoffed. "I don't care what sort of debaucheries his daughter avails herself of. Children are children. It's the industry that concerns me."

"Then allow me to ease your worries. Even if Lord Patruinus fails to supply, others are waiting in the wings. I know Lord Macro has indicated interest."

"Macro? Hah. I shudder to think what sorts of monstrosities he would stitch together and call 'golems.' He's an utter madman."

"It would be impolitic of me to disparage the fine minds of the Senate," the monk ventured. "But I will agree that Lord Macro may better serve working with his beasts. But he is merely the most prominent of names that come to mind. Lord Vibianus has expressed interest, for example."

"Vibianus? Hm. His sister is a sharp sort, may have what it takes. No history of quality to back on, but I am already finding myself longing for the days of Patruinus's grandfather. Perhaps some shuffling is due about now. If, of course, Patruinus is truly failing to meet our needs."

"Indeed," the monk agreed. "Have you, perhaps, been keeping abreast of our agricultural situation?"

"What of it?"

"Our outlying farms have been having trouble producing. Fertility is faltering again."

"Then we will increase imports from the province. That is what the Gate is for."

"Yes. Though we might expect the price of grain to increase all the same."

"Then we send more farmers to the outlands. The city is crowded enough as is," Lord Galbrio said. "Did Hirtius set you up on this?"

The monk demurred. "Lady Hirtius has been speaking of agricultural reforms with me. She will be seeking support before the upcoming session."

"I'm not a farmer," Galbrio said. "I don't pretend to know anything about it."

"But you can speak to her, let her make her case, yes?"

"I'll think about it," he mumbled, and turned around. "You three, are you going to introduce yourselves? Or just tiptoe around as if we do not know you are there?"

The three of them looked at each other sheepishly.

"We apologize, Lord Galbrio," Alain said. "We were heading in the same direction, but we didn't want to interrupt your conversation."

"Hmph. Well, I want to be interrupted right about now," he declared. The monk didn't seem perturbed by the comment.

Now that he had a better look at him, Stas realized that Lord Galbrio was far older than he had assumed. The lines on his face pointed to a man past his prime. The monk also had an aged face, one dotted with a pair of spectacles.

Both of them might be around Ludo's age, if not older, though they held themselves better for it.

Zola bowed deferentially. "Pleased to meet you, Lord Galbrio. I am Zola. I've heard many great things about you. Your eye for talent is second to none, and your skill as an instructor is unsurpassable," she said, flattering shamelessly.

"People have a high opinion of me." He smiled. "The three of you, you are from the school we passed? Luno's school?"

"Ludo," the monk corrected him.

"Ludo." Galbrio nodded. "I have not had the chance to meet with the man much. He moved into the estates recently, I want to say seven years ago? Back when Thrace retired."

"That is correct, sir." Alain bowed his head.

"I was wondering, your lordship," Zola ventured, "if you had any advice? For gladiators such as ourselves? The feats of your students are well known."

"Hmph." Galbrio's smile grew, proud and amused. "My gladiators' feats are their own. Anything they accomplish is through their own skill. I just ensure they have what they need. But as for advice ... What really sets my students apart is the refusal to be satisfied. Ambition, that's the word. You can't have victory without ambition."

Stas took the words to heart. Though he would have preferred something more specific, he could hardly expect Lord Galbrio to aid his students' competition.

"Thank you, your lordship." Zola bowed deeply. "Perhaps you might see us at one of our matches. We'd be honored if you could."

"Likely as not. I do tour the arenas often, to catch sight of the talent. It's my favorite pastime, as it were."

Zola smiled, no doubt taking it as an offer to scout her, rather than the polite dismissal Stas knew it to be. People sometimes heard what they wanted to hear.

He turned his attention to the quiet monk.

"I heard," Stas began, "that you could use magic without elixirs."

The monk's eyes lit up. "Indeed. You have heard correctly. I have delved into powers beyond the limits of this world. Are you aware that a thousand years ago there were no elixirs? Nothing in those scattered histories that remain points to their existence, not in the shreds of shreds of histories in which magic is mentioned at all?"

Stas shook his head.

"We know magic existed, but the nature of that magic was lost," the monk continued, in a manner akin to an oft-repeated lecture. Lord Galbrio already seemed to be tuning the man out. "In my youth, I was fascinated with the topic. I ventured out of the city, beyond the outlands, to the great mountains that engulf the sky in the far east. And, hidden among the ruined temples and crumbling stone, I found what I sought. Records, treatises, meditations on that lost arcanum, untouched for ages. I spent years deciphering them, first in translating that dead language into our own, years more making sense of the words. But I was able to learn the secrets, to recreate the magic. I do not need elixirs, no. Not when I can forge my own mind and willpower into fuel."

"Can you demonstrate?" Stas inquired.

The monk hesitated. "Ah, it is no small thing to expend one's will. This world will not allow it to be restored easily. I would prefer to avoid needless exertions."

The realization was as disappointing for Stas as it was expected. The man was a charlatan. There was no cost to arcanum like Stas's.

The Dominus was either oblivious or amused by the lies. But the Mad Monk would be useless to him.

"If you wish, I can teach you what I know. I am always looking for students so that this art will not be lost again with me."

If the man weren't a member of the Dominus's court, he'd tell him exactly what he felt. But Stas kept his tongue in check. "I don't believe I am in the best position. I am busy training most every day, and I do not believe it would be easy to fit such lessons between my regimens."

"Hm. I believe what I know could help you in your goals more than you expect, but I will not push." The monk stared into his eyes as though he was dissecting him in his mind. Stas suddenly understood why Zola had referred to the man as *creepy*. "Perhaps in the future you will be of a more amenable mindset."

Stas did not think that likely.

Lord Galbrio was not recruiting, and the Mad Monk was a fraud. Stas had no reason to remain. He would be better served by training, so that he could impress the noble lanista when he next had the opportunity.

This excursion was not a solution to his problem, and he had been too optimistic in hoping that it would be.

He sighed. "I'll be heading off."

Alain glanced at him. "I thought you were coming to the race with us?"

He shook his head. "No, I was just seeing you off. I'll head back to the yard."

Zola frowned but didn't say anything.

Alain sighed. "Alright. Well, maybe next time."

Stas grunted and, after showing proper respect to Lord Galbrio, turned back.

Perhaps, he mused, Enjolras might know someone who could teach him. Some swordsmanship instructor or something. It was a long shot, but it wouldn't hurt to ask.

But that was in the future.

He had taken a long enough break as it was. He needed to get back to the damn posts.

# Twelve

Cassandra was a meek woman, Stas had quickly discovered. She was vastly uncomfortable being in a position of authority over him, and with him intruding on her work.

But he had dutifully spent his evenings with her over the last week, aiding her in her tasks as he had been ordered. Neither spoke. Stas did not have anything to say to Ludo's servant.

Taking advantage of her nature, he had requested leave to finish early that evening, citing exhaustion. She had granted it out of hand.

Ludo had placed Cassandra in charge of him. The lanista wouldn't be able to complain if she was the one to let him off for the night.

He would be heading out again tonight, but this time, there would be key differences. He had a dagger hidden under his pants leg now. It was a risk. Weapons were illegal in the city. But Stas figured it was worse to be caught without one than to be caught with one.

He had a mask as well, of sorts. He had procured a rag from the laundry and torn some holes in it. It was ugly, but he did not expect to actually need it. As with the knife, it was a precaution.

And, most importantly, Ludo would not catch him this time. He had been practicing a trick in secret for this purpose, a remnant of a failed experiment from years before that could serve him now.

Stas crawled under the covers of his bed, pulling them tight around himself. Then he got up again, leaving his reflection behind.

The lifeless image would not stand up to true scrutiny, but it could mock his sleeping form well enough.

Decoy in place, Stas carefully *reflected* out of the window and to the forum. He walked past the many bird-masked watchers on his way to the bar where Eponine would be waiting.

He arrived at the meeting place eventually. Strolling down the streets was a much slower process compared to reflecting across the roofs.

He found Eponine easily, leaning against the brick wall of the bar. Or rather, she found him.

She waved. "Stas, glad to see you could come."

Stas grunted. He didn't have anything else he would be doing right now. The laundry didn't count.

"Come on, then." She grabbed his hand, pulling it. "Let's head out."

"How far are we going?" Stas asked as he allowed her to drag him. "And where are we going?"

"A good location to meet up with friends. It's a bit of a walk. Across the city and a bit."

She led him back the way he had come. Stas frowned. "If we're crossing the city, why couldn't we meet in the forums?"

Eponine shook her head. "Meeting in such crowded places is a major pain. Besides, I don't feel like attracting so much attention from the watchers. They say that the Dominus has eyes everywhere, but most of those eyes are pointed at the forum. Speaking of ..."

Ahead of them, on a rooftop, was a watcher, masked face locked on the street below. Stas ducked his head, keeping his eyes to the ground.

Eponine, on the other hand, waved, a smile on her face.

"Didn't you just say you wanted to avoid attention?" he hissed.

"Acting like you have something to hide is the easiest way to get eyes on you," she whispered from behind her smile, eyes still locked on the guard. "You're lucky. Most people dip their heads. But I don't."

The watcher on the roof didn't outwardly react, but his masked gaze did fall upon Eponine for a moment. His attention turned elsewhere quickly and Eponine stopped waving.

"See. Nothing to it. Now, the forum is closing for the evening so we will have to take the long way around. I hope you enjoy the scenic route."

The "scenic route" was far from direct. Eponine led him around the city in a twisting manner. It was hard to keep the chaotic streets straight in his head. The roads they traversed were in a better part of town, but they still paled in comparison to the majesty of the estate. Drab, simple, sparse, the buildings and roads served their purpose. The oft-trod stone was worn down from regular use.

Like the city itself, the people he saw in this area were drab, faceless. No stone-faced men carved like mobile decorations, or palanquins carrying women and men adorned in finery. Children were huddled close to their parents, not playing freely.

And, even here, there seemed to be idle people on the side, sprawled against the stone and brickwork. Not beggars, but restless.

Eponine chatted idly, but Stas did not pay much attention. Eventually, as the sun began to set, she led him to a decrepit building on a crumbling road.

The doorway was bricked up and the windows were boarded shut. The street itself was near vacant, outside of a ragged man with bloodshot eyes who was slumped on a wall.

"Here we are."

Stas wrinkled his nose in disgust. "This is the meeting place." He could smell the distinct scent of piss from an alleyway adjacent to the building. He wouldn't have been surprised if there was some vomit mixed in. "How do you even get in? Do you pry open the windows and nail them shut every time someone comes?"

"There's a side door." Eponine waved to the scraggly man, who returned it with a nod. She then walked to a boarded-up window in an alley. She pressed a discolored brick, and pushed in the window, which swung on a hinge inward. Eponine stepped gingerly though the entrance.

She gestured and Stas followed suit. She shut the window behind him.

The inside was underwhelming, an unlit expanse of a single room. The ground was covered in a layer of straw, with a number of aging barrels haphazardly distributed across the space. Sacks of grain, sealed shut, lined the walls.

Stas frowned. "Are we the first ones here?" This "better meeting location" was falling far short of the promise.

Eponine held up a hand and walked to a barrel. She opened the side, revealing an opening in the floor with a dangling ladder. She climbed down without fear, and Stas followed. The barrel closed behind them.

Below was a long hallway lit with some magic sconces. They traveled for perhaps five city blocks in the dim darkness, over a well-paved path.

Along the way, Stas could make out the muffled sounds of some commotion, and some subtle stanzas of music.

He soon reached the end of the tunnel, where a thick metal door stood. The sounds emanated strongly from behind it.

Eponine knocked, three raps in quick succession, followed by two slow knocks, and finally three more.

Locks jostled. The door opened, revealing a weedy-looking woman and unleashing the noise. She glanced at Eponine, a neutral expression on her face. She noticed Stas, and it turned suspicious.

"Maria," Eponine said. She jutted her elbow into Stas lightly. "He's with me."

Maria frowned but stood aside.

The gathering area stood in stark contrast with the fake storehouse above. It was large, near the size of the Bell, with more doors leading off to further areas of unknown size. It was brightly lit, with sconces lining the sides, brightly painted walls, and comfortable furnishings.

It was also well populated. A few dozen people occupied the space, sharing drinks, speaking loudly to one another as if it were a bar and not a hidden enclosure. There was even a bartender, polishing mugs behind a counter that guarded a large number of tankards. A young boy darted between tables bringing the brews to the thankful men and women. A musician played a hearty tune in the corner, providing a background to the general noise.

Their entrance drew a great deal of attention, and a break in conversation. A dozen suspicious glances turned their way.

"Everyone," Eponine announced, "this is Stas."

Years of image training took over in an instant. Stas held still and strong to allow the people to take a look at him.

"The gladiator?" a plump red-haired man to the side called, words slurred slightly.

Eponine did not answer, looking instead towards Stas.

He nodded. "Yes. I am a student of Lanista Ludo's school and—"

"A gladiator!" a man cheered. "Come here, mister gladiator! Have a drink with me."

Stas glanced at Eponine, who shrugged. He made his way to the table.

"Hah, a bona fide gladiator joining us, who would have thought?" the drunk redhead cheered. "I am Lucian. This," he reached around and grabbed the shoulder of the bald man next to him, "is my friend, Romeo."

Romeo grinned. His face was sharp but his expression was kind. "I hope you're good at your job, because if you're one of us, I'll have to bet on you every single match."

"Yes," Lucian said. "Be kind to his wallet, please. I rely on Romeo to buy my drinks."

Romeo responded in kind, punching him in the shoulder. "When you cannot mooch them off somebody else."

"Ah ... yes." Stas looked to Eponine for direction.

She smiled and waved him off. "Enjolras will explain best."

"Cheers to Enjolras," Romeo declared, taking a large gulp of wine.

"Gladiator," Lucian slurred, "tell me, what did you think of today's match at the Grand?"

Stas blinked. "I didn't catch any of them. Which do you mean?"

"The beasts, the beasts." He jumped. "Of course the beasts. Nothing could compare."

"Ah, I am a duelist, not a venatio. I do not fight beasts."

Romeo snorted. "A good thing, that."

Stas quirked his head. "The venatio are a respectable group." There was more valor in fighting an intelligent opponent, but Stas would not disparage his near fellows. The coordination their efforts required was admirable.

"Aye, respectable," Romeo agreed. "But not fortunate."

"I suppose you hadn't heard then." Eponine brought herself into the conversation. "But the chimera of today's hunt slew every single venatio in the event."

Stas blanched.

"Who would have thought they would live to see the day the beast won." Lucian grinned. "The panic after was almost as fun, the beast handlers scrambling to secure the monster, the organizers running to and fro. It was the sight of a lifetime. Ah, so what do you think?"

Stas calmed himself. The accidental disrespect of a drunken man was not to be taken seriously. "The venatio know every hunt may be their last." He spoke solemnly. "We should honor their bravery, but not mourn them unduly."

"Of course, of course. To those brave gladiators. May their deeds be forever remembered. Let us drink in their honor!" Lucian raised a glass, as did some nearby listeners.

"Venatio, not gladiator," Stas corrected quietly. They were different professions, kept separate intentionally, even after the merger of most other categories of pit fighter. It was a distinction Stas would insist upon.

He had no desire to fight beasts.

"Romeo, where is Henri? Is he here yet?"

Romeo gestured to one of the open doorways, from where loud jeers emanated. "He's in the back room with Sanson."

"Of course," Eponine muttered. "Come along, Stas."

"Hey, let the gladiator stay and get a drink," Lucian cried. "Our wines are the best. Our spirits, phenomenal. Our ales … adequate."

The last time Stas drank, he had suffered for it dearly the morning after. He was not interested.

Even if the wine sounded tempting.

So he followed Eponine. She reached the door and stopped abruptly, staring within. Stas could soon see why.

The room was a small cove, speckled with a desk and a few chairs. An ornate shield was mounted prominently on the wall. Four men and a woman were circled around a recognizable pockmarked face standing upon a chair.

Hanging from the ugly man's hands, held aloft by ethereal thread, was the rotting corpse of a bird-masked man. It danced in the air like a marionette on arcane strings. Its head bobbed up and down on its sliced throat. Sanson sang a miserable falsetto with each movement in mockery of the deceased watcher.

"What the fuck is this?" Eponine growled.

"Hm?" The corpse puppet drooped as Sanson turned his attention to the door. "Ah, Eponine. What great timing. I was just showing off my new puppet." He twitched his fingers, making it flop.

"It's revolting." She spat.

Sanson chuckled cruelly. "Now, now, don't be like that. Everyone else is having good fun with the bastard, right?"

Two of the men cheered. The rest looked down guilty, but Sanson didn't seem to mind them.

"It's horrific! And moronic! What were you thinking, Sanson? Killing a watcher? We can't afford that sort of heat. And the rest of you just watched this idiocy."

One of the men in the circle, a short, handsome fellow with clean brown hair, pulled at his collar. "Erm, it's not as bad as you think, Eponine. We didn't kill him. We just found him like this. So … it's fine right?"

"And what if you were seen dragging that corpse around, Henri? Bringing something like that to the hideout?"

Henri shrank in on himself.

Sanson rolled his eyes. "We weren't caught. I made sure of it, you pansy. This is just some fun."

"It's a waste of elixirs, that's what it is. How many did you take for this disgusting little show?"

Sanson grinned. "It's not a waste if I am getting practice in. See?" The threads from his hand twitched and the body lurched forward, taking large, monstrous steps in the air. More twitches saw the body spin in place, raise and lower, and fall to the floor.

Eponine's gaze fell pointedly on Stas. "You are making a terrible impression."

Sanson scoffed. "He's a gladiator, isn't he? This is tamer than those fucking executions. If he can't stomach it, it's not my problem."

Eponine clenched her fist. A cheerful cry of "Enjolras" echoed from the front room.

Stas turned around and caught sight of the man entering through the thick metal door. The mood of the room seemed to elevate at his arrival. Slouched backs straightened. Smiles grew. Enjolras's presence brightened the place and pulled attention, like some strange arcanum.

Enjolras surveyed the room until he reached Stas. He smiled.

The warmth took Stas aback. His silver eyes were as earnest and joyful as before, despite Stas feeling it unearned. Stas could not bring himself to hold his gaze.

"Stas! I'm so glad you decided to join us. Did you find your way here easily enough?" he called.

He halted when he came close to the door, and the smile vanished from his face.

The corpse puppet sagged to the floor.

Enjolras pulled the door shut behind him. "Would somebody please explain the meaning of this?" he said, voice soft.

Sanson scratched his neck. "Well, erm. Henri found a dead watcher, so I thought we could have a bit of fun with it. No real harm to it. We were careful dragging it here. Made sure nobody saw us."

Enjolras sighed, directing his gaze to the corpse. "It is debasement. Mockery for the sake of cruelty. You know that as well as I, Sanson."

"It's just a fucking watcher, Enjolras," Sanson bit back. "It doesn't need your sympathy."

"Does he not?" Enjolras said. "Behind that mask is, was, a citizen. Same as you or I. He was born in this city, lived in this city, died in it. He donned his cloak not out of cruelty or desire to oppress, but for duty, misplaced as it may be. The watchers suffer from the same ills we do, suffer the same grievances. Their ignorance does not change this. Though we may come into conflict with them, that does not change who they are. We must grant our foes respect. The respect to fight them properly, the respect to treat them properly afterwards. Lest we fail as citizens."

Enjolras turned to face the room. "I understand that you are angry.

You have good reason to feel it. My own rage burns brightly in my chest from dawn to dusk. But your targets have become misplaced. We should not hate our poor foes. Whether they are deceived or desperate, whether they oppress because they view it as proper or because they fear being under that same lash, they are not the cause. The rank and file are victims too."

The room was still. Stas watched it in rapt attention.

"You will take him to the outlands," he declared to Sanson, "with all the care you took in sneaking him here. There, you will give him a proper burial. Find a gravestone, mark it as appropriate."

Sanson blanched. "Can't we just dispose of him like normal? Get something out of it at least?"

Enjolras looked down at the corpse. "No. He has been defiled enough. You will treat him properly in recompense."

Sanson grit his teeth. "Fine. Henri, help me out." Sanson removed his threads and grabbed the body from under the shoulders.

Henri grimaced, but nodded. "I'll grab the legs, I guess?" He did so, and the two of them walked out. Cries of disgust filled the bar area as they passed.

Enjolras sighed once again. "If I might ask you all to clear the room? I wish to speak with Stas. Eponine, please remain."

The others in the room left without complaint and the door closed.

# Thirteen

"I apologize for such a display." Enjolras bowed his head. "It was badly done."

Stas nodded, unsure of what to say.

"I suppose you must have some questions."

Stas nodded again. "Who are you? I know you fight the watchers, so you are criminals of some sort, but ..." He couldn't really formulate the question properly.

But Enjolras seemed to understand it all the same. He nodded. "Criminals? By necessity, perhaps. Before I answer your question, Stas, might I turn it around? You wish to know who we are? I wish to explain who we want to be."

Stas blinked, unsure of what he meant.

"I don't mean to deflect," Enjolras explained. "Only to provide context. I find there is value in acknowledging the differences between reality and desire, the *is* and the *ought*. The goal matters, separate from the state of things ... ah, but I am rambling. Stas, are you aware of the population of the city? The number of citizens that can claim residence?"

"No?" This felt irrelevant, but Stas did not feel comfortable challenging the man on it. "I know the arenas can seat a few hundred thousand people, and that not everyone can find seats. So ..." He made a quick guess. "Maybe eight hundred thousand in total?" The number was massive. He hoped he was not overestimating by much.

Enjolras shook his head. "True numbers are hard to come by, but estimates range between four and six million."

"What?"

Enjolras continued. "Though the number you came to is not inaccurate from a certain point of view. If I were to ask how many citizens could afford tickets to the arena without relying on the whims of the lots, you could count a few hundred thousand. But they are a mere fraction. Perhaps four in five citizens are unemployed, and rely entirely on the grain dole for survival." Enjolras smiled, but it was mirthless. "The number of people that are both employed and have the means to enjoy the fruits of the city, the forum, the grand baths, the magic market, number in the tens of thousands. Patricians, from whom the body of the Senate is exclusively chosen, number in the thousands. And yet, in the city that holds this five million and among all the farms in the outlands, patricians are the only ones that are permitted to own land. And the average patrician is closer to a plebeian than they are to the fantastic wealth of the hundred senators.

"The problem is obvious, yes?" He shook his head mournfully. "In this grand, wonderful, wealthy city, four million people sit idle and destitute, robbed of their dignity, kept as beggars to the Dominus's teat. Their labor is lost, their personhood ignored. They should be able to work their own fields as owners of their own land, rather than spend their lives waiting in line for their daily grain. They should be employed to produce greater works for them to enjoy. The shackles of bread and circus keep them suffering under the yoke, but it is an all too fragile state. If they were to miss a meal—"

"We are a revolutionary group," Eponine said suddenly. "We are trying to overthrow the Senate."

Enjolras deflated, pouting. "Did you have to interrupt me? I was getting there."

"You were taking too long," she declared. "You can explain your manifesto at any time, but not when somebody is waiting for a straight answer."

Stas had to make sure he was hearing correctly. "You want to replace the Senate?"

Eponine nodded. "The Senate, some of the patricians, and the Dominus too."

Stas nearly choked. "The Dominus?" It was the definition of unthinkable. The Dominus was the Dominus. The founder of the city was eternal.

"A daunting task, yes." Enjolras nodded solemnly. "Ultimately, they are responsible for the complacency of the Senate. We feel that the citizens of the city would be better served by a different government structure, which empowers the individual citizen to—"

"You're getting too bogged down in the details again," Eponine said. "Policy particulars don't matter right now. Do you have any questions about this?"

Stas had managed to wrap his head around the idea, if only barely. "Where do I fit into this?"

Eponine jumped in to answer. "You are a gold mine. Your combat training, for one, is extremely valuable. But way more important than that is your social value. Fame, influence, money ... if your career blossoms you'll get all of that. The people will love you. You'll have the ear of patricians, senators even. You'll have a level of trust and access that we could only dream about. Even as a complete novice, you're already living on the palatial estate. None of the rest of us have that privilege."

"Your status is indeed a boon, I'll admit," Enjolras cut in, stepping in front of his companion. "But character matters more to me than that. More than the fact you are willing to fight the watchers. As I said before, I consider myself a good judge of character. And I feel that you are the sort of person who cares about this plight, who is motivated to act. A person who understands justice and seeks it, even if they don't know how. I know you are a good man, and we are eager to have good men join us."

Stas clenched his teeth. Again, he was being called a good man. It was a difficult compliment to accept. Eponine's position at least made sense. Enjolras, in comparison, seemed to trust him far too much with far too little reason for comfort. It would be too easy to disappoint him.

"Please do not feel pressured. Our goal is a dangerous and difficult one, we have no delusions about it. You should only join us if you have no reservations in your heart."

"What happens if I say no?"

"Then, regrettably, Eponine would erase your memories, and you would be escorted out of the hideout. It would be for both your safety and ours."

The idea sat badly with Stas.

"Please," Enjolras implored, hand on his heart, "ask me whatever it is you wish to help you decide. Test my virtue, and I will answer your every question."

His words were too earnest, like baring one's neck. It made Stas feel guilty for some reason. He swallowed. "You say you are a revolutionary group, but what does that mean? What do you do?"

Enjolras nodded. "Of course. That is straight to the point. The simple answer is that we do whatever we must to advance our cause. We gather information. We write and distribute pamphlets. We are creating a network among the people, to better know what ails them and to know what actions our foes are taking."

Eponine jumped in. "And we take necessary action. Arson. Sabotage. Bombings. Assassinations."

Enjolras frowned. "Only with the greatest deliberation. Terrorism is a tool to be used only when necessary, and only when it advances the people's interests. Far more often than not, the death and destruction would fail to have a positive effect, or the missions are infeasible. The truly heinous individuals are well protected."

"We'd probably do it more if we knew we could do it safely and stealthily," Eponine said with a shrug. "But risk to reward currently makes it not worth it most of the time."

Enjolras frowned sharply but did not disagree with the notion. "As it stands, the lives of our comrades are more valuable than the deaths of our enemies. That is very unlikely to change. Our goal is to help the city, not destroy it."

Stas nodded. "This group of yours, how did it come about?"

"It is hardly my own group. Libertas belongs to all of us, to the city itself." Enjolras blinked. "Ah, did I not mention the name until now? Our group takes the name Libertas, after an ancient being who stood for freedom from bondage. We, like our namesake, work to that end. As for our history ... we are not the first to seek revolution. The pain of the citizens existed long before us, and the will for change did not come from nowhere."

Enjolras gestured to the shield hanging from the wall. The shining metal gleamed in the light of the room. It looked to be quite a fine implement, a strong metal core gilded with a thin layer of gold. "Do you see that shield? It is a relic we hold dear, one I was granted by my predecessor." Enjolras took the shield off the wall and held it between his hands. "Do you have a dagger? A weapon of some sort? Ah, it doesn't matter. Eponine, please hand him yours."

Eponine retrieved a small blade from under her shirt. She handed it to Stas. Confused, he accepted it.

"I imagine you are quite proficient with a blade," Enjolras said. "Please strike it."

Stas hesitated. "Are you sure? I'd hate to mar it with a scratch."

Enjolras grinned, some grand amusement visible in his silver eyes. "Please. As hard as you can."

Frowning, Stas did as he was instructed, striking the shield with as much strength as he could muster. To his shock, the moment the blade touched the metal sheen, he felt all the force of his arm leave him. The blade slid across the shield harmlessly, not even leaving a crease in the gold.

"This is no ordinary shield," Enjolras explained, deep satisfaction on his face. "It is a perfect implement: indestructible, more than a match for any blow. Its creator put their heart and soul into the work, invoking the absolute ideal in the form of a shield, eternal and unequaled. We have had this for years, and it does not even gather dust."

A magic shield. Like Radek's sword. Stas swallowed.

Enjolras returned the shield to its mantle. "My predecessor's organization met an unfortunate end." He sighed mournfully. "They were a righteous group, but flawed in methodology. The mistakes they made are known to us, and we take the lesson to heart. It is perhaps as great a gift as the shield itself.

"But with the shield came the group's purpose, their dreams, their creed. We inherited their mission and made it our own. The shield itself is the perfect symbol. Just as it protects all those that wield it, so too do we protect the city from its ills. Just as its arcanum and craft make it indestructible, so too is our will unbreakable, our passion indefatigable. Just as it remains ever unmarred, so too will we remain pure in our spirit. Our revolution shall last as long as the shield, and the shield shall last eternal."

"Do you ever use it?" Stas inquired.

"Of course. Sitting on a wall is of no value. But we are careful to ensure that it is used where best needed, and only when it cannot be lost."

Eponine smirked, catching his eye. "You know, if you were to join, you would probably get to use it. None of us are trained like you are. You'd be able to make the most out of it."

That was almost a reason enough to join on its own. Eponine's grin grew, seeming to read his thoughts.

"You got it from your predecessor, but do you know where they got it?" Stas asked.

Enjolras shook his head. "Sadly, no. The organization's records burned with them. Their history is lost to us, and with it, any hint to such matters. I would love to meet the smith talented enough to produce a soul-crafted item, but we have no idea where it came from originally."

It was a pity. Stas was dearly interested in other equipment from such a smith. "One last question. If I were to join, would I have access to training?"

Enjolras looked confused. "Training? Well, we do have some practice sessions to help people learn arcanum or dagger-play, but it is an informal thing. Anything we teach would pale in comparison to the lessons you would have access to at your school."

Stas scratched his neck, a new wave of awkwardness overwhelming him. "Aha, yes. Of course. I shouldn't have expected otherwise."

Stas felt too ashamed to admit that he had lost that privilege. He would just have to find some other means of getting an instructor.

"So," Eponine ventured. "If that was your last question, you must have decided?"

Stas nodded. "I will join."

She smirked. Enjolras beamed. "Wonderful! I am ecstatic that you will be joining us. Come, let's get you introduced to everyone."

He opened the door, pulling Stas out with him. "My comrades." His voice projected across the room with authority. The rowdy crowd quieted near instantly. "I would like to formally introduce our newest member, Stas!" He gestured to Stas.

"Hah!" Lucian's voice screamed out. "Told you! Cheers to the gladiator!" He beat his hand on the table rhythmically, soon joined by others.

"Come now, Stas. Allow me to introduce you to everyone. If you wish for a drink first, then, by all means, we can grab one. Our hideout is kept stocked by Agnes and Simon. They run a bar in the south side of the city."

"Ah …" Stas swallowed, mouth dry. "Some sweet wine, perhaps?"

Enjolras nodded. "I remember which one you liked. I know one just like it."

A wine glass found its way to his hands very quickly.

Stas was dragged from person to person, hearing a name, a short description, some platitudes. He had trouble keeping track of the people, the faces and names blurring together more than he wished to admit.

Thirty-six people in total, not counting the two that had been sent to dispose of the corpse. In some ways, it was a great number. But compared to the goals, it felt like very few.

Stas kept a lookout for a particular figure, a body shape he hoped to recognize, but none of the individuals present matched it enough to be certain. He decided to ask directly.

"I ran into somebody last week, right after we met. I thought he was one of yours, but I don't think I see him here." He had managed to keep to a single glass of wine this night, sipping the sweet liquid slowly.

Enjolras looked up over his own cup. "Hm? I'm not sure what you mean. Recognize somebody?"

"He wore a mask. A blue one, with the image of an eye on the right side. On my right side," Stas said. "I encountered him attacking some watchers, a few blocks outside of the forum."

"A blue mask you say?"

"Oh, you met the masked man?" a woman beside him said.

"Do you know him?"

Eponine answered. "He's a rumor, going back for the last couple of years. A secretive character that stalks the night, wearing a mask with an evil eye, attacking people with no rhyme or reason. Practically a myth. But it's a useful one."

"Enjolras," a man off to the side called. "Help me settle a dispute."

"Ah, begging your pardon." Enjolras got up and headed over, leaving Stas with Eponine and a few strangers.

Stas decided against following him, opting to continue the conversation. "How so?"

"Well, he mucks up investigations. I know at least one watcher outpost that has wasted effort trying to track him down. And, despite the rumors, nobody knows anyone who's been attacked by him. But if he's going after watchers, that would explain things."

At Stas's confused expression, she explained. "The watchers never disclose losses. If any of them die, they refuse to let anyone know. It's part of why they wear masks: prevent people from knowing how many there are, and prevent people from being able to tell which particular ones are where. We only recently managed to get a halfway decent estimate of them."

"And how many is that?"

"There are nearly ten thousand watchers active in the city, across forty-eight headquarters. Minus the one Henri found today."

"Six," Stas corrected, drawing some attention. He clarified. "Six fewer. I saw the masked man kill five that day. So adding in today's corpse makes six." From the wounds, Stas had a suspicion that the masked man had been responsible for that one as well.

"Making our lives easier." The woman, Katriane was her name, spoke lightly. "Maybe we should see about recruiting him."

Eponine shook her head. "Enjolras wouldn't approve, likely. He's still trying to get sympathizers within the watchers' ranks. If we recruit a serial watcher killer, that plan would fall apart more than it already is."

"What's this about it falling apart already?" A man—named either Orval or Orville—asked. "Something happened?"

"No. Nothing happened. It's just as much of a fool's errand as it has been. Enjolras has been beating at it for nearly a year. He hasn't made any headway. There're better uses of his time than that."

"Hmph." Orval shook his head. "I think getting some insiders in the guard is more than worth the effort."

"Nobody is saying it wouldn't be valuable. It's just that it's far harder than we hoped. Finding a watcher who lives off their base is hard enough. Getting into contact with them is even harder, to say nothing of actually getting them on our side."

Stas sipped his wine, nursing it to last. He might need a second glass soon. The young boy was quick to bring him one.

"Though I don't even know why Enjolras cares so much about it. His contact already gets us all the watcher routes and schedules."

"Contact?"

"Enjolras has a contact who feeds us information. It's part of why we've been so successful. I've got no idea who it is, though." Eponine shrugged. "Enjolras is very tight-lipped about him. I suspect even he might not know for sure."

"Probably not a watcher," Katriane said. "Unless he's just spending so much time on that for no reason."

"Right," Eponine agreed. "I'd guess it to be some jealous patrician. Somebody who wants to get one over a rival and is trying to use us as much as we use them. Maybe even a senator. Enjolras is a patrician himself, so he's got access to those kinds of people."

"He's a noble? He seemed to hate them."

"A second son of Lord Julianus." Eponine nodded. "He renounced the institution and moved from the eastern quarter to be among the plebeians. But he still visits and speaks to his family and fellows when it serves his purposes. It's not a secret." She grinned conspiratorially. "If you want to annoy him, all you have to do is call him 'Lord.'"

Now that he was looking for it, Stas could see it easily. The man's clothing was a step beyond everyone else's in the hideout, as was his bearing and manner of speech. Only a few compared, including Eponine. And himself, he supposed.

"Are you a patrician?" he asked Eponine.

"No." Her answer was swift and sharp. Perhaps she had a grudge.

Not that it mattered much to him. There were no patricians in the provinces, only plebs. And it was an exceedingly rare day when a lord decided to become a gladiator.

He didn't even think that Ludo was a patrician. Nobody referred to the man as a lord of anything, despite his wealth.

Lord Galbrio might have been the only patrician he had met, unless the Mad Monk counted, which Stas did not think was the case.

"Henri's a patrician's brat too," Katriane said. "You wouldn't know it from the way he acts, but he's an heir even. Sanson really dug into him when he joined up. Ah, I don't know if you met him. Sanson is the big guy that left with Henri a bit back. He focuses on … 'counterespionage,' he claims. I think he just likes needling people."

"I've met him," Stas grunted.

"Since you're a gladiator, you get to live on the palace estate with all the others, right? You ever met Horatio Undaunted? What's he like in person?"

Stas shook his head. "I haven't had the chance yet. I've only been in the city for a few months. But once I meet him, I can let you know."

Conversation stayed like that, with people dancing between topics and asking him questions on various aspects of his life. It was a nice experience, having people take an interest in him, even if he was disappointed that he could not live up to their grandiose ideals of the gladiator lifestyle.

Hours whittled away in the casual setting before Stas had to beg off, with a promise to return for the next meeting in two weeks' time.

But he was not heading back to the school. Not yet. The night was still young, and he needed to resolve his lack-of-instructor issue.

He was going to see if he could find the masked man once again.

# Fourteen

Finding a single individual in a city of millions was an impossible task, by most accounts. Stas had no idea how another person might manage it. But he had a particular advantage.

Stas's magic, as he had tried to explain to Eponine, was not teleportation. For all that it was his most practiced and most useful expression, it failed to represent the full extent of his unique arcanum. Stas did not move. He *saw*.

The world and its *reflections* were always laid bare before him. He did not have to scour the city to find a person. He only needed to catch sight of their *reflection*.

Not that it was an easy task. There were countless mirrors, unveiling every part of the world from every direction, not even counting the unnerving mirrors that Stas did not dare gaze into. To peer through them all was just as impossible as checking each building one by one, if not worse.

But Stas did not need to look at them all. The masked man was unique in this city. And he kept to the rooftops where none other than himself or the bird-masked watchers frequented. If the assassin was out and about as he had been that night, clad in his one-eyed mask, then Stas might have a chance to find him.

Of course, if he was hiding as a normal plebian or asleep in bed, he would be impossible to find. But Stas had waited until the late hour to give himself a better chance.

He climbed up to the rooftop and gazed upon the mirrors, searching for people upon the roofs, searching for any glimpse of that distinctive blue mask in the expanse that was the world.

There were watchers aplenty. Hundreds. Thousands, perhaps. The number did not matter to him. A few dirty plebeians curled up on decaying roofs. Stas *reflected* to another rooftop, shifting perspective around the taller buildings that blocked his view. He stretched his sight obliquely around them, taking care to avoid the unnerving mirrors.

And then ... It was the barest hint, a flash of blue with a single white eye. Stas twisted his mind's eye for a better picture of the moving man. The assassin was present on this night, far across the city.

His head throbbed, burning from the task. But he had done it. It would have been convenient to *reflect* at that moment, but the distance was great. Stas had to take the further step of finding a path across the city, heading to where the assassin was traveling. Despite the pain, he set forth on the trail, an almost mindless state as his target's reflection darted into and out of sight lines.

It took some time to catch up, but eventually he could see the masked man, and not just his reflection. He had positioned himself in the open, facing Stas, a hand on his dagger.

"Why are you following me?" The assassin glowered. "Just because I didn't kill you before doesn't mean I won't if you become a bother."

Stas jolted out of his fugue. The pain in his head was near unbearable, and his skin itched intently. But he forced himself to respond. "Ah, you remember me."

"I'm old, not senile. It's only been a week."

"Are you killing more watchers tonight?" Stas inquired. "There aren't any around here."

"What do you know about that?" the man asked. "And what I'm

doing has nothing to do with you."

"I want you to train me, Masked Man."

The man put his hand to his forehead. "Brat, there is being stubborn and there's just being obnoxious. I already told you no."

Stas held himself firm. "No. You said that I had nothing you wanted. But that's not true." He forced his voice calm and attempted to project a level of professionalism. "You want elixirs. You looted them from the watchers. Well, I have elixirs."

The man said nothing.

"I'm a gladiator," he said. "My school supplies me with elixirs. But I don't need them for my arcanum." Stas had never bothered to explain his magic to the school, meaning they wouldn't question him about the potions. Ludo might have cut off his access to training, but the commissar's services were still open to him. "If you train me, I will provide them all to you. Far more convenient than fighting watchers, wouldn't you say?"

To his great irritation, the man remained unresponsive.

Stas clenched his teeth in frustration. If he had a problem with the offer, he should just come out and say it. Standing silently helped nobody.

But as Stas opened his mouth, the man spoke. "The elixirs. What quality are they? How many do you have access to?"

Stas didn't actually know. But he was hardly going to tell the man that. "The highest quality. We're gladiators. They don't scrimp on our equipment." He thought back to his experience at the Bell. "It's far better than those cruddy snuff boxes."

The masked man seemed to consider it.

"As for the amount …" He paused, thinking. Nobody had told him about any limit, but there was only so much he could request before being suspected. Or before Ludo accused him of wastefulness. "I can acquire three vials a day," he estimated.

He might need to fake drinking vials. It might be a good idea to do that on the arena sands as well. He would hate to be tarred by the brush of bad sportsmanship for "drinking an elixir before the match." While Stas knew he was innocent of such bad faith, future audiences might be ignorant.

The assassin sucked a breath through his teeth. "I am not a teacher, you realize? I have no practice in pedagogy or any of that shit."

"I don't care," Stas said. "You are skilled enough." He wasn't in a position to be too picky. He was good enough to make up for bad teachers, so long as they provided direction.

The man clenched his fists and sighed deeply. "Fine, brat. I'll be your instructor."

Stas grinned. "Excellent!" This evening was going great. Far better than last week. "I'd like to start with—"

The assassin held up a hand. "No. Not tonight, brat. I'm busy."

Stas glared. "Fine, not tonight. But if I am going to be your student, you cannot refer to me as 'brat.' My name is Stas, Masked Man."

"If I'm going to be your teacher, I will call you whatever I damn please. And it's Phobos, not 'Masked Man.'"

"Phobos, then." The man was looking to be abrasive, but Stas could work with unpleasant people if it meant getting stronger. "If not tonight, then when?"

"In a week's time. At the Trajan Bell Tower in the north of the city. Bring a week's worth of elixirs with you."

"Unacceptable." Stas had lost too much time already. "A week is far too long away. We will meet tomorrow."

From behind the single eye hole, Phobos glared. "Fine, tomorrow, same place. But you still need to bring a week's worth of elixirs."

Stas considered. He could probably acquire what he needed. "This is not for a single lesson. If I am paying so much, I would expect more."

Phobos huffed. "Six per lesson. The up-front payment for good faith."

"Agreeable." Stas nodded.

"I will be at the top of the tower an hour after sunset. You will bring the elixirs. If you waste my time, I will make you regret it."

"And if you waste mine, I will do the same," Stas retorted.

Phobos did not seem to be concerned by the threat, ignoring it entirely.

He turned away. "You've taken up enough of my time tonight. Don't follow me any further." And with that, the man leaped off the roof for a railing on a building opposite the wide street. He then pulled himself up with the dexterity of a cat and returned to running. The city's rooftops were no obstacle to him.

Phobos was very skilled. Stas had made the correct choice in seeking him out.

He looked forward to the lesson. But for now, he needed to return before his decoy faded.

# Fifteen

The rooftop of the Trajan Bell Tower was a precarious location. It was small and steeply inclined, and Stas could barely keep steady. Every gust of wind threatened to send him plummeting off the side, down so very far to the streets down below. Worse, perhaps, he might keep falling into the chasm, that dried-up riverbed that split the city in two. The ramshackle huts built into the side of that expansive gap did not look sturdy enough to catch him if he were unlucky enough to fall past the bridge.

Phobos did not share his concern. The man was completely at ease at the height, seeming to bask in the blustering wind.

"This doesn't seem like a good place to train," Stas murmured.

"It's a safe spot from the guards," Phobos said. "Out of sight and out of hearing. The few of them that could make it up here won't bother."

"I don't blame them. It was a pain to get up here," Stas grumbled. Even with his arcanum he'd had to climb more than he wished. Finding grips in the crumbling edifice was not a pleasant experience.

"Consider it training," Phobos said. "Regardless, hand over the vials."

Stas removed the bandoleer of elixirs and passed it to the man. "What if the climb damaged them?"

Phobos shrugged. "That would be your problem, not mine." He took a vial from the middle and examined it. Uncorking it, he dipped his finger into the vial, extracted a drop, and dragged it across his skin, which reddened, irritated.

He nodded to himself and resealed the vial.

"The strap isn't yours," Stas reminded him.

The masked man grunted; he took each vial one by one, securing them somewhere on his person. He tossed the empty sash back to Stas, who caught it.

"There. Payment met. So, what are we starting with?"

"Observation," the man said simply.

Stas scoffed. "Yeah, no. I'm paying for this. We are going to do something real."

Phobos seemed to glare, even through the opaque mask. "There are two things you can train from up this high: observation skills, or getting shoved off from this height and seeing how you land. Which do you prefer?"

"The second, obviously." Stas nodded to himself.

Phobos rubbed his hand against his forehead. "Brat ..." He seemed to bite back words. "Observation is important."

Stas rolled his eyes. "I know that. A blind gladiator is a dead gladiator. But I am observant enough already. We can skip the basics."

"Observant enough, you say? How many wagons have driven by since you arrived?"

"What?"

"It's not a hard question. The wagons are all lit—you have no excuse for missing them. So, how many?"

Stas frowned. "That's not fair. I didn't know to pay attention."

Phobos flicked him in the forehead. "That's the point. You're never going to know what you need to pay attention to in advance. You need to be aware of every little thing. Otherwise you'll miss the crossbows being pointed at you."

Phobos gestured, and Stas whirled around.

On the spine in the center of the bell tower's roof, hidden by the growing shadows of sunset, was a loaded crossbow aiming straight for him.

Phobos raised a hand, letting Stas see the thread that connected to it.

Stas swallowed and stepped out of the weapon's path.

"Not everything is the arena," Phobos said, moving towards the crossbow. "Not every fight is clean." He removed the weapon from its perch. The bolt was removed, and the weighted lever was released, firing blank and loudly.

Stas inhaled. "Fine. I may not be as observant as I had assumed. But I am not training for everything, only the arena."

Phobos took a deep breath. "Perhaps we should start with your weaknesses, then. Are you aware of why I was able to defeat you?"

Stas shrugged. "You are better at hand to hand than me. I usually practice with weapons, and it seems I have fallen into those habits when it comes to using my arcanum. Now that I am aware, I can work to correct it." Stas was not an unarmed fighter, nor did he desire to become one. But he wouldn't let himself be helpless if he ever got disarmed. Or if he were ever forced to go without again.

"No," Phobos grunted. "That's not why you lost. If you had a sword, I'd still beat you."

Stas narrowed his eyes. "I assure you that, while I might have not acquitted myself well with my fists alone, I am far more practiced with a blade. I can demonstrate, if you wish. Do not underestimate me."

"You could be a perfect sword master and it still wouldn't matter. Your problem is mindset, not skill."

Stas bit back a retort. The man was acting as his teacher, so he would try to heed him. He didn't have other options.

"We fought for less than a minute, but you're such an open book it may as well have been a lifetime," Phobos said. "You're used to winning, aren't you? Used to being stronger, faster, more skilled than your opponent. Used to your magic overwhelming people. Tell me if I am wrong."

"You are not wrong." Stas took pride in it. He had earned his strength, his skill, with dedication and training. He had honed that useless burden that had been his arcanum into a tool that could demolish any peer.

He won because he worked for it. Because he earned it.

"It's given you terrible habits," Phobos said. "You fight assuming you're going to overwhelm your opponent. You use your magic carelessly, assuming nobody can adapt. You only know how to win by being better."

"But I am better!" Stas insisted. "If not now, then in the future. So long as I can train and learn, I will always achieve victory."

"Feh. There's always someone stronger. That will never change. The people ahead of you ... do you expect them to rest on their laurels? Are you just going to hope they wait for you? Do you plan on just rolling over for anyone stronger, faster, more skilled?"

Stas grit his teeth. "What are you suggesting?"

"You're familiar with chess, right?"

"No? What is it?"

Phobos cursed under his breath. "Never mind that. Okay, consider this. Suppose you summon a ring of fire around your opponent, but there's a gap in it—"

"If I could summon a ring of fire, why would I leave a gap in it?"

The blue mask glared. "Don't interrupt me, brat. This is hypothetical. You summon a ring of fire, but there is a gap in it. What do you think your opponent would do?"

Stas considered.

"This isn't a trick question, brat," Phobos spat.

"He would escape through the gap."

117

Phobos nodded. "Good. Now, knowing that, what should you do?"

"I could attack him there?" Stas mused. "Or set a trap where the gap is?"

"Right. Now, switch this around. You have just been surrounded by a ring of fire, but there is a gap in it. What should you do?"

Stas frowned. "Go through the fire instead?"

"And get your fool self burned? Are you fireproof?"

Stas shook his head.

"Then don't act like you are fireproof." Phobos grunted. "Try again."

"I would reflect through the gap in the fire, past where any traps might be set up."

Phobos nodded again. "Good. This," he gestured vaguely, "is what I am getting at. Winning a fight is not about being better. It's about the flow. Force your enemies to do what you want—prevent them from controlling you. Limit their options, maximize your own. Do you understand?"

It sounded pretty obvious to Stas, but he nodded.

"That's what you are missing. You're like a narcissist, only focused on what you can do. Your strategies are shallow, and you flounder when you can't browbeat. If I'm going to teach you, that's what I'll fix." Phobos held up a finger. "The first step is observation. If you fail to notice something, your planning will be useless. You need to be able to take in everything quickly, effectively, and accurately. That's what tonight is for."

Stas took a deep breath. "Perhaps there is wisdom in your direction. But 'observation' cannot be all that you would teach me. Surely your weapon skills are on the table as well. It was your use of the chain that drew my eye." Unique weapons made for crowd favorites. Sword and shield was a classic for a reason, but it did not make for a brand all on its own.

Phobos shrugged. "Can't help you there. My style depends on the hook, and that's one of a kind."

Stas's eyes widened. "You have a magic weapon?"

"No." The response was immediate. "I have a magic hook. I just happen to use it as a weapon."

Stas didn't really see the distinction. "What can it do?"

"You saw me fight. What do you think? Consider this part of your observation training."

"More memory game than observation," Stas grumbled, but he did as instructed and thought back to the fight. "I saw it grab hold of a man, who you pulled in. The watcher attempted to resist with arcanum, but it was worthless. Does the hook disrupt arcanum?" Stas shook his head. "No, the acid-wielder was able to destroy the chain even after being snared. Does the hook ensure that any it catches can be pulled in?"

Phobos nodded. "Anything else?"

More confident after the approval, Stas continued. "I saw the hook change course mid-flight. I imagine it can fix your aim as well."

Phobos nodded again. "Seems you aren't horrendous at noticing things. You just need to work on your tunnel vision. To answer your question, the hook does three things. Or one, depending on how you count it. It attaches itself, it stays in until I want it out, and it lets me reel them in. Nothing can get in the way of that. Essentially, it's the perfect fishhook. That's what it is supposed to be after all."

Stas blanched. "A magic fishhook? What sort of madman would waste the effort on such a thing?"

Phobos shrugged. "I wouldn't know. Lucky for me, the perfect fishhook makes for a decent weapon. And no. I am not selling it. So there's no point in you learning how to use it."

Stas frowned. "I see. But your knife skills are exemplary, as is your unarmed. You should teach me that."

The masked man sighed. "Fine. When it makes sense. But not

tonight. This isn't the place for that."

"Acceptable. Can we start now?"

"Of course. Take a good look around the city, because I am going to be quizzing you on it." Phobos took out a piece of cloth from somewhere on his person. "I hope you paid attention while climbing up here, because you are going to be going back down blindfolded."

Stas held his tongue. At least this wasn't as boring as simply counting wagons.

# Sixteen

The sands of the Stellar arena were no different from any other. While Stas had been reliably informed that each stadium represented a unique experience for the adoring throngs, the designers had taken care to ensure that the fights themselves would be unimpeded by the venue.

The rumblings of the crowd were identical.

This was to be the fourth match of his career. He had enjoyed victory in the previous three and did not wish for his perfect streak to end here.

"Presenting," the loud voice of the announcer echoed through the entrance hall, "of the Ludo School of the Forum! The undefeated provincial! Stas the Blink!" The music of the band drummed him forth. Stas stepped into the light, arms raised.

Cheers greeted him. Most were indecipherable: wordless and nameless, simple cries of excitement. But among the roaring throng, Stas could make out a distinctive rally.

"Stas! Stas! Stas!" they cried, to his pleasure. Less enjoyable were the equal number crying: "Blink! Blink! Blink!"

Stas held back a grimace. As far as titles went, "Blink" was not the worst, but it ranked quite low. If he ever met the clever announcer who had coined the odious name ... well, his conduct would upset Ludo.

121

Still, cheers were cheers, and Stas basked in them. He wondered how many members of Libertas were in the stands, if Enjolras had come to see his victory.

The band changed its tune, and the announcer resumed his duties.

"And presenting," the voice bellowed, "also of the Ludo School of the Forum! Usurper of the Lion's Beard! Thrice victorious this year! Zola the Tigress!"

And with the proclamation declared, Zola entered the arena from the entrance opposite him. She was bedecked in her armor, helmet held in her arms. On her back a long flowing cape advertised some cart repair shop.

The calls of "Zola" and "Tigress" were louder than his own. Stas did not begrudge Zola her fans. She had been establishing her career for longer. He was, however, envious of her nickname.

With a flourish, Zola unclipped the cape from her shoulders and whipped it around, allowing everyone in the audience to read its bold lettering. She let it fall to the ground behind her, to be retrieved by an attendant before it could interfere with the fight.

This was her second match with the sponsorship, and she had handily won the first. Stas wondered if the shop would pursue his endorsement if he proved victorious today.

After ensuring everyone had a chance to see her face, Zola secured her helmet. Stas took a moment to appraise her equipment. Her armor was heavier than his own, offering full coverage. He wore simple padding. She sported two short swords, sheathed at her hips. He had a sword and shield. She wore a belt of three elixirs. He had a bandoleer with three vials of water.

The two of them stepped forwards to meet in the center.

Zola grinned. "Well, well, well. Seeing us matched up like this. You've had such a nice streak going too, my friend. Shame I have to be the one to ruin it for you."

There was no heat in her words. Stas offered a smirk in return. "I'm just happy not to have to say the same. After all, you don't have a real streak for me to break."

"Hah." Zola barked out a short laugh before unsheathing her blades. "Well, we'll see who comes out on top. You better not hold anything back, Stas."

"So long as you do the same, Zola," he retorted, grasping the silver hilt of his own sword.

Zola's blades were smaller, designed to get inside a larger sword's guard. They were also notched to catch an opposing blade.

He would have to watch out for that.

In their readied stances, they both turned to the aedile, awaiting his command.

The signal was delivered, and the band roared into action.

Immediately Zola tossed her knife into the air, sending it spinning. With the freed hand, she brought an elixir to her lips. The well-practiced trick was a proper crowd-pleaser, and the audience roared her name with joy.

After so many weeks with Phobos, however, Stas could not see it as anything but an opening. The smart move would be to strike now, before the liquid touched her lips. Zola's arcanum could only make the fight more difficult.

And yet that would be terrible sportsmanship. So he simply watched as Zola caught her knife deftly.

Zola struck her knives together, grinning wildly. "I hope you are ready, my friend, because I developed this little trick just for you."

Yellow sparks jolted from the tips of her blades, jumping from one to the other in a vibrant bolt of lightning. The magic expanded outwards, arcing around her in a splendid, crackling shield.

The accompanying sound was as loud as thunder. It overwhelmed the crowd for an instant.

The lightning faded just as quickly as it arrived. He could see the slagged bits of sand where some of the bolts had diverted.

"Careful, my friend," she said with a grin. "I don't know if you'll be able to survive if you get hit by it."

She pulsed her arcanum once more, unleashing the lightning shield once again.

Approaching Zola, from any side, was a fool's endeavor. He would be electrocuted before he could retaliate. The obvious solution would be to run out the elixirs. Zola had only brought three, and the magic looked wasteful.

But such a victory would be unsatisfying, both for the crowd and himself. Stas would not be a coward.

Stas shifted his stance.

Just as Stas had witnessed in the training yards many times before, Zola clanged her knives together. This time the lightning went straight for him.

Stas twisted to the side, letting his shield block the stray fringes of the branching bolt. The leather handle offered him a manner of protection from the magical lightning, but he felt his hand grip the hilt of his sword, feeling the cool touch of the silver plating.

Ironic. A cheaper sword would have had a wooden hilt. The decorative metal made for an unfortunate liability.

Stas did not hesitate, dropping the sword to the sands below. He banged his fist against his shield to prove to the crowd that the action was intentional.

With his free hand, Stas grabbed a vial from his bandoleer and brought the disguised water to his lips.

The crowd jeered and cheered in equal measure. The musicians picked up in tempo.

Zola unleashed another salvo. Stas pulled his arm back, winding up for a throw, eyes focused on a spot far behind her.

At the last possible moment, right before the lighting would have struck his shield, Stas *reflected* to the spot and threw the empty bottle.

Zola blindly unleashed her lighting shield, but Stas had not been foolish enough to be so close. She twisted around in time to catch the projectile with her blades. Had the vial been cheaper, it would have shattered in her face. But the vials for fights were sturdy, so it broke far less aggressively, batted into the sand.

Once again, quality disfavored Stas.

Not that he had great expectations for the attack. Both of them knew Zola's trick gave her advantage in melee, and Stas lacked ranged options. Throwing elixir vials was hardly unorthodox, though it was rarely successful.

To force her advantage, Zola immediately followed through by dashing to close the distance, sending another bolt of lightning as her vanguard.

Again, Stas was able to dodge the brunt of the attack, twisting to the side, and allowing his shield to catch the fringes. As Zola approached, he leaped back, eyes peeled for a location behind and to the side of her.

Zola's eyes darted to follow his gaze, one of her knives slashing out towards it, releasing a bolt in the same instant Stas teleported.

Momentum from his jump carried him even further from his target, safely out of the way of the lightning. Zola turned to face him once again.

This was a dodging game now, and the music reflected it. *Reflection* followed *reflection*, oftentimes at the tail of a bolt of magic. At one point, Zola consumed her second bottle, with far less flair, because she was forced to surround herself with her arc of lightning lest Stas take advantage. And so the game continued.

Stas had to take care not to fall into the rhythm of the band's beats. It was an amateur mistake, and any proper gladiator knew how to exploit it.

It was the band's purpose to match their tempo to him. Stas did not plan on making their job easy.

But his movement wasn't without purpose. He was not trying to waste time. Every *reflection* moved him and Zola as he desired.

Sat banged his shield once again. Zola met his challenge, unleashing two scattered bolts of arcanum, one from each blade.

The attacks were far weaker than her mainstay, but they covered a greater area. Stas could not dodge.

So, staring at a position away from Zola, he *reflected*.

Zola, well used to the motion, was quick to twist around and force him back in view. What she did not expect was the bottle flying at her face.

Throwing an empty vial was normal. Wasting a *full* bottle? Unthinkable.

Zola was as confused as the crowd, losing precious moments. Instead of catching the bottle as she had done before, she threw herself to the side, obstructing her sight.

Taking advantage, Stas *reflected* once more, tossing out his third and final bottle at Zola's head.

Through sheer luck or battle-honed instinct, Zola threw herself out of the way blindly, avoiding the projectile. Safety secured, she swung her sword, deflecting the container, cracking it into the sand.

That was the last of Stas's missiles. Only a single option seemed to remain, and Zola seemed to realize it too.

Stas *reflected*. This time, Zola did not react. She anticipated. Her arcanum flew for the sands by the second bottle, the sole intact one.

Caught in the position, Stas could not dodge. He braced himself fully behind his shield, falling to a kneel behind it.

From this semi-prone position, he could not properly move. By all accounts, the situation appeared dire.

And yet, this was exactly where he wanted to be.

With the large shield positioned to obscure Zola's view, he let go of its handle and *reflected*.

He arrived right next to Zola, right next to the sword he had left on the ground. With the empty leather bandolier wrapped around his hand, and in the perfect position to reach it, Stas reclaimed his blade. In that same motion, he struck.

Zola lost precious moments staring at the abandoned shield. But she was well trained. She managed to catch his blade before it could pierce her skin, barely deflecting with her knife.

Lightning crackled, but the leather of his makeshift hilt-cover insulated him. Stas forced his blade through the notches in Zola's knives and twisted with all his might. Zola, still reeling from surprise, only managed to keep a hold of one of them.

She was not prepared for Stas's armguard to slam into her helmeted face.

The band surged. Stas capitalized on the momentum and forced Zola's other blade from her hands. Both were quickly kicked away.

Zola grit her teeth and sucked a breath. She quietly signaled her defeat. Surrendering while standing was an unpopular action, no matter how reasonable it may be. His school had taught them to make the endings look more impactful if required.

With Zola's acceptance, he "forced" her through the dance of a grapple, which ended with her on her back, his foot on her stomach, his sword aimed for her exposed throat.

Even the worst seats could see this ending.

The crowd erupted in cheers, louder and greater than any Stas had garnered before. "Stas! Stas! Stas!" they recited to his joy. The complementary cries of "Blink! Blink! Blink!" did not sound as sweet.

Through the gaps in her helmet, Stas could see Zola smile.

"Hah ..." she groaned, good humor in her voice. "Seems like you

127

got me, my friend."

"Good match," Stas agreed with a grin.

The aedile signaled the match's end, allowing the white- and black-masked officials for the event to enter the arena. The two professionals quickly made their examinations and signaled the lack of injuries to the cheering audience.

At that, Stas was free to offer his hand. Zola accepted it and he pulled her to her feet.

The two clasped each other's backs in friendship and turned to face the audience.

"Stas! Stas! Stas!" The cheers continued, intermingled with cries of "Zola" and "Tigress."

"They really liked this match." Zola grinned.

Stas nodded in agreement. It was a pale shadow compared to the praise Radek and Daxton and Horatio Undaunted had earned, but it was a treasure in itself.

He would have to thank his teacher for it. As much as Phobos claimed his tactics were for fighting, not sport, they definitely made for a better show. Another bit of irony.

"Don't count on having the same luck next time," Zola said next to him. "Once I figure out how to imbue my whole armor without killing myself, there will be nothing you can do about it."

"I'll look forward to it," Stas admitted truthfully.

The aedile let them bask in glory for a bit more time, until the pressures of the schedule forced them off the stage.

Zola and Stas allowed the attendants to collect their weapons and shields as they walked back, arm clasped in arm, to the arena entrance. Though other matches were scheduled, he would be heading straight for the baths. The heat had been so brutal today and he was certain he smelled just as bad as Zola.

# Seventeen

Over his months in residence at Ludo's school, Stas had gotten adept at sneaking out. His unjust punishment detail had given him a better sense of when and how the school's staff made their rounds. Not all of them served as Ludo's constant eyes and ears, and of the select few that did, Stas had learned to avoid their gaze.

Learning about the ventilation shafts and the servant entrances had given him a hiding place for the elixirs Phobos charged, along with a purloined dagger, as well as a makeshift cloth mask. He would not be unprepared ever again.

He had solidified his habit of "retiring early" to some minor jeering from his fellows. But it ensured that he could escape without comment. His arcanum had improved with practice; the decoy he left behind was no longer so lifeless. A close observer would think the illusion was sleeping, not dead.

He had also found a better way to exit the forum. Off the beaten trail, tucked away behind another lanista's school was a simple garden. The plants and grass were dead from lack of maintenance, and the fountain in the center was eternally dry. Nobody seemed to come here, visitor or estate worker alike, and the little alcove had been left to dry up. The only exception was a large black slab of stone, carved in the shape of a mirror that cast no reflection. It retained its sheen alone in the garden. Whatever material it was constructed from resisted the crumbling dust.

But that was unimportant. What mattered was that nobody came here, and, from the top of the dead fountain, Stas could *reflect* to the rooftops of the city proper, to one that had the distinct benefit of *not* serving as a nest for the bird-masked watchers that plagued the city.

It was ideal for his purposes.

As a bonus, it allowed Stas to avoid the forum entirely. Months in the city had done well in inuring Stas to the pressure of crowds, but the ostentatious throngs of the marketplace still brought some anxiety. He couldn't escape the worry that he might trip over some fabric or step on a coattail, ruining some dress that a senator's wife had spent far too much money on. He had heard stories of one of his fellows making such a blunder, and being forced to work as a bodyguard to pay off the outrageous debt. It was almost certainly an exaggeration, but Stas did not want to worry about the hassle.

When one left the forum, left the dazzling streets that paved the way from the Gate to the stadiums, from the grand patrician districts to the palatial estate where the Senate met and the Dominus resided, where the bird-masked watchers kept eternal vigil, Stas encountered a different sort of discomfort. Beggars, drunkards, would-be pickpockets ... with Phobos's training, Stas could not shake their presence from his mind.

He felt their eyes, felt his freshly laundered clothes. He felt how his natural stride and bearing marked him as *other*. As yet, he had managed to avoid trouble, but it was only a matter of time.

The winding path was necessary, but Stas disliked it all the same. He let out a held breath when he was through the hidden entryway, descending to those dimly lit tunnels.

Reaching the metal door at the end, Stas rapped his knuckles against it. Two slow knocks, a pause, and two more rapid ones: the code of the day.

Locks disengaged with their regular steadiness. The door slid open to reveal the door guard.

"Maria," Stas said with a respectful nod towards the older woman. Maria's lips turned upwards. "Stas." She stood back, opening the door to allow him through.

"And here he is!" Lucian's voice proclaimed loudly. "The undefeated champion of Libertas! The man whose matches have paid for the good wines! Our very own Blink!" The proclamation was met with cheers from the usual suspects. Many members enjoyed the games. Others simply liked to cheer.

Stas sighed. "Oh, piss on that name." He stepped forward to allow Maria to close the door behind him. "There will be a new one next month if I have any say in it."

His declaration was met with good-natured laughter.

"Hm ... I don't know," Eponine mused from her side of the table. "I think it's appropriate. Easy to remember. Rolls well off the tongue. Stas the Blink. I'm sure everyone here agrees." She held up her mug high. "So, let's cheer for Stas the Blink."

Again, more laughter and cheering. Stas resigned himself to the ribbing. He sat down and grabbed a glass of sweet wine from the serving boy. The drink went smoothly down his throat.

"It is a memorable name." Henri nodded. "I mean, I understand why you would want something more awe-inspiring or glorious. But it's unique and, as Eponine said, rolls off the tongue. It's a short name and that's kind of special on its own." With growing confidence, Henri continued. "Plus, it's unique. There have been a handful of 'Lionhearts' over the years, a dozen 'Braves,' or 'Immortals.' But you are probably the first 'Blink' ever, and may just be the last."

Stas let the thought mull in his mouth with the wine. "If you put it that way, I suppose it isn't so bad."

"Hah." Sanson's large meaty hand slapped his back. Stas almost spilled his drink under the force. "I'm sure we can come up with a better name for our little gladiator. Stas the Swatter? Stas of the Sweetwine?" Sanson's rancid breath was a perfect match for his rancid words. "Do you think you'll brave a real brew today, Sweetwine, or are you sticking with the watery piss once again?"

Stas rankled. "Unlike some, I am not content to make a drunken fool of myself. I drink to suit my palate, not to forget about my miserable life."

Sanson roared in laughter, and slapped Stas's back again. He was less lucky this time; his drink stained his shirt.

Henri beside him winced.

"Oops." Sanson shrugged without contrition. "Sorry about that, Blinky Boy. I'll go get you a towel."

Eponine snickered. "Perhaps you should be the Sweetwine. It would be the best smelling of all gladiators."

"That title would still belong to Secunda the Lavender," Henri said. "But I'm sure Stas will earn a much better title he can enjoy, should 'Blink' not be to his satisfaction."

"Well, if not 'Blink,' why not 'Ever Triumphant'?" Lucian prompted. "If anyone can take the title from Heracles, it would be Stas. It has been … what, one hundred years?"

"One hundred and eighty-seven since Heracles Ever Triumphant was ascended by the Dominus," Henri said. "After a perfect career of forty-seven matches."

Romeo agreed. "More than enough time for someone else to earn the title, well more than enough. Four matches, four victories, he's certainly on track. If he never loses, never ties, then I will die a very rich man." A grin etched itself on his face. "So, what do you say? Will you make me a fortune?"

As much as the dream appealed to him, Stas was not so arrogant. His sparring with Phobos had proven that some people could trounce him even now. Stas shook his head. "Being undefeated at this point of my career ... It is unusual, but not so unexpected. As I am a fresh gladiator, the aediles will not agree to schedule matches for me against the fiercest of competitors until I have proven my worth properly. Against the likes of Horatio Undaunted or Radek Twinblade ..." Stas swirled the remaining wine in his cup, letting the scent waft from it more than from his shirt. "I could only beat them nine times out of ten."

Lucian and Romeo roared in laughter, loud and free.

"You are far too humble, Stas," Lucian declared. "I'm certain you could trounce the two with both your arms behind your back."

"Defeat them both in the blink of an eye," Eponine teased.

"Get them drunk off your sweet wine," Sanson rumbled as he approached. He tossed a dry rag out for Stas to catch. "I will say one thing, Blink. Your recent matches have been good for our funds, if nothing else."

Stas tilted his head in confusion. "You bet on me? You?"

"Me, bet?" Sanson belted out a short laugh. "What do you take me for? A moron like Romeo over there? Gambling's a fool's game. No. I run the games. Taking the cut ... setting the odds in my favor. The stories you tell, well, bookies earn their keep by being in the know. Means you aren't a complete waste of space sitting there drinking our expensive wines."

"You're wasting a lot more space than Stas, you fat tub of lard." Eponine grinned. "Blinky here has a chance to actually make a difference for us. Imagine, two, three years from now—he might be picked by the Dominus. Having a spy holding the ear of the government. Nothing could compare."

Sanson's jovial cheer turned sour. "Oh, fuck that shit." He spat. "If this brat comes anywhere even near that, we cut him loose. Nothing, absolutely nothing you could learn would be worth that much damn scrutiny."

"Bit paranoid, aren't you?" Romeo interjected. "Worrying like that. Stas here is a great guy. We don't need to be so concerned."

"Psh. This isn't even about the bastard." Sanson grunted. "I don't trust anyone, not you, not me, not even Enjolras himself, to spend time around the fucking Dominus." Sanson's mug cracked in his hand. "You think Eponine here is unique? You think the Dominus doesn't have a dozen Eponines in the wing waiting to root through the minds of anyone he requests? They'll get your secrets whether you help them or not!" Sanson slammed his meaty fist on the table. "And where the fuck do you get off trusting so quickly? Drinking with someone, making a few bits and bobs from betting on them? That's nothing but shit, and begging to get all of us killed!"

The conversation, though nominally about Stas, sounded like some regular argument that had long predated him.

Eponine scoffed. "You think you are the only one considering these things? Don't be so self-absorbed. You can't just refuse all risks. Staying back, doing nothing—"

Sanson spat. "There's a big difference between doing nothing and …"

Stas felt a hand tap on his shoulder.

"Ah, yeah, this happens every once in a while," Henri explained, letting the loud and belligerent conversation continue. "Sanson gets argumentative when drunk and, well, Eponine likes to argue back, and it gets kind of loud. Enjolras can settle it down when he's here, but until then it can get pretty distracting." Henri scratched the back of his neck. "There's a quiet place I go when this happens. Do you want to join me?"

Stas looked around. People were watching the growing argument or off in their own conversations. Nobody really seemed to be paying attention to anything else, other than Maria, ever vigilant at the door.

Stas nodded, and Henri gave a weak smile.

"Right." Henri nodded, rising to his feet. "Follow me."

Ducking away from the crowd, Henri led Stas to one of the back rooms and knelt down to grasp at the rung of a trapdoor situated within.

"It's not a long ladder," Henri said as he descended. "Ah, can you close the trapdoor behind you? It can muffle the noise."

Stas nodded, stepping on the ladder to follow. He shut the trapdoor, leaving them in complete darkness for a moment.

He heard Henri shuffling and a small red light flickered from on the walls. It was a flameless torch like those lining the tunnels to the hideout, but it was far dimmer.

Stas could barely make out the outline of Henri's face.

"Sorry it's so dark. The light down here is broken, but nobody cares about fixing it. Let me ..." Henri stumbled a bit, hugging against the wall. He procured some small thing Stas couldn't make out and pulled back the lid, which caused a small flame to jut forth. The piddling fire was only a small improvement. "It's a bit damp, but I like how cool it gets down here. And the quiet."

It was indeed quiet. Stas could hear the barest muffles of shouting. "What's that? A sort of magic candle?"

Henri nodded, his face flickering in his flame's dim light. "Er, sort of. It's more for lighting candles than for being one, but it's a substitute. I, ah, keep it on me for times like this."

Henri seemed a bit more nervous than usual, but Stas did not have much sense as to why.

"Seems useful." Something small enough to fit in Henri's pockets but able to make a fire so easily. He wondered how long its fuel lasted. "So, what is this? A storage room?"

"Yeah." Henri nodded. "Something like that. It's a stockpile for supplies, but we hardly ever touch them, so I just use it as a place to get away sometimes. Mostly for the quiet. I've thought of bringing a chair or two down here. If I did that and fixed up the light, it would be pretty comfortable."

Stas nodded. "I see."

And conversation halted there. Henri, it seemed, didn't really have anything to say to him. And Stas didn't have much to say in turn. Henri, Stas had learned, was quite passive by nature. He eagerly contributed when those around him laid the groundwork, but he did not try to direct anything if he could help it. There really wasn't much between the two of them.

Stas did appreciate the break from Sanson's bellowing.

A few minutes passed in idleness, with no noise but for the sound of their breathing. Stas had somewhat expected that Henri had dragged him here with the intention of saying something private, but it seemed he rather just wished to share the silence.

Stas didn't really know what to make of it.

He frowned. "How long do you usually stay down here?"

"Ah, a few minutes. Maybe longer if I need a break. I've napped down here once or twice. But the worst of it blows over quickly enough. You can head back up whenever you like."

"Perhaps," Stas ventured. The muffled sounds from above were changing. Stas heard the tread of feet.

A foot knocked against the trapdoor. "Henri? You down there?" A muffled voice, that of an older woman whose name Stas believed might be Odette, called down. The trapdoor opened, letting the noise and light in freely. "Sanson was looking for ..." The woman stopped abruptly, face aghast. "Henri, you blithering imbecile! Are you insane? Put that fire out instantly! Are you trying to kill us all?"

Henri jumped in place and struggled for a moment, fumbling with the tool before shutting it.

"And Stas." The woman's glare turned to him. "I can understand

136

Henri being so thoughtless, but I would have thought you too sensible for this nonsense."

"What are you talking about?" Stas held stiff against the unexpected antagonism.

"You don't know?" Odette asked. "This is our supply arsenal. Pitches, tars, powders, fuels ... everything we might need to destroy a building or set a fire. And everything we need to keep away from fools gallivanting about, especially with an open flame." The woman shook her hands in exasperation. Stas flinched with every word.

Henri meekly defended himself. "It's a small fire. And I was keeping to the far side. If we just fixed the light ..."

"None of those excuses," Odette grumbled. "Out! Out! Both of you! I'll keep this foolishness quiet this time, Henri, but if I ever catch you doing anything so monumentally stupid again, I'll hold you in place myself so Sanson can skin your hide."

Chastised and despondent, Henri climbed up the ladder to leave the cool storage room. Stas himself followed with perhaps more haste than strictly required.

Odette stood, hands on her hips, ready for them at the top. "Sanson was looking for you, Henri. So don't keep him waiting." She shooed him to the back room door and exhaled sharply.

She turned to Stas with a shake of her head. "Honestly, that boy. He's harmless most of the time, but then he goes and pulls stunts like this. We all have to keep an eye on his foolishness."

Stas didn't really know what to say to that. Odette was not really someone he'd had dealings with. But thankfully the woman didn't seem to expect anything from him.

Nothing had been broken during the argument between Sanson and Eponine, so it couldn't have been that bad. The two were on opposite sides of the room, no longer looking at one another.

Stas took his seat once again, surrounding himself with an ongoing conversation about chariot races, which he had no opinions on, and gladiator fights, which he happily participated in. As he waited for Enjolras, he procured another glass from the serving boy.

# Eighteen

Over the next few minutes, a handful of Libertas members trickled into the hideout. Each time, Stas found his eyes drawn to the opening door, only to be disappointed. But he was not left waiting for long.

When Enjolras arrived, everyone knew it. The room erupted in inescapable noise and cheer. Enjolras barely took two steps into the room before he was swarmed; the denizens of the hideout were eager to blather about their reports, to share their thoughts, or to demand information from their unquestioned leader. Stas could only make out the barest glimpses of the man's silver hair through the mess.

Enjolras could spend the entire evening chatting away. He deftly glided through the conversations, from matters of dire importance to simple jokes. He happily matched the enthusiasm of all who crowded him, never rejecting or visibly tiring. He was a constant nexus of discussion, and it was almost impossible to find an opening without shoving in.

Stas held himself away from the annoyance.

Through the throng of people, Enjolras's silver eyes caught Stas's own. Stas found himself on the receiving end of one of the unflappable man's smiles. He swallowed and averted his gaze. He took another gulp of his drink to treat the dryness in his throat.

The crowd fell apart as Sanson barreled through it. The heavy-stocked man had no shame about literally pushing others aside.

Enjolras offered him a nod and allowed himself to be led to the back room that held the magic shield.

But, as they passed Stas's table, Enjolras pulled aside. "Stas," he said, with his ever-present smile. "I am glad you could make it."

Stas nodded in turn. "You did ask me to be here tonight."

"That I did." Enjolras nodded. "But it does not escape me that the trip is more difficult for you than for anyone else. I appreciate you making the time."

"It really isn't a problem." Stas enjoyed coming to Enjolras's hideout. Enjoyed the atmosphere. Enjoyed speaking with his growing fanbase. He couldn't think of it as an imposition.

Sanson grumbled loudly. "You can chitchat later, Enjolras. We need to sort this business out."

"Of course." He nodded to Sanson. "We will need to speak tonight, Stas. But for now, duty calls."

Stas watched him follow Sanson through the side door, which closed behind them both.

Eponine plopped down beside him, mug settling on the table.

Stas raised an eyebrow at her. "Are you not part of that meeting?" he inquired, directing a finger toward the backroom door.

While Enjolras refused to dole out official ranks, going as far as to avoid referring to himself as leader despite the obvious, the realities of organization left decision-making powers in the hands of specific individuals. Sanson was one of them. Eponine was another.

Eponine shrugged. "Enjolras doesn't tell me about every little thing. Nor do I care. If Sanson is speaking with him alone, it has something to do with finances, or supplies. Maria isn't with them, so it's not the armory or training. If it is something important, I'll weigh in when all the little details are decided." She took a large gulp of her bitter-smelling drink. "Alternatively, Sanson has a terrible idea and he wants to try and convince Enjolras without me shooting it down.

He does that sometimes." She shook her head. "Maybe he's got it in his head that I'm a traitor." She chuckled.

Stas frowned into his drink. "Why is Sanson so paranoid?" Some caution made sense, but almost everyone here was relaxed and trusting. Only abrasive, smelly Sanson would get into shouting matches over the matter.

Eponine chuckled. "Sanson was in a group before this one. More aggressive, less intelligent. They got found out by the watchers. Got rooted out almost to a man. Sanson claims it was a betrayal, but I'm pretty sure some drunken thug just bragged to the wrong person. Enjolras fished him out of the burning wreckage they found themselves in. Now the fat tub of lard is convinced our group will end the same. As if I hadn't rooted through the memories of everyone here to check for that risk."

Eponine finished her assessment with a wry grin.

Stas found himself uncomfortable. "You checked everyone's memories?"

"Everyone we let in here, from Maria's brat serving you wine to Enjolras himself."

Stas struggled to put the strange, uncomfortable sensation he now felt into words. "When?" he inquired, bereft of any other coming to mind.

"Don't worry so much, Stas." Eponine chuckled. "Your embarrassing memories can't compare to the worst I've seen. Henri's been in some pathetic messes. Romeo's gotten up to absolute nonsense in his days."

"You spent the night at the Bell looking through my mind. Was Sanson just there to distract me so you could?"

"Sanson ... something like that, yes. Usually Sanson bullies people around for a month or so before I come in. But I thought you were worth the elixirs. And it's not like I saw everything that night, Blinky

Boy. I was focusing on whether you knew about us, if you had spoken with the watchers, senators, the Dominus. That sort of thing."

Stas had trouble understanding what he was feeling. He had never fully considered the matter before, but the idea that Eponine could have used her arcanum without him ever knowing ...

Unbidden, his training with Phobos brought some unpleasant thoughts to mind. What else could Eponine do without him realizing? He imagined this was one of those hypotheticals the grumpy teacher loved. If *he* could read memories, change them, mess about with minds all without any sign ... with all that, how could he go about destroying his enemies? How could he break them? Remake them? Switch friend and foe in their mind? Outside of the arena with time on his side ... what couldn't he do?

It was unpleasant.

"You aren't going to do it again, are you?"

"What? Waste elixirs checking what I already know? Why would I bother with that? You're one of us, now, Stas. And you're going to help us do great things. No need to sour anything by acting like Sanson."

"Do you swear," Stas pressed, "to not use your arcanum on me ever again?"

Eponine shrugged. "I mean, as I said, I don't have much reason to. But it isn't up to me, you know? If Enjolras asks me to or something comes up, then I'm going to do it. It's not like it hurts you at all."

"What do you mean by 'something?'"

Eponine waved her hand vaguely. "You know, 'something.' Why do you care? It's no big deal."

"If it is no big deal, you can swear to not do it," Stas argued. He hadn't drunk much tonight, but his head seemed to be spinning. "Don't use your magic on me. Or at least, don't do it without telling me."

"Sure, sure, fine. Whatever you say."

Stas glared.

Eponine sighed. "Does this really matter that much to you? Fine. I swear."

"Swear it explicitly."

Eponine, in a show of mock seriousness, placed her hand upon her heart. "I swear to never use my magic upon you without asking first, and may chimeras rip me apart if I am lying." Her voice echoed with exaggerated solemnity.

She rolled her eyes. "Does that work for you, Stas?"

Stas swallowed. Did it work for him? She didn't seem to care much, but he couldn't force her to be sincere. She either meant it or she didn't, and no amount of badgering would change that.

He would just have to live with it. That was what a good man would do.

"It's as much as I could ask for. Thank you."

"Feh." Eponine popped her lips, eyes rolling. "What's got you so bothered about that now? It's not like I make a secret of what I can do. Is it because of Sanson being a paranoid prick?"

Stas deflected. "You did say his last organization was rooted out and killed."

"Honestly. Even calling what Sanson was in an 'organization' is three steps too far. They were a bunch of disgruntled thugs. Angry violent drunkards who mugged and stole from whomever they pleased. We're nothing alike. The fact that Sanson thinks we'll have the same problems is a fucking insult of mind-boggling proportions. Sometimes I just want to sock the bloated tub of booze and stench in his pox-filled face when he goes on another paranoid rant." Eponine's eyes burned in a contained rage, and then calmed. "Sadly, Sanson is actually good at his job, so we have to deal with him."

"Hm." Stas sipped his drink.

He should probably pull the matter back to lighter topics. "So," he said, "were you able to catch my match yesterday? You were speaking about it, but I couldn't tell if you had acquired a ticket or only heard of it second hand."

"You mean the match where you threw your sword away and spent cowering back and forth?" Eponine grinned. "Lucian was singing praises about your heroic feats, but that could not possibly have been the same as the match I saw."

"Hah." Stas chuckled. "Everything in that match was part of my plan. I had the Tigress dancing to my tune from the very start." He let his well-justified pride surface for all to see. "As for removing my sword, I wouldn't expect you to know this—you have little reason to be so well versed in arcanum—but when faced with lightning, metal is not your friend."

"Interesting," Eponine said. "Is that what they teach at your gladiator schools?"

"That and much more," Stas asserted with a nod. "It is a vigorous curriculum, for both mind and body, to ensure our survival on the treacherous sands of the arena. Fools who fail to take to the lessons will find themselves dead even before the aedile can make their judgment."

"With only four matches to your name," Eponine said, "it might take some more time before you prove to be a fool."

"I invite you to come watch me, then, to prove myself again and again. Eventually, you'll be forced to admit to my might, both in body and in mind."

Eponine demurred with a grin. "I don't know … Your matches usually coincide with races. I might prefer to watch a superior show."

"Hah! Chariot races. Where the horses do most of the work while the riders ineffectually batter against one another. Anything and everything the charioteers do in their miserable moving battles is better done by gladiators in the arena, or even the venatio." Stas nodded to himself. "The hippodrome is too specialized. The moving platforms and obstacles are good for nothing else. But in the arena you can enjoy the gladiators, the acrobats, the venatio—"

"The executions."

Stas frowned. "And the executions. But don't pretend prisoners aren't also trampled in the hippodrome. At least in the arena there is a performance to the act."

"The costumes and set pieces are nicer, I will grant. But the unwilling actors are the same."

"That may be true." In truth, Stas often wished the executions could be set apart. Gladiators, venatio, acrobats, even charioteers, all practiced for their events. An execution play was simple slaughter set to narration.

"For all that you nag about charioteers, I'm wondering if you have ever been to the hippodrome. I doubt they have any in the provinces."

"Of course I have been to a race," Stas grumbled in affront. "Yes, there are no races in the province. But I have been here for months now." His peers had dragged him to a few events. His opinions were founded in fact and experience, not bias for his own craft.

"Oh, so do you have enough experience to have an opinion of the teams?"

"If you must know," Stas sniffed, "based on my professional opinion, the Blue team were the most skilled with their arcanum."

"The Blues?" Eponine asked with a tilt of her head. "Not the Reds or the Greens, but the Blues? What a day this is, to find someone who is a fan of the worst team of the three. You are truly a unique specimen, Stas."

Stas scowled. "They are not the worst. The aedile is just biased against them in favor of the Reds. As are the crowds for the Greens."

"There's no need for bias when the team is terrible. Ah, Katriane, come here." Eponine called out to the woman walking by. "Stas here is a fan of the Blues."

"What?" Katriane stopped, eyes widened. "That's adorable. How can you suffer to be a fan of the team that loses all the time? Are you a masochist? A practicing stoic?"

"I never said I was a fan," Stas said. "I simply noted that they are the most skilled with magic. And they had the best accuracy. Besides, I had heard that they took a championship six years ago." Alain had been insistent on that point.

"Six years ago is forever ago. The Blue team of today is not a contender. Now the Reds—" Katriane began.

"Enough about your silly Reds, Katriane," Romeo called from across the room. "It is the year of the Greens! The Greens! I have money on it!"

And so the room once again erupted in arguments over chariot teams, much to Eponine's visible amusement. The eternal conversation lasted for minutes this time, drowning nearly everything else out. It served as a decent distraction until Enjolras finally emerged with Sanson.

Enjolras took note of the ongoing argument. "Ah, it seems like everyone is quite lively this evening." There was some satisfaction in his words. "Stas, perhaps we can converse in the back room for some quiet? Eponine, if you would come as well?"

Sanson rolled his eyes before charging into the room, declaring his undying support for whichever team happened to be on the losing side of the argument. Today that turned out to be the Greens.

Stas left his empty wine glass on the table. Eponine followed suit. The two of them found their way to the back room with Enjolras, who closed the door behind him, muffling the drunken argument.

"Thank you, again, for coming, Stas," Enjolras began. "And I apologize once again for making you wait. Ah, no need to stand, please, sit down. I can have Dion bring you some wine if you would like."

Stas shook his head. "I've had enough for the moment." He moved to take a seat but found Eponine had stolen the nearest chair for herself. Offering her a frown, Stas moved to the next chair over and sat. Enjolras joined them. "What did you wish to see me about?"

Enjolras nodded solemnly. "To say it simply, I have a mission for you."

"A mission?" This was the first time Enjolras had made a request of him. Stas had dutifully attended meetings, but, as yet, Libertas had only requested that he keep his ear to the ground. To Stas's despair, for all the he listened in rapt attention to his reports of rumors, jokes, injuries, and moods, he had yet to hear anything important.

The uselessness had been grinding at him. He would jump at the chance to help.

"It is completely optional," Enjolras was quick to assert. "I understand if you are not willing to risk your public figure, especially now that your renown is growing. We can find a suitable substitute if necessary."

"No," Stas quickly said. "No need for a substitute. I am more than happy to do the mission."

"Perhaps," Eponine said wryly, "you should wait until you hear the details before you agree so readily. You don't want to be too eager, after all."

Stas's glare was met with an innocent smile.

"Indeed," Enjolras said. "I would not ask you to make a decision until you have heard the details. After all, this comes at quite short notice." Enjolras coughed lightly. "I won't waste your time further, so let me explain. I do not know if you were aware, but recently, an organization we conducted business with was discovered by the watchers."

Stas had indeed heard a bit of this. It was the subject of a few whispers.

Enjolras continued. "We did what we could and managed to save a few lives, but the organization itself is not in any position to continue acting. The surviving members have been driven underground, their hideout destroyed, and their operations completely dismantled. This represents a particular problem for us, because this group was the source of a vast majority of our elixirs."

Stas frowned. "I can see why that is a problem."

Enjolras nodded solemnly. "Indeed. It is a painful blow, beyond the deaths alone."

Eponine cut in. "Obviously, we've been searching for an alternative. Even with money, that's not something you can just buy, you know?"

Enjolras continued. "We believe we have found a possible partner, and we are looking to meet with them this very evening, to start the process of securing a deal. Usually, this would be a matter I would handle on my own. But those in the elixir trade tend towards a more," Enjolras searched for a description, "cutthroat inclination."

"Violent, immoral criminals," Eponine asserted. "Scum of the street. If their product wasn't so necessary, they'd find themselves thrown out of the slums."

Enjolras frowned. "I wish I could object to that description, but that is the tendency. I have made efforts to find a group that is less objectionable but …" He sighed. "Our needs force our hands. It is my hope that any arrangement we broker would curtail the worst offenses. But I am rambling." He turned back to Stas. "Simply put, I would ask for you to be my bodyguard for this meeting tonight."

Stas frowned. "You expect trouble."

"Expect it? I have no particular reason to. Even businesses of violence are still businesses in the end. They will not get far by attacking potential customers, though it remains a possibility. But guards are expected. If I were to arrive without a visible guard, I would appear either naive or arrogant. Both portend badly for any deals."

"And having a slab of beef like you as a guard might make everything easier," Eponine added with a smile. "A trained fighter with a proper physique is far more intimidating than whatever back-alley thug these criminals can scrounge up."

"More than that," Enjolras interjected. "Should something go wrong, nobody would be more suited to see all three of us safely delivered from harm. Again, I do not expect this to be the case, but I would have nobody else at my back for this."

Stas swallowed. The amount of trust this man so casually showed was uncomfortable. Stas wondered if Enjolras had been watching his matches, to be so confident. He hoped it was the case. He did not wish to ask, for fear of disappointment.

But his mind caught on the particular word choice. "All three of us?" he inquired, eyes darting to Eponine.

"Correct. I am permitted to bring two others. If you are both amenable, it would be the three of us tonight."

"Enjolras to talk, you to menace, and me to be the eye candy," Eponine added, idly inspecting her nails.

"To ensure matters go smoothly," Enjolras said. "Far more valuable than simple eye candy."

"Of course, of course." Eponine nodded her head sagely. "I can do that as well. I'll make the most of losing out on my beauty sleep."

Enjolras continued. "You won't have to say anything, or do anything, but be a visible guard. If you see an issue, I trust you to act with your best judgment. The meeting is scheduled for late tonight, in some hours' time. Do you believe you are up for the task? Will you join us?"

Stas nodded. "Of course. I will ensure your safety."

"Excellent." Enjolras clapped. "We will reconvene in a few hours. Enjoy your time until then. I will trust that you won't overindulge. I look forward to working with you, Stas."

Stas nodded and swallowed, unsure of what else to say. Eponine did not waste time heading out of the room, likely to join back into the ongoing argument.

"Ah, but a moment, Stas," Enjolras called as he was leaving. "As a public figure, I know it is important to keep your identity concealed. For tonight, I have something for you." Enjolras moved towards a chest against the wall. He opened it and picked up an item that had clearly been sitting on the top of it.

"This is for you, Stas. I hope it makes matters easier. Do with it what you wish."

He handed the item over. It was a mask, ornate and well-crafted. The front was a mixture of gold and silver, stylized with the simple symbol of Libertas: the same insignia that marked the shield. The smooth back cloth and padding promised a comfortable fit. The sash to secure it was silken.

Stas tested it against his face. It rested comfortably without adjustment. It was built for him.

"Ah ..." Stas, once again, was left speechless. "Thank you. It's grand." How much money had such an item cost? How long did it take to make? When had Enjolras commissioned it? Stas did not know the answers to these questions, nor could he vocalize them.

Enjolras offered a soft smile. "Let our first mission together be just as grand." And, with a nod, he left the room.

Stas followed shortly after, mask grasped tightly in hand.

# Nineteen

At the appointed time, Stas, Enjolras, and Eponine made their way out of the hideout through the tunnels to one of the exits. There, their silver-haired leader led them to a waiting cargo carriage. Enjolras took a moment to speak with the driver before directing them to take seats in the back, under the cover of a tarp.

Stas experienced the second most uncomfortable ride of his life. The trip through the Gate had been far, far worse. But being disguised as cargo, hidden in darkness on a bumpy road with little idea as to where they were going was its own sort of trouble. Stas was made acutely aware of just how close he was to the other two hidden passengers.

The three of them did not risk making noise. The paths traveled by carriage were well patrolled, and they did not want to draw attention to themselves. Breaking curfew was risky enough, but being visibly armed would cause a commotion among the bird-masked watchers.

Eventually they ended up where they needed to be. The carriage ground to a halt, and the tarp was pulled back.

"You're here," the driver announced in a whisper. "Out quickly, now."

"Thank you, Rupert," Enjolras said with a nod. "I'll ensure the rest of your payment makes its way to you in the next few days." He grabbed a lantern from the carriage back.

"I'll hold you to it."

Stas jumped down next and helped Eponine to the ground.

Enjolras and the driver reset the tarp and, with a mutual nod, the man drove off.

Enjolras took a deep breath. "We are still a few blocks from the meeting place, but we are set to arrive right on time. It should be good to stretch our legs, I would think."

Eponine rolled her shoulders. "I'll say." She turned to Stas. "This part of the city doesn't have much bird-face presence, so we don't need to worry about being spotted. We're more likely to run into muggers. But do keep an eye out, just in case."

"For muggers?" Stas said, looking around. This part of the city was definitely more run down than where they had started the trip. Though hard to see in the moonlight, the buildings seemed to be rotten in parts. Off to the side he clearly saw the dozing form of a homeless man on the ground, back up against a wall.

"No lone mugger would target a group," Eponine said. "The ones that work in groups? That's who we're meeting. And they're pretty territorial."

Stas frowned, but accepted the words. He would assure their safety regardless. This was his first mission and he wouldn't dare mess it up.

"Try not to call them muggers to their face," Enjolras chided. "They are making a show of civility in meeting with us, so we should respect it."

"Respect it, right." Though it was dark, Stas could imagine how Eponine rolled her eyes. "Well, I suppose 'mugger' is inaccurate. If they are moving into the elixir market, then they're a little more organized than that base rabble." She exhaled loudly. "If there is one big disappointment in my life, it was learning how much of a bore common criminals are. They definitely fail to live up to the stories." She offered what Stas believed to be a grin in his direction. "Thankfully gladiators might be living up to the hype. But it's hard to say for certain."

"We don't want to be late," Enjolras said, though his eyes seemed to be locked on the homeless man. "So let's head to the meeting point."

He headed towards the alleyway, right past the homeless man. As he passed, he quietly knelt down and left a handful of coins, which he hid from obvious view. The man would be well positioned to see them when he woke up.

Stas regretted his lack of money. A good man would have contributed without comment, as Enjolras so deftly demonstrated.

Eponine huffed at the display, walking past without care. Enjolras asserted his lead quickly, leaving Stas to scope out any potential threats. Enjolras lit a dim lantern.

"Is a light necessary?" Stas asked quietly.

"As Eponine mentioned, there are few watchers in this part of the city. And none of them will care to enforce curfew this far from the central districts," Enjolras answered, voice low but clear. "Letting our hosts know of our presence is only a boon."

Stas caught the sound of rustling clothes, and saw in the corner of his eye a small shadow darting away. He tracked it as it fled down an alleyway but made no move to pursue.

Enjolras nodded in the direction of the fleeing shadow. "Indeed, I suspect they will be amply forewarned of our arrival."

"Good. I'd hate to be stuck waiting for them," Eponine grumbled. "I wonder if they even have a clock."

"I assume they have something." Enjolras swung his lantern out to examine a building, some warehouse that seemed near identical to all the others. But there must have been something to distinguish it because Enjolras nodded. "Ah, here we are, I believe."

Enjolras moved to open the door, but Stas intercepted. He interposed himself and made to examine the situation. After determining it was safe, he checked inside the building.

There was no one there.

"It's empty. Should they not be here waiting for us?" Stas asked.

"This should be a meeting ground, not their headquarters." Enjolras entered the near empty building and sat himself fearlessly on a pile of straw, keeping the lantern on his lap. He removed its hood, letting it shine freely across the open area. "I do not expect to be kept waiting for long."

"Really?" Eponine mused. "I bet they keep us waiting to try to unnerve us."

"I can only hope they are more polite than that."

Stas and Eponine situated themselves near Enjolras. Eponine took a seat herself, imperiously leaning back to stare at the ceiling. Stas himself remained standing, examining the room as Phobos had taught him.

It was a simple warehouse filled with straw, a single broken cart, and not much else. There were no obvious vantage points. It reminded him greatly of the first entrance he had visited when going to Libertas's hideout. He wondered if this warehouse, too, had a secret entrance concealed within.

The three waited without speaking. Eponine hummed something softly, clearly unconcerned.

As it turned out, Enjolras was closer to correct. They did not wait long before the doors slammed open. Three men entered: a pair of burly men in ragged clothes with a lantern and an ugly club between them, followed by a taller, thin man, who appraised the room.

The weapon was pitiful, as were the thugs. From their builds, it was obvious the men were laborers, not fighters. Their muscles might have helped them stack crates, but they wouldn't be much use in a brawl.

Stas dismissed them quickly. If there was any danger, it would come from duplicity or ambush. He would be on the lookout.

Enjolras rose to greet them. "Mister Sartre, I am glad you found the time to meet with us." He stepped forward, hand extended.

The club-wielding man interposed, glaring menacingly. Stas stepped forward to meet him, but Eponine's hand on his shoulder stopped him.

Enjolras nodded and took a step back in irritating deference.

"Feh," the taller man spat. "Save the niceties for patricians, brat. And don't have any misconceptions. I don't want anything to do with the sort of nonsense you represent—nothing but trouble for me and mine. But my nephew vouches for you, so I'll hear you out before slamming the door in your face."

Stas bristled, but Enjolras held firm. "Ah, how is Quentin doing?" he said. "It has been some weeks since we have had the chance to converse. Last, I heard, his wife had graced him with a little girl. Gabrielle, was it?"

"He's fine." The man, Sartre, huffed. "And I'd tell you to keep your nose out of it if I thought it'd do any good. People like you, groups like yours, it's bad business all around."

"I wonder if you may have some misconceptions as to our aims. I am happy to address them," Enjolras said with a smile. "Or we can skip to the meat of the business, if that is your preference."

"I don't have any damn misconceptions." The man's eyes narrowed. "I know exactly who you are, exactly what you want. You think I don't have information? You think I'm some sort of small time who can't keep track of my competitors? Who got them wiped out?" He spat again, and the man wielding the wooden club palmed at the weapon. "Let me make this clear. I'm not some moron like Varne was. I ain't gonna be swayed by some whimsical cause, or pitiful calls to aid my fellow man. I ain't gonna end up dead like him, and you can bet your ass that I ain't gonna divert my hard-earned money, or my product, to your little group. If that's what you are looking for, you can get the fuck outta my territory."

This time, Stas couldn't hold himself back. "Why bother agreeing to a meeting if you're so dead set on refusing everything? Is your time so worthless that you think nothing of wasting ours?"

"You shut your fucking mouth, brat," the man with the club rumbled, brandishing his weapon high.

"Your form is pathetic." Stas said, coldly. "Have you ever held a club in your life? It's just going to fly out from your fingers as soon as you swing it. Worthless." Stas held himself strong and found silent joy when the club-wielder flinched under his glare.

He moved to step forward, but a hand was placed once again on his shoulder.

A jolt of shame swept through him at Enjolras's touch.

It was the wine he wanted to blame, and the late night. But that didn't change the fact that he had acted against his instructions. But did those instructions even matter when this insolent criminal was refusing to even discuss matters?

Sartre took a deep breath, eyes locked with Enjolras. "Your guard has quite the mouth on him. Like a whiny little dog. Not that I'd expect more from little kids playing dress up, pretending they're heroes."

Enjolras remained serene in the face of the insults. He did not rise or respond, letting the awkward silence fall back to the criminal.

The man huffed. "Your masked dog is correct on one matter. This is a waste of time. But I made a promise to my dear nephew that I'd hear you out, so here we are. I'll hear you out, then I'll have you escorted out of my territory. Easy enough."

Stas had already spoken. He did not hold his tongue back again. "Setting up a meeting in bad faith … Why even pretend you're keeping a promise?"

This time, Sartre's gaze left Enjolras. His glare turned to focus on Stas's masked form. "Deluded kids like you only care about what sounds nice, but in the business world, a man's word is his everything. Nothing, absolutely nothing, is more important than keeping your word. In this shitty world you can't trust anything or anyone. Can't rely on a single fucking thing. All a man can do is ensure his will is followed and his promises are kept. No matter what. Anything else and you'll just drown in all the shit."

Sartre spat. An ugly, hawking bit of phlegm fell to the straw below. "Fuck you, implying my word ain't gold. I promised I'd hear you out, so I will. But when what you want is something I'm never gonna give, I don't need to consider it long. I'm a businessman. I'll always put my business first."

Here Enjolras asserted himself with all the calm of a man whose plans were proceeding smoothly. "Of course, Mister Sartre. That is a perfectly reasonable position to take. I understand if you have no desire for indulging in acts of charity, or for greater cooperation agreements. While I would gladly enjoy such a relationship, it was not my intention tonight to request such from you. Rather, my hope was, and is, to form a business partnership. Not only between ourselves, but also with some other parties you might be interested in."

Sartre did not seem convinced by the words, but he did not interrupt.

Enjolras took the tacit permission to continue. "Like with your nephew, I make a point to try to make friends of all sorts in this grand city, from those in positions of great privilege, like yourself, to those in troubled times. In my correspondence, I am often in a position to identify problems and opportunities in equal turn. After learning of your new business expansion from Quentin, I realized that another friend of mine might be in a position to help you."

"Cut to the chase," Sartre grumbled.

"Ah, yes. To put it bluntly, one of my friends holds a position of executive control over an unofficial sewage treatment facility in the far south of the city. The throughput is admittedly minor, but it has the fortune to avoid oversight from the city government."

The criminal rolled his eyes. "You think we've got problems with raw materials? Really? That's your proposal? I may be new to this aspect of the business, but I'm practically rolling in untreated product. Everywhere you go, people are jumping at the chance to sell. And my normal operation is full of opportunities to harvest for myself."

Enjolras remained undeterred. "You wouldn't be expanding into the elixir trade if you were not in a secure position with your supply line. But, as a businessman, clearly you are able to see the advantages. Safety, security, reduced scrutiny … unless I am mistaken it would be cheaper for you as well. From a simple business perspective, there are only benefits."

"Everything depends on the cost," Sartre retorted. "I'm not lacking for options, and you're just a fucking middleman. I won't give you elixirs for setting up a meeting."

Enjolras held up a hand in a placating gesture. "Of course, of course. I wouldn't dream of assuming something so momentary would be worth anything tangible." The continued show of humility bothered Stas greatly, but he refused to make matters worse by interrupting again. Not now that Enjolras had managed to get matters back on track. "No, Mister Sartre. What I wish is to secure the right of first purchase of your elixirs from you."

Sartre blinks. "What?" The simple lack of comprehension painted the word with a long brush.

"Ah, allow me to elaborate." Enjolras struck, employing the calm he had engendered this whole conversation. "You wish to sell your product. And we are in the market to buy elixirs in bulk. Allow us to be your primary customer, then. Whenever you are able to produce a batch, all that we ask is that you let us know, so that we can purchase them from you. At full price." Enjolras smiled. "Our need is great and our coffers are not empty. If, at a time, we do not elect to purchase your wares, you would be perfectly free to sell your product to someone else. We simply wish for the opportunity to buy them first."

The criminal paused, lips pursed. "That's your offer? You set us up with that sewer man of yours so you can buy from us?" There seemed to be a simple lack of comprehension in the man's eyes, fueled by distrust. He was looking for an angle, Stas believed. The man seemed to be convinced that Enjolras was trying to make a fool of him, and was bothered by the fact that he could not figure out the method.

Obviously Enjolras had no angle. Anyone with eyes could see that the man preferred honest deals in good faith. Stas found himself pitying the scum, who seemed incapable of believing that people could possess common decency.

"Indeed," Enjolras confirmed. "You would secure a consistent customer. We would enjoy a consistent supplier. And my friend gets to benefit from the fruits of whatever deal you strike with them. It is a good deal for everyone involved."

Sartre grunted, eyes narrowing. "And that's all you want? Not a speck more?"

"Ah." Enjolras scratched the back of his neck in a little show of embarrassment. And it was a show, Stas knew, because the man had nothing to be embarrassed about. "I will admit that I have some additional hopes for the benefits of dealing with a group in your position. As you might imagine, we sometimes find ourselves in possession of ... raw elixir materials, as it were. Not often, nor lightly, but it occurs enough that it would be helpful to have a proper disposal process. With Mister Varne's group no longer in the picture, we no longer have clean arrangements."

"We are not a fucking clean-up crew," Sartre spat. "And I'll be fucking damned if you treat us like one. We aren't taking any of your fucking heat." Despite the clear anger in his voice, he seemed calmer now. Likely he was satisfied at having caught Enjolras's 'ploy,' even if Stas didn't understand the implications of it.

Again, Enjolras raised his hands. "Of course, of course. We would not dream of requesting anything from you that would put you at risk. Despite what you may have been led to believe, we are perfectly capable of discretion. In our arrangements with Mister Varne, we took great strides to assure there was no additional scrutiny due to our … materials. You could simply consider us another seller in this matter. We would not even require money to change hands, because we would be immediately placing it towards the purchase of your final product."

"I ain't gonna discuss this right now," Sartre said. "Nothing like this is even close to being on the table tonight."

"I understand. Such would only be a possibility after our partnership, should we develop one, is well established. But if I may ask about the larger arrangement?"

"I am not making any deals tonight." He placed the full weight of his words on the *not*. "I am not making any promises. What I'm gonna do is look into that 'friend' of yours. If I don't like what I see, that's the end of this. Done. If I think it might be useful, I'll consider matters. Consider them," he reemphasized. "I'm making the decision that is best for me and mine. None of your wants compare to it."

"I would ask for nothing more. Shall I inform my friend he should get in contact with your group? It would be more convenient, I imagine, if you were able to meet in your own territory."

Sartre chewed his lip. "Do so. Before the end of the week," he ordered, as if he had the power to make demands. "And now that you've said your piece, get the fuck outta my territory. My man will escort you out," he snapped, and the lantern man stepped forth.

Enjolras bowed his head once more. "We will not tarry. Thank you, once again, for seeing us."

Sartre grunted, turned away and went out the building door, the club-wielding man following after. His eyes were locked on Stas. The lantern man himself kept his watchful eyes on the three of them. Only after the sound of Sartre's and his lumbering thug's footsteps faded away did he make for the door, motioning for the three of them to follow.

They did so, and allowed themselves to be led by the man some number of blocks down. Once again they found themselves near the homeless man.

The lumbering man grunted and gestured vaguely.

"We appreciate the escort, sir," Enjolras said, "and bid you good evening."

The man said nothing in return. He simply turned back and lumbered onward.

After he had left, Enjolras exhaled with a nod. "I believe that went well. Come. Rupert should be circling around soon." He lifted his lantern to shine the way. "We can talk on the way there. I don't believe we will disturb anyone."

Stas frowned. "Was that it? I was expecting…"

"Something more exciting?" Eponine said. "I'm with you. Sadly, life is usually boring. We have to make our own excitement."

"I just feel as if I didn't do anything…" Stas mumbled. More than that, he was concerned he had made matters worse by his presence.

"Have no worries, my friend." Enjolras spoke with a soft shake of his head. "Just because you were not forced to employ your skills did not mean you weren't necessary. The risk existed regardless of the results. And, more than that, I believe that your words served our aims in the end, so do not feel ashamed for having spoken up."

Stas swallowed. Of course Enjolras had been aware of his actual concerns. He was the sort to see through people quickly. But Stas could not take the words to heart, because Enjolras was also a man who saw the best in everything. He was too kind to scold Stas for his failure.

"It did keep their eyes off me," Eponine added, "which definitely helped. I doubt those wastes of space had any sense of what I was doing."

Stas blinked. "What were you doing?"

"Ensuring everything worked smoothly." Eponine shrugged. "Messing with their memories. That wanna-be crime boss was mine from the start. By tomorrow, he'll be convinced that he managed to pull a big one over a bunch of naive patrician brats. He'll be stupidly giddy over how much he thinks he'll be fleecing us for."

Stas couldn't imagine why she would want that. "Why would you do that?"

"People who think they won are less likely to go back on a deal," she said. "That goes double for criminals. They assume there is only ever one winner. If they believe they managed to swindle the other person, they'll work to keep everything smooth. But if they're worried they might have lost, they'll squirm and fight it every step of the way. We can't trust jerks like Sartre to keep to anything, but we know how they think."

"I greatly prefer to deal honestly," Enjolras added. "And the deal, despite what Mister Sartre might believe of it, is a fair one. But for matters like this, it is safer to take advantage of our skills to ensure matters move apace." He shook his head. "It really is a shame that Mister Varne is no longer with us. He was a good man who did not require nudging: a rare trait when it comes to the elixir trade."

Stas frowned in thought. "What is so special about elixirs anyway? I know that the city controls its production, and that people get executed if they're caught trying it. But why is the trade so bad?" And another matter occurred to him. "And what does it have to do with sewage treatment?"

"You don't know?" Eponine asked with honest surprise. "I know the city goes out of its way to prevent plebeians from learning. But I assumed gladiators like you were in on the secret. After all, you actually work with the stuff."

"No. I do not know," Stas asserted. "We are only taught to make use of them. Not how they are produced."

"Ah ..." Enjolras frowned deeply. "Well, there is no value in keeping it a secret. Though there are many ingredients involved in the process, most of which are known only to the official production centers, the primary component is human remains."

"What?"

"I am not perfectly familiar with the mechanics myself," Enjolras continued. "The black market keeps their process a secret as much as the city does. But I am aware that human corpses are the primary ingredient. Human excrement, in vast quantities, can serve as a substitute, if at the cost of quality." Enjolras gestured vaguely. "At its core, the elixir trade is the corpse trade, with all sorts of related, unpleasant industries. Commonly, the producers or their suppliers will offer predatory loans, and demand bodies as collateral. In many cases, the gangs will ... source their own corpses, as it were. It encourages them to be far more violent in their regular dealings. And their presence as buyers will cause desperate communities to turn on one another, to scrape out of their dismal circumstances."

Enjolras sighed. "The trade is disgusting at its core. I hope to direct suppliers to work with the less horrific material, but the city watches the sewer workers closely, in a manner they fail to apply to the violent gangs. I consider this whole mess to be one of the greatest failures of the Senate."

Enjolras had been speaking for a while, but Stas had little will to pay attention. "It's corpses and shit?" he said in disbelief. "Corpses and shit?"

"Don't worry, Stas." Eponine patted him on the back in reassurance. "The official stuff you get doesn't have the shit. And they refine it greatly. Very clean, unlike the dredge the black market makes. You're fine."

"It doesn't matter how much they clean it," Stas squawked. "That doesn't change what it is." Never in his life had Stas been so grateful that he did not require elixirs for his magic. The memories of trying out "normal" arcanum burned.

Eponine tutted. "You aren't the first to have that sort of reaction. If you want, I can make you forget about it. Do you think that would help?"

Would it help? Stas considered for a moment. In some ways he wanted nothing more than to go back to simple ignorance, when elixirs just were potions that happened to exist, and where his entire industry wasn't based on magical cannibalism.

But, if he did forget, he might make the mistake of actually drinking an elixir in the future. And that was unacceptable.

"No," he decided, firmly.

"Suit yourself." Eponine shrugged. "Believe me, I find it as gross as you do, but you just have to deal with the world that we live in."

"We are here," Enjolras announced at a street corner, forcing the subject to a halt. "Rupert should arrive shortly."

Stas looked forward to putting this far-too-long night behind him. Perhaps, once he got back to his bed, his thoughts would no longer be consumed by corpses and shit.

# Twenty

The days following Stas's first mission were anxious. He fretted over the matter constantly; the idea that he had ruined the mission, once it had taken hold, refused to leave him. Enjolras claimed matters were proceeding smoothly, but Stas still worried.

Moreover, the revelations from the night tormented him. It took all Stas's will to avoid gagging whenever he saw his fellows imbibe the cursed drink. He did not know if he would ever be able to see it the same way again. Gathering the foul vials to deliver to Phobos became a far more disgusting chore. He wondered if the man already knew. Perhaps, like Enjolras, the blue-masked man was a patrician, already aware of the process. His skill and weapons were evidence of that fact; most plebs wouldn't have access to either.

Stas resolved to ask him that night.

As Stas made his way to the dead garden, from where he staged his regular escape, he heard voices. His mood soured. The value of the garden was that nobody ever visited. He debated turning away, but curiosity got the better of him.

As he approached, the muffled sounds became audible.

"The political will exists, I am certain." Stas recognized the dry, humorless voice, but he could not properly place it. "Those who favor the reforms outnumber those who oppose them."

"And those who are apathetic outnumber them both." The other

165

voice was quite similar, but more muffled, cast from a different position. "Which seems to be a common problem with the Senate of late. Lethargy and willful ignorance, content to blindly follow the party line. Marcellus and Gratidianus both encourage it of their followers."

"Gratidianus has been attempting to make inroads with Hirtius, though she remains spiteful because of his previous transgressions. And Marcellus has been unduly influenced by her detractors. My inclination is to direct her to Gratidianus."

"In the short term, that may be prudent, but allowing Hirtius to fall into the Antiquiores might lead to her estrangement from our purposes. Moreover, any reform led by Gratidianus will be slow and guarded. Perhaps too slow."

"The Honori are more prepared to act with the swiftness demanded by circumstances," the first speaker agreed. "And Marcellus is in a better position to shut down opposition in his party. But to even speak with them would annihilate any chance of Antiquiores' support. Marcellus himself is fickle, unreliable. And purging Hirtius's detractors from his camp would weaken them greatly."

Stas edged closer, attempting to get a view of the speakers. He was, technically, permitted to walk the estate, but he didn't want anyone to know he came to this garden.

"Solving the current crisis at the cost of the next is unacceptable. Allowing Hirtius to establish an independent voting block for herself would be ideal."

"Ideal, yet infeasible. Marcellus and Gratidianus would both fight any new party. They covet their stranglehold. Hirtius is many things, but adept politician is not one of them. Perhaps this will require direct intervention."

Stas took care to *reflect* to a better vantage point.

"Direct intervention is always tempting, but counterproductive.

The city must be self-sufficient and capable of self-governance. And we cannot risk the Dominus's attention."

From behind the dead hedge, Stas was able to see the occupants … or rather the sole occupant. It was quite easy to recognize the flimsy man with strange garb—the Dominus's Mad Monk. He stood before the statue of the mirror that did not cast a reflection.

Standing alone in a dead garden, arguing with himself. If Stas had been confused as to why this man was considered mad, this would have cleared the matter quickly.

The madman sighed to himself. "Perhaps the Senate is incapable of this task, and we must rely on other investments. Though I will attempt to garner the cooperation of either Gratidianus or Marcellus. As for determining which … perhaps an impacted individual might provide some insight."

The monk exhaled and closed his eyes. "Stas, correct? I would ask for your opinion on this matter, as a citizen of the city."

Stas froze. The man had not even been looking in his direction, had not shown even a hint that he knew he was being watched.

The monk turned to face Stas's hiding spot. "Come now, no need to be concerned. I was not making an effort to conceal my words."

Stas was tempted to *reflect* away and pretend this had never happened. Except that the Mad Monk, for all his insanity, was a member of the Dominus's court. And he was speaking about the Senate. Enjolras and Eponine had recruited him for his access to these sorts of people.

This was a chance to be of use, since he had failed to be any in his first mission.

Stas stepped out, looking down. "Greetings …" He stumbled, realizing that he didn't know the monk's name. "Ah, Greetings," he repeated awkwardly. "I didn't mean to interrupt your deliberations. I didn't know anyone visited this garden."

"Hm. I often come here to speak to myself when dealing with particular issues. It helps to put my thoughts in order when decisions need to be made."

Stas frowned, glancing at the stone mirror statue. "You might want to use an actual mirror if you are speaking with your reflection."

The Mad Monk gave a wry grin. "Ah, but I am not trying to speak to my reflection. I am speaking with myself. A reflection is not good for much intellectual debate, though I do understand why you might have a different opinion."

Stas forced himself to remember that the man was possibly mad. Or pretending to be such. All his words needed to be viewed within that context.

"But that is not a concern at this moment," the monk continued. "You have yet to answer my question."

"I am uncertain what your question is," Stas replied.

"Perhaps I should make a habit of speaking to myself more loudly," he mused, "for the benefit of any onlookers. But I shall clarify. A member of the Senate has identified a potential crisis in the works and, being a practical woman, has devised a solution to said crisis in the form of a package of legislation. However, the necessary components of her solution will be very unpopular among the senatorial body. While the body acknowledges the crisis, she necessarily requires the support of one of the major power blocs if she wishes to see her reforms passed. Her options are to work with the Antiquiores or the Honori. Which should she work with? Lord Gratidianus or Lord Marcellus?"

"Ah ..." Stas floundered under the question. "I do not know enough to make the decision. The matters of the Senate do not concern me, so I don't keep myself informed."

"Hm." The monk frowned deeply. "Matters of the Senate impact everyone. You, as a citizen, should strive to be aware of their actions and politics. But the particulars are unimportant to the dilemma.

What you must know is that in choosing the Antiquiores, the crisis will not be solved quickly or totally, to the detriment of the populace. In choosing the Honori, you risk failing completely, and you will leave the Senate fractured and weak, unable to address the next crisis. Neither option is good, but which is preferable?"

"That ... I do not believe I am the best person to ask when it comes to lofty matters like this. But ..." Stas was not one to settle for a bad option. His training had taught him to always seek victory, wherever he could find it. He did not allow himself to fall into false dilemmas. "Does the solution need to come from the Senate?"

"No," the monk said, "it does not. If the Senate fails its duties, then the Dominus might step in. Or perhaps the citizenry might handle matters on their own. The plebeians do have some power, even if the patricians are vastly better positioned. Famine is a difficult beast to tackle without empowered policy."

"Famine?"

"It's not a secret that the price of grain is rising, that the bread lines are more restrictive. The situation is stable for the moment, but we can expect great difficulties if further harvest failures cut into the city's shrinking stockpiles."

Stas had not been aware. He'd had no need to know. Perhaps Enjolras was aware.

The monk hummed to himself. "Very well, then. I have asked my question and you have answered to your ability. It is only fair that I offer reciprocity. What is your question for me?"

Stas blinked. The turns of this man were sudden and without any warning. "My question regarding?"

He waved his hand vaguely. "Whatever you may wish. In whatever direction your curiosity may direct you. My offer of instruction remains, if you have changed your mind. If not, does anything pique your interest?"

Stas had absolutely not changed his mind. He already had his arcanum, and it was superior to anything the fraud might teach. But his duties to Enjolras and Libertas forced him to consider the matter. Was it worth spending time with the man?

His time already felt frayed, between regular training, Phobos, and Libertas. It was unlikely the man was of true use, compared to other members of the court. Stas did not want to tie his reputation to the Mad Monk. But he did need to come up with something.

Stas jumped to the first thing that came to mind. "Where can one acquire magic weapons?" And the first thing to come to mind was a pretty good question. Getting a hold of a magic weapon like Radek's sword, or Enjolras's shield, or Phobos's fishing hook would be a major boon for his career. If it were iconic enough, it might help supplant his title of "Blink."

"Magic weapons? If your goal is a weapon that uses elixirs, I imagine the novelty makers in the forum might be able to help you. The toy smiths, the artificers, or the golem makers would accept commission. But there is a reason most don't employ such frivolities. Generally, it is far more efficient to imbibe an elixir directly than to feed it to a device. I would advise training your arcanum over relying upon a tool."

Stas shook his head. "I don't mean weapons that use elixirs. I mean weapons that are themselves magic." The weapons that Stas were thinking of had no room for fuel. They simply worked.

"Ah." The monk nodded in understanding. "You speak of soul craft."

That was how Enjolras had described the unbreakable shield, Stas recalled. "That's the name for it, yes. I do not know much on the topic."

"If a soul-crafted weapon is something you seek, you may never be satisfied." He spoke solemnly. "There is no craftsman in the city capable of such a feat. It would be better to consider soul crafting to be a mystery more than a craft—a unique phenomenon that I personally find fascinating. If you would allow me to explain ..."

Stas realized he was waiting for his approval for some reason, so he gave a nod.

"The nature of soul-crafted items is one that I have studied extensively. The items are extraordinarily rare, and their circumstances are painfully strange. Much that I seek to describe is, unfortunately, conjecture, but it is my best understanding of the facts available." He cleared his throat. "When an artisan makes a work—any work, be it a weapon as you seek, or a suit of armor, or a cart, or even a toy—when they truly strive for excellence, they put a bit of themselves in their product. This is mostly metaphorical, but there is some literal truth to it as well."

The Mad Monk nodded to himself. "In very unusual circumstances, a craftsman, perhaps struck by a great and powerful inspiration, will put too much of themselves in. This would be a mania: an all-encompassing need to craft their masterpiece. They would forgo food and sleep, forgo the needs of their mortal shell in the all-consuming pursuit of their work. And the result is soul craft: a work of perfection. All at the cost of the craftsman."

Stas frowned. "So the craftsman dies at the end?" In some ways that sounded like elixirs: sacrifice for arcanum.

"No," he said sharply. "The craftsman does not die. The soul is not some component of the body, like blood or innards. The soul is the person—their existence, their history, their ontology. One's past, present, and future all reside in the immortal soul. If a soul-crafted item exists, then its crafter does not, and never did. They are erased from the memory of the world, cut from the cloth of history. It is an acausal paradox." He offered a small smile. "By all evidence, the soul-crafted item simply sprang into existence without a source, or it had always existed. As I said, it is quite a fascinating phenomenon."

Stas was not a fool to miss the weakness of the theory. "If soul-crafted items seem to come out of nowhere, then how do you explain your knowledge?"

The monk's smile only grew. "Of course, that is the great difficulty of this subject, and why my explanation will forever remain in the realm of conjecture. If I am correct, you would never be able to prove it. You cannot observe something that never happens."

Stas held his tongue on how convenient the explanation was. Like with the Mad Monk's arcanum, he somehow did not need to prove it.

"We can, of course, observe the properties of soul-crafted items, extremely few as they may be, in order to make our guess at their nature. I have had the chance to examine three, in my years. For all three, the creator was unknown, and the history of its acquisition was muddled. I searched extensively for each, but I could not find a proper chain of ownership or origin.

"Beyond that, all three shared the property of being ideal examples of their purpose. They were, as you described, outright supernatural in their ability to accomplish their tasks. So long as it served the purpose of the tool, the tool would not fail. And they were utterly indestructible. I expended a large amount of time and resources attempting to damage soul-crafted items, to complete failure. Though that seems a natural consequence of their perfection—a tool that can be destroyed is not perfect."

The monk nodded. "And that, more than anything else, is what convinces me of my theory. Nothing in the world is indestructible. Nothing is immortal. Even the world itself will fade and crumble with time. Nothing but the soul that is ... the ontological tautology of things that exist, existed. If the soul provides the fuel for craft, it can explain the impossibility."

The contents of the speech felt like the ravings of a madman, and yet the dry tone was more reminiscent of discussing the weather. It was a strange juxtaposition. And a time-consuming one at that. The weight of the elixirs on Stas's bandoleer almost burned against him, reminding him that he really did need to go.

"But all of that is theory," the monk continued. "As you are likely more interested in the practicalities, I will summarize. You will not be able to commission a soul-crafted weapon. It is a technological dead end, more a miracle of circumstance than anything else. The items you have already had the fortune to encounter are likely to be the only examples you encounter in your lifetime. I would advise pursuing the ones you have already discovered, rather than looking to find more."

That ... Stas considered for a moment. Was there a circumstance where Stas would be able to use Enjolras's shield? To have the item serve him in the arena?

"Stas the Shieldwall" was far superior to "Stas the Blink." It could only be a boon for his career.

But Stas discarded the thought almost as quickly as he considered it. It felt ... dirty, somehow to use Enjolras's shield in the arena. It was a symbol, the silver-eyed man had claimed, of Libertas's mission: to defend the weak and the exploited. Using it selfishly might tarnish its eternally polished sheen.

"Hm. I believe I have used up more than enough of your time," the monk said without warning. "I will allow you to use the garden for yourself. I thank you for your time."

"Ah, thank you for the explanation," Stas managed to say in time. The whole scenario was decidedly something, though Stas did not know what to make of it. At the moment he simply felt joy that the monk was leaving.

And with that, the monk walked away down the path, eyes shut, humming some strange, mad tune softly, closing himself off from the world. Stas waited for a good bit for the man to properly leave.

Once he was satisfied with his caution, he climbed up the fountain

and *reflected* to the opposite rooftop. Liberal teleportation would see
him at the meeting point in time.

# Twenty-One

Stas's rendezvous point with Phobos placed him in one of the poorer regions of the city this time. The blue-masked assassin regularly changed where they met, which had given the gladiator a ample experience navigating the city. And with it, he had gotten a sense of it. It allowed him to notice the changes.

Even over a few months, they were noticeable. The buildings were much the same, of course. Notably the only repairs or new construction Stas had ever witnessed all took place in the richer districts. The poor districts seemed to be left to crumble and rot.

The people, though ... Perhaps his conversation with the Mad Monk had primed him, but the people looked more tired, more hungry. More drunkards walked the streets, and more idle men hugged the alleys. A district Stas had previously seen as vibrant and healthy had adopted a more pallid air. The homeless of another district seemed sicker and more plentiful.

Stas's travels happened to bring him past the Bell, that disgusting den of misery he'd had the misfortune of visiting. The ugly, misshapen, homeless boy was absent from his alley. A woman had taken his place.

Stas hurried past.

His mind churned upon the Mad Monk's question. The knowledge that the city was worsening, and that the Senate had the power to prevent it but did not ... he felt the nobility of his cause all the stronger.

This was what Enjolras and Libertas fought against.

That was the solution to the false dilemma: cut through the politicking and unnecessary compromise. Allow a man like Enjolras—benevolent, charismatic, and competent—to wield the power and the unnecessary suffering would cease. There would be no need for simple "acceptable" solutions.

Of course, Stas was not enough of a fool to voice these thoughts to a member of the Dominus's court. But the fact that the man had even considered it a conundrum exemplified the failures of the government.

As dusk fell upon the city, Stas found his way to the designated rooftop. Once there, he secured his mask to his face. The gift remained as comfortable today as it had been the day Enjolras gave it to him.

Stas waited, as he was accustomed, keeping an eye out for his mentor. The sign came in the form of the slight creak of the roof tile behind him, quiet enough that Stas felt the vibration more than he heard the noise.

He turned to face the masked man, who stopped.

"When I said to bring a mask, I didn't think it'd be so god-awful gaudy," Phobos grumbled.

Stas rolled his eyes before realizing it wouldn't be visible. "Coming from someone with your taste, I'll take it as a compliment. It's far less ugly than yours, and I assume far more comfortable besides."

Phobos scoffed and extended his hand in a familiar demand.

With well-practiced ease, Stas tossed the elixirs from his bandoleer to the older man. "You know those are made of human shit and corpses, right?"

"Yeah," Phobos caught each bottle without much fanfare, securing them on his body. "Of course I know. I've seen them get made. Blown up a production facility or two. And, unless you're fleecing me, there shouldn't be crap in these ones. Just bodies."

"Why didn't you tell me?" Stas demanded.

"Because it doesn't matter. Elixirs are elixirs. The crud that goes in them is irrelevant. All that matters is what you can do with it. Don't bother thinking about it too much. You have to use what you have, no point letting it go to waste." The man scoffed. "Feh—you think I like drinking that shit? Fat chance. But there's no alternative in this twisted world, so, for as long as I'm here, I have to deal with it. Not everyone is as lucky as you."

Something stuck out in Stas's mind. "Did you say you blew up production facilities?"

"Yeah. I do have a life outside of making sure you can wipe your own ass, you know."

"A life that involves destroying government production facilities? No, it's ... if you're fighting the city, there are people I could get you in contact with. Individuals who might be able to help, or better direct you." Stas tried to make the pitch, but he realized that there was little he actually knew about Phobos. He had sort of been assuming that Phobos was some deranged maniac, who killed for fun. Or someone with a grudge against the watchers. Or someone addicted to elixirs.

But actually destroying an elixir production facility was a level beyond that, and didn't make much sense for an addict or a simple grudge holder. It spoke of loftier ambitions, or greater hate.

If Phobos was an enemy of the government itself, it would make sense to coordinate.

But Stas was no Enjolras. He could not grasp the goals of a man and make him understand their shared aims. He could not portray the righteousness of Enjolras's cause, could not do justice to its aims. He could only fumble and flounder in vague hopes.

It was a weak pitch, and Stas knew it well.

Phobos ignored it entirely. "Enough of that. I want to get this lesson over with. You brought a mask, so you didn't fail out of the gate at least."

Stas huffed and said nothing.

"Today's lesson is different, more practical. I've been drilling you with exercises and thought experiments, but the only way to truly test you is through experience. For this lesson, I will be giving you a task to complete as you see fit. I will offer no input nor any commentary, nor will I provide any aid but what you explicitly request. If you request something I deem trivial, you fail. If I am forced to intervene that will also be a failure. Do you understand?"

This was a strange request, but it did not stray too far from the eccentricities of Phobos's tutelage. Stas did not bother to inquire as to the consequences of failure. Phobos had shown his creativity in devising his penalties often enough. Stas had no further desire to engage in calisthenics in a fetid horse stable, or to dodge rotten fruits on the rooftops again. The smells left a distinctly unpleasant memory.

Instead, he began with the obvious question. "What is the task?"

"There is a man, a senator's nephew by the name of Elagabalus. Your task is to ensure he dies before midnight."

Stas bristled under his mask. "I am not," he seethed, "an assassin. I am not a killer for hire, or some lowlife thug. I am definitely not some catspaw for you to throw your perverse work at. What in your despicable mind makes you believe this is anything close to appropriate? I have half a mind to strike you down for even offering such an insult to me, scum."

Phobos's posture was unamused. The single painted eye seemed to stare through him, unblinking. "Cute. Are you forfeiting, then? Don't assume your arrogant morality changes anything. Elagabalus is a marked man. He will die tonight with or without your participation. I am making it a task for you entirely to aid your tutelage."

That his masked instructor was completely unperturbed by Stas's threats gave him pause. The man might have been a better fighter, but the gladiator had grown rapidly under his tutelage. His apathy was enough to halt Stas's building wrath.

"What is so special about this man that he needs to die?"

"Hmph." Phobos exhaled sharply. "Maybe you should be asking why he deserves to live instead. Elagabalus is a predator, a sick, twisted excuse for a man who trawls the markets for the vulnerable. He invites them, women and children, back to his estate, in the guise of a benevolent host. Once there, he keeps them until he has had his sick thrills in 'recompense' for his hospitality. Sometimes he does not release them. Sometimes he only releases them part by part, keeping pieces for himself to enjoy." The voice delivering the lines was blank, clinical. "Elagabalus is a rapist and a murderer. He does not deserve the consideration of your morals. You should not spend any effort defending him."

Stas held himself still. "How certain are you of this?"

"I learned of it from one of his victims. I found her after hearing about the rumors. Then I spent the last two days traipsing the estate to confirm the matter. I saw more than enough."

Stas felt indignation boil. If Phobos had seen these crimes, why did he not do something already? Why had he not rescued the victims immediately?

But the paradox of his gut reaction became apparent. Had he not just lambasted the man for his assassinations? How fickle would he be, decrying a man for murder, then immediately accuse him of being too slow? His instincts were flawed, somehow.

What was the proper response, then? How should one treat a villain as vile as Phobos claimed Elagabalus to be? What would a good man do? A good man wouldn't seek the death of a foe, as an assassin would. But a good man would not allow innocents to suffer.

"I imagine," Stas mused aloud, "that this is not a matter the lawmen would concern themselves with?"

In a just society, in the society that Enjolras sought, there would be no conundrum. Any villain could simply be trusted to the courts, and justice would follow. Society executing a criminal is just. But a single man cannot both judge and execute; they can only murder.

"He keeps himself to poor plebeians. He is not stupid enough to target anyone who matters. So the watchers have no reason to care."

Stas grit his teeth. Of course that would be the case. A senator's nephew was in a position of privilege. To make an enemy of a senator was not a light matter.

The lawmen would not, could not, solve the issue. What was the alternative? Confinement was infeasible. Maiming would not stop the crimes. Castration could stop lust, but not cruelty. And any punishment would enrage the Senate. Nothing but the complete destruction of the man could guarantee the safety of the victims.

Death seemed to be the proper course, but Stas could not believe it with a whole heart. He would be delighted to hear that the man suffered an accident, but he could not demand it. Certainly, if Stas ever had the fortune to face the villain Elagabalus in the arena, he would not hesitate to slay him immediately. Such could be the justice of the sands, where death was permitted.

But Elagabalus was not a gladiator, nor, Stas expected, a fighter at all. To kill a man who knowingly faced death, who fought on equal terms, was a world away from simple slaughter.

Elagabalus was a villain who deserved to die. Stas was certain of this. But only a villain could deliver the sentence. A good man could not murder. They could defend themselves or others, but they could not seek the death of others.

But was a good man still good if they permitted evil?

This dilemma was far more concerning than the Mad Monk's miserable Senate. There the right action was clear, but pathetic men made it difficult. Here, even the nature of correct action was at stake.

Stas was not a philosopher, to ponder these questions. He was a student of the world, and looked to learn from those around him. To answer what a man should do to be good, he only had to consider a good man, and what they would do.

What would Enjolras do? Stas considered the silver-eyed man and let him act in his stead. Enjolras would not hesitate to decide, his virtues apparent. Stas pictured him taking each course of action. Ultimately, Stas could not picture Enjolras committing murder. It was irreconcilable with everything he knew about the man. As for sitting back and letting the villain act … that also didn't work.

But Enjolras would not sit back. He would act tirelessly to fix society, to make a world where justice could be enacted. Indeed, that was what he was doing, now and today and every day. He worked to address not just Elagabolus but every other failure of the city, in perpetuity.

In the end, this, like the Mad Monk's conundrum, was a false dilemma. In the proper light, the answer was clear.

Stas bolstered his resolve. "I refuse. I will not kill a man who cannot fight back. If I must fail your test, then so be it, but I will not allow myself to be a murderer. Not even for a villain like you describe."

Phobos stood silently for a long while. He was always difficult to read, but he did not appear angry. Rather, he seemed to be caught in a quandary of his own.

After a while, Phobos finally spoke. "You don't need to stain your hands," he declared. "I can do so. But for this task you must do absolutely everything else. Is that acceptable to you?"

Stas considered. It was a tricky matter, but Phobos's own villainy simplified it. If Elagabalus were certain to die by the assassin's hands regardless, then Stas was not culpable. It would be akin to the misfortune Stas wished upon the senator's nephew. He could learn, as Phobos intended, and he could ensure the matter was handled delicately.

"Nobody else will die," Stas declared. "Not servants, not guards, not witnesses. Not even watchers. Just your target."

"It is your task to do as you see fit."

Stas counted it as victory. He closed his eyes in thought as he set himself to the task in truth.

"You spent two days investigating Elagabalus," Stas began. "Might I ask you about it? Or would that be considered a failure for relying too much upon you?"

"You can ask any questions you like, so long as they aren't about what you should do," Phobos answered without hesitation. "But I won't volunteer any information you do not request."

From how quickly Phobos had responded, Stas knew he was on the right track.

"In that case ..." Stas considered the first question. "Based on what you know of the man's schedule, when will he be in bed? Does he sleep in his own estate, or will he be out tonight? Who else lives with the man? How often does he host visitors? Would anyone be visiting at this time?"

"Elagabalus will be asleep in two hours. He will be in his own estate tonight—he has not received any invitations today. Elagabalus is a bachelor. No wife, and no children he acknowledges. He often hosts debaucherous parties, but there is not one scheduled for tonight."

Stas nodded. "How many night guards does the man employ? How do the watchers' patrols intersect with his estate?" He immediately corrected himself. "Actually, are you able to provide a floor plan for the estate and the rooms within, including the surrounding buildings? Can you include patrol patterns upon it?"

Phobos nodded at each request, without a word. He produced a slate from somewhere on his person, as well as a thin piece of chalk. He began to draw, the implement flying across the blacked slate with practiced speed.

He was quite prepared for this request. Stas knew he was asking the right questions. Phobos had gone over abstract scenarios enough that Stas had a good idea as to the sorts of facts his teacher felt were important.

He waited for Phobos to finish the drawing, which did not require much time at all. In the fading sun, the details were quite hard to make out, but Phobos's smooth, quick lines did not seem hampered by the lack of light. That he was drawing it all from memory with such confidence was impressive on its own.

Phobos procured a rod from his cloak. Its resemblance to the flameless torches that lit up the revolutionary hideout was proven when it emitted a soft glow. Its directed beam cast light upon the slate, and not much else.

Stas gave Phobos a side glance. "A slate, chalk, a magic torch, who knows how many elixirs," he listed aloud. "I know you have weapons too, the hook and chain and some throwing knives. Just how much are you carrying, Phobos?"

"Irrelevant," the masked man declared gruffly.

Stas held up a hand. "I'm just curious. And impressed. I honestly don't know how you can carry so much without any of it showing. Is it arcanum? Or do you simply have scores of hidden pockets?"

"Focus on the task, brat.".

Stas rolled his eyes and focused on the floor plan. Upon his direction, Phobos highlighted the patrol patterns, both of the guards employed in the estate, and the watchers that surveyed the hill upon which Elagabalus's estate lay. Of the first, there were only four, two stationary, one patrolling within, and one patrolling without. Of the latter, there were quite a number. The residential area for patricians was filled with watchers. That said, their patrols were not focused on the specific estate. But it was certain that, should any alarm be raised, the bird-masked lawmen would be very quick to act.

Stas further inquired about servants of the estate, of which there were many, but few would be active at night. He also remembered to ask about the guards of neighboring estates, a question that elicited a special grunt of acknowledgment.

After getting a layout of the people, Stas focused his mind on deciphering the floor plan, paying special attention to the possible entrances and egresses, as well as the location of the villain's bedroom. He asked Phobos about the nature of the estate's roof, and quickly dismissed it as an option. It was far too open to the view of patrols. Better to pit himself against the night guards alone, and not the Dominus's lawmen.

He did not believe the guards would be a great threat. Any true combatant, current gladiators or those retired from the arena sands, would be employed as day guards. Half the reason they were so sought after was for the prestige. Patricians wanted to be seen employing famous gladiators as they went about their day. They would not be wasted on the night shift.

A night guard would be as skilled as a watcher, at best. And Stas was far superior. The only difficulty would be dispatching the guards without raising the alarm. And without killing them. He would need to plot a route to accomplish the task.

He asked Phobos if he had the tools to bind and silence defeated foes, to which he responded by unveiling rolls of linen. Just another surprising item the man happened to be carrying. It would serve as bindings and gags if needed.

Phobos waited patiently as Stas plotted. Stas took his chalk to the slate, deliberating over possible moves.

Ultimately, he determined his route. It would take him from an entrance to the bedroom, and allow quiet exfiltration. Phobos offered no comment. Stas was tempted to ask what he thought of his plot, but he knew his teacher would simply refuse to comment. So instead he imagined himself as Phobos, offering critique to his work with a dispassionate eye. He harshly judged the plan, seeking its failure. In turn, he offered a defense of each of the plan's facets to the imagined teacher.

The imaginary Phobos was gruffly satisfied. He had to imagine the real one would be too.

There were risks, of course, but Stas would not be paralyzed by the need for perfection. He had a course he could trust and room to adapt as required.

Satisfied, Stas declared aloud that his plan was solidified, and that he wished to carry it out in an hour's time. Even if Elagabalus had stayed awake longer than expected, he would be deep asleep at the time they met him. Phobos offered no comment.

He inquired as to the directions to the man's estate, and Phobos offered counsel. Stas took the time to determine the best way to cross the city. This was not as meticulous a plot as that of the mission itself, but speaking of the patrol routes with Phobos did pass the time.

He also requested the right to use Phobos's magic torch and was somewhat surprised to be granted it. The dim light would make the mission far simpler when he needed visibility. That said, he would avoid using it too much. Light allowed one to be seen as much as it could help one see. Phobos showed him how to use it, which turned out to be as simple as pressing a switch.

# Twenty-Two

The two of them made their way across the rooftops to Elegabalus's manor. According to Phobos, Stas was to act as though he were alone. It was quite an easy task, seeing as Phobos had immediately imbibed an elixir and vanished from view. He seldom used arcanum in Stas's presence, but he had great skill in hiding from the senses.

He also was effective at traversing the city. The man could keep pace with Stas even as he made full use of his *reflections*.

That said, it wasn't like Stas could see his teacher any more. It was conceivable that he had managed to outpace him. But Stas had been outshone by Phobos too often to fall into that trap. He would just assume that he was there, watching him, as he had stated he would be.

He focused his mind instead on navigating the moonlit city, watching for bird-masked watchers and light posts that might give him away. His path was indirect for good reason.

Ultimately, Stas situated himself on a rooftop, looking down on an expansive manor. He waited a short moment before speaking softly. "This is the place, correct?"

Phobos's grunt of a response proved both that it was and that he had indeed kept pace.

Stas steeled himself and *reflected* for a better vantage point. He did not want to deal with the outdoor patrolmen. Once he had caught sight of them, he would enter the manor proper behind their backs.

On cue, as per Phobos's description, one of the guards made their rounds through the grounds. As soon as he had passed, Stas *reflected* to a window by the servants' quarters, and *reflected* inside.

He quickly and quietly moved to the main section of the estate, making sure not to wake up any of the sleeping staff. This was perhaps the most risky part of the venture. Servants did not have the regular patterns of guardsmen. He did not want to be forced to subdue them, nor risk their raising an alarm.

But Stas did not encounter anyone awake in the hallway. The laundry room he found himself in was empty, as was the narrow hallway that led to the estate grounds proper. With careful deliberation and occasional *reflections*, Stas found his way to the dining hall of the estate. He lit Phobos's magic torch and took careful stock.

It was egregiously opulent—gold and gemstones and rich woods and a chandelier that twinkled in the night. Couches and tapestries deeply dyed with outrageous colors lined the room, almost haphazard in arrangement. The amount of wealth on display in this reception room was off-putting. Stas wondered if the estate's sole occupant even found the arrangement attractive, or if it was all just as brazen a showing as it appeared.

The entire area was also suffused with the pungent scent of strong soaps and perfumes. Stas did not want to consider what sort of odors they were covering up. That he could smell so much through his mask boded ill.

When not utilized for Elegabalus's many parties, this room would be seldom touched. Or so Stas surmised. None of the patrol patterns passed through this den. It was a good room to catch his bearings.

Stas took a deep breath. He immediately regretted it as the perfumes assaulted his nostrils. Shaking his head, he turned off Phobos's torch. Then he reached for his magic.

Stas gazed upon the infinite mirrors of the world, seeking for the *reflections* of the manor. Compared to scanning the great expanse of the city, this task was a simple matter. He simply needed to find the *reflections* of the patrolling guards. If not for the unnerving mirrors and their unpleasant sights, he would have no issue at all.

The guardsman he sought was patrolling, as expected, through the house. Stas followed the reflection, moving his gaze across the infinite mirrors so that he would be able to keep track of his location. And, when the backwards inverted reflection of the man entered the backwards inverted room furthest from Elegabalus's bedroom, Stas quickly *reflected* forth.

His fists were flying before the guardsman had the chance to respond. His gag was secured before he could utter a word of pain. The shocked man fell to the ground, his muffled yell cutting into the gag even as Stas worked to tie it more securely. He kept a hand around the man's neck to secure it, so that it would not break in the sudden jerking.

The man struggled, but Stas was stronger, and had better leverage besides. It was a trivial matter to keep the man's arms and legs at bay. A well-timed kick provided the pressure. A foot stomped to the ground near the man's fingers threatened him towards compliance. Deft movement of his hands prevented the lantern the man was carrying from clanging loudly against the floor.

From there, Stas was able to tie the guard's hands and feet together behind his back. He hoped it would be tight enough to secure him, but not too tight as to induce harm, though Stas was admittedly unpracticed, and hedged on the side of too tight. He snuffed out the guard's lantern and secured it against himself, then he lifted the heavyset man up and slung him over his shoulder.

He *reflected*.

Months ago, Stas would never have been able to *reflect* with something so heavy. It had been difficult enough to learn to travel with his clothes at the start, and carrying his equipment had been a great hurdle for the longest time. But Phobos had insisted that Stas practice the skill, assigning him sacks of grain over and over again. It was exhausting, but fruitful.

Stas brought the man back to the dining room and hid him behind the couch, alongside the lantern. The man would not be discovered in the night, but could be easily found in the morning.

The next step was the bedroom guard, stationary before Elegabalus's door. He would need to strike quickly before the man noticed his fellow was not returning. Stas gazed through the mirrors to confirm the solitary man had yet to move.

He took another deep breath and *reflected*.

This takedown was as smooth as the last. With the element of surprise, he muffled and dispatched the hapless guard. Soon enough he was deposited next to his fellow. He quickly returned to the patrician's bedroom door.

Stas's heart raced and his blood beat in his throat. Everything was going to plan, but he couldn't help but feel nervous all the same. Every moment felt like the one in which he would be discovered. It was irrational, he knew, but he felt it all the same.

Stas steeled himself. He opened the bedroom door.

It was dark, but he could make out the faint outlines of a large bed, and heard the sounds of breathing. He did not dare to set a light, fearing it might wake the occupant.

He entered the room, and slowly closed the door behind him.

Stas didn't know what to do at this point. The situation was far less dramatic than anything he had imagined. The villain whose death he had helped plot simply lay in bed, asleep, relaxed upon a mound of pillows, beneath a luxurious blanket. There was no great sign of guilt here, no trapped victim. Nothing about this scene screamed villainy.

In the midst of his contemplation, his masked teacher shimmered into view ahead of him, standing above the bed, knife extended.

A single, short stab plunged it into the sleeping man's neck, severing his spine. Phobos extracted the knife with a similarly smooth motion. He flicked the blood clean off the weapon and concealed it back on his person.

Elagabalus had died in his sleep without a sound. Stas found himself watching in shock.

Phobos turned to face him, a dispassionate face hidden behind the one-eyed mask. "Wait for me at the Trajan Bell Tower," he commanded, snatching the magic torch from Stas's hands. "I will meet you there after I complete my business. Don't get caught."

Stas did not have a moment to respond before Phobos faded from view once again. Stas took a moment to shake himself out of his stupor.

Blood gushed into the rich linens in the unlit room. The smell stained the air.

Stas clenched his teeth and turned away from the dark sight. A series of *reflections* saw him out of the building, away from the prying eyes of the night guards and the bird-faced watchers. Several more and he had made his way across the city to the meeting point where his first lesson had taken place. There he ascended to the top and waited, alone but for his thoughts.

Had he made the right decision? Was he acting as a good man should? Mere hours ago he had been so certain, but after watching a sleeping man die before him, could he truly claim his innocence?

Stas had been so eager to believe Phobos about Elagabalus's evil deeds. He had not thought to ask for proof. Stas did not believe Phobos to be a liar, but he didn't even consider the possibility.

Could a villain truly sleep so peacefully? Would not their conscience make for an uneasy slumber?

Stas pulled off his mask and stared at the metal-coated symbol on it. Did he even deserve to wear Enjolras's gift?

He had imagined a glorious adventure, and a foul villain to be slain. But the ease of it shook him as much as the violence of Phobos's act. Stas festered in his dark thoughts.

# Twenty-Three

After nearly an hour, Phobos arrived.

"What took you so long?" Stas demanded. "Did you take the time to murder another patrician? Perhaps the neighbors?"

Phobos offered a blank stare. "I was searching the manor for any prisoners."

The bite fell away from Stas's retort. "Did you find any?"

"Three," Phobos announced calmly. "All in a sorry state. Two of them required treatment. The third demanded a mercy killing."

Stas froze, not wishing to ask if Phobos had granted it.

"My time was spent escorting them to safety. More important than humoring you, I would say."

Stas bit his tongue, reassessing his thoughts. "I could have helped," he said.

Phobos shook his head. "It wasn't part of your test. It has nothing to do with what I was training you in, so there was no point."

Stas felt the need to argue the point, but Phobos continued. "Speaking of, I don't have much to complain about your performance. You planned out the matter properly and executed it to your own specifications. As I expected, I really don't have much more to teach you."

Stas blinked in confusion. "Can you really call it a proper test? It felt too easy. I don't really understand how everything went so cleanly.

My plan was simple and did not require great skill. Surely there is a better means of testing my knowledge of your lessons."

"The test only felt easy to you because of your magic. For anyone else, it would have been far more difficult."

"But does that not mean it is an improper test for me? Should you not have told me to go about it as anyone else might?"

Phobos shook his head. "No. You have your magic. You'll always have your magic. If it were elixir magic, that would be one thing, since you can run out. Telling you not to use it is like telling you not to use your legs." He inhaled. "That said, you should never be relying entirely on your teleportation tricks. Knowing when to use the proper tool for the proper job is important. But there is nothing wrong with using it when it is proper."

Stas chewed on the thought. The logic made sense, and, honestly, if Phobos had demanded he refrain from his arcanum, he would have complained. But to go so far as to say he had nothing left to teach? Ridiculous. That Phobos could still trounce him in a spar was proof enough. Until the student fully surpassed the master there was always more to learn.

But there was another matter bothering him.

"In Elagabalus's bedroom, when you killed him, why did you not first wake him up?"

Phobos paused. "Why the hell would I have done a fool thing like that?"

Stas frowned. "So that the man might know why he was being executed? So that he might prepare to face death with open eyes? So that he could be given a moment to repent?"

"There's quite a few problems with that, brat," Phobos said. "First, it's an unnecessary risk. If I had woken him up he might have raised an alarm. Or escaped. And any delay is a risk by itself."

"You could have bound and gagged him as I did the guards," Stas said. "Perhaps it might have been an issue, but I don't see how he could have escaped. And an added minute could hardly muddle matters. Perhaps if I had been sloppier, or if an alarm had already been raised, I would understand the argument. But we could have made it work."

Phobos posture radiated disapproval. The painted eye blankly stared in time with his visible eye. "There is no value in it, for any amount of risk. Wishing to have your target witness their own death is either a mark of sadism or pointless sentimentality. Is that it, brat? Did you want to see him cry and shit himself?"

Stas scoffed. "Of course not. But a man should be aware of their own sentencing."

"Execution is for the audience," Phobos said. "The pain and suffering exists for the sake of driving terror into the witnesses, and to stoke the imaginations of all who hear about it. The goal of cruel punishment, of ugly deaths, is to prevent others from repeating the crime. To the man who is dying, death is the punishment. The pain does not have a purpose. It is entirely superfluous. In the same way that repentance before death is pointless. The dead do not, cannot, care if they died in pain or died peacefully. They don't care if they died for 'justice' or out of malice. Insisting your victim must know why they die … the only value is assuaging your ego as the killer. Feh. I'm shocked this sort of drivel is festering in your head."

"If you do not see the value in justice, then why do you even care who your victims are?" Stas said. "Was it simply advantageous for you to kill this man? Were you hired to do so?"

"The point," Phobos stressed, "is for the victims. For the still living ones. Those living in fear, who suffer every moment they know their oppressor is alive. The value in death is the satisfaction and serenity the action brings to those that are alive to be impacted by it. The dead victims don't have the capacity to care."

"So, then, a murderer is not worth stopping because their victims can never benefit from the death? A thief or a mugger is more a criminal than an assassin?" Stas extracted the ridiculous conclusion from the nonsense. Rhetoric was never his favorite subject in his youth, but he had learned some from the classes. "I suppose, as a murderer yourself, you enjoy such a distinction."

Phobos huffed. "You are being argumentative and you know it, brat. You stop a murderer to protect their future victims, and to aid all the victims' friends and relatives. But you are correct in that there is no value to the victims. Nor is there any value in ensuring the murderer experiences 'justice' for the crime. The dead cannot appreciate it."

"No." Stas held firm to his arguments. "You are pretending that justice is some irrelevant force, that all that determines the value in an action is its impact on people. You would have justice perverted to serve the goals of your values. But justice is an end in itself. Avenging a person, allowing a villain to face the weight of their crimes before death ... it is irrelevant that they will not live beyond the moment, because justice does not require a witness. It is still proper."

There was a long pause. Stas enjoyed that the weight of his words seemed to have an impact on the man.

"You claim you are not a murderer," Phobos said, with some great heat. "Well, I am not a torturer. I will kill and steal and maim and destroy, but I will never, ever, inflict pain for the joy of it. Every ounce of suffering I produce is deliberate and purposeful. If a clean kill is possible, then I will make it clean. And no calls for justice will ever change my mind."

There was steel to the masked man's voice, an unshaken resolve that Stas was enthralled by. He could hear the will and anger, the vows forged and promises kept. More than anything else Phobos had ever spoken aloud, this declaration seemed to be the most true to his psyche. It forced Stas to question just what he knew about the man.

"Who are you?" he asked. "You aren't some mere assassin or thug for hire, or some serial killer or trained fighter with a petty grudge. So who are you? What are you after?"

It was not as if Stas hadn't wondered about it before. The eternally masked man was some small mystery in his mind. In truth, though, Stas had decided long before that the answer didn't matter in the slightest. It did not matter if his teacher was a killer for hire or for pleasure, so long as he could serve as a teacher as Stas required. In the end, Phobos was a man with skills that he was willing to impart in exchange for the elixirs that Stas had access to. Anything beyond that hadn't mattered in the slightest.

But now, after the test tonight and after Phobos's declaration regarding morality, the basis of which the man had certainly considered before, Stas felt that the answer was beginning to matter.

The mystery gnawed at him. He needed to know.

"What sort of question is that?" was the gruff response. "Who do you think I am?"

"I had assumed you were a former gladiator, who took up a life of crime for pleasure or thrills. Or perhaps a defector from the watchers, who took the training and used it for your own ends. I assumed you were a mercenary, or that you found satisfaction in murder. And yet you chose a target on the basis of his crimes. More than that, you seem to have a code of honor. A strange one that permits murder and assassination, but it exists all the same." Stas took a breath. "So who are you, Phobos?"

Phobos inhaled. "Who am I? I'm simply an old man, aging night by night. I do what I must, because I can't accept otherwise."

"What you 'must?'"

"I made a vow, long ago," Phobos explained, with a light tilt to his voice, "years and years ago when I first took on this mask. I vowed that whenever I donned it, I would ensure the world would be made a better place before I was permitted to remove it. I vowed to eradicate the evils I found. I vowed to seek them out when they weren't apparent. I vowed to use whatever means were required to see my mission through. Assassin, thief, saboteur, or even a teacher for a nosy brat, I am whatever I need to be to ensure nobody will suffer from the depredations of the strong and callous."

A declaration like that was almost enough to make Stas forget. But for all that he said, it was the actions that made a man good or evil.

To disparage justice, to permit any method, to show no remorse for one's own victims, casting their lives away from behind like a coward because you needed the elixirs they held ...

Stas respected the skills of his masked teacher. He trusted him to keep to their deals, and he believed him to be an excellent pedagogue in his own rough way. But Stas would never trust the virtues of the masked man. He would never be able to see him as a force of righteousness. Not when he fell so short against true paragons.

The nobility of the man's mission was betrayed by the man himself, his virtues corroded by the deeds he so regularly engaged in. No wonder he wore a mask. All the better for this world to never see his ugly visage.

A just society would not allow Phobos to engage in his mission. But at the same time, a just society would not require Phobos's mission. Perhaps that was the simple truth of the matter.

Regardless of anything else, Stas could not see a virtuous world being created by anyone but a virtuous man. That was the flaw in Phobos's vow. If all men of justice were like Phobos, their work would never cease.

But the work itself was vague, and the man's explanation demanded further elaboration.

"What do you need elixirs for, that you have been so willing to tutor me? Also, I resent the implication that doing so is equivalent to slaughtering watchers for their supplies."

Phobos huffed sharply. "I'm not even sure why I am telling you this, but it hardly matters if you know. I am stockpiling as many elixirs as I can so that I have the best shot at eliminating the greatest source of evil in this world. The Dominus."

"You wish to assassinate the Dominus?" Even after months in Libertas's company, the idea of removing the undisputed and eternal leader of the city was still daunting. Even with the repeated assurances of his fellows, the self-aggrandized bragging, the repeated explanations of the necessity, it felt like the greatest hurdle.

Libertas wished to overturn the Senate and force the Dominus to accept the change as *faitaccompli*. They wanted to convince the lord of the city to accept a ceremonial role outside the day-to-day matters of governance.

The thought of actually killing the immortal emperor ... Phobos was far more mad than the Dominus's monk.

"The Dominus is a parasite," Phobos declared. "Perhaps in a literal sense. They are an invader from another world, sucking this one dry for his own satisfaction. This city existed long before him, but they came and conquered it, and have been feasting on it for hundreds of years now. The Dominus is the greatest evil in this world, and I am certain that is the reason I have been brought here. It is the greatest good I can accomplish in this world."

Madness. Utter madness. "Even beyond all that ... you are trying to kill the Dominus, a person renowned for their absolute mastery of arcanum, with elixirs? Are you certain you have taken your own lessons to heart? Because if I had proposed such a mind-bogglingly moronic plan, I am certain you would have taken a switch to my backside."

"I have thought it through many times, brat," the man spat.

"Have you? Because it isn't clear, since it seems you are trying to defeat the Dominus with arcanum and elixirs. If this is truly your goal, wouldn't your time be far better spent sabotaging the Domunis's own supply? If you could deny the Dominus access to their arcanum, and their bodyguards, and the legions of watchers they employ, then maybe your moronic assassination would have a chance of succeeding."

"I can't negate the Dominus's arcanum any more than I could negate yours," Phobos declared. "They have no need of elixirs. Their magic predates them."

For perhaps the fifth time in this long night, Stas was forced to process some new revelation. "The Dominus has elixirless magic? The Dominus is like me?" Stas had, for the longest time, assumed that his situation was unique. After the false hope from the Mad Monk, he had accepted it as a fact. After all, if someone could use magic without elixirs, they were certain to be famous.

But, then again, who else but the Dominus fit that description? Stas had never dreamed of comparing himself to the august emperor before, but it made sense in a way that nothing else did.

Was Stas himself immortal like the city's ruler? He was far too young to know for sure. And he was not foolish enough to test the matter. So it might be a long, long time before he ever discovered the truth.

Considering that matter, how was Phobos hoping to kill an immortal? Likely the elixirs were there to achieve that, because arcanum was certainly the solution. He decided to ask.

Phobos scoffed. "The Dominus is not immortal. They just won't die of age or disease. But you are correct in that the elixirs are for that purpose. I don't pretend that I have any chance of defeating the Dominus in a straight fight, despite what you might think of me. The elixirs are necessary for a trap I am helping devise."

"But how do you know so much about the Dominus?" Stas asked.

"I have a contact. Did my own digging. But never mind that. Is your curiosity settled, brat?"

Was it? Phobos was definitely annoyed at this point, so Stas doubted he was willing to answer any more questions. Honestly, Stas was surprised that he had deigned to answer so many and so honestly already. Normally the man was quite taciturn or dismissive about anything that didn't have direct relevance to his lessons. He even got annoyed enough when Stas discussed anything but the lesson directly at hand.

Something tonight must have shaken him in some way, for him to be so talkative. But enough had happened in the night that Stas could not determine what in particular.

Except there was one matter. "Before the task, there was a matter I wished to bring up. A group of individuals that you might benefit from contacting."

Phobos held a hand up. "Save it, brat. I don't want anything to do with that sort of operation. My task is my own. I won't get mucked up in anyone else's fool dreams or let anyone else get mired into mine. I am not interested."

Stas sighed, biting back his immediate response. It was choices like this that ensured he could not see Phobos as a truly righteous individual.

Phobos spat out a harsh breath. "We'll meet again next week at the usual time. I'll figure out a lesson. But we may see about wrapping these up soon enough. Get back to your cozy bed then and get some actual sleep."

And with that final command, Phobos dove off the rooftop for the city below.

Stas did not spend much time grumbling before he headed back to his school. Phobos was right about one thing. It was far too late. He needed to get to bed if he wanted to be in shape for sword lessons in the morning.

# Twenty-Four

The underground bar was in an uproar when Stas arrived. For once, nobody seemed to be drinking.

"It's the money! The money, I'm telling you!" Lucian's screeching voice rose above the din. "The coins are watching us, those damned eyes!"

"Shut up about the fucking money, you damn drunkard!" someone yelled. "You were his partner! Why didn't you save him?"

"It wasn't Lucian's neighborhood, you daft fool. It was yours!"

"I didn't even know about the fucking operation! Why didn't you let me know about it, Sanson?"

"You don't need to know every fucking thing. Everyone already knows too much. That's why we're in this fucking mess!"

In the doorway, Stas stood awkwardly, watching the roaring argument grow. Beside him Eponine's anger visibly rose. The door closed softly behind them. The older door guard, Maria, also seemed distraught with the situation.

"How can you waste your time on that shit, Sanson? It's obvious Romeo's own damn incompetence is why he got caught. Why bother setting up your damn purges, when he could be squealing right now?"

"How dare you besmirch Romeo? He'd never get himself caught for any fault of his own."

"Yeah? Well—"

Whatever Odette was about to say was interrupted by Eponine's loud, echoing scream. "Will everybody shut up!"

As she commanded, the room fell silent.

She cast her angered gaze across the room. "Now, will someone calmly explain what's going on?"

Immediately, half a dozen people began shouting at once.

Eponine's eyebrows twitched. "What did I just say?" she yelled, shutting the rabble down once again. "Nobody's going to speak unless spoken to. Henri, tell me what's going on."

"Me?" Henri jumped. "I mean, I wasn't involved. I didn't see anything myself, I just heard it from everyone else, so ..." He paused, gulped, and continued. "Romeo was trying to destroy one of the communication towers. You know, one of the ones Enjolras told us about? But apparently somebody was there waiting for him. And Romeo got captured."

"Captured?" Eponine asked. "Not killed?"

"That's, um ..." Henri gulped. "That's what they said. The watchers subdued him, right at the start, and yeah ..."

Eponine nodded, and then turned to Stas. "Are there matches tomorrow?"

Stas blinked. "Yes. Both the Solar and the Stellar arenas have matches set for tomorrow at the usual times."

Eponine nodded. "Good. If Romeo's been caught, he won't be executed until tomorrow. Orval, Maria taught you the eye trick, right? Go check the Solar and the Stellar. See if you can find where Romeo is being held. Don't get caught. Katriane, you should check the hippodrome just in case. Either way, we have time." She nodded to herself and glared at Orval. "What did I just say, Orval? Hop to it!"

The young man jumped to his feet, running for the supply room. He passed Katriane who was already moving.

Eponine exhaled sharply. "We'll wait until Enjolras arrives to plan our next move. We can argue about whose fault it was when Romeo's back. Until then, keep your shit to yourself. Am I understood?"

The crowd offered some muttered acceptance and wilted under the weight of Eponine's growing glare. The anger had died, but fear remained. Stas felt the task was left half done. Eponine was effective, far more than Stas himself would have been, but Enjolras would have handled the matter with far greater ability.

"Good," Eponine concluded. "We're going to get through this. Don't worry about Romeo. Don't worry about if he squealed. We will figure it out. Calm your nerves and prepare yourselves. We are going to act soon. Sanson, a word in the back. Stas, join us as well."

Stas blinked, but followed Eponine as directed. Sanson too moved for the back without complaint. He was unusually silent. There was a dark cast to his gaze. They reached the back room and closed the door behind them.

As soon as it had shut them from view, Eponine slumped over. "By the Dominus, I hate having to do Enjolras's job. Damn it ..." She rubbed her forehead, and directed a harsh glare to Sanson. "Why the fuck did you let everyone get so riled up?"

"It was Enjolras's fucking informant," Sanson seethed. "He was the one that told us about the towers. I made damned sure nobody knew about Romeo's mission. But they were there, waiting for him. That fucking backstabbing piece of shit."

"I don't give a damn about that right now. I want to know why you were letting everyone tear into each other, why was I forced to calm them all? You were right there, and you let it happen."

Sanson defended himself. "It isn't my job to deal with that shit. That's all on Enjolras. And it'd've been fine if he weren't so late."

"It isn't my job either, you fat fuck. And you weren't just sitting back. You were pouring oil on the damn fire. Why are you so obstinate?"

"Why did you bitch about my methods? Working out who leaked is more important than anything else."

"I thought you said it was the informant," Stas said.

For the first time in the evening, the large man laid his beady eyes on Stas. "Aye. It was the informant, most likely. But there's always the chance it wasn't. And there is never just one leak." His gaze dug into Stas with an accusing glare.

"Oh, come off it, Sanson." Eponine rolled her eyes. "Stas didn't know anything about the towers or Romeo's mission. And we don't even know if there was a betrayal. Romeo might have slipped, or maybe it was bad luck. But we have to get to him to figure out the truth before anything else."

Sanson nodded. "Hmph. That I agree on. We need to know what he spilled. Best case? He managed to off himself before giving anything up."

"Feh. The guards don't allow suicide. They want their big executions. He's alive, so we can rescue him. And you'll have your chance to figure out what they forced out of him. And that's why you're here, Stas." Eponine turned suddenly and rummaged through a drawer for a stack of paper, a pen, and an inkwell.

Stas stared at the implement as she thrust it into his hand. He had never used paper or ink before. He had learned writing on slate tablets and wax practice tools, or with sticks in the dirt.

"I want you to draw out floor plans for the arena dungeons, as accurately as you can. The Solar and the Stellar."

"Ah." Stas hesitated a moment. "I have not toured the prison cells myself. I've only been in the designated areas. I don't know the layouts for certain."

"But you know more than anyone else, so mark out what you can."

"Can I have some slate to start with? I'd like to work it through on something less permanent before I commit it to ink. I don't want to waste any paper."

"Fine. I'm sure we have some somewhere." Eponine rummaged through the chests in the room.

Stas was far more comfortable with the chalk in his hand. He began drawing as best as he could remember. Even for the portions he hadn't seen, he had some sense of the layout simply from what he knew would be taking up space.

"The arenas are not patrolled often," he explained. "They rely on the watchers in the forum for the brunt of their guard work. The watchers don't pay much mind to the stadiums, but they are within easy reinforcement distance. The only on-site defenses would be the prison guards. There should be between four and eight of those. The cells aren't built to house more than twenty prisoners. The Grand Arena would be a different matter. I've heard they have an entire floor to hold victims for mass executions."

Stas raised his chalk-covered hand to his mouth as he considered the matter. "You aren't going to have much luck sneaking by the guards … or rather, the problem is more about sneaking the prisoners out without getting caught. We will need to overwhelm the guards in some way, all of them. The difficulty will be preventing them from calling for reinforcements. Loud noises under the stadium are not audible above the ground, so they are certain to have some dedicated means of sounding an alarm. I don't know for certain where it would be held, but it is most likely to be somewhere around here." He gestured at a region on his map. "For this arena, at least. When I draw the other one, I can show you the corresponding location, but the logic is the same. Any plan would need to start by dealing with all the guards near the alarm device, whatever it may be. The remainder can be taken out at our leisure."

Both Eponine and Sanson stared at him.

Eponine blinked. "I didn't realize they taught assault planning in those gladiator schools of yours. I wouldn't expect it from looking at you."

"What's that supposed to mean?"

Eponine shrugged. "I figured you were more of a meathead. I mean, you have to be, for your profession."

"Combat is a battle of wits as much as it is a battle of might," Stas exclaimed. "Anyone who cannot think on their feet will soon find themselves at the mercy of one who can." Just because he hadn't fully realized the sublime importance of that lesson until Phobos had drilled it into him did not make him a liar for speaking it. "And arcanum is a difficult art that requires great intellect to master. As do sword forms in their own way. We are far from 'meatheads.'"

Eponine waved her hand lazily in a sign of surrender. Stas decided to accept it as an unspoken apology.

"But it is true that I did not learn this at my school. This is something I picked up in my own time."

"Hmph." Sanson huffed. "We don't need amateur advice. We know what we are doing. Don't waste our time when you can be doing something useful, like drawing the other map. This one is worthless if it turns out we aren't storming the Solar."

Stas rolled his eyes, but internally, he was pleased. If Sanson had seen any flaw in Stas's analysis, the ugly man would not have hesitated to drag it through the mud. That he hadn't called out anything in specific proved that Stas was perfectly on the mark.

With a steady hand practiced from the first map, and with his memory jogged through that process, Stas was far more efficient in producing the second. The arrangements of the Stellar and the Solar arenas were not that different, ultimately.

As he worked on his slate, he saw with half an eye Eponine opening the back room door and calling for Henri, who arrived quickly.

She shoved the first slate into Henri's hands. "Stas is making us maps of the arenas. We'd be fools if we only had one copy of them.

So, make some copies."

Henri nodded. "Of course. I'm happy to help." Immediately he procured some paper and a pen and inkwell and set himself on a desk across from Stas's position. Stas idly noticed, with some small envy, that the pen sat far more easily in Henri's hand than his own.

Stas assuaged himself with the knowledge that Henri was a patrician. The boy had likely spent his whole life around paper and writing. There was a reason he was the one called in to scribe.

After finishing the slate, he transitioned to helping Henri make permanent copies of the maps.

Sanson and Eponine returned to the bar, leaving Stas alone with the younger man. It was somewhat awkward, but he was able to focus on the task at hand. Henri seemed to be doing the same.

Occasionally Henri would inquire as to some sloppier notes, which Stas would provide a proper explanation for. It was not a real distraction.

"Ah ..." Henri exclaimed softly. "This is the chimera pit, then?"

Stas nodded. "Yes. What about it?"

"I'm just wondering. Do they keep the chimeras in the arena overnight? Or do they just bring them in the morning?"

"The monsters are transferred into the facility a day or two in advance," Stas explained. "The process is laborious, for safety reasons." Stas frowned. "I've had to prepare for some matches with the chimeras secured nearby. Nasty things. Loud even through the soundproofing. They smell absolutely horrendous too. Venatio must lose all sense of smell if they have to deal with that."

"Ah, I've heard about that," Henri commented. "The smell thing, I mean. One of my father's colleagues was trying to petition Lord Macro into doing something about his chimera's scents, but Lord Macro was unwilling to spend the time investigating the cause of the odor, since it didn't interest him. I think Lord Macro must be nose blind, or at least some rumors paint him as such, among other things." Henri shook his head. "But I'm losing track of myself. Is there a chimera hunt scheduled for tomorrow?"

"The Stellar never hosts chimera hunts. But there is supposed to be a venatio troupe at the Solar tomorrow, so there are probably a few beasts there now. Why do you ask?"

"I was just thinking." Henri fiddled with his fingers. "If we end up attacking the Solar arena tonight, if Romeo is being held there, well … wouldn't setting all the chimeras loose make for a great distraction?"

Stas blanched. "Setting the chimeras loose? A distraction would be the least of it. A single chimera is designed to be a challenge for a whole team of venatio. And they are equipped for, and specialize in, beast hunting. In the narrow halls below the arena …" Stas did not wish to imagine such a challenge. The chimeras of recent months were death on four legs. Or six legs. Or eight legs. Or on long, sinuous tails. Venatio succeeded by surrounding and corralling their opponents. One on one, they would be completely outmatched. A single chimera would be terrifying. Letting multiple chimeras free sounded more akin to a horror story than anything worth contemplating.

"That's good, right? We could let them dispatch the watchers without us having to lift a finger."

"Yes, they would likely dispatch the watchers with ease. As well as the prisoners. And us. And any staff that have the misfortune to be in the area. And then they might escape."

By the Dominus, if a chimera escaped into the open city … how long would it be able to avoid capture? In a city of millions, of winding streets and decrepit buildings, where the force of arms was concentrated only in the most well-off areas, how long could a predator survive? Chimera were hand-crafted killers, born to fight and die for the glory of the venatio. Unchecked …

Stas shook his head. "It is a terrible, terrible idea."

"Oh." Henri spoke softly, head lowered after the chastisement.

Their work continued in silence after that, Stas answering the few questions his companion had. But after Henri had assured him he had the rest of it handled, he left the matter to the younger man.

Creaking his back to stretch from the awkward position of writing, Stas went for the back room's exit. From the muffled sounds, it seemed like Enjolras had arrived, and was addressing everyone at the moment. Opening the door and letting the unfiltered sound in confirmed it.

"Is the situation dire?" Enjolras called from his raised platform. "I would be a liar if I claimed otherwise. But this is not our darkest hour. It is a challenge, one we can rise to meet. A hurdle in our path, but one we can handle with grace. When we look back on this night, we will not remember it as tragedy, but triumph! Of overcoming adversity! Of proving that the cruel grip the watchers hold upon the city is weaker than our wills."

The crowd was listening in rapt attention, proof of the silver-eyed man's deft control over the situation.

"We must trust in Romeo, know with our hearts that he will not allow himself to be an instrument of betrayal. And we must validate his trust in us. Do not do him the disservice of imagining him crumbling before his captors. Why would he do so? Romeo is not afraid, because he knows we will rescue him. No, like as not, Romeo is lounged up against a cell wall, enjoying a comfortable nap with an easy mind, because he knows there is no reason to worry."

The last pronouncement was met with a laugh.

From his position, Stas could see behind the cheering crowd. The door to the hideout opened, revealing a panting Orval. Eponine, situated at the door, spoke with the man quickly and quietly. She then signaled Enjolras on stage with some strange signs he did not understand. But from Enjorlas's expression he understood them perfectly. He offered a subtle nod of acknowledgment and continued

209

his speech.

"So, my friends, my brothers and sisters in arms, my fellow seekers of justice and liberty. Do not despair. Our work is stronger than our adversity. Our brotherhood is inexhaustible, our will is indestructible. For we have put our hearts and souls into our efforts, just as countless men and women have invested their own hearts and souls into this legacy of freedom. So long as we can trust in one another, we will never truly die." Enjolras raised a hand. "We are the incarnation of Libertas, the true spirit of our city, and we will not falter!"

His declaration roused greater cheers. The smiles here were real, the anxieties soothed. This was Enjolras's talent, this absolute command over all who listened. Enjolras could convey his sincerity with an ease that left Stas speechless. Those silver eyes exposed the convictions behind them, to the point one could not help but share them.

It was like arcanum, his skill working a crowd. It was the mark of a virtuous individual, espousing honest beliefs.

Eponine's earlier flailing could not compare. And Sanson was not even a contender. If Enjolras was a feast to a starving mass then Eponine was simple water, only capable of quelling the harshness of thirst … and Sanson was shards of ground-up glass.

Enjolras allowed the cheering to die down before resuming. "And I have good news, my friends. Our intrepid Orval has just returned from the forum with his report. I can confirm that Romeo is indeed alive and well, housed within the Solar arena's cells. We will be mounting a rescue tonight."

Enjolras did not wait for the cheering to die down entirely this time. He continued speaking even over the roar. "I will allow Sanson to see to the matter of securing volunteers. I hope you all consider the matter with all the weight it requires. But seeing the spirit of all of you, I trust we will have no issues."

Enjolras climbed down from his raised platform with a solemn nod of his head. Sanson wasted no time and rose up to take his place, bellowing to the gathered crowd. "All right, you sorry lot! We've got a rescue mission on our hands, and we need volunteers. The open bar is officially closed, because the only party happening is the eternal dance of kicking ass. This will involve active combat. Any coward who's not up to the task, get the fuck out of here. Anyone who's not got the skills for anything helpful, get the fuck out of here. I know who you are and I know what you can do, so I will personally boot your ass if you try to waste my time. We are taking the fight to the watchers. We don't need anyone who can't even swing a damn fist."

Sanson's diatribe continued, but Stas was not paying attention. Enjolras was looking at him, his silver eyes boring into Stas's own. The nobleman tilted his head to the side, towards the back room. Stas blinked and made a questioning gesture for the same, which was met with a steady nod.

So Stas returned to the back room he had just exited and was met by a look of confusion from the still working Henri.

Enjolras entered shortly. His entrance caused Henri to stiffen in greeting. "Ah, Enjolras," he exclaimed with halting enthusiasm. "I was just about finished with this map."

Enjolras cast a discerning gaze upon the maps. "This is the layout of the Stellar arena, is it not?"

Stas nodded. "Yes. It's the Stellar's staging area, and the cells. I drew the original from what I could remember. Henri is making a copy, cleaning it up a bit."

Enjolras nodded with closed eyes. "I have to thank you both, Stas, Henri. These are certain to be invaluable. Not just for tonight but for any future mission. We will likely find ourselves benefiting from this information in the days to come." He turned to the shorter, brown-haired boy. "Henri, your work is appreciated. Feel free to take a break, if you wish."

211

Henri shook his head. "I'm almost done. I don't mind finishing up, it's …" He paused, and looked between Enjolras and Stas. "Oh. Oh." He flinched a bit, rising to his feet quickly. "I'll, um, take a break. Leave the two of you to your privacy. I can finish any time, after all …" He meekly darted to the door.

"Have a good evening, Henri," Enjolras called.

"I'll try. Ah, have a good evening, Enjolras." Henri carefully opened the door and slipped through its gap before letting it shut behind him.

Enjolras moved over to the maps and examined the layouts. Stas noted, with some small annoyance, that the man's focus was on Henri's copy and not his own original.

They stood in silence for a few moments.

Enjolras sighed. "I wish to be honest with you, Stas.," Enjorlas spoke in a somber tone. "I have a great deal of trust in our comrades. They are driven, and unflinching in courage. And I have nothing but respect for what they can accomplish. But we are not fighters by trade." His eyes locked ton the pictures of the cells. He traced his fingers on the freshly dried ink. "We have our strengths, and we can take pride in them. But, staging a rescue … it is not a simple matter. I don't like the look of these narrow corridors." His fingers dragged across the paper in emphasis., "This assault upon a stronghold is new ground for us."

He exhaled deeply, eyes closed. "I have made a point to structure my command on the basis of volunteering. The burden of responsibility should never fall on the shoulders of any one man or woman. But it seems that for my lack of preparation, I have failed tonight."

He opened his eyes and Stas was caught in them. The silver shimmered in the flickering light of the room's flameless torches. "Stas, I do not believe this rescue mission can succeed without your aid. I would never force you to partake in any mission. I don't have the right. But I would ask you … no, I will beg you."

Enjolras lowered his head deeply in a bow. "Please, Stas, I beg your aid. For Romeo's sake. For my sake. For the sake of everyone volunteering for this mission." He bowed even deeper. "Please help us in this rescue mission."

The entire display was deeply uncomfortable. Enjolras was a man who should never be forced to prostrate. That he would do so bothered Stas in a way that he could not properly describe.

It took Stas a moment to realize he had not responded. "Of course." He almost stuttered his words, but held firm. "Absolutely. You did not even have to ask. I am more than happy to lend my skill for this endeavor."

Enjolras smiled. It was a good, honest smile. Stas felt the image burn itself into his memory. "Thank you, my friend. I do not know what I would have done without you."

Enjolras rose to his feet and moved to the wall of the back room, to the shield hanging on the wall. He grasped it in his hands and walked it over to Stas.

"I want you to use this," he proclaimed, "for the rescue mission."

"The shield?" Stas found his words failing him. Of course it was the shield. Enjolras was perfectly clear, both in action and in words. And yet Stas mindlessly spoke the words dancing in his mind. He felt like an idiot.

Enjolras nodded, ignoring the inanity of Stas's pointless question. "Yes, the shield. It is a bulwark of justice, and a wall for the innocent. Its purpose is to defend us, and the people of this city through us. I can think of no better use than in rescuing our fellow. And I can think of no one better to wield it." He passed the shield forward, outstretched for Stas's hand. "I can think of no better tool to help you. Please, use it well."

Stas, struggling to keep his fingers from trembling, accepted the shield. His hand traced across its metal. It felt cool to the touch. Strong. Comforting. The soul-craft weapon almost seemed to purr under his touch.

The whole shield felt like it had a weight to it, as much as any tower shield or suit of armor. And yet it offered no strain to his arm. He strapped it to his shield arm. The strap fitted perfectly.

"We will see about providing you with a sword as well. I cannot promise its quality will match that of the shield, or even the swords you enjoy for your matches. But it will be good, quality steel. And we have enough variety that you should be able to find one that suits you. And elixirs as well."

"I don't need elixirs." Was Enjolras not aware of the quirk in his magic? It must have come up at some point.

Enjolras nodded, not missing a beat. "Of course. We have bits of armor, something to suit you. And you are free to peruse our arsenal for anything you feel will be of aid. Whatever it takes for you to succeed."

Stas closed his eyes. He embraced himself in that strange, comforting weight of the shield. The reflection of the polished metal shined brightly.

"I won't let you down," he declared. Tonight he would finally prove his worth.

# Twenty-Five

The plan was simple. Overwhelming the watchers in a direct confrontation was not an option. Infiltration was the only way, and every unnecessary body added to the risk. To that end, only four people would be invading the Solar: himself, Eponine, Sanson, and Lucian. Their task would be to deal with the guards on site and free all the prisoners within.

A second, much larger, group would cause a distraction, to ensure that the many watchers of the forum did not interfere. This, apparently, would involve a great deal of arson.

Stas did not feel particularly comfortable with that part of the plan. While he agreed it would be an effective distraction, it struck him as a horrific risk. But he held his tongue and allowed himself to trust that his comrades would not allow the city to burn to the ground. And that they would occupy the bird-masked watchers without themselves being caught.

His mind was better focused on his own task. Stas had been given command of the infiltration team, much to the loud grumbling of Sanson. And the bulk of the effort would rest on his shoulders. He would be the one to dispatch all the guards within, starting with what they believed to be the alarm room. Sanson and Lucian would be placed at a chokepoint, to ensure that no guard was able to escape his efforts. Stas was not sure he trusted the disfigured man to manage that much, so he resolved to make their post unnecessary.

Once they had secured the area, they would free all the prisoners and escape into the chaos of the burning city in scattered directions.

While their task was to free all the prisoners in this raid, it was subtly understood that the goal was Romeo's rescue alone. Eponine had been instructed to ensure that the man would escape without issue.

Stas, privately, set himself to the task of ensuring that no prisoner would be recaptured. He knew Enjolras would want it that way. This was his first *real* mission, and he would ensure it went perfectly. All he needed to do was defeat half a dozen trained combatants who specialized in arcanum and coordination in a battleground that limited his movement.

Stas felt very good about his odds. Justice was on their side for this, unequivocally and without exception. And with the soul-crafted shield, it wasn't even a contest.

With the matter set, he had his team pour over the arena map. Even Sanson did not complain about that.

The distraction team exited the hideout first, offering their well wishes. Stas accepted them with the meaning they intended. But he did not need them. He was not worried.

After allowing the distraction team time to get in place, Stas, Eponine, Lucian, and Sanson left for the forum. Sanson was, to Stas's great surprise and enjoyment, perfectly silent. The surly man's face was the picture of professional conduct. That the man was capable of shutting up was annoying in its own way. It proved that his regular conduct was intentional.

They made their way across the city inconspicuously. Of the four, Lucian seemed to be the most nervous. The plump man's hands shook in place. But he kept himself on task, firming up as they moved.

They positioned themselves in one of the districts neighboring the stadiums, where their presence would go without remark. There they awaited the plumes of smoke that would signal the start of the operation. Stas kept a special eye out for any patrolling watchers, making sure to note whenever they passed.

Against the darkness of the setting sun, the smoke made for a great spectacle: a tower of ash that blotted out swaths of the sky. It captured the eye like a demonic shroud of death. Flickering flames reached above the rooftops of the city's uneven skyline.

Even from this distance, he heard the shouts, the tumult and confusion. Stas swallowed his nerves and reaffirmed his trust that his fellows had the matter under control.

As they desired, dozens of bird-masked watchers rushed across the rooftops for the fire. None paid them a moment's attention.

Stas and his fellows put on their masks and, at his command, they all rushed for the Solar arena. Lucian and Eponine each gulped down an elixir and began working their arcanum. According to Eponine, their magic would make them harder to spot, but Stas did not want to test it. He made sure to keep them all outside the watchers' view.

They were able to reach the stadium without incident. Stas led them through the staff entrance. The entry used by his peers was far less visible than the awe-inspiring grand threshold used by the masses.

By all accounts they had arrived undetected.

They found their way to the chokepoint.

Stas gestured to the other two men. "From here you should be able to catch any fleeing watchers. Between the two of you, you should be able to monitor it properly. If you are forced into a fight, shout for me so I can come to deal with it. Don't worry about noise. They won't be able to hear it aboveground."

Sanson grunted. "We've been at this far longer than you, boy. We know how to handle the fucking bird-faces. If anything gets screwed up, it will be on your end, not ours."

Stas bristled but decided against escalating. "Just worry about yourself and there will be no problems."

Sanson huffed. "Get on with it, then. The fire isn't going to last forever."

Sanson was not in command of the mission. He had no need or right to give orders. But once again, for the sake of civility and group cohesion, Stas weathered the insult.

He nodded to Eponine, whose face was still clenched in concentration. "Let's go."

They only had a general sense of where the room with the alarm would be. It would be separated from the cells, but otherwise near the prison area.

For the Solar arena, the prison area was completely separated from the gladiator suites, unlike in the Lunar, where the prisoners could be seen in their cages from the benches; you might not even know they were there if not for the executions. The gladiator suites and staff areas took up half of the great circular expanse. The prison area took up the other half. The thick metal walls of chimera pits served as the dividing lines between them. The beasts could be lifted by a raised platform onto the sands of the arena.

The gladiator suites were empty. Stas and Eponine could travel fearlessly through them.

They situated themselves just outside the entrance to the prison. With a nod to Eponine, he creaked the door open by a crack. Eponine's magic should limit the attention of any prison guards who happened to be looking in that direction.

With a small gap secured, Stas looked through the mirrors.

The prison suites seemed to consist of a long, curving hallway; tightly packing both sides of the hall were heavy doors with conspicuous locks. The rooms behind seemed positively tiny, built for perhaps only a single person each.

218

Stas had underestimated just how many prisoners could fit into the Solar arena's cells. He hadn't realized that the accommodations were so cramped.

Through the gap in the door, Stas could hear a number of voices in various states of despair. They were shouting incessantly: clamoring for food, hurling insults, protesting innocence, crying, shouting for quiet. It was an ugly symphony, muffled by thick prison doors. Stas had had the misfortune of hearing this cacophony of the condemned many times before.

Eponine, from the look of distaste in her expression, had not had the pleasure.

One of the voices, hurling insults of a very colorful variety that Stas had only heard uttered by Sanson before, seemed to be Romeo. He sounded quite hoarse. Likely the man had been shouting for quite some time now. Outside of them, Stas also heard the movements of men in armor. Through the mirrors he could see them patrolling.

More importantly, Stas could also see his target. The door immediately inside the area to their left was different from the rest. It allowed for more space than the other cramped doorways, and lacked a lock.

He silently signaled to Eponine, and, when he knew the guards were in other parts of the curved hallway, they entered the prison and placed themselves against the door.

Stas turned to Eponine and silently counted down on his fingers from three.

She raised another elixir to her lips, reinforcing her arcanum.

When his last finger fell, Stas quickly shoved open the door.

One of the lessons Phobos had devised for Stas was the ability to immediately take in a scene and *reflect* across it. Stas had originally been satisfied with his ability. It only took him a few seconds to identify a proper mirror in a new room.

Phobos had been unsatisfied with *a few seconds*. His standards were as brutal as his training methods. Stas had spent hours upon hours back at the school practicing to avoid repeating the issues.

As a result, Stas could *reflect* across the room before he even fully processed its contents.

The bird-masked watcher situated on a bench to the side of the room, its sole occupant, had even less time to react. Stas's sword barreled for the surprised man's neck.

He did not enjoy ambushing opponents. But this man was a guard. If he failed to be alert, that was on him. Or so Stas told himself as his sword cut through the man's throat.

Eponine, closing the door behind herself, watched on dispassion-ately. "Hm." She nodded. "Good show."

Stas frowned. "Should we be talking?"

Eponine shrugged. "I am muting the sounds. It should be fine."

"I see." Stas's eyes fell back to the blood dripping from the sword. "Do you have anything for this? I'd rather not let the blade have a chance to rust." In the arena and at the school, there were servants for such trivialities. But this was a borrowed blade from Enjolras's armory. He'd hate to leave it worse off.

"Here." Eponine tossed him some cloth, some spare bit of clothing that must have belonged to one of the guards. Stas grabbed the bundle and wiped away the warm red ichor.

Eponine moved to the wall behind him, examining a smooth metal box with an extended lever.

"This must be the alarm."

Stas nodded. "It must be."

"I wonder if I can break it. Rip out the lever, perhaps?" Eponine mused. "If there is more than one alarm nearby, I won't be able to guard both."

Stas shook his head. "I don't think it's worth the risk. The prison is small, so this should be the only guard room. It is likely the only alarm."

"Well, why don't you get to it, then?" Eponine said. "I don't really care to stand around here all night."

Stas tossed the bloody rag to the ground. "Give me a moment." He wanted his heart to settle. This was far more stressful than a fight on the stands.

"My arcanum is not going to last forever. I only brought so many elixirs."

"I don't need long." Stas closed his eyes and caught his breath. He set his mind's eyes back to the mirrors, and the reflections of the hallway. The bird-masked watchers were still patrolling the small corridor. Only two remained, and neither had noticed the invasion.

The distraction was proving a great success.

"I'll be back shortly." Stas braced himself and *reflected*.

He swung his sword for a guard's nape. Astoundingly, he missed.

Or rather, the watcher dodged. A sudden movement turned the fatal blow into a shallow cut. Whether through preternatural instinct, a mistake on Stas's part, or some magic of the watcher, he had been noticed.

The guard's head slammed backwards with great force. Stas pulled back in time to avoid the brunt of the skull bash, but he felt it smash against his mask.

Stas's next strike was interrupted as the guard twisted in place with a leg sweep.

If he were performing for an audience, Stas would have leaped over it. But Phobos would tan his hide if he engaged in such folly. He instead maintained his footing and stepped out of range.

Mask to mask with the watcher now, he felt the weight of the guard's glare. With a quick flick, the watcher extended a pair of daggers from their wrists. The quick release left no room for interception.

At the same time, the other guard was reaching for an elixir flask.

Stas *reflected* quickly. His blade tore easily into the watcher's flesh. This one seemed to lack the competence of his fellow. It was a small shame, to be denied the challenge, but a one-on-one bout was more proper.

As the elixir drinker crumpled to the ground, the first watcher adopted a loose stance, ready to pounce in any direction. It was an appropriate response to the gladiator's magic.

Masked eyes met masked eyes. Stas *reflected*.

The watcher launched himself forward to avoid a surprise blow from the back. He had gleaned matters quickly. But Stas was a step ahead, appearing at the watcher's side instead. But the guard's reflexes proved as potent as his intuition. He caught Stas's strike with his blade.

By standard account, a steady strike would overcome an off-guard defense. But the watcher once again proved his mettle. Stas struggled to keep his grip as the force proved far greater than he had expected.

Stas's stance fell open and the watcher capitalized. His other dagger stuck forth for Stas's staggered form with lethal intent. And yet it passed through empty air. The decoy *reflection* Stas had left behind dispersed in an instant. Stas, from his true position, was able to get a solid blow on the overextended watcher. His sword crushed through the guard's vambrace and drew a thin line of blood.

His foe took the blow expertly, recovering his bearings in spite of his injury. He resumed his stance, intent and ready.

Stas could not account for the strength and skill of the guard. Perhaps he had the honor of facing a former gladiator. He did not know why a gladiator would ever don the bird mask, lower himself to guarding prisoners. But the man's prowess was undeniable. He would treat the battle with the respect it deserved.

Stas struck forth, blade clashing with blade. His foe proved his overpowering strength in this clash as well, forcing Stas back. He *reflected*, but the guard was ready again, forcing Stas to abandon the strike. Enjolras's shield practically leaped to block the retaliation, effortlessly deflecting the powerful blow. The sound of clanging metal resounded through the corridor.

The sound was attracting attention. The prisoners seemed to be getting an inkling of matters. The moans and screams were slowly being replaced by growing realization and some hesitant cheers. In this stark prison beneath the glorious sands of the arena, their fight was turning into a facsimile of a real match, complete with spectators.

The soul-crafted tool was almost unfair. While the watcher could force through any clash of sword against dagger, the shield could effortlessly capture any blow the man attempted in turn. He adjusted his stance to compensate, leading with the shield as much as he could. It seemed to hum in joy, resounding with fervor at each blocked blow, delighting in its purpose for this just mission.

The shield would not, could not let him down. Stas could only fail if he made a mistake. And he would not make any mistake.

And that included ignoring the other watcher, bleeding out on the floor and grasping for his elixir. Stas deliberately positioned himself to make it seem like he had not noticed the movement. His dagger-wielding foe was clearly counting on the surprise aid of his fellow to turn the tide.

And Stas was intentionally fostering that hope. For the moment it made the dagger-wielder manageable. If the guard lost hope, he might do something unpredictable, or try to flee. And in crushing that hope, Stas would be able to land a decisive blow.

"Fuck you," the dying voice behind him rasped, blood spitting from his lips. And they tapped the floor. Stas prepared to *reflect* at a moment's notice. A crack emerged in the stone floor and grew quickly, not towards Stas, but instead towards the wall.

It expanded rapidly in an explosion of debris, leaving a large hole in the thick wall. Stas did not understand the point of it all.

"Oh, you fucking bastard!" the dagger-wielder exclaimed.

A low, resounding rumble emerged from the hole. A scampering of feet. A terrible, rotting smell.

One did not have to be a fan of the venatio to know their sport. The hunts were many, and they often dominated conversation. Stas himself had witnessed three in his time.

The monsters of the arena, the chimeras, varied as wildly as one could imagine. Stas had seen a snake the size of a full carriage, with venomous fangs that melted through stone. He had seen a lumbering beast in the mocking shape of a man thrice the size, with a single, bulging eye centered in its mouthless head. He had seen a misshapen, three-legged shell, whose porous back housed thousands of swarming insects poised to drain a man dry.

He had heard tales of elephants that crushed the earth with each step, horses that feasted on the flesh of man, and an enormous raptor that spent most of its match trying to fly from the arena to feast upon the audience. Only the arena's shield had kept the hundred-eyed, winged beast contained.

One could never predict what monstrosity would emerge before a hunt. Only madmen could think to create one. Only the venatio could think to slay them. Each was unique, bound only by their hatred for all life. They came close to matching the horrors that lurked behind the unnerving mirrors.

The beast that crawled out of the hole and clung to the wall in defiance of gravity was no exception. Onyx scales covered the entirety of its flesh, gleaming like the black marble of the forum. Its round-bellied torso, the size of a man on its own, was supported by four thick, muscular legs, each marked by four sinuous toes. Its tail was half as long again, whipping lazily in the air.

And its head ... with a neck like a snake but as thick as the tail, a round, scaled bulb protruded. It lacked adornment: no eyes, nor ears, nor nose. Instead the bulb was split, lengthwise and vertically, leaving four identical wedges for a mouth.

Scaled lips peeled backwards like a flower. The insides were coated with hundreds of glistening white, needle-like teeth. No tongue graced its widening maw.

And, from this hideous opening, a high-pitched sound screeched forth. Stas felt his blood boil, his veins pinch. His bones rumbled, threatening to break, and his head almost exploded from the pain. His stomach rebelled, from the noise and odor both. He found himself spewing bile on the floor. He could not even remove his mask in time.

The bird-masked watchers were in no better shape.

The chimera's scream halted. Its head tracked the room. Then, as quick as a lash, its tail speared the crumpled corpse of the guard who released it. The body dangled on the tail, like meat on a skewer stick.

Once more the flowered lips parted, and the beast brought the body to its maw. Razor-sharp teeth scraped against the armored chest of the deceased watcher. The metal shredded under its assault, flesh and bone and viscera following suit. The four petals clamped closed around its morsel, and the body fell apart.

Nothing about the creature's mouth made for clean consumption. Gore stained its scaled lips, as more of its meal fell to the floor than made its way to the creature's gullet.

Letting the mass of the body fall to the floor, it turned towards Stas. The flower bulb opened once again.

Stas braced himself for the screech as much as he could manage. He *reflected* away to avoid the weakness that was sure to come with it.

Even still, he fell to his knees, barely able to hold his vomit. Blood dripped from his face. From where, he did not know.

The chimera, still screeching, launched itself from the wall towards the watcher. Thick forelegs reached for the staggered guard. Twin daggers rose in defense, but they were knocked aside by the chimera's falling bulk. The monster's tail stabbed through the guard's armor, and the eyeless face feasted upon new prey.

The corpse was discarded as quickly as the last.

The chimera hunted not to eat, but to kill. It was no true animal, but a monstrosity made to murder. Its eyeless head locked onto Stas.

The beast launched itself, screeching once again. Stas was sick to the stomach, ears ringing painfully, and on the brink of losing consciousness, and the third round of screaming only seemed to exacerbate what was already there.

On well-trained reflex, Stas *reflected*. He appeared by the creature's side, avoiding the tail and head both.

He slammed his borrowed blade into the creature's scales with as much force as he could muster. The chimera did not buckle. His sword, however, did. The metal bent pitifully, the blade ruined. He let it fall to the floor.

Stas *reflected*, leaving a decoy in his place. But the beast ignored it, its tail speeding for his true position. The eyeless chimera's senses defied explanation. Stas *reflected* once more.

The beast twisted, finding his new position with ease. Its bulbous head seemed to stare at him. Abruptly, it turned away, looking instead at one of the prison doors.

The beast's tail slammed through the metal, puncturing a hole the size of Stas's fist. Its jagged mouth ripped at the perforated edges, forcing the hole larger and larger. In a few short moments it was large enough for the chimera to fit its head through.

And to Stas's horror, that was what the monster did. The prisoner inside the tiny cell screamed in pain and terror as the scaled beast ripped through the unfortunate woman.

Stas was left frozen in place. Nothing could harm the chimera. It had already taken his sword without any issue, and his arcanum was of no aid. Helpless as he was, he could picture the beast breaking through cells one by one, feasting upon the prisoners he was supposed to save, before escaping to the city at large.

But Stas was not completely without weapons. His mind turned to Enjolras's shield. If he could turn the indestructible edge of the soul-crafted shield against the beast's scales, perhaps it cut through the monster.

As soon as the thought ran through his mind, Stas felt a sharp, painful burn from the shield. The very idea seemed to repel him, and his nausea redoubled. The shield was a shield, he knew with an excruciating jolt. Anything else would be folly.

Stas *reflected* back into the guard room, much to Eponine's shock.

"Stas?" she questioned. "Did ..."

"Chimera got loose!" Stas interrupted with a shout. "Stay here!" He found a key ring quickly and ripped it from the dead watcher's belt.

"What ..." Eponine began, but Stas did not wait for her question. He *reflected* back to the cells, where the chimera was devouring its second prisoner. He forced the sight from his mind, instead grabbing a key from the ring at random. He struggled to read the tiny number on it, his mind in a daze.

He forced his shaking hand to get the key in the lock and yanked the door open.

The prisoner inside was near insensate: clear marks of torture lined their body, as did blood and bile from the chimera's scream. Stas forced them through the door.

"Run!" he commanded. "Run for your life!"

Stas pushed the man out, but he didn't seem to comprehend. The chimera was upon the man in a second, ripping him to shreds with teeth and tail. Stas *reflected* out of the way.

He did not allow himself to stop. He focused on the next key and the next cage. He opened them, one by one, as fast as he was able.

"Run!" he screamed. "Scatter! It can't get all of you, so run!"

It was a miserable routine. Stas was able to release prisoners faster than the chimera could devour them, but only just. As more and more prisoners escaped their cells, the more chance they had to escape even as their fellows died miserably. The chimera danced between them, killing as it desired. Stas worked almost mindlessly, trying to blot out the death. When the last door was opened, he *reflected* towards the chimera, using Enjolras's shield to divert and delay.

He intercepted a snap of the jaws only for another prisoner to be impaled by the tail. He blocked a pounce only to be forced to *reflect* away from another blow.

It was gruesome. It was miserable. It was hopeless. Perhaps one in four made it out of the prison block. But that was a one in four that would have died had he not let them free. Stas did not have the presence of mind to note whether Romeo was among them, or if his mangled corpse littered the floor with the rest.

Stas pulled the mask away from his throat to retch. The situation was horrible, and it was going to get worse. Once the chimera escaped the prison block, its hunt would resume. The prisoners he saved might all die regardless.

Except … it didn't seem to be heading for the exit. Rather, its location seemed to have slipped Stas's mind. His thoughts screamed, but could not find purchase or understanding.

Stas *reflected* into the guard room past the door his mind wasn't capable of noticing. Eponine shrank in the corner as the chimera pounced. He placed himself in front of her, shielding her with his entire body. Enjolras's shield interposed itself.

The chimera's jaws clamped around the unblemished shield, but the soul-crafted tool held steady. The beast's mouth was locked open, its head secured by Stas's will.

"Knife, now!" he yelled.

228

Eponine did not waste time. She grasped for her hidden blade and placed it in his awaiting hand.

Stas shoved it into the creature's open maw. The monster's teeth scraped viciously against his arm, but he ignored the pain.

The blade reached the back of the black beast's throat. It met solid, unscaled flesh. And, like Stas's sword before it, the knife crumpled uselessly.

Stas felt despair build up inside him. It was unfair. Why was the inside of the beast as tough as the out? There were no eyes to stab, no conspicuous openings. The monster was too strong by far. What were its crafters thinking, making its flesh so impervious? Were they trying to slaughter all the venatio?

The beast's tail sped for the two of them. He grabbed a hold of Eponine and *reflected* to safety.

Eponine gasped. "That was, by far, the strangest sensation I've even felt."

"I've stopped noticing," he stated blandly. His mind was focused on the beast and its reflections.

"My magic did nothing," Eponine said morosely. "Absolutely nothing. I had thought myself safe. If a watcher came I could make them forget about me, if they could even remember the guard room in the first place. But ..." She trailed off, eyes falling to the many, many bodies for the first time. "How did it get out?"

Stas grit his teeth. "One of the watcher's released it intentionally. As a dying curse, perhaps. I was able to rescue a few prisoners, but ..." He exhaled.

"You can kill it, right?" There was a certainty to Eponine's question, some blind trust.

Stas swallowed. Bravado demanded he affirm, but ... "I don't know if I can. I can defend myself, but I don't know how to slay it. The chimera is designed to match a whole squad of venatio." And he was just one person, but he did not say.

"I see. We should flee, then. We have freed who we could. Our mission is over. The watchers can deal with the chimera. If we're lucky, it will slaughter a good number of them before it's brought down."

Stas frowned. "I don't trust that it will stay in the arena. If it reaches the city ..." Stas grimaced. "Perhaps we should pull the alarm."

"No," Eponine said firmly. "If we call the watchers, we will be captured. Us and the prisoners. We can't risk that." Her expression softened. "Stas, I'd hate it if the monster escaped, but if it does, it wouldn't be your fault. The watcher who released it would be to blame."

Fault? Blame? If a young child was torn apart by a beast, would their last thoughts be about who allowed it to happen? They would be dead, regardless.

"If you can't kill it," Eponine continued gently, "then we have to flee. There is nothing else we can do."

Stas considered the matter. It was true, he could not kill it. Even with his arcanum and the shield, the scales were too impervious. But the chimera had been safely encaged until the vindictive watcher had freed it. Stas had no method of fixing the wall, but that was not the only enclosure.

Stas resolved himself. "There's another option. There's more than one enclosure. If I can get it inside one of the intact ones, it won't be able to escape."

Eponine frowned. "You shouldn't risk yourself for this. There's nothing wrong with running away."

Stas shook his head. "It's not a risk. Not much of one anyway. I don't need to defeat it, I just need to grab a hold of it." In his mind's eye he could see the other enclosure. He could easily get inside. The only question was if he could take the monster with him. If he couldn't handle something so large, or if the madmen had somehow made it immune to arcanum ...

"Okay." Eponine nodded. "I trust you."

Stas inhaled deeply, an unpleasant action considering the aroma. Then he *reflected*. The chimera lashed out instantly, tail swiping. But Stas was ready. The blow bounced off Enjolras's shield as though it were a simple pillow. With his free hand, he hugged himself tightly against the scaled body.

And with a force of exertion he had not felt for years, Stas *reflected*. The black-scaled lizard came with him.

Stas nearly collapsed immediately. A foul substance within the enclosure assaulted his lungs. In the dim light, he could make out the light purple haze that suffused the air. He felt the dust burn his throat through his mask. His body seized.

In the corner of the room, gazing with three, massive, bulbous, unblinking eyes, was a stout chimera. It reminded him of the toads that lived among the ponds and riverbeds that dotted the provinces. Unlike a toad, it stood taller than him, with a gaping mouth large enough to swallow three men whole. On its back were numerous mushroom caps that emitted the purple haze.

The black-scaled chimera was just as pained by the spores. It seized in place, and then opened its flower-lipped mouth to scream. The horrific noise washed over Stas, forcing him to release the beast. The toad-chimera winced in turn.

A large, bulging tongue covered in sacs of ooze shot out of the toad-chimera's mouth. It snagged onto the scaled chimera, securing it tightly. And, like an angler with a fish on the line, it reeled its prey backwards towards its cavernous gullet. The lizard-like chimera was no easy prey. Its indestructible maw tore into the other beast's fleshy tongue, its tail raised to skewer the toad in turn.

It seemed, for the moment, Stas was being ignored. It was a great fortune, because his muscles, assailed by spore and sound alike, failed to respond.

Thankfully, he did not need them to *reflect*. He arrived back with Eponine, where the air was gloriously clear.

"Is it done?"

Stas coughed, a raspy, ugly action. He desperately craved water. Or better yet, a hard drink to burn the sensation out.

When he was finally able to, he spoke. "Yes," he croaked. "The two chimeras are fighting one another." Which would emerge triumphant, he had no idea. But he could guess that neither would stop until the other was dead.

"Hah." Eponine exhaled deeply. "I thought this would be a mess, but I didn't think that it would get so bad."

"Everything was going perfectly until the watcher let the chimera loose." Perhaps that should have been the sign things would go wrong. Romeo often claimed a winning streak foretold a great loss, just as a losing streak guaranteed a win. It was nonsense, but the gambler swore by it.

Speaking of ... Stas checked the reflections of the arena basement and spotted the ragged Romeo being interrogated by Sanson and an ecstatic Lucian. It seemed that their night had not been completely uneventful—a single watcher corpse lay beside them.

"Romeo survived," Stas said. "He's with Sanson and Lucian, and some of the surviving prisoners. We should let them know that the chimera has been dealt with."

Eponine agreed. "I'm tempted to let them panic, but we don't want them doing anything stupid. It looks like our mission was a success. But it's definitely given me a new hatred for chimeras. And a new respect for the venatio troupes."

"Indeed." Stas nodded. "I think I might wish to catch a hunt or two. Seeing chimeras get slaughtered would be cathartic."

"Can you snag me a ticket? I'd like to join you."

"I can try." One of his fellows would know how to get tickets for regular audience members.

"Hm. Well, let's get out of here before something else goes wrong. Can you teleport me again? I'm pretty sure you've made me left-handed."

"Really? I didn't know my magic could do that."

"I'm surprised you didn't notice, what with all the teleporting you do."

"Well, I am ambidextrous. Most gladiators train to be."

"Interesting." Eponine nodded and extended her hand daintily. "Let us go, then. We still need to sneak the living prisoners out. Your work might be done for the night, but I have a good deal left to do."

Stas grabbed the hand. "I just want to collapse in bed and sleep for a week."

"And miss your next arena match? Perish the thought."

"Don't remind me." Stas *reflected*, and the two of them left the awful, corpse-ridden prison.

# Twenty-Six

It had been a week since the chimera incident, and Stas was still feeling its mark. His stomach had never settled properly—something between the lizard's screech and the toad's spores had likely left him with an undercurrent of nausea that never truly subsided. Purging his stomach did little, and his arcanum seemed to make it worse. Even the simplest *reflection* sent a shudder through his body.

Still, it was manageable. Stas was learning to adapt to his weaker stomach. It hadn't cost him his match, and that was the best judge of things. The greater concern was his arm.

The scratches from the chimera's teeth were not healing properly. The scabs and scrapes had grown back smooth and shiny, almost metallic in nature. Stas did not dare imagine what sort of horrific substance could cause such a transformation. He was only glad it was not spreading.

The problem was that he had no good way to explain it. He had taken to keeping the arm concealed to avoid questions.

He was getting a negative reputation with the general physician for avoiding checkups, unfortunately. But the health professional would do no more than grumble. Perhaps Stas could take a blow from some arcanum when he next had the opportunity. Then he could allow it to be seen. Or perhaps it would heal in time.

Making sure to secure the wrapping, Stas headed to the cafeteria for breakfast. The morning hours were well attended. He received his personal plate from the dietitian and sat next to Alain, who was already present. Zola joined them shortly after. She was followed by one of the new gladiators, a short red-haired girl named Vita.

They ate slowly, and their conversation was light. But all four knew they were awaiting news.

As expected, Ludo entered the cafeteria and made his way to the four of them. He was followed, as always, by a servant.

"Alain, you have been invited to Senator Marcellus's soiree tomorrow evening. You will be accompanying me. I recommend you limit training until then. I would also ask that you avail yourself of the baths. If you require formal dress, speak with Tana and she will provide you with something suitable. Or speak with the commissary for some money and purchase something for yourself from the forum today. I can trust you to not pick anything outrageous."

Alain spoke with a bow. "I have already purchased a formal gown, Lanista." The invitation was of no surprise to anyone. It was a tradition for all gladiators participating in a Kalends fight to be invited to the party the night before.

"Good," Ludo concluded with a nod, moving to leave.

"Lanista," Stas asked. "Has anyone else been invited?" While the Kalends fighters served as the guests of honor, they were far from the only guests. The hosting senator could invite whomever they desired, and, quite often, anyone who caught their eye could expect admittance. A simple invitation was not as great acclaim as fighting in the Kalends. But it represented the greatest of opportunities. Whether one sought to change schools, desired more prestigious matches, or wished to secure employment after retirement, the senators and patricians attending would be the ones to speak with.

More than that, having access to a senator's estate would be a great boon for Libertas. Who knew what opportunities would be available at such an exclusive event?

"No." Ludo spoke succinctly. "No other invitations were received."

Stas, Zola, Vita, and a number of nearby eavesdroppers all deflated.

"I would not concern yourself with patricians and their parties at this stage of your career," Ludo advised. "It is an undesirable distraction. If you train and make a proper showing in the arena, recognition will follow, just as it has for Alain. It is better to focus on yourself and what you can control."

Stas hid a frown. He had the distinct impression that a different, superior lanista would have done a better job promoting his students to the senators. Doubtless, the gladiators under Lord Galbrio were all invited. But he held his tongue.

"Good day to you all," Ludo concluded. "I hope your training goes well." With a final nod, he exited, his servant trailing behind.

As soon as he had left, Zola punched Alain in the shoulder. "Look at you, my friend. Getting into the big leagues. Do not forget about all us little people when you are out there fighting the likes of Esmae and Horatio."

Alain rubbed the back of his head. "It's nothing like that. My match is only against Lamorak of the Dollabella school. Only the date is anything special."

"Don't count yourself short," Stas interjected. "You have been doing well, and have been at it the longest. You deserve the honor." He sighed. "I just wish Ludo put more effort into getting more of us better matches."

Zola smirked. "Are you jealous, my friend? Are you bitter for not being invited?"

"You weren't invited either, Zola."

She waved it off. "I know that. But I also know where I stand. I have no reason to feel snubbed or left out."

"I'm not feeling snubbed," Stas said. "I just think that our school should be represented more for things like this."

Vita jumped in. "And you want it to be you representing our school, right?"

What was he supposed to say to that? "Yes? Of course I would like to be invited. It's not like I am not undefeated."

It was, perhaps, not the best response because it left the two girls grinning.

But before they could say anything more, Alain spoke. "In truth, I wonder if I am the best choice for this match." He gently dragged his cutlery along his plate. His eyes did not leave the table. "Being the first for the honor, being selected at all … for all that I have been here the longest, I am aware that you are a more spectacular fighter, Stas, and with a better record as well. Perhaps the honor should have gone to you." His words were calm but morose.

In truth, Stas agreed with the assessment. Alain was strong; his broad shoulders and cleaving swings could shatter stone. And he was skilled; wielding a two-handed blade, he was perhaps the most technically proficient fighter in the school. In a fight without arcanum, Stas's senior might crush him ninety-nine times out of a hundred.

But in a true match, there was nothing Alain would be able to do against him. The man lacked arcanum beyond strengthening himself and toughening his skin. Ludo's nominally "best" student was helpless against him.

If Stas had fought more prestigious matches, if Ludo promoted him more aggressively, he would have received an invite, perhaps even months before now.

But it would be impolite to speak of such observations. It was hardly Alain's fault. The man's success did not detract from Stas's own.

So he shook his head. "Spectacle is hardly everything. A good, solid technique matters far more. Balance, strength, awareness … you excel at all of these."

Zola nodded. "Not every gladiator relies on arcanum. Radek Twinblade, Alexandros of the Spear ... even Horatio Undaunted have been known to win matches without imbibing an elixir."

"So says the woman who relies on arcanum the most of all of us," Vita mocked with a smile. Zola shoved her to the side.

"I appreciate the sentiment, but I cannot help but feel nervous."

"You have no need," Stas said. "This is only Lamorak's second Kalends fight, and he lost the last. At worst, you will prove his equal."

"Stas is right." Zola slapped Alain on the back. "So relax, my friend. Enjoy your rest day and the party in your honor. I know I will."

"And how will you be enjoying a party you have not been invited to, Zola?" Stas inquired.

"I will simply scour the forums for some senator's handsome son or nephew. Those types would fall upon themselves to escort a gladiatrix like myself. Suffering their attention is the least I can do to ensure poor Alain is not alone with all those wealthy patricians and influential aediles," Zola remarked with a grin.

That was an interesting thought. Perhaps Enjolras would know somebody who could take him. Or Henri.

"Good luck with that," Vita said. "I don't think I'll bother. Even if I did get in, it's too early in my career to get anyone's attention."

It was a fair point. The girl only had two matches to her name.

"Changing the topic," Vita continued, "are any of you planning on catching tomorrow's chariot race? It's an auspicious month for the Reds."

Stas let out a good-natured groan as conversation reverted to the casual topic of chariot racing. It was a good diversion, at the very least. Nothing of true import ever happened in the races.

As they were finishing their meals, a servant entered the cafeteria. It took Stas a moment to realize that she was coming towards their table. He could not place the servant's name. All he knew for sure is that she was not Cassandra. His month with the laundress was not easily forgotten.

Alain greeted the servant with a nod. "Ophelia, do you require something of us?"

"Yes, Master Alain." She turned to address Stas specifically. "Master Stas, you have a visitor."

A visitor? From what he recalled, visitors were not permitted in the morning.

"Who?" Stas asked, but found the answer quickly as Eponine sauntered into the school's cafeteria. That, he knew, was definitely not permitted.

Eponine must have been using her arcanum for everyone to ignore her trespassing.

"Stas!" Eponine said with strange cheerfulness. "It's so good to see you."

"That would be her," the servant concluded. "Have a pleasant day, masters, mistresses." With a deferential bow, the servant exited the cafeteria, leaving Stas's unauthorized guest behind.

"Oh?" Zola's lips perked up. "Stas, who is this?"

"Really, Stas? You haven't mentioned me before?" Eponine pouted deeply. "Are you ashamed of me?"

"Ah. This is Eponine. She's my ..." He trailed off, not knowing how to describe the relationship. The truth was out of the question by far.

Thankfully, Eponine opted to step in. "I'm his number one fan," she declared. "I caught his debut match and, well," her fingers brushed through her hair as she looked away. "Well, I was captivated. I had the good fortune to meet him, and—" she giggled "—he's been very accommodating."

Stas suppressed a grimace.

"Oh Stas, you sly dog." Vita grinned. "Is this where you've been sneaking off to in the evenings?"

"Now, now, Vita." Zola chastised her with a grin of her own. "I'm sure our friend has been a perfect gentleman, 'accommodating' this lady however she required. And I must say, he has surprisingly good taste in women to 'accommodate.'"

Stas could not help a blush. Eponine seemed to be blushing a deep scarlet as well. Stas was unaware she was such a proficient actor.

"Erm," Alain said, himself blushing at the conversation. "Miss Eponine, I don't believe you should be here right now. We aren't supposed to be receiving visitors at this hour."

Eponine's eyes widened. "Oh, I'm so sorry. I didn't realize! I just needed to speak with Stas quickly. I'll be right out of everybody's hair as soon as I can. Is that alright, Stas?"

If it was important enough that Eponine needed to seek him out, then it was worth listening to. "Fine. Let's get some privacy and keep it short."

"Hopefully not too short," Vita jeered. "Make sure to 'accommodate' her to her satisfaction."

"And take proper precautions." Zola smirked. "I'm too young to be an aunt."

"Really, you two," Alain said. "You're being very rude ..."

Stas and Eponine were out of the cafeteria before he heard anything else. He directed them towards an isolated spot.

"What are you doing here, Eponine? Why are you risking things like this?"

Immediately her vapid persona dropped. "It's fine, Stas. Everyone expects fans to try to get in. With a little bit of my arcanum, nobody is going to think anything of it. Just ... don't mention it to anyone, right?" She was blushing. "I'm just making the most of assumptions."

"Fine, I won't mention it. If you're willing to waste the elixirs, there's no real problem. What's so important that you needed to see me?"

"There's a mission. Are you aware of the Kalends feast?"

"Yes? What about it? It happens every month."

"What matters is that this one is taking place at Marcellus's estate. And Marcellus leads the largest faction of the Senate. It's a perfect opportunity to get an ear on what's been happening there, and a little more on the side. As a gladiator, you have a perfect excuse to attend."

Stas exhaled sharply. "I was not invited. I can't help this time."

Eponine waved him off. "Don't worry about it. I can get an invitation for both of us. You'll just be my plus one instead of the other way around. And it has to be this one. Who knows when Marcellus will be hosting again?"

"Why me, then? Isn't Henri a patrician? He shouldn't have any trouble getting an invitation, if you need someone else."

Eponine scoffed. "I can handle the spying and sabotage myself. I need someone reliable in case things go wrong. Plus, Henri avoids these kinds of events. If he shows up, there will be too many eyes on us. Nobody would bat an eye if I took a gladiator as a date."

"I see. How are you going to get an invitation?"

"Don't worry about it," Eponine said quickly. "Find something nice to wear. You can escort me from here at sundown." She nodded to herself. "Goodbye, Stas." And she walked away. After taking a few steps, she stopped and turned around. Her voice reverted to the act from before, carrying loudly. "Thank you, Stas. Goodbye. And good luck with your training." She giggled and scurried off.

Stas huffed and headed back to breakfast.

# Twenty-Seven

Despite Eponine's assurances, Stas was on edge until the very moment they were let into the estate. He didn't exactly trust Eponine's hastily acquired invitation, and the elite senatorial guards overseeing the event were not the sort to fall for forgery, or even Eponine's arcanum. But they passed through the gate unhindered.

It was strange, being in the noble district. Stas could not help but reflect on his last illicit visit. It was, bluntly, night and day. Elegabalus's mansion had been opulent and empty. Marcellus's manor, in contrast, was thronging with people ... it felt alive and luxurious instead of dead and gaudy.

In size and in spectacle, the estate of a senator far outshone that of a simple nephew. The grandest element was the conspicuous use of arcanum. Hundreds of magical torches cast their brightly colored light wherever one gazed. The air inside wafted with a cool breeze, in spite of the stale air of the city. And the golems ... wherever one might expect a servant, a stone-faced automaton served instead. Gardeners, doormen, waiters, cleaners ... a dozen golems followed along the garden path with no purpose but to be seen.

It would take a flood of elixirs to power the estate. A single day's worth of fuel might bankrupt patricians.

Eponine interrupted his gaping. "We need to introduce ourselves to the host."

"How will we find him?" Stas inquired. "I don't even know what Senator Marcellus looks like."

"Not a problem, because I do," Eponine countered. "He'll be easy to find. Everyone needs to greet him when they arrive. When we get there, wait for him to address us first."

"I know that much." Stas only knew bits and pieces of patrician protocol. Some lanistae ensured their students learned decorum. Ludo did not think it so vital. And, on this, Stas agreed. If it came down to hiring a swords instructor or one for etiquette, Stas was glad his lanista had chosen the former.

There would be opportunities to learn as his career progressed. For now, he could rely on Eponine. She led him further through the extravagant mansion, past rooms filled with bound paper and illustrations where guests marveled at the contents, past lounges where guests reclined on darkly dyed cushions, enjoying dark wines in crystal glasses served by stone-faced golems, past open dance rooms where even more golems plied their instruments and guests frolicked.

Every part of the manor screamed luxury.

Eponine led him into a massive indoor atrium. Sconces and ceiling lights made the space as bright as the day outside. Proper sense would simply have had the roof opened for daylight. But there was no need for proper sense in the senator's domain. Here, the majority of the guests mingled, either before them, or up on the balconies overlooking the space, accessible via marble staircases.

In the corner was a tall, blond-haired man in a brilliant white suit with golden accents, sporting a tall hat to match. He was flanked by a pair of golems, and laughing with a man and woman before him. The man and woman left and another, older man, moved to speak with him.

This could only be Senator Marcellus.

As Stas approached, he made out the small glass spectacles on the man's face, as well as the small, neatly trimmed triangle of blond hair on his chin. The ensemble, combined with his suit, produced a rather foppish effect in Stas's opinion. But he was not well read on the courtly fashions.

The senator's easy smile fell into a glare as the old man in front of him spoke.

"Please understand, this is not meant to be an insult."

"Of course it is an insult," the senator growled. "How can it be anything but? Even miserly Gratidianus availed himself of my hospitality for a few minutes. But Lady Hirtius sends a servant to beg off? How can I take this as anything but an insult?"

"My lady is feeling ill, Lord Senator. No offense is meant."

"Your lady was certainly feeling well this morning when denouncing my proposal. Quite a healthy rant of hers." The senator rubbed his forehead. "By the Dominus, that woman takes everything so personally. Does she not understand that grudges of the Senate House end when one leaves the Senate House? She would turn a simple political difference into a blood feud."

"My lady has no such wish …" the flustered servant stammered.

"I will not waste more words on a mere footboy," the senator declared. "Begone! And let Lady Hirtius know that her insult has been acknowledged."

The older man bowed. "Of course, Lord Senator." He scampered away as fast as could be managed without breaching decorum.

Senator Marcellus took off his spectacles and rubbed his eyes. His gaze turned towards them. "Ah, could it be? Lady Claudia! How good to see you. I was afraid you would not receive my invitation. How is your mother doing?"

Eponine bowed her head deferentially. "She is doing well, Senator Marcellus."

"Good, good. And your grandfather? I hope he is as well after that unfortunate bit of unpleasantness. No hard feelings there?"

"It is as you say, Senator Marcellus," Eponine said with a subservient expression. "Grudges of the Senate floor should remain on the Senate floor."

"Good, good. I am glad to hear it." The foppish man beamed. "Your grandfather was something of an inspiration to me, back in the day. Hearing he is recovering well is a boon for my soul. If only others would emulate Lord Claudius and yourself." He tutted to himself. "Lady Hirtius could certainly learn from your virtues."

"Lady Hirtius?" Eponine inquired.

"Oh, it's a simple Senate matter, nothing to worry about." Marcellus waved the question off, and then immediately contradicted himself. "The lady senator and I had a disagreement today. While we can greatly appreciate my fellow senator's intelligence, her suggestions leave much to be desired. Far too extreme. No need to bring the heavy hand of the state to play when a simple reduction of the grain dole would suffice. Ah, I apologize for my rudeness, Lady Claudia. Would you do me the honor of introducing your escort this fine evening?"

"Indeed." Eponine pushed Stas forward a step. "This is Stas, a gladiator under the tutelage of the lanista Ludo. He has done me the honor of agreeing to escort me this evening."

"Pleased to meet you, Lord Senator," Stas said with a bow.

"Ah, yes, one of Ludo's students. Forgive me for not recognizing you. I have little time these days for recreation, so I must prioritize my attendance to the prestigious bouts."

The jab, intentional or not, chafed.

"I must admit," the senator continued, "that I have a greater preference for the venatio. Not to disparage your profession, but there is something noble, I feel, about the triumph of man over beast." Marcellus blinked and frowned. "When they triumph, that is. The event has turned into an unfortunate bloodbath as of late. Lord Macro

245

does a disservice to his position, making such monsters."

Recalling the chimeras, Stas couldn't help but agree, if only with the sentiment.

"You will not have to worry about running into the man at this party, for sure. Ah, but the reason I bring it up is that all of tomorrow's hunters are present. Have you ever considered becoming a beast fighter? It might do you some good to talk with them about career prospects. There is always room for more hunters."

Stas nodded. "I will keep your advice in mind." He had no intention of lowering himself to do so, but he could keep his seething to himself.

The foppish man grinned. "Excellent. Lady Claudia, I hope you and your escort enjoy my hospitality this evening."

"Thank you, Senator Marcellus. I'm sure we will."

"Thank you," Stas echoed, and Eponine pulled him away.

Behind him the conversation continued.

"Ah, Lord Patruinus! So glad to see you! I must thank you for your wonderful gifts."

"Of course, Senator Marcellus. I hope they are serving you well—I spy many of them within your staff tonight," a middle-aged man in simpler finery responded.

"As always. As always. Your creations are ever delightful."

The din of the crowd soon overtook the voices as Eponine led Stas to an alcove. With the manor so large, it was easy enough to find a discreet place. Eponine's tight expression turned into one of fury. "I can't stand rotten snakes like Marcellus. I'll be glad when he and his ilk are dead and rotting."

Stas frowned. "I thought you said you weren't a patrician. Is 'Lady Claudia' a cover, or is it your true name?"

She stilled. "Never call me that. I'm Eponine, got it?"

There was a deep vehemence in her command. Stas raised a placating hand. "As you wish." He opted to change the topic. "Do you think Katriane knows? About the change to the grain dole, I mean?" The revolutionary worked for the city distributing grain. The change would directly impact her work.

Eponine huffed and calmed down. "I don't know. The Senate likes to keep laws to themselves until they go into effect. She'd probably appreciate the heads up." Eponine shook her head. "We were seen speaking with Marcellus, so now we need to be seen around the party. So go and mingle. I'll do the same. When there's an opportunity, I'll come get you. Got it?"

Stas nodded. And with that, they separated. Eponine headed off towards a gaggle of patricians she seemed to know and Stas, lacking knowledge or connections, headed towards the banquet layout.

The food was excessive. Meats and sweets and breads and cakes and roasts and fish and fruits and many dishes Stas could not identify, all served on crystalline and golden plates. Behind it all were stone-faced golems, ready to serve.

In truth, the food sickened Stas. It all looked far too rich. His dietitian would be aghast by the gluttonous fair. So he turned aside from the banquet with only a few choice pieces of fruit, some meager bread slices, and a single choice cut of a sirloin that looked palatable.

He did end up snagging a crystal goblet of sweet wine from a golem.

Out of the corner of his eye, Stas spotted the Dominus's Mad Monk. The unassuming man in plain garb was speaking with some patrician or other. Stas turned to move away. He did not want to deal with the unsettling man tonight.

Stas spotted a few gladiators he recognized. They were easy to find, dressed in their arena armor, happily speaking with enthralled guests. The likes of Radek and Esmae were clear centers of attention.

Stas felt a surge of embarrassment. These were the greats who achieved an invitation on their own merit. He could only ever approach them as an inferior.

He turned away from the guests of honor. He would meet them for the first time on the arena sands, not in this decadent manor.

He turned his gaze to look for any other recognizable sight. Up on the balcony, he spotted Zola conversing with two young patrician women. Lacking any other direction, Stas made his way up the marble stairs towards the three of them.

Zola caught his eye as he ascended and waved him over with a smile. "My friend," she said. "I am surprised to see you here. I hope you are not party crashing?"

"I wouldn't dare," he replied with a frown. "Eponine was able to get an invitation and I am escorting her. We are going our own ways for the moment." Both of the patrician women were staring at him. One seemed to be giggling.

"I would have assumed she would be hanging off you the whole night," Zola said, "but it's good to get some space."

"And you?" Stas asked. "Did you manage to find a senator's son as you planned? If so, where is he?"

Zola shrugged. "I'm not sure, nor do I care. He was a boor. I have found better company." She gestured to the two women. "Stas, these are Ladies Tusca and Limenia, whom I have had the pleasure of meeting this evening. Ladies, this is Stas, my junior. He is famed as the Blink."

Stas suppressed a bristle, opting to bow instead. "Greetings, Lady Patricians. A pleasant evening to you both."

The two women smiled. "A pleasure to meet you," Limenia said affably.

The giggling one, Tusca, tittered some more. "It's always so nice to meet gladiators. Do you use two swords like the Tigress does?"

"No." Stas shook his head. "I have some training with such, but I prefer to use a sword and shield. And the style I learned differs greatly from Zola's. Her emphasis is on arcanum, and mine on more traditional maneuvers."

Tusca hung on the words he spoke. "I see. Are there many different styles of sword fighting? Even among those that use two blades?"

"Indeed," he answered. Falling back to expertise was easy. "Outside of Zola's own style, I am aware of at least three different schools of swordsmanship that use twin blades."

"I see. How fascinating. If one were interested in learning a two-blade style, which would you recommend?"

"That depends on the student, I would say. There are strengths and weaknesses of each. For a gladiator, it is important to have a basic grasp of each style to understand how one's opponent might respond. But for a hobby, it would depend on inclination. I sadly cannot make that judgment by sight."

"I've seen you fight, Stas the Blink," Limenia said, "against the Tigress and one other time. You defeated her, did you not?"

"Ah, yes. It was a good fight," he answered simply.

Zola added to his answer. "He did indeed. Stas is a talented fighter, and I am blessed to share a school with him. I imagine few can respond to his blinks." She grinned at the prodding mock. "Lady Limenia, why don't you ask Stas about the offer you brought to me?"

"An offer?" Stas asked.

Limenia nodded. "My mother runs a brewery of some renown. I was hoping to offer a sponsorship to the Tigress so that it may find more success."

"Unfortunately," Zola continued, "my current deals preclude other sponsorships. I was planning on trying to speak with Alain about it, but since you are here, that is even better."

"I've seen enough of your skill to think it a fine proposition," Limenia said with a nod, "and if the Tigress is vouching for you, then I have no qualms in the slightest."

Zola pressed on. "A sponsorship is a great way to have some money for yourself, Stas. I can vouch for the product." She grinned wryly. "And I would be happy to avail myself of access to good beer."

Stas swallowed. "I am not against the proposition," he stated calmly, "but I would need to know the exact details before I could give an answer." He would need to do something nice for Zola, to thank her for the opportunity

"Of course, I could not ask otherwise," Limenia agreed. "My mother would be the one to speak with, but she is not attending this evening. If you come to our manor, she would gladly discuss terms."

"I would like that, I think." Stas swallowed. Honestly, he had no idea how these terms were negotiated. He would need to ask Zola about it after the party. Or Enjolras, with his patrician ties.

Or Eponine. Tonight was proving that she, too, had connections.

Stas cleared his throat. "You mentioned Alain, but I haven't seen him anywhere. Where is he?"

"The man of the hour? He is on the other balcony, being badgered by fans." Zola pointed across the atrium. Stas could see a crowd of people there, one of which was certainly Alain, for the size alone. "Ludo is with him, having a miserable time as you would expect from the old bore. Geoffrey is here too." Zola pointed down to the atrium.

Geoffrey was easier to make out; the people around him were less packed together. He seemed to be addressing a great many of them, eliciting laughter with his quips.

Stas noted, with no lack of jealousy, that the vaunted Lord Galbrio himself was among that number.

He clenched his fists.

"Ah, my friend." Zola interrupted his thoughts, perhaps intentionally. "Perhaps you can help me. Lady Tusca here was disparaging the use of arcanum. As a fellow user of the mystical arts, perhaps you might lend your words to mine?"

"Oh, I didn't mean to disparage any skill," Tusca quickly said. "I just feel that it is more admirable when one strives for prowess of one's own will, over magic from a bottle. All else being equal, I would root for the fighter who uses fewer elixirs." The formerly giggling girl seemed quite bashful of her opinion.

"See, Stas?" Zola spoke with a light smile. "We have to defend our honor."

"I actually agree with Lady Tusca," Stas said. "Martial prowess is a base that everyone needs. Arcanum is a powerful tool, but it isn't a foundation in the same way."

"Really, Stas the Blink?" Zola asked. "You of all people?"

"Most of my time in the yard is focused on my physical abilities for a reason, Zola."

"Alas, I have been betrayed by my own comrade," Zola moaned. "Lady Limenia, I require your aid in helping defend my honor."

"Of course, Tigress." The patrician spoke the words solemnly. She immediately lost it with a small fit of giggles.

Conversation continued in that vein. It was easy to speak of things like this. He almost managed to forget about his mission with Eponine.

Eventually the ladies begged off to go and speak with others present, and Zola went her own separate way. This left Stas to resume his wandering. Perhaps an hour passed without Eponine contacting him.

Then, suddenly, the air seemed to still. A silent, haunting bell rang through the air. Everyone stopped as one. An unnatural sensation cast a blanket over all, and an eerie silence reigned.

The doors to the atrium opened. A large shadow crawled forth in defiance of the great light.

At the source was a large, cloaked figure: a man whose very image cast a quiet pall over the entire party.

It was the Dominus. There was no room for doubt. The fact seemed to engrave itself in Stas's heart. This was the unimpeachable lord, the very soul of the city and all within.

That Horatio Undaunted, the greatest gladiator of the modern era, walked beside and behind the Dominus was an unimportant note. Everyone in the atrium fell into a deep bow, the stone-faced golems included.

Well, not everyone. The Mad Monk stood alone, unperturbed, offering only an incline of the head. The disrespect went unacknowledged.

Senator Marcellus walked forward to offer supplication. He stood with a bow, waiting to be addressed.

Stas felt something pull at his arm.

"Come on," Eponine declared.

Stas shook himself from his daze and followed her. This must have been the opportunity Eponine was waiting for. Nobody else seemed willing to take their eyes off the Dominus. Nobody would notice them slinking away.

When they had gone far enough, Stas exhaled deeply.

"Was that your first time?" Eponine asked.

Stas nodded. He had seen the figure in a box before, but being in the same room was its own experience. The closest he had ever felt to that atmosphere was when the chimera was bearing down on him. He was glad to be away from it.

"You can get used to it, but it never goes away. I don't know what the Dominus is, but they have that effect on people." Eponine shook her head. "Regardless, it's an amazing distraction."

"What are we doing exactly?" Stas asked. "Are we looking for anything specific?"

"Senator Marcellus uses golems for almost everything," Eponine began. "He's famous for it. And one of the jobs is scribe. A bit of laziness on his part. Since only senators are permitted in the chamber, most take notes for themselves. But Marcellus considers himself 'above' that type of labor."

Eponine led him down corridors as she spoke, keeping an eye out for any guards.

"He brings the same golem to every single meeting, where it takes notes for him on everything anyone says. I've found where he keeps it."

"So we are going to look through its notes?"

"Better. We are going to replace its pen with this one." She produced a simple pen from somewhere in her dress. "It's an arcanum construct, linked to a similar one back at the hideout. Anything written down by this one will also be written by the other."

The implications churned through his mind. "Amazing."

Eponine grinned. "The fop's laziness is doing us quite a bit of good. Ah, here we are." She stopped in front of an opulent wooden door and pressed her hand against its keyhole. There was a small flash of light from her magic. "Here's the study. Stand guard for me and let me know if anyone is coming. I shouldn't be too long."

Stas nodded and set himself to guard the corridor without making it obvious. He cast his sight out, through the reflections, to see further down the hallways towards the patrolling guards and other guests.

And so he waited, and waited. Stas felt his anxiety grow as time passed. The guards, who had been so far away at the start, were coming closer now. He could hear Eponine's muffled movement through the thick wooden door, but he had no idea when she would finish.

It was taking too long. He opened the door.

There he saw Eponine tearing through paper, ripping sheets apart. Her face seethed in rage.

"What are you doing?" Stas hissed.

"Don't question me," she barked. "I am not in the mood."

"They are going to find the papers," Stas hissed back. "They are going to know somebody was in here."

"It doesn't matter,"

Stas closed his eyes and exhaled. "A guard is coming." He cast his view out. "I think he heard something, because he's coming straight for this room."

The rage in Eponine's eyes drained, replaced with fear.

"Did you make the swap?" Stas asked.

Eponine nodded. "Yes. It's done."

"Then let's get out of here," he moved to grab her.

Eponine dodged his grip. "No," she insisted. "If he heard us, then finding nothing but a mess will just raise his suspicion. We can't risk them discovering the pen." She looked Stas straight in the eye. "I have an idea."

"What …" Stas was interrupted by Eponine's lips latching on to his. In his distracted state, he was unprepared when Eponine's foot swept under his own.

Stas fell to the floor, papers scattering with him as he struggled and failed to maintain balance. Eponine fell on top of him, her lips still sealed to his own. He could feel her hands gripping at his clothing, making a mess of them.

The door to the room opened. The guard stared.

Stas stared back, mind blank. He pushed Eponine off him. She turned to the guard, her expression full of fear and embarrassment, a burning blush on her cheeks.

"What …" The guard was clearly confused.

"Please don't tell anyone!" Eponine's voice matched the embarrassment on her face. "We're so sorry, we thought this place was out of the way."

Understanding dawned, and the guard's confusion turned into annoyance. "You shouldn't be here," he growled. "This is the Lord Senator's private study."

"We're so sorry, we didn't know. We were looking for a place away from the party and the door wasn't locked …"

"Wasn't locked?" That seemed to throw the guard through a loop.

Irritation returned but it didn't only seem to be directed at the two of them. "Regardless, you were somewhere you shouldn't be and have made a mess of it. The both of you are coming with me to see the Lord Senator."

"We can clean up the mess," Stas offered. "Nobody needs to know, right?"

"No. This is a senator's private study. He needs to be informed." The guard huffed. "Of all the places ... what's next, an orgy in the treasury?" The man muttered to himself. "Now come along. Make yourself presentable. We're going to the Lord Senator." The guard turned around and beckoned for them to follow.

"Should I ..." Stas asked quietly, raising a fist.

"No," Eponine whispered quickly, refusing to meet his eyes. "Too suspicious. This is bad but manageable. We do what he says. Let me do the talking."

Stas held his annoyance. The two followed the guard back towards the bulk of the party.

"Hm?" a voice called out as they approached. "What's going on here?"

"Sir," the guard declared. "I found this pair being indiscreet in a non-public area. I need to report the matter to the host."

The Mad Monk looked over them with a dull eye. "The Lord Senator is currently speaking with the Dominus. This may not be the best time."

The guard blanched.

"As for the 'indiscreet' individuals," the monk continued, "I do not believe the Lord Senator would be surprised to hear of it. Likely as not, there are many pairs doing the same at this moment."

"It's a matter of where they were," the guard continued.

The monk interrupted. "I doubt it is of any true concern. Going above and beyond your duty is commendable, but in this case I do not believe it is warranted. These two have been appropriately chastised, so it is better to return to your duties."

The guard sighed and turned to the two of them. "If you are looking for privacy, please use the bedrooms. Don't wander around the senator's private wing."

Eponine, still blushing scarlet, bowed her head. "We will keep that in mind."

The guard didn't bother responding, opting to return to his patrol. Stas released a sigh of relief as he departed.

"I hope your evening is productive, Stas, Lady Eponine," the monk murmured with a bow of his head. "Perhaps it would be best to get back to the festivities."

"Perhaps," Stas agreed. He needed another drink.

# Twenty-Eight

Ludo's arena box was far more crowded today. Given that one of their number was fighting a Kalends match, that was to be expected. Sadly, that meant Stas's choice of seating was limited. Having dallied before departing, he found himself seated next to Ludo.

The lanista greeted him with a silent nod.

"It's a good day for a match," Stas said. "The weather is quite pleasant."

"Hm ..." Ludo's face was blank, eyes affixed into the distance. The man never seemed to smile, not even at matches. Ludo did not seem to enjoy gladiatorial bouts. Stas often wondered why he had made a career out of it. His dour lanista would seem far better suited as an accountant. Or a gravedigger.

Ludo spoke after a moment. "I dislike the look of the crowd today."

The crowd? Stas looked out to see what he might have meant. The audience seemed as lively as ever, enraptured by the acrobats.

"I don't understand what you mean." According to Katriane, the grain dole had been halved as of this morning. But Stas wouldn't have known from hearing the exuberant cheers.

"Hm ..." Ludo closed his eyes and sighed. "Perhaps I am overthinking matters. We will see how the match goes."

The acrobats cleared the field and the announcer strode forth.

"Presenting!" The announcer's voice carried far and wide. "Of the

Dollabella School of the Aventine—the mist-cloaked spear! Trickster of the sands! Lamorak the Legion!" The band played in triumph as Alain's opponent entered the sands. He wore a set of light armor much like Stas's own, and wielded a long, ornate spear. The crowds roared in anticipation.

"And presenting! Of the Ludo School of the Forum! The giant of the Stellar! The Atlas who carries the world! Alain the Tower!"

Alain's signature music played as the man himself stepped forward. His large meat cleaver of a sword hung on his back. The cheers doubled, and shouts of "Tower" and "Alain" joined those of "Lamorak" and "Legion." The roars outshone those of any match Stas had attended. Such was the popularity of Kalends fights.

The two gladiators met in the center. They spoke to one another, but their voices were inaudible. They shook each other's hands, to great cheer, then separated.

The band drummed up suspense, mixing the music of the two competitors. Alain drew his oversized sword. Lamorak drew his spear.

The signal fell, and they moved. Alain went for his elixir, using his large sword as a shield. Lamorak went on the offense, charging forward to disrupt. But Alain was able to catch the blow and drink the magic brew.

The magic was obvious. Lamorak jumped backwards to escape as Alain grew in size rapidly. His cleaver fit neatly in a single hand now. The crowd roared and the music was dominated by the heavy rhythms of Alain.

"It's a shame Lamorak uses a spear, not a shield," one of Stas's fellows proclaimed.

"Huh? Why?" Vita asked.

"Alain's strength is in crushing defenses," Stas explained. "But Lamorak, with a spear, will rely on dodging and range instead." That said, with Alain's size, the two had about the same reach.

The two fighters exchanged blows. Alain's large size was no detriment to him, but Lamorak proved to be the more nimble, escaping the heavy swings of Alain's massive blade.

Lamorak jumped backwards in an acrobatic display and imbibed his own elixir. In a flash, a cloud of mist erupted. One Lamorak became five and the five charged.

"Has anyone here fought Lamorak before?" Stas inquired. "How does his arcanum work?"

"Lamorak's copies are more mist than man," a gladiator explained. "They can't exert much force, but the spears can still make you bleed. One small hit, though, and the copies dissipate."

"One small hit from Alain and Lamarak himself would dissipate," another jeered.

"True, but the problem is knowing which is which."

The five spearmen moved to surround the swordsman. The giant did not remain idle, dashing to the side to avoid entrapment.

A single Lamorak charged. Alain caught him with his blade, and the figure burst into mist. The other Lamoraks took position. Alain blindly slammed his elbow backwards, destroying another Lamorak.

Stas took credit for the instinct. Attacking from behind was natural with his arcanum, and he made regular use of such in their practice bouts.

"None of the bodies are disturbing the sand," Stas noted aloud.

"You can see that?" his fellow asked. "Well, he's probably learned how to hide that. Lamorak wouldn't let his foes find him so easily."

The three remaining bodies split into seven with another burst of mist. The music crescendoed towards the spearman's tune.

They coordinated, keeping Alain on his toes. Any motion from either side risked punishment. It was not a true stalemate, though. Every few strokes one of the spears would manage to nick into Alain's skin, drawing a drop of blood. And, every few strokes, Alain would manage to disperse one of the Lamoraks, only for it to be replaced.

Stas would need to know how many elixirs Lamorak had brought and how difficult the copies were to create in order to judge the winner of these exchanges. But from the perspective of the audience, the Legion was slowly slaying the Tower, one pinprick at a time.

Perhaps that was what drove Alain to change his strategy. With a roar, Stas's peer swung his sword not at the copy of Lamorak before him, but at the sand of the arena. He struck deep and heaved in a spin, sending the grains of sand outward all around him.

The forceful wave burst through the Lamoraks, each and every one of them exploding into mist. Alain was left alone, to the great confusion of the audience.

Lamorak emerged from the mist, spear raised. Alain reacted instantly, cutting through the spearman, who burst. From behind the giant another Lamorak shimmered into view, his spear extended for Alain's neck. The point pressed against the giant's skin.

"So Lamorak learned to turn himself invisible …" one of Stas's peers muttered. "That's going to be irritating."

Invisibility was an unpopular ability on the sands, given that it deprived the audience of a show. But for Lamorak, with his mist duplicates, Stas could see how it would be valuable.

Being Alain's friend and peer, Stas knew that a spear to the throat was not a killing blow. The gladiator's arcanum made him quite durable. But the threat was a good ending for the audience. The sporting response was concession.

Alain, ever a man of fair play, did just that. He shrank back to his regular, still massive, form, and signaled his surrender.

The crowd roared. The band played a triumphant tune. Cheers for "Lamorak" and "Legion" reigned.

"It was a good match," Stas acknowledged. "Shame that Alain lost."

"Hmm." Ludo's eyes were locked on the crowd and not the fighters. Alain and Lamorak accepted the cheers with a bow. The aedile in his box prepared to end the match.

Then something shifted. Or perhaps it was always that way and only now he noticed.

Stas did not know where it had begun—with crowds it was always hard to determine such things. But at some point the cheers for Lamorak were joined by those of a darker tone. The blurry waves of excited faces mixed with darker grins. A pallid wave spread across the crowd, and with it came cries for blood.

In mere moments, the same crowd that had been enthralled in the show was now clamoring for execution.

Stas turned to the aedile in his box. With horror, he saw that the man was contemplating.

His fellows were clamoring. Ludo's face was as still as the stone-faced golems.

The aedile gave a signal. Lamorak bowed. Alain closed his eyes with a nod.

A spear pierced Alain's heart.

The crowd roared.

Stas fell back into his seat. The box was a mess of shouting, anger. Somebody was crying. And Ludo, damn Ludo, was above it all as always.

"Don't you care?" Stas was unable to keep the anger from his voice. "One of us has been killed. Do you not care?"

Ludo turned to him, his face tired but stoic. "Do you wish for me to wail? I can assure you that mine sounds no better than anyone else's."

"Alain died," Stas seethed. "I would expect you to acknowledge it."

"The fact has been acknowledged, I can assure you. A death in a fight is to be expected. The fact that you had not considered the possibility is a failing on your part, not mine."

"You don't care, do you?" Stas accused him. "We are just numbers on a ledger to you. As long as you get the blood money, this is just another damned transaction."

"Minus some to account for the costs Alain incurred, I will be delivering the money to his mother," Ludo declared blithely.

It wasn't the death that was so painful, Stas realized, but the injustice of it. If Alain had been felled in the fight, the blow would not have been so tragic. Instead he had conceded honorably and had been slaughtered for it.

"Alain did everything right." Stas tried to force his words into the lanista's insufferable mind. "Everything. He fought well. He held himself with honor. He acknowledged his opponent's skill by letting the match end on a good note. He accepted the aedile's verdict without complaint. And he died anyway."

"Correct. Alain did everything right, and he died. That is the nature of a gladiator. That is the nature of life. You can do everything right, and you will die. You can do everything wrong, and you will still die. Death in the arena, a sudden seizure of the heart, slain by a mugger ... the one constant is death. It is uncaring and ever present and beyond our control. That is why we must strive for excellence in matters that we do control." Ludo spoke with a note of finality. "Wailing accomplishes nothing. Honor Alain by following his example and be a better gladiator for it." Ludo rose. "If you would excuse me, I need to speak with the aedile."

Stas did not watch him leave. His mind was on the crowd. They cheered for Alain's death just as happily as they cheered for the executions that interspersed the fights. They saw no difference between the blood of an honorable man and that of criminals.

One missed meal turned them to this. They killed a man with their chants and they loved it.

Stas could no longer see a glorious crowd of adoring fans. No, he could only see the patrons of the Bell: disgusting drunks clamoring for the blood of poor, indebted fools. Had there ever been a difference? Stas felt his bile rise.

The black-feathered official directed his assistants to cart Alain's body out of the arena. Something precious had been taken with it.

Stas left the arena box. Many left with him.

# Twenty-Nine

Stas frequented the Libertas hideout more often these days. The idle pleasures of life had lost their appeal, and he was already training more than the school's physician permitted.

With little to occupy his time, his options were to sleep, or to idle his time away with Libertas. And his bed lacked sweet wine.

The revolutionaries could be bothersome at times, but the din was usually easy to ignore. Now marked an exception.

"My friends!" Lucian proclaimed. The plump man was making a spectacle of himself by climbing on top of a table. "I have learned of a great opportunity! A marvelous opportunity! A noble chance to stick our blade deep into the city's heart!"

Through the drunken cheers and jeers was a call to "Get on with it!"

"Through my glorious network of spies—"

He was interrupted by a mocking shout from Romeo: "Stop lying, you sap!"

"Through some gossip I happened to overhear—"

Romeo laughed drunkenly, eliciting a slap on the back from Katriane. He had taken to excessive drink after his ordeal, but few called him out on it.

"As I was saying," Lucian continued, "I have managed to learn of an opportunity. The city has been consolidating elixirs ... purchasing stockpiles from patricians, or confiscating them from the saps that can't grease the wheels ... where was I going with this again? Ah, yes. One of my clients has sold a big stockpile. A truly stupendous amount. The transfer is set for two days' time. But—" Lucian placed his hand over his heart and grinned at the assembled room "—I learned which warehouse they are gathering it to."

"Three cheers for Lucian!" Romeo shouted. "We keep him for the wine, but sometimes he acts useful!" Some people joined in his cheer.

"My brothers! My comrades!" Lucian declared. "This is an opportunity. We are people of the city, are we not? So if the city is buying the elixirs, then why not save those poor day laborers the work of transporting it?"

The cheering resumed. Stas found himself joining. This, at least, he could enjoy.

"Really?" Sanson bellowed. "How the fuck do you expect us to pull that off? Two fucking days? And what the fuck are you talking about 'overhearing?' Have you got any brains in your head at all? Or have you drowned them out enjoying your own product?"

"Oh, shut up, Sanson." Stas didn't hide his irritation. "Patricians don't think anything of talking. They love bragging about their importance." The banal conversation at the party had proven such. "As for what we can accomplish ... we are Libertas, aren't we? We can abscond with every single vial if we put in the effort." Stas raised his glass high, the wine threatening to spill.

"Well said, Stas." Enjolras rose. "We are Libertas, the soul of the city. And no mission is beyond us. If we are willing to grasp it, then it is ours for the taking."

"Enjolras ..." Sanson's heavy voice was low, but carried.

"No, Sanson. You know why this task could be so vital." Enjolras dismissed Sanson's concerns. His voice elevated. "But for a mission such as this, we will need volunteers. Brave souls that exemplify our spirit to carry this opportunity into reality."

Voices clamored, Stas's among them.

Enjolras raised a hand. "Do not rush. Take the night to consider matters. Think about your capabilities. And tomorrow, when you have a clearer head, I will be honored to count on you."

Enjolras let the happy crowd return to a rumble, and his voice turned back to a conversational pitch. His silver eyes caught Stas. "Stas, Sanson, if the two of you would join me?" He led them to the back room with the shield.

When the door had closed behind them, Sanson loomed. "What the flying fuck, Enjolras?"

Stas moved to intercede, but Enjolras pressed his hand on his shoulder. "Would you please be more specific, Sanson?"

"We have a protocol for a reason, Enjolras. One, I'll remind you, that you insisted on. Why the fuck are you gathering volunteers for this nonsense?" Sanson pointed at Stas. "And why the fuck is he here?"

Stas bristled, but the hand on his shoulder kept him grounded. If not for that, he might have thrown himself at the pox-faced pile of fat.

"Stas is here because I trust him and because his insight is valuable."

Stas felt a warm grace permeate through him. That Sanson looked pained only added to the joy.

"As for why I am so hasty ... I do not believe we can afford to wait." Enjolras turned to Stas. "My contact has informed me that the city is planning an imminent crackdown. Lucian's information adds daunting credence."

"The watchers are always cracking down," Sanson argued. "They are never not cracking down. Half the reason they exist is to find bodies for the executions, crimes be damned. Nothing different about this."

"How strange for you to be the optimistic one, Sanson." Enjolras smiled ruefully. "Though I hope I am wrong, my contact has yet to steer me astray. I fear there is a plan in the works, and I would rather be proactive than reactive."

"You and your damn fucking contact ..." Sanson grumbled.

"Who is your contact?" Stas questioned.

"I am unable to say," Enjolras replied. "We communicate through dead drops. But I know they are highly placed in the Dominus's court. The information they provided speaks to great privilege. I have suspicions, but ..." He shook his head. "Regardless, the reason I asked for you, Stas, is because I would like you to lead the mission."

Stas felt his chest tighten. "You would?"

"I have not forgotten your success in rescuing Romeo. I haven't forgotten how you led both the execution, and the planning. While our members are brave, we do not have a true tactician. Your proven skill makes you the ideal candidate."

Sanson grumbled, but did not interject.

"This is an important mission, Stas. I feel deeply that it may prove the difference between survival and extinction. A true stockpile of elixirs could ensure our triumph for years to come, to say nothing of the great stroke it would be against our foes. I know I am asking a great deal of you, but will you do me this favor, my friend?"

Stas swallowed and nodded. "I will. I will do everything I can to ensure the mission goes smoothly." Because this was something that mattered, far beyond satisfying the bloodthirsty wastes on the arena sands. "It will be done, I swear."

Enjolras beamed. It was a gentle smile that held far too much trust in its silver eyes. Stas would move heaven and earth to prove it correct. Enjolras moved across the room and grasped the indestructible shield. "You made great use of this before. I see no reason not to grant it to you again."

Stas nodded.

"Of course, if you need further supplies, the armory is open to you. We will have our volunteers tomorrow so that you can make your plan."

Stas nodded. "There's something I need to get. I will return tomorrow."

After all, Stas had sworn to do everything he could to help. And there was one particular person who could help.

\* \* \*

"No." Phobos's response was immediate.

Stas frowned. "Why not? This is exactly the sort of thing you do." Phobos was the first person to come to mind when the mission came up. "You should be jumping for the chance. You could take as many vials as you can carry as payment. There's more than enough."

Phobos looked unmoved, so Stas continued. "Think of how many patrols you would have to ambush to make up for this single operation. Or how hard it would be to infiltrate a better-defended stockpile. You're willing to spend far more time teaching me for a few vials. This should be perfect for you."

"I said no."

The man could be infuriating at times. "Can you explain why?" Nobody else had his experience fighting watchers. Stas had vowed to do his best. Recruiting Phobos was part of that.

"Hm, let me think …" Phobos tilted his head to the side and placed a fist on the bottom of his strange mask. "Let's go with *no*, brat."

"If you would simply give a reason, I might relent." Not that Stas planned on relenting. He just wanted an explanation so he could dismantle it. There was no conceivable reason for Phobos to be against this.

"I have no interest in working with vainglorious fools. I am done with that nonsense."

Stas held back from punching him. The man clearly knew nothing about Enjolras, or Libertas. This was an insult of ignorance, not malice.

"You spoke to me of your vows before," Stas said. "Of how your mask drives you to eradicate evil, and make the city a better place for all. Maybe you have run into fools before, but is it so strange to imagine that others are driven by a similar creed? That they would stand together to fight the same tyranny you seek to destroy? From what I have witnessed, Libertas exemplifies the virtues of your mask better than you do."

"You misunderstood, brat." Phobos sneered, his fingers tracing the blue material on his face. "This mask isn't a sign of virtue, far from it. This mask has passed through tyrants, murderers, thieves, torturers, madmen. I wear this cursed thing not to celebrate its history, but out of damn spite. I hate it with every fiber of my being." The assassin's voice was harsh and heavy. "The only reason I wear the cursed thing is because the bastard I took it from would have hated every single thing I am doing with it. And that brings me endless joy." Phobos gave a sardonic sigh. "If your group actually did exemplify this mask, I would tear your throats out one by one."

There was silence, broken by an angry huff. "This isn't up for debate, brat. I work alone. End of story."

It was a dismissal, but Stas wasn't done yet. If Phobos was completely against the proposal, he would have fled by now.

So, he instead attempted to change tracks.

"I find it strange," Stas mused aloud. "You are willing to do many distasteful things for your goals. You have no qualms attacking from ambush, stealing, sabotaging, murdering ... No method seems to be too horrible if you believe it leads to beneficial ends. And yet, the act of coordinating seems to be a step too far."

Phobos stilled as if struck by his words.

Stas remained silent, letting him stew. After waiting a period his childhood rhetoric instructor would have praised, he added the deadly blow. "I suppose you must care about your own pride more than your objectives."

"Damn you, brat," Phobos cursed. Stas knew he had won. In some ways, his teacher took a strange pride in his lack of pride.

"I will let you know the time and place when it is set." Stas spoke definitively.

He *reflected* away before Phobos could argue.

# Thirty

They stood before the warehouse, nine in total. They had spent the day observing the area, keeping track of patrols, mapping it out as best they could, preparing the horses and carts for the trip.

The four bird-faced watchers who patrolled the surroundings had already been dealt with. Ambush and coordination made short work of them. They had plenty of time before the watchers' absence would be discovered.

Stas took a final scan of the surroundings. Satisfied with their thoroughness, he led them forward. The doors creaked silently. The arcanum they employed would ensure no one paid any mind.

The light of the moon shone through the cracks of the patrician's warehouse. Their target was awash with dim light when clouds gave way.

The contents of the building were distinctive: barrels upon barrels stacked up to the rafters, each marked with the sign of their premier producer. Stas had seen a few of these barrels in Ludo's school, secured tightly, where only the commissar was permitted. A single barrel served the needs of the entire roster for an entire month. Libertas possessed a mere two from which they rationed scrupulously. And the contents were of far lower quality.

Stas could scarcely comprehend the amount before him. What grand magic could be accomplished with such fuel? How many corpses had this treasure trove demanded?

Stas was not alone in his stupor, but he was the first to escape it. He gestured for his band to head forth. Lucian was the first, scrambling up the stack of barrels to the top of the heap. Perhaps his familiarity with wine casks gave him confidence. He took one from the top and handed it down for another to grab.

The barrel made its way down, ending in the hands of a member who stopped. "Isn't this supposed to be heavier?"

Stas felt his stomach sink. The clouds parted and moonlight shone through the warehouse. The shadows deepened, twisted, coiled.

From the shadows a dozen figures emerged, then a dozen more. Shadows pooled into men, attired with beaked masks.

Two dozen watchers appeared in but a single moment. They arrayed themselves between Stas's band and the door.

Panic and shouts reigned, and a crossbow bolt smashed into Lucian's chest. The man crumpled, falling pitifully down the barrels to the floor.

Stas could not process it. The many, many watchers advanced. Another pair of bolts were fired. This time Stas found himself moving—Enjolras's shield caught both effortlessly.

A watcher gurgled and fell, a dagger lodged in his throat. From the rafters, Phobos, invisible, cast his hook. It caught his prey and threw him into another confused guard.

Stas forced his mind back to center. He *reflected* behind an unguarded crossbowman and slit his throat. "Well?" he shouted, projecting his voice as he had been taught. He *reflected* again before the watchers could converge on him. "What are you sorry lot waiting for? Let's get them!"

It was hardly the best speech, but it served his purpose in rousing his fellows. Maria took her short bow and launched an arrow, catching a guard in his shoulder through the gambeson. Katriane readied her sling.

Another fighter, Raoul, brought a vial to his lips. A bolt went for the boy, but Stas intercepted it. Raoul lobbed a ball of darkness at the mass of watchers.

The battle was on. They were outnumbered, almost three to one, but they had their own advantages. The empty barrels served as a good barricade, both as shields and as impromptu projectiles. Libertas scrambled to higher ground, under the cover of Maria, Katriane, and Raoul. The bird-faced watchers could not make use of their full numbers without approaching, and they risked slaughter by Phobos or Stas if they were incautious.

Few of the watchers possessed ranged weapons or arcanum. For those that did, Enjolras's shield proved implacable: Stas could keep his fellows safe from their projectiles with constant success.

The watchers had not been prepared for such resistance, and it showed. But they were slowly consolidating, adapting to the situation as they had been trained. They did not break, but neither did Libertas.

Stas felt his hope growing. The battle was in his hands.

Then, without him obvious cause, his stomach sank. He felt it before he saw it, the shadows coalescing under the moonlight once more.

The air seemed to still. A silent, haunting bell rang through the air. Watcher and revolutionary alike froze as an unnatural chill blanketed the warehouse. The shadows, long and sinuous, danced in spite of the moonlight.

The pool of shadows grew deeper, coalescing around a large ornate cloak, an imposing figure enshrouded within.

"Lord Dominus," a watcher said with a deep bow. His fellows joined him.

"Hm ..." The Dominus hummed softly to themself, dark eyes scanning the room. "So these are the mice who've caught themselves in our trap, are they?" The emperor's tone was bland, their expression disinterested and disdainful. "I expected more, somehow."

To Stas's shame, he was not the first to break their stupor. Rather it was Maria, the stern-faced door guard. She raised her short bow for the Dominus's heart.

The soul of the city raised a single hand. Before the arrow was fully loose from its string, a burst of shadow erupted from the Dominus's outstretched arm. It smashed into Maria, throwing her backwards, and crushed her against the warehouse wall. The wood creaked; the body snapped.

Stas was horrified to note that the column of shadows seemed to disguise a mass of discolored flesh. Blinking eyes and gaping teeth hid beneath the wisps of darkness, joined by scales and fangs and ears and tumors, like a scene from beyond the unnerving mirrors. All of it was out of sight, but his arcanum could see the truth.

The shadow-cloaked column of flesh pulled away from Maria's body. Her corpse was mangled and torn, as though a hundred people had taken a bite out of her. The splatter of blood blended with wisps of shadow in the air.

The flesh column fell back into the shadows, dissolving from view, and the shadows themselves faded away under the moonlight. The attack had taken but a single blink.

The Dominus lowered its arm and sighed. "Disappointing." The weight of the ruler's shadow kept everyone frozen in place.

"Well?" The Dominus spoke with wry impatience. "Get on with it. I'm hardly going to do your jobs for you. Kill them all."

The watchers jolted and the fight resumed. But the situation was different.

With the Dominus came the death of morale. The revolutionaries fought weakly, cursed by the knowledge that the immortal sovereign of the city could end matters at their leisure. Maria was dead. Raoul was in a useless panic. The makeshift barrels were of no real use. And

Phobos had disappeared.

It was all Stas could do to hold the line as the bird-faced watchers crawled up the barrels, fending off the faltering strikes of the revolutionaries upon them.

Libertas was crumbling as the Dominus watched with boredom.

A throwing dagger shot forth, aimed for the Dominus's neck. The ruler's arm shot out to catch it, and its hand clasped around the blade. The Dominus frowned. "Impudence." Its hand clenched. The dagger crumpled.

Another dagger shot out from another angle. Again, the Dominus caught it without a care. This time, to the emperor's surprise, it exploded. The Dominus staggered in place, clearly disoriented. Phobos faded into view behind the cloaked figure, a strange knife at the ready. It was covered with markings Stas had only seen on the arcanum toys in the market.

Phobos slashed for the back of the Dominus's neck, but the figure twisted into shadow. A new head with an unsettling face emerged out of the Dominus's neck, facing Phobos. Two new hands, cloaked in wisping shadow, sprouted forth, grasping for their masked assailant.

Phobos abandoned his strike smoothly and dodged out of reach. A column of shadow-cloaked flesh, akin to that which slew Maria, burst forth. But Phobos had predicted it, moving himself out of the way even before the attack even began.

Phobos threw a smoke bomb at the ground. In the confusion, he disappeared from view.

"Vermin," the Dominus huffed with annoyance. "You cannot hide from me."

A wave of shadow pooled out from the Dominus. It spread out on the floor of the warehouse, covering the surface, creeping up the walls. To Stas's horror, it was like the other attacks: a thin layer of shadow hiding unblinking eyes and grasping teeth. The medley of flesh oozed outward, emanating from beneath the Dominus's cloak.

Stas *reflected* away, both from a watcher's swipe and the writhing patchwork of meat. Watchers too fled from the monstrous arcanum, focused more on staying out of the way than on completing their murderous task.

Flesh and shadow crept towards the rafters. A cruel smirk grew on the Dominus's impassive face. "I have found you."

The shadows and flesh retracted to the source. The snagged prey was pulled in rapidly. But it was not Phobos.

The Dominus seemed to stop to contemplate the corpse they had caught: a watcher entangled with a recognizable fishhook. At the end of the hook's line was that strange dagger.

It swung forth in the movement. When it touched the immortal's flesh, it reacted.

A great white blinding light exploded upward. A great column of pure brightness expanded outward in a wide beam towards the moon. The beam was silent beyond possibility, deafening the warehouse in empty quiet. It pierced through the Dominus's body, expanding to engulf it entirely.

Stas stopped to gape as did the watchers. The arcanum in the dagger was far beyond anything Stas had ever seen. The beam of brightness obscured the Dominus's body. The wooden roof in its wake crumbled to nothingness, as did the floor and the earth beneath.

After some mesmerizing time, the beam petered out, revealing the Dominus's tattered body. Gaping nothingness replaced more than half the emperor's form. The watcher's corpse and the dagger had been completely obliterated. Stas did catch the glint of Phobos's fishing hook, undamaged on the tattered ground.

The Dominus's flesh twisted, with no shadows to disguise it. The empty spaces were filled quickly, and the body reverted to form. Even the Dominus's cloak seemed to patch itself together.

"An admirable effort," it droned. "But worthless." The ruler of the city stood unharmed among the devastation. "Tell me where you learned of such arcanum, outlaw. That form of the art is not one I have allowed to be taught. Answer me, and I shall allow you to die swiftly."

Phobos did not respond, and Stas had lost track of him.

"Do not bother hiding, villain. I can find you easily enough."

Phobos jumped down from the rafters, landing before the Dominus. In each hand he grasped a copy of the strange dagger.

"One might not have been enough," Phobos growled. "But I have nine more where that came from."

The Dominus scoffed. "Do you take me for a fool? I can sense that those toys lack the willpower of the first. Such wasteful implements. Is that why you have been stealing my elixirs? Disgraceful."

Phobos held steady. "Are you so certain, Dominus? The blades of an assassin can deceive the senses."

"They cannot deceive mine, you hapless fool. Do you know how many people have tried to kill me across the ages? You are not nearly as threatening as …" The Dominus stopped, some recognition dawning. "That mask … where did you get that mask?"

Phobos said nothing, stepping forward.

The previously aloof Dominus shuddered, emotion boiling forth. "It should not be here. There is no room for such blasphemies in my world! In my paradise! This is my domain, and I will not have the line of Phobos taint it!"

Phobos took another step forward. The Dominus almost took a step back, but they steeled themselves, rage overtaking fear.

"I will slaughter you!" the Dominus screamed. An all-encompassing wall of flesh broke like a wave towards Phobos.

Stas *reflected*. His blade cut into the Dominus's back, but failed to find any purchase. The skin was as tough as the chimera. It did serve the purpose of distraction, though. The wall of flesh fell aside for a moment.

"Cockroaches," the Dominus growled. "Are my men truly so incompetent?" It swatted its arm at Stas, faster than he could raise Enjolras's shield. The gladiator found himself thrown to the side by the force of the casual blow.

The Dominus was strong. Impossibly so. But the form of its attack was pathetic to Stas's discerning eye. The Dominus was not a trained fighter. But it did not need to be when it overpowered anyone before it with strength and arcanum both.

And for all the Dominus's lack, Stas would never be able to defeat it. The immortal ruler of the city was too far beyond him: more like a chimera than a man.

A column of flesh, lacking the coat of shadows, rushed for Stas's position. He raised Enjolras's shield to defend himself. The attack pressed against him, but the shield held firm. But it was of little aid. The flesh pooled around the shield, creeping towards him.

Stas *reflected*, leaving a decoy in his place. The Dominus's arcanum crushed it into the warehouse floor, pulping the frail magic.

The Dominus did not pay it much mind, focused on Phobos. "You are alone now, pretender of Phobos," it mocked. "How many have claimed that accursed name? After centuries in this world, I have not been keeping track."

Phobos said nothing, his form resolute. The bird-faced watchers all turned to observe the scene. Everyone else in the accursed warehouse had perished.

Phobos turned his head slightly, appraising Stas's position with a glare. Stas did not know what it meant. Was Phobos ordering him to run away? Was he asking for Stas's aid? Was he cursing Stas's name for getting him involved? Stas had no way to know, no way to act. His strength was leaving his body, his mind was deserting him. The nightmare was too much.

A wave of flesh cascaded over Phobos. He did not dodge this time. Stas could hear the cruel snap of bones breaking, flesh liquefying under pressure. The tumorous mass of meat nearly engulfed every part of Phobos. Stas could see a glint of metal, another of those strange daggers. It stabbed into the Dominus's wall.

Once more a bright light engulfed the warehouse and the Dominus with it. This time it lasted only a few seconds, and the immortal ruler of the city was no more harmed.

Phobos's body was reduced to nothingness. Only the strange blue mask survived.

The Dominus huffed. "Inconsiderate. Ruining his own body like that." A tendril of flesh, once more covered in shadow, snatched Phobos's mask. The monster tossed it towards a watcher who caught it after a moment.

"Keep a hold of that," the Dominus commanded. "I am going to mount it in my study. The current bearer was a fool, but the originals were worthy of respect. I will need to find someone more intact."

Stas watched as the Dominus made their way to the nearest body, that of Katriane. A tendril of flesh and shadow grabbed the woman's corpse. The immortal seemed to unhinge, flesh turning to a gaping maw, a mass of teeth and sinew, all hidden underneath a cloak of shadow. The monstrous figure engulfed the corpse entirely, bulging outward from the mass. Then the Dominous bubbled and bulged and shifted.

From the shadow Katriane emerged, creaking her muscles in distaste. The expression on her lips was disturbed. "It seems these vermin have built themselves a nest in the twenty-first district." The voice sounded exactly like Katriane's, but the tone and words would have never passed through the woman's lips. "Raze the district to the ground. Don't let a single person escape."

The watchers nodded, and all but the one carrying Phobos's mask were engulfed in a wave of shadow. They faded from view just as they had arrived.

Katriane's body twisted and folded, bulging beneath a cloak of shadow. Once more the Dominus stood in her place.

"I must remember to discipline the commander of the twenty-first," the Dominus muttered to itself. "Forcing me to graft a weakling ... the rancid taste will bother me for weeks."

Stas could not allow himself to wait any longer. He *reflected* to the warehouse floor, behind the watcher.

"What?" the Dominus murmured in surprise.

He punched the man and caught Phobos's mask when the man dropped it. Then, he *reflected* to the fishhook and snatched it too. He teleported as far as he could manage.

Speed was his only concern. Libertas was in danger and needed to be informed.

There was a great distance to cover but he pushed himself, reflecting as fast as he was able as far as he was able. Nothing else mattered. He had ruined everything already, and he would not accept ruining anything more.

When he arrived at the hideout, it was already too late. The warehouse disguising the hideout was on fire. Bird-faced watchers swarmed the district in outrageous numbers, tearing people from their homes, slaughtering them in the street. He saw watchers swarming the tunnels through the mirrors. He saw the hideout burning.

Everything had fallen apart. The world went white.

Stas grasped the mask on his face, that ornate cloth that bore the symbol of freedom, and tore it off. How could a wretched person like himself wear such a thing? How could he hope to deserve it after failing? After ruining everything? After getting everyone killed?

The mask of a murderer was far more appropriate. Stas brought the smooth blue veil to his face. It was far less comfortable: both too big and too small at once. The painted nazar blocked his vision and the single eyehole clung inadequately.

The watchers continued their slaughter as Stas watched from above. He considered jumping down there, killing every single one until he exhausted himself fully. Dying in a fight would be honorable.

But even that thought could not rouse him. There was no point to it. No matter how many he killed there would be no impact. His friends would still be dead and the monster would still rule the city.

He was a coward in the end.

So Stas went back to Ludo's school, back to his room. He sat on his bed and stared at the wall until morning came.

# Thirty-One

The days since the incident had been like a haze, a nebulous dream he might escape at any moment. But he never awoke. Phobos's mask rested on his dresser, taunting.

Every day was the same. He woke. He ate. He trained. He slept. There was no purpose to his actions, only routine. He was like those stone-faced golems, following tasks for lack of will.

Perhaps Ludo would enjoy that ...

A knock interrupted his thoughts. He watched blankly as a servant opened the door.

"Master Stas?" the servant called. "There is a visitor for you at the front entrance."

Stas blinked, trying to shift through the haze of his mind. Who could it be? The sponsorship girl, perhaps? Limenia? The opportunity had slipped his thoughts after Kalends.

"Shall I send her away, Master Stas?"

Stas shook his head. "No." If he was to be a golem for Ludo, this would be part of that. "I will go see her."

The servant bowed. "As you wish, Master Stas. I will inform the lady that you will be present shortly, after you have had a moment to make yourself presentable."

Presentable, right. He nodded and the servant left.

Stas changed to more appropriate attire. He took care to change the bandages on his arm. The mirror-like scars had grown in recent days. Maybe he would be lucky and it would kill him soon.

After securing the wrap, he donned a cloak. Then he grabbed Phobos's mask. He did not like being with it, but he hated being without it more. Enjolras's shield and the fishhook were procured as well. He did not like leaving them unattended.

Prepared, he made his way outside.

He stilled when he saw the long dark hair.

"Good to see you're still kicking, Stas." Eponine grinned.

Stas froze. Had he snapped? Was he dreaming? Was he finally waking up? In a flash he crossed the distance and clasped his hands over both her shoulders.

"Ah …" A bit of red dusted Eponine's cheeks, their faces were close. "That's an unexpected greeting, Stas. Can you let go? Your grip is tight."

Stas released his grip, and almost gaped. "How are you alive? Is anyone else alive? Is Enjolras alive?"

"Be quiet about that," Eponine hissed. "We're rationing elixirs, so I'm not deflecting attention. We can talk about it at the new place."

"Who survived?"

"Shush, I said. Are you good to go right now? I understand if you can't leave before night."

"No," Stas answered quickly, barely keeping from shouting. "No, I can skip training. Please," he begged, "take me to them."

Eponine shrugged her shoulders. "Alright then. Enjolras will be happy I found you so quickly. Come along. I'll lead the way."

Stas nodded and followed her. He did not care if this was a dream, or a trap. If this 'Eponine' were an impostor, he would accept his death.

He silently followed Eponine through the busy city streets, clutching Phobos's mask as he walked.

She took him on a solid trek across the districts. They arrived at a modest home near indistinguishable from any around it.

Eponine walked in without a care. Stas followed. From there, she led him up a floor to a thick wooden door that muffled the noise behind it.

Some rancorous argument erupted through the opening crack. It fell to silence as Eponine opened the door fully.

"I managed to find Stas," she announced.

A cacophony erupted. Stas could not make out the words. He was too distracted by the sight: Sanson, Henri, Romeo, Odette … everyone who had not joined him on that ill-fated raid was present, cramped together in a small room.

Standing above it all, with a smile on his face and brightness in his piercing silver eyes, was Enjolras.

"I'm glad to see you found us, Stas." Enjolras's words carried over the din. "We have a number of questions for you. What happened on the mission?"

"What happened on the mission?" Stas repeated. "What happened to you all?" he demanded in return. "How did you escape? I saw the tunnels burn. I saw all the watchers swarm the district."

Enjolras nodded. "I can imagine the confusion. It was a grisly scene from what I heard. In truth, we did not manage to escape in the traditional sense. Rather, by providence, none of us happened to be present."

"What?"

Romeo answered. "It was Henri's fault." He grinned, pointing at the smaller man who wilted. "The daft idiot was playing around in the arsenal and set a fire. The whole place went up. We all had to run out of there." He chuckled. "Boy, Odette looked like she was going to string him up by his innards. We fled the fire before we even knew the watchers were about."

"That sounds unreasonably lucky," Stas said. Impossibly lucky, even. Such a coincidence beggared belief. Stas almost imagined that someone had somehow orchestrated matters, but it was too horrifically stupid of a method to be anything but an actual accident. To say nothing of how convoluted it would have been.

"I know, right? I'm thinking of gambling since my luck is so great," Romeo joked, breaking him from his contemplation.

"You already waste too much money gambling, you drunk," Eponine chided, and turned to Stas. "And I wouldn't call it that lucky. We lost a great deal. We grabbed the important things, but we had to leave most of our supplies behind."

"Alas, the booze!" Romeo moaned. "Our precious, delicious alcohol!"

"Enough of that," Sanson bellowed. "The real question is how the hell did the fucking watchers know where we were? What happened on that fucking mission, Stas? We can't contact anyone else."

Stas's eyes widened. They didn't know. He wanted to laugh at the irony.

The pain was fresh. He wanted to cry. He refused to cry.

"Dead." He spoke quietly.

"What?"

"They're dead. All of them. There was no stockpile. It was a trap. An ambush. Two dozen watchers and the fucking Dominus were waiting for us." His voice cracked. "They died."

Pandemonium followed. Shouting. Disbelief. Denial.

"You fucking traitor," Sanson screamed, his loud voice carrying. "Is that what happened then? You sold us out? Gave those fuckers the hideout in exchange for your own sorry hide? I bet the Dominus was pleased as shit to deal with one of his pet gladiators, letting you waltz back to your life in exchange for ours."

Stas froze. For the first time in days, rage boiled through the misery.

He moved to speak but found someone else beat him to it.

"How dare you, Sanson, you unwashed pig shit," Eponine growled. "You have some fucking gall, blaming Stas for your own fuckup. The only reason we put up with your ugly, pox-ridden mug is because you're supposed to prevent shit like this. This was entirely on you. Or maybe you're just covering for your own treacherous hide?"

"Enough." Enjorlas spoke and his voice carried over the crowd. "These accusations are pointless. Sanson, you know as well as I that the Dominus would not even allow a collaborator to walk the streets. Eponine, Sanson did caution against this mission. I made the decision to push matters through. The fact he was not able to perform his duties is my fault and my fault alone. As for the claims of treachery, they are beyond ridiculous. I know the characters of Sanson and Stas and I know them both to be above reproach."

Enjolras looked everyone in the eye one by one. "If you have a concern about my ability to judge character, or if you truly distrust your fellows so greatly, then I have failed as a leader. Please let me know so I can resign."

Nobody spoke. A weight hung over the room.

"Thank you. I understand tempers are hot. My own feelings are in distress. But it is clear to me that this was not an intentional betrayal. Rather, we fell for a trap set to catch us. This is the danger of our fight. It is a risk we have all accepted, not that it detracts from the tragedy in the least. I mourn for our lost companions as much as anyone else."

Sanson interjected. "A trap doesn't explain how they found the damn hideout. Somebody blabbed." Sanson glared at Stas, the implication hanging.

Stas took a deep breath and spoke. "The Dominus ... it's not a person. It's a monster of arcanum. A chimera more than a man. I saw it sprout masses of flesh, eyes and teeth. I saw it regrow from a third of its size. I saw it change faces." Stas did not know if he could convey the horror of the sight, but he tried his hardest. "After everything, it ate Katriane. And then it turned into her. It had her face, her body, her voice. And her memories. The Dominus teleported the watchers straight to the hideout. It knew without asking."

"That sounds like a complete crock of shit," Sanson said.

Eponine spoke up. "But it's the truth. I've read Stas's mind, watched his memories. It was disgusting." She glared at Sanson. "Unless you are calling both me and Stas a liar?"

"You read my mind?"

"But it's crazy!" Sanson shouted over him. "Arcanum doesn't work like that."

Henri spoke up quietly. "It can. I've heard of things like that ... worse than that." He didn't elaborate further.

"So ..." Romeo ventured. "You're saying the Dominus can just eat people and turn into them? Learn their memories and pretend to be them perfectly?"

With the direct address, Stas jostled back to the topic at hand. "That's what I saw, yes." He nodded.

Again, pandemonium reigned. The revelation shot a new wave of fear through the group, suspicion and terror at the implications. Sanson seemed especially incensed by the idea.

Once again, Enjolras interjected. "Peace, my friends. This is indeed disturbing to hear, but it is not as dire as it may appear. I have met the Dominus before. The simple truth is that he is an impatient man. Capricious. Petty. The Dominus does not have the nature to slink or to spy.

"More than that," he continued, "we have seized a great boon from this tragedy: the Dominus thinks us to be dead. He and the watchers think that their cowardly trap has slain us, destroyed us. But the Soul of Libertas shines as strong as ever. Our friends may fall, our supplies may burn, but our cause survives pristine."

Enjolras closed his eyes and inhaled. "We will always mourn those we lost. Lucian. Maria. Katriane. Raoul. Josselin. Basile. Arsene. We will remember their sacrifices to our dying day and beyond. Take the time you need to mourn. Celebrate their lives and all they stood for. Let us honor them by carrying onward, by making full use of the opportunities their sacrifice has won us. We will recover, stronger than ever. For we are Libertas, the enemy of tyranny!"

Somebody cheered, which set off a greater celebration.

Stas frowned, and tapped on Eponine's shoulder. "Eponine, did you say you read my mind?"

"Yes? What about it?"

Stas frowned, but he quashed those churning thoughts. This was not the time for that. Instead, he let himself bask in the rising elation of his fellows.

For the first time in days, Stas felt hope.

# Thirty-Two

The following months passed without excitement. Enjolras did not have any daring missions; Libertas was lying low as they recovered. Stas's scheduled matches had been banal; none of his opponents proved to be of any interest. And, without Phobos, Stas lacked evening pursuits.

New Year came and went, with Horatio Undaunted earning ascension into the Dominus's household. Stas had avoided the festivities.

And with each passing day the city seemed to decay. The streets seemed meaner, the residents leaner, and crime felt rampant. The bird-faced watchers patrolled aggressively, snatching up any poor sap they desired. Executions grew in number and scope, dominating the games, the races, the hunts.

Stas went through the motions, training himself to exhaustion every day, waiting for the moment something would change. The work and its promised rewards brought him no joy any more. He considered simply leaving to join Libertas full time. But his position here was valuable.

For that reason, he soldiered on, the perfect, stoic gladiator for the humorless Ludo and the bloodthirsty crowds.

Phobos's mask had become a constant companion, as had his hook. Stas would not allow himself to forget his failures. But the fishhook in particular had proved to be an annoyance. He had tried training with it, to use it as Phobos had. But every attempt in utilizing the weapon ended miserably. The so-called "perfect" tool would not strike even the post, and it seemed to burn his hand whenever he made the attempt.

Stas had no idea how the assassin had handled the finicky weapon. The simple thought of it seemed to make it burn in his pocket. At least it was a good reminder: that the man who might have killed the Dominus was dead, and it was Stas's fault.

The dreary routine was finally interrupted with a summons. Stas made his way to Libertas's new hideout with all haste.

Few members were present in the cramped home. Enjolras, Eponine, and Sanson were waiting for him, which was usual enough. A bit more surprising was Henri, sitting in the corner.

Enjolras greeted him warmly, but there was barely hidden exhaustion behind his silver eyes. "Stas. I wish I could give you cheerful tidings, but we have learned of a dire matter we must discuss."

"Is that damn pen finally showing its worth?" Sanson spoke in a bored tone. "Or is there another reason why the brat is present?" he asked, gesturing towards Henri. There was no heat in the insult, but Henri shrank all the same.

"That is indeed the source of the information. Henri was observing this morning's Senate session and brought the information to my attention. Henri, if you would?"

Henri nodded and passed out sheets of paper—transcriptions, Stas realized. Sanson grumbled, but set to read, as did he and Eponine.

It was dry and rambling. A lot of the flowery speech made it hard for Stas to parse, especially with the smaller lettering. Eponine was on the second page while Stas was only halfway through the first. To the gladiator's annoyance, Sanson also proved to be a faster reader.

"Those bloody fucking bastards," Sanson growled. "Senseless, immoral, fuckers!"

Eponine said nothing, her eyes narrowing in anger.

Enjolras watched with tired eyes.

"Is this ..." Stas struggled to believe what he was reading. "A cull? Exterminating people to deal with the famine?"

Sanson seethed. "Of course they fucking are. Can't cut back on banquets, obviously. And replacing the cotton fields with wheat is out of the question. Why the fuck not jump to mass murder?" Sanson spat. "I see quite a bit of debate here: fucking quibbling over fucking minutia of fucking goddamn murder!"

To Stas's horror, the transcript depicted the Senate considering the monstrous act as casually as they might discuss any other spending bill. The arguments centered more on how many to kill and who would pay for it than on whether it should happen. The greatest argument seemed to be over who would own the corpses.

Eponine, with a frown, gestured at her paper. "It cuts out here, skips a bit. What's missing?"

"Ah," Henri responded. "That's when the Dominus's monk took the floor. He argued against the plan ... Two senators also argued against it. It was long and nobody really listened to them, so I didn't transcribe that part when I made copies."

Sanson grunted. "Two ... out of five hundred bastards? Disgusting."

Stas continued to read. The paper detailed the potential logistics as the senators discussed the specifics. He skipped to the end, where it listed the vote. He was dismayed to see it passed.

"Enjolras," Stas asked their currently silent leader. "What's the plan?"

Silver eyes met his own. "We cannot allow this travesty to come to pass. To me, the answer is clear." Enjolras closed his eyes and exhaled. "We must stage a general revolt."

He tapped the transcript. "This is the key. The Senate relies on secrecy. They can act without consequence because they know the populace is ignorant. This mass slaughter relies on hapless compliance." His silver eyes widened in a smile. "Our course is simple. We must distribute these words to the people. We must ensure that everyone is ready for the slaughter to come. And we will allow the people to express their displeasure directly. The justice of the masses will see us through. We can empower the people to save themselves. The Senate will be destroyed for contemplating this horror."

Stas, Eponine, and Sanson all stared silently.

Sanson broke the silence first. "Are you daft, Enjolras?!"

The insult irked Stas, but he had to admit he was wondering something similar.

"You are planning a riot, Enjolras," Eponine stated simply. "Mass panic. The city would burn to the ground."

Enjolras frowned. "I understand your fears. But I am confident that with careful coordination, we can direct an organized resistance against the Senate. The people of this city are better than that. They are good people at heart, strong people. They will free themselves from their shackles once they know the true corruption of the Senate."

"No." Stas spoke softly. Images of the arena stands flashed through his eyes. The callousness, the misdirected rage. He imagined the selfish audience in a panic. "People are creatures of instinct. The masses break when there is not enough food in their belly. They turn on anyone, anything, with no care for fault." Alain had died for hunger. Who would be slaughtered for fear? "There is no justice in that."

Enjolras frowned deeply.

Sanson snorted. "I never thought I'd hear you speak sense, gladiator. When the hell did you learn some proper smarts?"

"When did you learn consideration, Sanson?" Stas spat back. "Here I thought you'd be overjoyed at the idea of the city burning down."

"Feh. Parts of it, maybe. And I'd rather ensure the Senate actually dies." Sanson turned to Enjolras. "It's a shitty plan, Enjolras. This isn't something we can let free. Not before we have solved the issue."

Enjolras frowned. "I feel this is something that people deserve to know. Are we to be no better than the Senate to decide who gets to know what in our wisdom? To place ourselves above the freedom of the people by dint of position alone?"

Eponine scoffed. "When that information will cause a panic, yes. And don't make bullshit comparisons with the Senate. They're the ones trying to cull a fifth of the city."

Enjolras inhaled deeply and closed his eyes. "Can I convince none of you of this? It feels to me that allowing the people to free themselves is the only just response."

They all remained silent. In some ways Stas wished he could be convinced, but he had seen the truth of the matter for himself. For once, Enjolras was wrong.

Enjolras sighed. "I suppose this is why I have advisors, to identify my failings."

Stas swallowed. "We should agree to keep this a secret." It seemed like a nightmare in his mind, almost worse than what the Senate described in their session. That at least would be swift and orderly. "We should swear to it."

Sanson rolled his eyes. "I'm not going to blab. It would be moronic."

Eponine nodded. "I feel the same way. I can't see any benefit of letting this leak."

Henri, from his corner, meekly spoke. "I won't say anything, I swear. I'll hide the copies so people don't find them."

Enjolras nodded. "If it would make you feel safer, Stas, then I will do so as well. I swear on my honor that I will abide by the decision of this meeting. I will not spread word of the Senate's heinous plan."

It did make Stas feel better. "Thank you."

Enjolras clasped his hands. "Then, if my plan is shot, how do we go about preventing this travesty?"

Sanson grunted and pulled out the last few pages. "This," he exclaimed, "it's a target list. Every single fucker who voted for this shit has forfeited their right to live. Mass assassination. If they're willing to slaughter us, it's only fair we get to kill them too. We should have done that a long time ago."

"It wouldn't have worked before," Eponine said. "People wouldn't have accepted it, especially not the patricians. But we have justification here. We pull it off, and then we publish it. If the problem is solved, there won't be a panic. We'd legitimize the new regime."

"Aye." Sanson nodded. "People love heroes. They'd accept the new government. But we need to destroy this one first. Everyone who voted *yes* needs to die. No exceptions. The ones that voted *no* get to live." Sanson spat. "Millions of lives are at stake, and we have a time limit. We need to go loud, Enjolras. Use all our stockpiles. Buy out the gangs."

Enjolras exhaled. "You do not have to convince me of the urgency, or the stakes. I would have preferred a cleaner coup, but I acknowledge that the matter has been forced. The Senate, in their callousness, has crossed a line that cannot be forgiven. The ones that proved their moral fiber may be valuable. I will scope them out for collaboration, or to at least see to their safety. Henri, I know your father courts with the Antiquiores. See if there are any social events planned for this month, so that we might catch them in a single location. I will check the same for the Honori."

The planning was moving quickly, but Stas felt there was a big issue being ignored. "What about the Dominus?" he asked softly.

The question cast a stark pall over them all.

Enjolras broke the silence. "Hopefully it will not be an issue. The Dominus does not care much about the particulars of governance. So long as they don't interfere, we can accomplish our coup and present it to them as fait accompli. We may need to offer some concessions, but the rule of the Senate would be broken."

"And what if the monster does interfere?" The question needed to be asked. "What if it refuses to accept the Senate's death? Or if it decides to fight? The Senate would not be making a plan this outrageous unless they felt their master approved. Do our plans rely on the whims of that rotten pile of flesh?"

Nobody responded for all that it looked like they wished they could. Not even Sanson interjected.

It was the cruel truth. The Dominus held sway and could not be opposed. The monster could not be overpowered. The immortal could not be outlasted.

"Ah ... what about the Legendary Hermit?" Henri inquired.

"What about that nonsense fairy tale, patrician brat?" Sanson glared.

Henri gulped. "Well, I'm just thinking. The Dominus is immortal. But the Legendary Hermit is also supposed to be immortal. The stories say that the Dominus chased the Legendary Hermit out of the city when he, the Dominus I mean, arrived. So, wouldn't that make them enemies?"

"The Legendary Hermit is just that, brat, a legend." Sanson scoffed. "A nonsense legend at that. How could the Dominus 'arrive' when he's the one that made the city? And how could someone use arcanum before the Dominus created the damn thing?"

"That's not ..." Henri struggled for his words. "I've read things in my father's collection. The city might be older than the Dominus. Arcanum too. Maybe the Legendary Hermit is a real person. And maybe they're still alive. And maybe they could help us."

"That's a shitload of maybes."

Stas considered the matter. Arcanum before elixirs must have been real. He himself was practically proof.

The Dominus was evil and unstoppable. It only made sense that there would be an equal and opposite. Why wouldn't it be the Legendary Hermit?

"I think it is worth investigating," Stas said, interrupting the argument. "I can cover a lot of ground. If the Legendary Hermit used to visit the city, then he couldn't have been that far outside of it. If he is real and alive, I can find him, bring him back."

Enjolras frowned. "Are you sure you wish to attempt it, Stas? I will admit that the legend strikes me as a tale more than anything of substance."

Stas shook his head. "We need something to deal with the Dominus. This is the best hope we can think of." Phobos was dead. His assassination plot was gone with him. "There's no reason not to try."

Eponine nodded. "I'm with Stas. The Dominus can't be unique. There have to be others like him. I don't want to depose the Senate and still be trapped under the Dominus's filthy claws. That's not enough for me. In fact, I think I should join Stas." She grinned and elbowed the gladiator in the side. "I'd do a much better job convincing some immortal arcanist to join us than a provincial gladiator. Right, Stas?"

Stas snorted and rolled his eyes.

"Are you sure, Eponine? Outside the city is not a hospitable place. And we could use your talents here," Enjolras said.

"I'm sure." She nodded. "I can handle bad weather. And you can handle things without me. Better to spend my time more productively."

"You actually think you're going to find him." Sanson scoffed. "Feh, better that the two of you are not mucking around now that we are doing important work."

Enjolras closed his eyes and inhaled deeply. "If the two of you believe there is value in this quest, then you should go. I will see that you have supplies for the trek. Sanson, Henri, and I will ready everyone to strike at the senators. I will ask that both of you be back within a week, with or without the Legendary Hermit. If you find him, then we will be forever grateful. But if your quest goes as I fear, we will proceed without such aid. Inaction is not a possibility any more. Too much is on the line." Enjolras bowed his head. "Make your preparations and return here in two hours. I will have supplies ready by then. May Libertas favor you."

Stas bowed his head.

# Thirty-Three

Stas had never actually been to the city's walls before. He had seen them a distance quite a few times; the grand structures loomed when he was up high enough. But they had always been a distant thing at the edge of his consciousness. This would be his first time actually visiting the stone structures, which were nearly as tall as the bell towers and thrice as thick.

The city gates were imposing, large enough to allow the passage of three full carts abreast, and with a height to match. The thick iron trellis barred their way under the stringent watch of a dedicated contingent of bird-faced guards. Nobody could get in or out of the city without the watchers' permission.

Stas took hold of Eponine and, under the cover of her arcanum, *reflected* through. It was his first time outside of the city since he had arrived through the Gate so many months ago.

The vision that greeted him was green. Lots and lots of green. A veritable endless ocean of farmland dedicated to wheat and maize and other core crops, vegetables of color with the occasional cotton bough and tobacco, divided into tidy little plots, separated by simple fences and irrigation channels with small streams of water.

Stone-faced golems were at work, harvesting, watering, planting, sowing, all tending to this sea of produce mechanically. Simple, well-worn paths carried horse-drawn wagons, each carting mountains of produce towards the gate where they were inspected by the bird-faced gate guards and granted passage in a slow, laborious process.

He could hardly imagine there was a famine.

Keeping hold of Eponine, Stas *reflected* away from the city. And he *reflected* again, and again. As he traveled, he took in the sights.

"Why aren't there any farmsteads?" The farmlands around the city were not like those of the provinces, built around manors and livable plots.

Eponine shrugged. "This close to the city? These are prime plots of land, owned by the wealthiest patricians, so they have golem workers, not plebeians."

Stas frowned and *reflected* again. "So the communities are further out?" They would be a good place to start looking. The people might be able to give directions.

"What communities? Plants can only grow near the city. Everybody knows that."

That didn't parse. "Really? If only the city can grow food, then where are the provinces?"

Eponine paused. "I hadn't really thought about it. I suppose there are other places where food can grow. They must be far. Good thing there's the Gate."

It was something to ponder. Stas *reflected* again.

As they got further and further from the city Stas noticed a trend. The glorious golden wheat stalks were browning. The orchard trees stood weaker, with fruit that wasn't as plump. The air was growing hotter, and the wind drier.

More golems stood in the fields, watering the worse crops. Stas saw some familiar barrels.

"Are they watering the plants with elixirs?"

"Hm? I suppose so." Eponine nodded. "Diluted probably. I know that the manufacturers sell their bad batches to farmers. As a fertilizer,

I imagine."

"It might be more than a fertilizer." The crops directly under the elixir product seemed to be healthier. A dead plant seemed to return to life with the infusion.

A poorer-looking farm with a human worker was using regular water in her plot. The crops were almost completely withered, with few fruits to show for it.

Stas *reflected* onward.

Elixirs to make food. Food to feed people. People to be rendered into elixirs. It was a disgusting cycle.

It was getting hotter now. The sun seemed to scream in the sky. The air felt hostile, like the wind wished it could peel off his skin. The crawling sensation, which he had been suffering ever since he had passed through the Gate, worsened under the glare of the sun. He was more tired than he should have been. Perhaps he wasn't pacing himself properly.

He took a quick stop to drink from his canteen and his eyes narrowed on the plot beside him.

"That's indigo," he said, pointing to a plot where a golem was deploying elixirs. "I recognize it from the provinces."

"Yes? What about it?" Eponine inquired lazily.

"Indigo is for dye, not food."

"A bit of a waste of elixir, yes."

"More than that, all these golems are fueled by elixirs. There are more than enough people in the city to work the land. Why not hire them?"

"It's a status thing." Eponine shrugged. "Does it matter?"

"It's sick." Stas recalled Enjolras's rage over the organization of the city. It seemed especially evident here. Why jump to culling when there was so much that could be done with what they already had?

"It is what it is." Her words were dismissive, as if the wastefulness was a given. "Do you want some bread?"

"Let's keep going." He needed to get far enough away from the city that he wouldn't be distracted by all the reflections of the city.

They kept on moving. The farm plots got worse and worse, despite the presence of elixir watering. The land seemed to dry up of any and all life as they traveled. Here the famine was obvious. Very little grew.

Soon enough, they reached the edge of it all: neatly parceled plots of completely dead wasteland. Not a single sprout grew here, and yet the plots continued onward some distance.

Stas could see into the horizon, around the hills in the distance. The wasteland stretched on and on and on, beyond his view. No plants. No water. No life. It was a sobering sight—all this land and nothing of value. The sun seemed to weigh like a heavy blanket; the air clawed at his lungs.

Stas shifted his awareness to the world of reflections to see what was on the other side of far-away mirrors. It was even worse than he had thought.

The wasteland appeared endless. Truly endless. Stas stretched his senses out further and further, looking for the reflections of the ever-growing distance. And there was nothing. Absolutely nothing. Barren hills crumbling to dust, mountain ranges as dry and desolate as a burned bone, deep trenches that went down and down and down into an abyss of nothing.

The entire world seemed to be the city, its farms, and the wasteland.

Where were the provinces? Stas could picture them in his mind: bland, dismal farmland where nothing happened, good or bad. He felt a profound sense of isolation, and the confusion clawed at him just as the sun and air did. He searched everywhere for anything.

And, in his search, he found something: a modest cottage surrounded by a garden, on the top of a rolling hill of browning green. It was an oasis in the middle of nowhere, surrounded by wasteland.

Stas swallowed. The air was dry and he hacked up a cough. Eponine handed him the water canteen and he gratefully took a sip. How long had he been searching?

"I think I've found something," he said. "It's a cottage all on its own. If the Legendary Hermit is anywhere, he'd be there."

Eponine grinned. "Excellent. And even if he isn't, we can ask whoever is about him."

"It's quite far away," Stas said. "It may be a few hours, even with teleportation."

Eponine shrugged. "Better get to it then."

Stas nodded and *reflected.*

Eponine stayed silent through it all. Likely she did not wish to speak with the air so dry. Or perhaps she had nothing to say. Stas would have agreed on both accounts.

Finally, after a great trek, they were at their destination. The sun here did not feel as harsh. The air was cooler, and the wind was gentle. The earth beneath their feet was a healthy colored dirt, not a scorched waste.

The hill had grass, leading up to a simple cottage. It sported a simple garden of flowers and food. In the center of the garden was a single tombstone, polished like marble.

Stas fell to his knees, panting, as the exhaustion of the journey caught up to him. Eponine handed him some water and cheese which he ravenously tore into. Eponine took a few bites of jerky. Stas grasped for some himself.

"Interesting place," Eponine commented, observing the hill. "Quaint. Quiet, too. I don't think there are any neighbors." She frowned. "I wonder where they get their food. That garden isn't big enough to feed a person."

"Somebody has been here to tend the garden," Stas observed. "The Legendary Hermit is supposed to be a master of arcanum. They might travel like I do."

"True, let's go see if anyone is home."

Eponine began walking up the small hill, rather than wait for Stas to *reflect* them both again. Stas shrugged and walked beside her.

He paused, instincts blaring. He *reflected* in front of Eponine, Enjolras's shield raised just in time to catch a blow from a long, rusted sword. The strike staggered him to a knee.

Eponine stumbled back, falling to the grass-covered ground.

Stas raised his shield to defend against another strike.

His opponent was a tall, elegant-looking woman in a simple, sharp dress. She wielded an engraved longsword in a two-handed style. The blade was racked with rust, but its edge seemed impossibly sharp.

The woman twisted, bringing her force to bear up and across Stas's shield; the blow aimed for his chest curved towards his head instead. Stas *reflected* out of the way, his own blade aimed for the woman's back.

His opponent caught his blade with her own, sapping him of momentum in a motion that would have seen his sword instructor nod in approval. She was unhampered by the change in position, and settled into her stance naturally. Her sword rested in her hands in a relaxed grip, belying the force behind them.

And the woman moved, quick as a whip, strong as a bull, graceful as a dancer. The soul-crafted shield saved him once more, bleeding the force of the textbook strike. Stas's counterblow was deflected by the woman's hilt catching it in the cross guard. In the same motion, the woman released a hand from her sword and punched Stas in the face. He dodged as much as he could, but the fist brushed against his skin at an angle.

Stas *reflected* away and reached up to feel his cheek. It was bleeding, and badly at that. It was as if the woman had nicked him with a dagger. Wary of arcanum tricks, Stas changed his guard. The woman was strong. And skilled.

The mystery fighter dismissed him for a moment, turning to Eponine with a scowl. "Dog of the parasite." Her voice was harsh and cracking, as if she had not spoken in years. "Your mind magics are an insult. Do you think your paltry attempts could control me?"

Eponine flinched for a moment, before standing firm. "I'm just trying to calm the situation down. Why are you attacking us? We mean you no harm."

"Why?" The woman scoffed. "All dogs of the parasite should die. It is all you deserve." She held her sword in a taunting pose. "Come then. If I am to whet myself with your blood, then make a fight of it. Cease your worthless magics and fight me in truth. I yearn for it."

There was a part of Stas that still resonated with the declaration. A true, honest fight was something to be treasured.

But they weren't here for that.

"By parasite, do you mean the Dominus?" Stas inquired. "We are looking for a way to fight the monster."

"Truly?" the woman asked with a frown. Her stance remained wary, but her form was less aggressive. "I don't hear deception in your words, so I would take them as truth. Monster is an apt description, and one she would not stomach, vain as she is." The woman exhaled. "You are free to depart my land. No …" She turned to the gravestone for a moment and reconsidered. "I would invite you into my home. Come."

She turned abruptly and began walking up the hill.

Stas turned to Eponine with a questioning look. She shrugged and followed after the woman fearlessly. Stas, a bit more wary, kept his sword at the ready.

The woman opened the door of the cottage and gestured for them to go inside. They entered a simple single-room home with a table, two chairs, and a bed off to the side. A cabinet was set against the wall and was stocked with cutlery and flatware and herbs from the garden. In the back of the room was a pedestal supporting a pillow, upon which an ornate dagger rested.

The woman tossed a bit of cloth at Stas. "For your cut," she declared, and went to the cabinet on the side. Stas applied it to the dripping wound on his face as a bandage. He wondered if it would scar.

The woman fiddled with two cups and, in a flash, they were both filled with boiling water. The rusty sword she had been carrying had disappeared at some point.

Both Stas and Eponine noted the arcanum usage with great interest.

Eponine spoke first. "Are you the Legendary Hermit?" Stas found it strange that a legend could contort a young, stern woman into an old man, but he was wondering the same thing, given the evidence before him.

"What legend?" the woman asked as she added some herbs and flower petals to the boiling water and allowed it to seep. She placed the cups before the two of them.

Stas gave his cup a wary glance, as did Eponine.

The woman scoffed. "I am not a coward to kill with poison. It's a simple tisane."

Stas frowned but understood the sentiment. He took a sip of the drink. It was slightly sweet, with a bitter tone. Eponine joined him.

"In the city, there are stories of an immortal hermit who lived far outside the city. He visited occasionally to talk and to trade, until he was driven out by the Dominus," Eponine explained.

The woman shook her head. "I have never been to that miserable city." She prepared a drink for herself using the same herb and petal mix, and sipped from it. "The stories likely refer to my husband. He was prone to that sort of foolishness." Her harsh voice rasped with a gentle fondness with a backdrop of simmering anger.

Stas swallowed. He hadn't actually thought their quest would bear fruit so quickly and easily. "Ah, miss …" He stopped as he realized he didn't know her name. "What may I call you?"

"I was granted the name Feddlebrine. Knowing it will give you no more control over me than your mind magics, so don't insult me by making the attempt."

"Miss Feddlebrine," Stas continued. "We were hoping to find people like yourself and your husband. Is he around so we can speak with you both?"

The cup in Feddlebrine's hand snapped. Scalding water spilled over her but she didn't seem to notice. "No," she rasped. "You cannot speak with that bastard. He was murdered by the parasite."

Intense pressure exuded from the woman, like the rusty sword digging into his skin.

"She came to this world to kill him, the ungrateful vulture. The damn bastard ordered me not to interfere. He didn't even fight back. Even when that sanctimonious parasite desecrated his body, my worthless, inconsiderate, unthinking, selfish bastard of a husband had me stand by and do nothing. So no, you cannot speak with my despicable, cowardly husband, because the parasite has already taken him from me."

Long, deep cuts etched into the cottage walls and floors as she talked. The pressure grew and grew with each word.

"If you hate the Dominus," Eponine began, unfazed, "would you fight him with us? We came in hopes of finding somebody capable of slaying him. Are you willing to be that person? For vengeance? The Dominus's stupendous treasury would be open to you, as would our own coffers."

"I would like nothing more than to tear the parasite's head from her shoulders," Feddlebrine growled. "But beyond anything else, I am loyal to my husband, even if he abandoned me. I will stand by the vow he forced upon me until I rust away to nothingness."

"Is there truly nothing we can do to convince you to aid us?" Eponine asked.

"There is not." The swordswoman spoke with finality. "Do not insult me by trying to bend my mind otherwise, lest I declare you to be enemies in truth." Her glare focused on Eponine at that, and she flinched at the piercing stare. Her gaze died down. "Even if I were so mercurial as to break my vow, it would do you little good. The parasite is beyond me. In my prime she would have been no match for my prowess. But I have been rusting away for centuries now."

Stas swallowed. Their objective was shot, but Feddlebrine seemed to know of the Dominus's past. Perhaps she had knowledge of some weakness. It was the least he could attempt.

"You said the Dominus was from another world," he began. "What do you mean by that?"

Feddlebrine looked at him askance. "Is that so confusing a concept? You yourself bear the stench of Gaia, one this dead world has lost. Like yourself, the parasite was not born on this world, in this timeline. She traveled here, same as you."

The Gate, Stas realized. It was not a link across distances, but across worlds. The reason he could not locate the provinces was because they were nowhere on this Earth.

Eponine seemed to reach the same conclusion. "The Dominus was born in the provinces? Being a provincial is the source of his arcanum?"

"Wyrd ones and their magics were common before this world died," Feddlebrine explained. "Gaia provided shelter to them from the voids beyond. A wyrd one would die young without her succor." She frowned. "Is this not taught in your accursed city?"

"No," Eponine replied. She was staring at Stas now. "That sort of knowledge is not known to us any more."

Feddlebrine spat to the side. "Truly, I thought my opinion could sink no lower, but the parasite proves herself regardless."

"Even if you will not fight," Stas began, "can you offer advice?"

"I cannot," the woman responded. "I do not know the bodies the parasite has stolen over these centuries. Be grateful that my husband thought to cripple himself before she stole his body. If he had not, your task would have been impossible."

Eponine rose from her seat. "Thank you for hosting us, Miss Feddlebrine. I believe we need to head back to the city now."

Stas blinked. "Are you sure we should go now?"

Eponine nodded. "I believe we've learned what we can. It's a pity she will not fight. Best to head back."

Stas frowned but rose himself. "Thank you," he said with a short bow. In truth, he was angry at the woman. How could she let something as simple as a promise made to a dead man centuries ago, a promise it was clear she did not wish to make, prevent her from doing the right thing? She would see an enemy live forever because of her pride.

As they turned for the door, the swordswoman called out to them. "Wait," she commanded.

They did. Eponine had a small smirk on her face that she quickly hid.

The woman turned to the pedestal in the room and the dagger upon it. She grasped the hilt of the implement gently, almost lovingly. After a silent moment, she presented the dagger to Stas.

"Take her," Feddlebrine commanded. "If you are enemies of the parasite, then she deserves to join you. She deserves a wielder other than me, someone who would give her the chance to avenge her father."

The dagger seemed to gleam as Stas took it. "Is this soul craft?" The weapon rang in his hands in a way that reminded him of the shield. It lacked the dust that had collected in other parts of the house.

"Soul craft?" The swordswoman considered. "In a sense, one could call it that. In a kinder world she would have been somebody. In a softer world …" Feddlebrine shook her head. "But there is no life for her here, with a lonely widow on a dead world. She has always been eager to taste the parasite's blood. Perhaps you can make that happen." The woman sighed. "Perhaps you can give her the life she deserves. Promise me you will give it to her."

"Thank you." Stas did not really know what to make of the swordswoman's ramblings. Perhaps she had gone mad in her time of isolation.

"Promise me," Feddlebrine demanded, her voice a steel blade.

Stas swallowed. "I promise." It was a strange promise. He did not know what it would involve. But the conviction of the woman cut deeply.

For all the madness of the widow, she had certainty: a will to keep her word with no exception. And Stas envied her for it.

"Good." Feddlebrine nodded and turned away. "Go before I change my mind." There was steel to her voice again, a promise of violence behind her dismissal.

Stas nodded. They left the sharp-edged widow to her solitude.

They walked down the hill slowly. Stas felt the weight of the truth press against his soul.

"There is no hope," he declared softly. "No chance. No hermit to fight the Dominus for us. No one to free us from its whims." He looked at Eponine. "I felt it in her blade. Feddlebrine was strong. Stronger than me, perhaps. But she was not nearly as powerful as that monster. Even if we had managed to convince her, she would have had no chance." Stas looked ruefully at the gravestone. "There was one bit of hope, and the Dominus killed him centuries ago."

"Is that it, then?" Eponine asked. "Are you giving up? Are you accepting that that bastard Dominus can do whatever it wants? Ruin whomever it wants? The Dominus isn't unique. From what we learned, there could be a dozen like it in the provinces. Aren't you willing to fight, knowing that?"

"No." Stas looked down, dejected. "Whatever I am, I am less than that monster. You weren't there that night. You don't realize how outmatched I would be. I am not suicidal." And he knew that for a fact. If Stas had any inclination towards such cowardice, he would have ended his own life months ago.

"The Dominus doesn't train. It wastes its time watching games. You train more than anyone else. The Dominus fights without weapons, but you have them. With the magic shield and this new dagger, don't you think it would make a difference? Don't you want to fight?"

The words resonated with Stas, like an echo that would not leave his head. Shouldn't it make a difference? In a just world, that would be enough, wouldn't it? With a blade from a hermit and a shield from Libertas ... it brought his mind to a rumble.

Eponine continued, her words wrapping around Stas like a scarf. "Doesn't it just make sense? You and the Dominus are similar: provincials. Wyrd ones. The Dominus chose a life of tyranny but you chose to fight against it. You survived a fight with it, quested for a solution, acquired magic tools. Why shouldn't this story end with you standing as the Dominus's equal and opposite? Why can't this end with your triumph?" Eponine's emotions were high; Stas could feel them pulsing like his own. "Wouldn't that be right? Wouldn't that be justice?"

The words fit easily in Stas's mind. He was being a fool, a coward. He had let the Dominus defeat him without even a proper fight. There was too much at stake: the lives of the city, Enjolras's dreams, Libertas. It didn't matter if he thought he might lose; he needed to fight and needed to win.

"I believe in you, Stas," Eponine continued. "You say that hope has been lost, but I still have it. You are still here. You can defeat the

Dominus. You can save me. You can save all of us. I believe in you."

Stas nodded. The urge to justify that belief lifted his spirits. He grabbed a hold of Eponine's hands and *reflected*.

# Thirty-Four

They made it back to the city quickly, spurred on by a great sense of urgency. The Dominus needed to be defeated before the Senate made their move. Supposedly they had a week, but Stas did not wish to risk matters.

If he had his way, he would have leaped into a fight immediately, but the limits of his body proved too restrictive. Instead, he was forced to rest.

When dawn broke and Stas was as recovered as his mind and body would allow, he gathered his gear. Enjolras's shield remained with him. It would serve the cause, so he was certain Enjolras would understand the delay of its return. Feddlebrine's dagger joined his arsenal. If it worked as he imagined, it would be the key to slaying the Dominus. The dagger seemed to sing happily at the thought. It was a marked change from the stalwart shield's silence and the obnoxious reticence from Phobos's hook.

As for the hook, he did not dare let it leave his person. He needed the reminder, now more than ever. He would avenge everyone who had died for the monster's cruelty. Not just in the ambush or in the razing of the district, but everyone who had died on the sands at the ruler's whim. Perhaps, once he had avenged Phobos, he would earn the hook's allegiance.

That the hook burned in his pocket indicated otherwise, but it was the only idea he had.

And the mask ... This was not simply a battle for justice. It was an execution. If Phobos's mask was one of tyrants and murderers and thieves, then the Dominus would be its victim on this day.

So, Stas donned the mask once more. It seemed to fit more smoothly against his face now that he had a purpose for it. It was appropriate, he believed, to complete Phobos's mission in Phobos's mask, when he was the one who had derailed it.

Stas made his way into the city, to the grand forum that maintained its splendor even in the midst of famine. He set his sights upon the bird-faced watchers, who guarded this slice of decadence with eternal vigil.

Stas *reflected* across the rooftops, making no effort to hide himself from the guards or the colorful rabble below. He produced Feddlebrine's dagger and thrust deeply.

The blade cut through the watcher's armor like it were simple cloth. It pierced the man's heart in a single swift stroke and the blood seemed to flee from the blade out and away. The dagger, and Stas's hand with it, remained as pristine as Enjolras's shield.

Feddlebrine's dagger felt right in his grip. The magic weapon was finer than anything he had ever wielded.

The knife seemed to preen at the compliment. It sang as he teleported and slit the throat of another hapless watcher.

Could a weapon feel joy? Perhaps these were Stas's own feelings, and he only ascribed them to the blade to avoid admitting to his own sanguinary impulses.

But his fracturing mind did not matter. Only the mission mattered.

The watchers responded to his actions, swarming from the rooftops, attacking him with all manner of weapons and magic. Stas did not put much thought into it all. He *reflected* with his arcanum. He blocked with Enjolras's shield. He killed with Feddlebrine's knife.

And the bird-faced men died.

The foes he faced were unending. The blows he suffered were many. Parts of him bruised and burned and bled. But it was all insignificant: the simple, necessary prelude. He was fighting the watchers, and he was seen fighting the watchers.

People were shouting. Scores of finely dressed patricians ran amok, trampling over one another, pushing past the stone-faced golems to escape, no better than the rabble that would be culled on their behalf. They fled and harmed themselves in fear, even though Stas had no reason to hurt them. He simply did not care. This was but a means to the important end.

"Where are you, oh Dominus? Where is the lord of this fair city?" Stas mocked. "Can you not see me poking out your eyes? Can you not hear me cutting off your ears? I am laying waste to your very heart, and yet you do nothing. Parasite! Corpse eater! Wretched husk! Come and fight me, oh Dominus! Come out and die!"

This needed to happen. Eponine's words kept resounding in his head. It would be righteous for him to slay the Dominus. There was nobody else who could do it but him. Enjolras's depressed resignation, his acceptance of the Dominus's rule, would be proven wrong. He would let the man lead Libertas to the ending it deserved, absent the Dominus.

Killing the Dominus was all Stas wanted.

He had nothing left but this task, this need to see something go right in a world that lacked meaning. Why fight to please the crowds he hated? Why fight to save the people he hated? That life of naivety was dead.

Stas had no purpose of his own. But if he could help a better man accomplish his, wasn't that something worth doing?

In a sense, this was the same as his hopes of boyhood. He sought challenge, recognition. Now, though, he was choosing the audience, the opponent, the arena. Libertas would witness his deeds, not some bloodthirsty crowd of nobodies. His enemy would be an unrepentant monster, not a fellow athlete. The arena would be the forum, not the sands of the Solar.

Stas held a hapless watcher in his grip. "Contact the Dominus," he demanded. "Let that coward know I will kill it. Let that monster come and try to save you. I may let you live."

He did not care if these bird-faced men lived or died. They were insignificant tools for his true foe.

"Die, you criminal bastard," the watcher seethed before erupting in a flash of brilliant light. Stas *reflected* away from the suicide attack. Enjolras's shield protected him from the dregs of the explosion.

This was tiresome. If he had invaded the Dominus's manor, he might have provoked a faster response. That was what Phobos would have done: studied the manor for its defenses, plotted an attack, struck for the weakness. But Stas was not an assassin. He was a gladiator. An open challenge suited him best. The Dominus would die before the whole city. That was how the narrative should go.

Finally, finally, his aim was achieved. After too much time fighting too many watchers, the shadows pooled in the center of the plaza.

Stas grinned under his mask as that haunting bell tolled.

The lord and master of the city rose from the shadows. Its vile gaze turned to him, to his mask. Rage erupted from its cloaked form.

"Insignificant insect," the Dominus seethed. "You think to make a mockery of me? Do you mistake your worthlessness for skill? Your survival for achievement? You draw breath only because I did not bother to seek your death. You mean nothing to me."

"And yet, you came." Stas stood defiantly on the rooftop, looking down upon the raging lord of the city.

"That mask is a blight. The face of Phobos is a curse on the world. You cannot comprehend the horrors its bearers have wrought," the

Dominus growled. "But you are not Phobos. The gnat I slew was not Phobos. You are fools, aping greater men. Nothing but a boil to be excised. The mask alone draws my attention."

"I don't care for the opinions of a walking corpse, parasite," Stas said. Rage was to be cultivated in one's foes. If the Dominus possessed a lick of training, it would not have responded to his insults. "You claim the name Phobos belongs to greater men? Well, I know myself to be greater than you. I am Phobos. My predecessor, too, was Phobos, superior in all aspects to you." Phobos had been an honorless cur, but he had a noble purpose. The miserable get below him was no comparison.

"None are greater than me," the Dominus roared. "I have slain anyone who could pretend to be my peer. I am growth, perpetual. In this world, I am a god!" A wall of flesh exploded towards Stas's position. He *reflected* out of the way. The building he was standing on collapsed under a wave of twitching flesh.

"You are a monster," Stas declared. "So bleed and die like one."

Feddlebrine's dagger cut into the Dominus's nape, drawing a line of blood. There was no resistance to the blade, none of that impossible durability he had felt before. The dagger was a true marvel. If only he had had it against the chimera. The experience would have been far less harrowing.

Four grasping arms erupted from the monster's back, but Stas *reflected* away.

And so began their dance, this fight on patterned stone so like that on burning sand. Stas held his weapons proudly.

Between a shield that could block anything, a dagger that could cut anything, and the arcanum to move anywhere, the fight was firmly in his hands. The Dominus was enraged, and Stas was deft in avoiding the monster's flailing.

Eponine was right. The proper ending to this story was imminent.

316

Stas avoided the monster's disgusting swings, blocked its pillars of squirming flesh, cut through its writhing skin. He kept light on his feet and quick with his arms. He was feeling the flow of battle completely, a clarity of mind that made each action trivial.

Nicks and cuts made their way across the Dominus's stolen body, and Stas felt his elation rising with each one. His dagger shared in his glee, laughing at each close dodge, delighting in each cut. The dagger was a joy to wield, a quick favorite over that solemn shield.

He felt free in this fight, freer than he had been in a long time.

Stas went for yet another stab, severing what would be a tendon in the Dominus's arm.

A pillar of flesh rose from the stone road beneath him, catching him by surprise. Stas flew through the air and his head cracked against the solid marble of the bathhouse.

And, with the pain of the head injury, the clarity of the fight left him. Or perhaps clarity finally returned.

What was he doing? The question pounded in Stas's mind. What had he been thinking? The certainty that had suffused his being for the past day seemed strange and alien. The words that had been echoing through his head had silenced. What had he thought he was accomplishing?

Bereft of the confidence he'd had mere moments before, it was obvious now that the Dominus was unhindered by his attacks. The monster's flesh knitted itself back up even faster than he could induce new injuries. The deepest of wounds were endured without issue or pain. His grand efforts had achieved precisely nothing.

Stas had been pushing himself to his limit, a perfect dance that permitted no mistake. The Dominus had not. It swatted about with casual disdain, uncaring and without urgency.

"You are a pest," the Dominus grumbled. "I had expected some trick, some magic worth my interest. I have granted you so many opportunities. All you can do is blink about," the monster scoffed. "Do you believe that keeps you safe? Fool. There is nothing beyond my reach." The Dominus grinned a cruel grin. "Allow me to demonstrate."

The earth rumbled. The buildings shook. The street cracked. All around the Dominus a sea of flesh erupted.

Everywhere Stas could see the ground crumbled away revealing flesh. The grand forum was engulfed, demolished, consumed, rendered to simple debris before an inexorable tide of human meat and organs. Grasping arms and crying faces of hundreds, thousands of bodies flooded the city. The Gate, that magic portal to his home, shuddered and fell.

Stas watched in horror as hapless people who had failed to flee, watchers and civilians both, were overcome. They were pulled in screaming, eaten alive. Each form was torn apart and incorporated into the sea of flesh, melting into agonized terror.

In the distance great, blinking walls of the monster's arcanum rose. They pulled upwards and inward, tearing the city apart as they moved towards the center. And, in the center of this infinite flood of grotesqueries, the Dominus stood, bored. The death and destruction it wrought meant nothing to the monster.

In a single act, the lord of the city had trivialized Stas's rampage. The grandest district of the city died to the horror's whim, consumed by this grasping maw that blotted out the sky.

There was no escape from this. Stas could not *reflect* through it. Nor could he cut through the great thickness. The ground below was just as hostile as the ramparts that surrounded him. Nor could Stas hope to slay the Dominus before his arcanum devoured him. The only hope seemed to come from that ever-shrinking patch of sky above.

Stas was reminded of Phobos's first lesson, of the circle of fire. In this circle of flesh, only a single exit remained. And so Stas knew without a shadow of doubt it would be his doom if he took it. The

Dominus would be ready.

To go up was to die. To try to cut through was to die. To go down was to fruitlessly perish. To attack the Dominus was to accomplish nothing.

And yet, there was another direction. One that the Dominus would not expect. One that Stas had spent his life fearing.

Stas teleported to the Dominus and placed a hand on its fleshy back.

He then looked for his reflection, not within the sane mirrors of this world, but in one of the many, many chasms of the world. The reflection on the other side was pained, distorted, *unnerving*. Stas grasped it.

Then he, the Dominus, and that endless sea of flesh all *reflected*.

There was no arrival, because there was no place to arrive to. There was no light to see in this void, no sound to hear. There was only himself, the Dominus, and the stretching, twisting void.

They were alone. There was no body to experience this world, no mind to process it. There was no pain, because there was nothing to sense it. Space and thought and logic did not exist in this strange, distorted void. There were many things present, but Stas could not comprehend them without a mind. He could not scream without a body, without a voice. There was no room for these concepts in this impossible realm.

Stas could not see anything, because he had no eyes. But the *reflections* remained. They persisted even when the object did not.

The Dominus was no longer a man in this not space. Nor was it a monster. It lacked its shadows, its cloak, its annoyance, its power. All that remained was the flesh: that ravenous, cloying, lonely flesh that yearned to embrace all it encountered. The Dominus was massive, but there was no mass. It was the process, consuming, adapting, joining, embracing, growing eternal.

Stas observed his own reflection. But there was nothing to see.

319

Unlike the Dominus, he lacked flesh. The reflection of his body tore apart without the body to cast it. The skin peeled, and the mirrors that had been growing underneath for all those months burst forth.

He was the mirror, the process of reflection. There was no mind to it, no action to it. There was no happiness or anger or glory or fame or pride or hope or despair. No reason or care. There was no room for any of that, when there was so much here, where "here" could not be, so many things that would be alien in any sane world. The mask and the shield and the hook and the laughing little girl he held were wisps of themselves.

The only constant was reflection. It was the sole link between reality and this chasm. The mirrors remained. The reflections remained. Stas remained.

And Stas found the mirror he had used to arrive. He *reflected*. He fell into the plaza, that broken, ruined place. His body screamed as it existed once more.

The Dominus did not come back with him.

# Thirty-Five

Stas woke abruptly. His body was overwhelmingly stiff, the whole of it throbbing in pain. He didn't recognize the ceiling above him. He was lying in something soft, covered in something warm. He was lying in a bed, but not his own.

He tried to sit up. It was an endeavor, but he managed it eventually. His head pounded. It was hard to put his thoughts in order. Last he recalled, he had been unraveling in the void with the Dominus. Now, though ...

He was in a simple room with a large bed and a closed door.

There was a mirror on the wall. He caught sight of his reflection. He looked awful. His body was thin, ragged, emaciated. His skin was pale and bandaged intensely. His hair had grown long and unruly. His clothing was ragged. He could barely recognize his own reflection. But Stas knew reflections. The poor fellow in the mirror was his own image.

A voice seemed to call to him, and Stas turned in place towards it. Lying on a dresser beside him was Feddlebrine's dagger ... his dagger, he supposed. She seemed to cheer as his attention turned to her. Beside it was Phobos's mask ... his mask now. Enjolras's shield was propped up with them.

The fishhook was missing.

Stas inhaled, but his lungs did not cooperate. He kept to a shallower breath. His empty stomach churned. He felt the nausea, greater than ever.

Stas peeled away the bandages on his arm and flinched at the sight. The sheen had spread completely. His skin had broken, replaced by mirrors, just as it had been that delirious void outside the world. The scars of his arcanum were deep. The limb felt dead. Carefully, he attempted to manipulate his fingers. They moved slowly but offered no sensation.

His nausea grew. He felt as sick as he looked. Stas carefully reapplied the bandages as much as he was able. He had no desire to see the mirror that used to be his flesh.

Trapped in his body, Stas's mind drifted to his arcanum. He gazed upon the mirrors, looking out through the reflections through the small gap in the window to the city beyond. He could not recognize the site.

It was a ruin, smoldering, crumbling. Bodies bled in the street; corpses rotted. Stas did not know where this wretched district might be, but it was far from the ruined forum. There was no explanation for its miserable state.

Stas heard faint footsteps. The door creaked open. Eponine walked through carrying a bowl of soup. She looked tired, ragged. Her clothes lacked their normal impeccable shape, and it seemed she had lost some weight. Her long dark hair looked frayed. She looked unhealthy, though not to his own degree.

Her eyes widened. She blinked twice as if to confirm the sight. From the bags, it looked like she had been troubled by a lack of sleep. "You're awake." She spoke softly as if to taste the words. Her expression shifted into a soft smile. "I can hardly believe it. It's amazing." She set the soup on the dresser next to her. "Honestly, I was losing hope. I thought you were never going to wake."

She looked so relieved at that.

"How ..." His voice rasped and turned into a cough.

Eponine grabbed the soup and strode forward. "Here." She held a spoon out. "It's not much, but it's something. It'll be good for your throat."

Stas flinched. It was galling to be treated as an invalid. But his body rejected his needs. He allowed Eponine to spoon-feed him. After a few bites, he managed to get enough control to grasp the spoon for himself. She held the bowl, but he could at least feed himself.

After eating the thin broth and the few vegetables within, Stas swallowed, and tried to speak again. "How long was I asleep?"

"It's been a month."

A month ... if he was alive for so long the Dominus must have perished. A triumph by most accounts, but Stas felt hollow.

"What happened?"

Eponine looked away. "You should rest," she said instead of answering. "You need to recover your strength."

"You aren't telling me something," Stas said. "What happened?"

Eponine looked down. Her tired eyes refused to meet Stas's own. "The city's gone to shit. I've kept you safe and hidden here with my arcanum. But the city isn't pretty right now." Eponine shook her head sadly.

Stas couldn't understand. "What? How?" Defeating the Dominus was supposed to pave the way for a good ending. The threat of the monster was what was holding them back. Enjolras had a plan for a better future, a method to ensure it came about. How could anything go wrong?

Eponine sighed. "After you defeated the Dominus, there was a lot of confusion. People didn't know what to do, or how to react. There was some worry that the Senate might take advantage of it, make a martyr of the Dominus or something. Enjolras ..." There was heat when she spoke his name. "Enjolras decided that the best thing was to strike first. He decided to tell everyone about the Senate's plan. He didn't hide anything."

Stas felt his heart still.

"The plebeians reacted poorly. There were riots. Attacks on patrician neighborhoods. Looting. Vandalism. It wasn't long before the richer plebs were targeted too. Most of all, it was about food. Granaries and shops were sacked. People turned on their fellows to conserve their meager scraps. The gangs were already organized, so they were able to take control. And the whole mess gave the Senate time to act."

Eponine clenched her fists.

"The Senate denied everything, blamed everything on the gangs, on 'terrorists.' They preached about how they and the Dominus had stood for peace and security. They fed people, raised an army. It looked like they would win. Then the senators turned on each other and everything fell back into a mess."

Eponine looked down miserably, the exhaustion clear in her voice. "It's chaos out there. Everyone is fighting everyone. The storehouses were ransacked and the farms were burned. And some fucker released a bunch of chimeras. It might have been Macro, before he got decapitated. Or maybe it was some moron who thought it was a good idea."

She inhaled, and her voice flattened. "Right now, it's a bit of a stalemate. The gangs control most of the city, and waste their time fighting each other. The Senate has its districts, but they've broken into factions ... Enjolras and Sanson were trying to carve out their own little fief with Libertas. I left before I learned how successful they were. I'm not going to have anything to do with those bastards any more."

Numbness. That was Stas's overwhelming feeling. Every word from Eponine's lips sapped his strength. The pain in his body was irrelevant; he could barely notice it any more. He could barely notice anything any more as the last bits of color seemed to drain from the world.

Stas forced himself to sit up. He pushed himself to the edge of the bed facing away from Eponine. The aches in his muscles didn't matter. The nausea didn't matter. His head was a fog, his thoughts a low, inaudible hum.

"The city has gone to shit, Stas." Her voice wavered. "Everything went wrong. And it's all Enjolras's fault. I can't … it wasn't supposed to go like this." Her voice cracked. "Run away with me, Stas."

Stas said nothing.

"When you recover, I mean. I can keep nursing you, protect you until you are better. But when you are … let's leave this damn place. Just you and me. Together."

"There is nowhere to run to." Stas spoke blandly. "The Dominus broke the Gate. We can't go through it." Stas reached for his dagger. The blade seemed to trill at his touch. The mask beside it was cold and dark and dead. He brushed his single flesh hand across the wood. The mask slid over his face easily. It seemed to fit better now.

"It doesn't have to be to the provinces. We can leave the city. Go beyond it, find something for ourselves out there, so long as it isn't here."

"There is nothing outside the city." Stas had seen that for himself. In some ways that endless wasteland was worse than the void he had left the Dominus in. The void, at least, never promised to be anything else. It was inhospitable and alien, but it was supposed to be that way. The wasteland was dead, a crumbling corpse of a world that should have been fruitful.

There was no hope in that wasteland. No escape outside the city.

"Please," Eponine begged. "Something has to work. There has to be something, some way to escape this. I don't even care what it is, as long as we are together. We can figure something out." Her voice hitched. "If … if that means going back to Libertas, I would accept that if it was with you."

Stas remained silent. He gazed at Enjolras's shield and felt its gleaming metal. The perfect sheen seemed dull to him now; the symbol on its face looked farcical.

He picked it up, keeping his back turned to the distraught woman behind him.

"No." He spoke quietly and *reflected* away.

He landed on the roof of a partially collapsed building and fell to his knees in pain, coughing. Slowly, very carefully, he brought himself up to his feet. Taking a few deep breaths, he *reflected* again.

The city was unrecognizable. Parts of its skyline remained, but it was hard to orient himself. Stas *reflected* with no destination in mind, simply taking it all in. The destruction the Dominus had wrought was a minuscule fraction of the damage he witnessed: buildings torn apart, streets cracked, barricades hastily assembled in the corridors. The bodies were a constant, as was the smoldering ash.

Stas *reflected* into an alley where he found dark black splotches of some strange substance seeping through the brick. A decapitated body lay among the ooze, being digested before his eyes. The distinct odor of a chimera assaulted his nose.

Stas *reflected* away quickly.

There were people still, huddling in broken houses, desperate, hungry. One street was cordoned off by a line of golems. The stone-faced machines waited in unblinking silence, wielding swords and bows. Another district was guarded by a company of watchers. The bird-faced men looked haggard, but vigilant.

Stas avoided both of those districts.

In his wandering, he discovered Libertas's symbol painted onto the side of a building.

Armed men patrolled this district, lacking any uniform. Barricades blocked off most of the streets, isolating the city blocks. Some enterprising fellow seemed to have created a functioning gate out of the rubble.

There were people here, as there were everywhere. They lined up in great numbers before a marked building, under the watchful eyes of twitchy guards. At the head of the line Stas could see Odette, doling out simple loaves of bread and small cups of soup. Beside her, glaring at all who approached, was the pockmarked face of Sanson.

In the center of this district was another walled-off area. Buildings had been toppled, with dirt spread over the cleared plot. In it, simple grains and vegetables grew, and barrels full of clean water stood at the ready. This section of makeshift farmland served as a district within the district, overseen by a compartment of visibly armed guards.

In many ways they looked the same as the watchers, or the golems. It all looked pointless ... interchangeable.

Stas kept himself out of sight. He couldn't bear to stay in the district any longer. The numbness in his mind was overwhelming. He *reflected* and gently placed the soul-crafted shield in one of the district's alleyways. The gleaming metal would be discovered quickly.

Stas could not say what he was any more: gladiator, revolutionary, criminal, victim. But he was not a thief. Enjolras's shield was a weight he refused to bear.

Stas *reflected* out of the district.

There was no end to Stas's wandering. The whole of the city was before him. The four arenas stood, strongholds of the Senate's power. The hippodrome had been converted into farmland, heavily guarded by golems.

Stas observed, alone with his thoughts. Nobody seemed to notice him or care. He watched a battle in the streets end with three deaths. Nobody seemed to care about that either.

At some point, as the sun was setting in the sky, Stas found his way to the ruins of the forums, and the palatial estate beside it. The gates that had guarded the estate had fallen, crushed by the Dominus's waves of flesh. The grand palace had been burnt down, its treasures certainly looted. The schools that had lined the estate had been left as empty wrecks.

Stas found himself before Ludo's school. It was a husk of itself. The tasteful building was in tatters. The gardens that surrounded it were trampled over. Parts of the buildings Stas had known as home had collapsed into rubble.

And yet a single individual remained within. Ludo sat at his broken desk, writing upon torn papers with a pen that dripped with a very muddy ink. The man was emaciated, but his clothing was clean and his face was well-shaven. It was a stark contrast.

Stas *reflected* into Ludo's office and stood before the lanista.

"Do you have an appointment?" the man asked without looking up from his work.

"An appointment?" Stas wondered. "Of course not. How could I have an appointment?"

"I would not expect it, since my staff is unfortunately unavailable," Ludo replied. "But that does not excuse the rudeness of bursting into my office without one."

"Hardly an office when it lacks a wall," Stas commented, noting the open air of the outside.

"It serves its purpose." Ludo spoke dryly. "And I would insist you leave if you do not have business with me."

Stas felt his annoyance at the man push through his numbness. "Am I actually interrupting? What could you possibly be doing?"

"I am settling this upcoming month's budget, if you must know. My school is a business, and it is important to have my ledgers in order."

"A budget? How can you have a budget with your school in the shape it is? Do you imagine there is a need for games with the city like this? Is there even anything to buy?" Stas looked around at the deserted building. "Do you even have any students to send to fight on those damned sands?"

"The budget is particularly simple at this time, but that doesn't mean it isn't important." Ludo did not bother hiding the annoyance in his voice. "Surplus or deficit. Fortune or misfortune. Consistency is a virtue when it comes to one's business. The circumstances of the world cannot change the value of one's actions."

"You don't have a business," Stas retorted in frustration. "The city is dead, killing itself over the remaining scraps. Do you not understand this?"

Ludo looked up. Stas caught his tired eyes through Phobos's mask. "I am not blind. But what does it matter? Perhaps it will all settle and there will be a market for games again. Or perhaps it won't, and the city will die as you say. All of that is beyond my power, unlike my business. A man might be crippled, but that doesn't make exercise less valuable. The tragedy of the city cannot diminish the purpose of my work. If it mattered before, it still matters now."

"Where are your students?" Stas did not hide the harshness of his rebuke. "What happened to them?"

Ludo shrugged. "I do not know. I would have preferred if they had remained as our contracts dictated, but one cannot control other people." Ludo rubbed his forehead and sighed. "Are you here to kill me or rob me? If so, I would ask that you get on with it. Otherwise, please leave my office. I have work to do."

Stas spat, his disgust for the lanista overcoming his numbness. This was what the man had always been, in the end. This was the insanity beneath his virtue.

Stas *reflected* away.

# Epilogue

Soft footsteps broke Stas from his morose contemplation. Inhaling deeply, he allowed himself to fall from his perch. He landed gently, having *reflected* down the short distance before gravity had a chance to make a mess of things. The magic was almost a thoughtless action at this point.

He did not bother hiding himself. He had no need. It wasn't like he was here to sneak out as he had done so many times before.

And so Stas found himself, once again, face to face with the Mad Monk in the Dominus's hidden statue garden. It figured. After all, nobody else ever seemed to come to this place, but for this nameless madman. Even the looters hadn't vandalized the statues, and they had hit everywhere else on the palatial grounds.

"Hm," Stas grunted, finding his voice still sore from the smoke of the smoldering city, "it seems you managed to survive."

Stas hadn't put much thought into the monk's state. That the man had lived through chaos was both surprising and not.

"Indeed," the monk acknowledged. He sounded healthy. Undamaged. Stas found himself on guard. "I am known to do such. Your own survival is more noteworthy. I would never have been so bold as to challenge the Dominus."

Bold. That was a charitable way to describe it. "I'm surprised you know about that."

"I try to keep abreast of important matters, regardless of circumstances. Especially when said matters led to circumstances like this."

The man gestured vaguely.

For a moment, rage overcame morosity. "This was not my fault," Stas hissed. He had made mistakes in his time here, true, but he refused to be blamed for the death of the city.

"No, it was not," the monk said. "Far too many hands were at play in this tragedy for any one individual to claim responsibility. But your actions did contribute. Regardless of anything else, the Dominus was a stabilizing influence for the city."

Stas's hand traced across the smooth face of his mask. Memories of the sea of writhing flesh that aped at being a man burned into his mind. "The Dominus was a monster." He felt his dagger chirping in agreement, offering comfort.

"Physically? Perhaps. Living on a dead world is not good for the body. I would expect, if you too live for a few centuries, your own arcanum would mutate in a similar manner. Morally? I've had a great many disagreements with the Dominus in my tenure, but it is not my place to make judgments. I simply work with what I have towards what I view as best."

"And how is that working out for you?" Stas scoffed. "The city dead and its remnants fighting over the scraps?"

"The situation is far from optimal, I would agree, but I do not consider this a failure case. Some level of suffering was, perhaps, inevitable. It is a simple matter of energy: life is not sustainable in a dead world. We can only scavenge for as long as we can. And perhaps, as a result of this cataclysm, we may yet be able to scavenge for much longer. A stronger and better society with less risk of starvation is still a possibility, I would say."

"Didn't you object to the Senate's planned slaughter? Or was that just an act?"

"I did not fundamentally object to the culling of the population if it would properly address the problem. But the senators were more concerned with maintaining their wealth than with effective policy. It would not have been my preferred solution, but I can see the reason for it."

The casual declaration irritated Stas. Or perhaps he felt as if he were supposed to be irritated. "Maybe you are also a monster. Maybe I should kill you too."

"Perhaps." The monk spoke as though he were commenting on the weather. "Though I don't believe it would be of any aid to anyone. If you wish to slay monsters, one of the late Lord Macro's chimeras has taken residence in the former southern slums. The residents that remain would be grateful for its removal."

A voice in his head that sounded like Enjolras agreed that would be a true and noble thing to do. The dagger at his side seemed to agree, thinking it fun. He squashed both voices down, hard. Stas sighed and sat on a marble bench. The Mad Monk took a seat across from him.

Silence resumed.

Eventually it was too much for Stas. "What was your preferred solution? What did you want to happen?"

"'Want' is a strange term," the monk mused. "Every possible policy was a matter of mitigating fundamental facts. Food production is unsustainable. The cyclical nature of the famines makes matters worse. That human sacrifice can be employed to draw out the process leads to perverse incentives. The whole situation is undesirable." His tone remained bland as he spoke, despite the morbidity of his statements.

He continued. "Lady Hirtius had a novel goal of incentivized sterilization and suicide. In the ideal case, it could have allowed for a slow, gentle euthanasia of the city. Of the options, I found this the most agreeable." He adopted a small, wry grin. "It is amusing that such a simple solution had not occurred to me, but Lady Hirtius was an exemplar in many ways, may she rest in peace."

Stas closed his eyes and exhaled. "If that's what you wanted, why did you support Libertas? Or was somebody else Enjolras's mysterious contact?"

"Did you just figure that out now?" He seemed amused by the comment, more than by anything else in the conversation so far. "As I said, it is a matter of mitigation. There were a number of outcomes I would have found acceptable, and I worked towards all of them. Lady Hirtius's plan was just one of them. A more impartial decimation of the city was another. Allowing a revolutionary group to seize control of the government was a third. In the initial days of a new government, it would have been simple enough to ensure that enough enemies of the new state died to stave off the current famine, and the resulting government could be better placed to deal with the next." His lips turned to a frown. "I must admit I am disappointed Enjolras was unsuccessful in seizing power. I had thought him more competent than this."

At this, Stas felt the need to laugh. "If that was your plan, it never would have worked. Libertas is the perfect revolution. It can never die, never be quashed, never end. No different from the magic tools you described to me. And what is a victory but another type of ending?"

The Mad Monk blinked. "A soul-crafted movement? Fascinating. I did not think such a thing was possible. But it would explain a great deal." He bowed his head. "I must thank you, Stas. Your insight will save me a lot of wasted effort in the challenges ahead."

"Challenges ahead?" Stas scoffed. "The city is dead. The Gate is destroyed. People are killing each other over the last stockpiles. There is nothing to do but die."

"Quite a morbid assessment, but I disagree. With the reduced population from this ... civil war, shall we call it, the restraining factor on food is no longer production, but distribution. The labor force remaining is large enough to grow and process a new batch of crops, if the blood of the deceased can be harvested in time. If one of the current factions emerges victorious and properly puts the city to work, I imagine society will resume in as little as a year. A reborn city to last another few centuries, lacking the flaws of the old."

"No wonder they call you mad." Stas huffed. "In this fantasy of yours, do you imagine yourself ruling this decrepit husk?"

"Traditionally, that honor would go to the one who defeated the prior ruler."

Stas gaped. "What?" The mask on his face seemed to cling tighter. The horrifying thought brought a wave of nausea from his stomach to his throat. "No. Absolutely not. I refuse." The dagger at his side seemed to laugh.

The Mad Monk sighed. "A pity. A strong, unifying individual with a semblance of legitimacy would have made this upcoming matter much simpler. And since Libertas is not an option as you have explained, I must select the best among the former senatorial factions to lead. Far from ideal ... Are you sure I cannot convince you otherwise?"

Stas glared at the madman.

"Well, I have no desire to force you. Perhaps it is for the best. I suspect the Dominus is not as lost as you might hope. Should they return in the coming years or decades, discovering someone else has taken their title would certainly enrage them."

Stas shook his head, the dagger at his side burning at the thought. He felt it trying to leap to his hand. "No. Impossible," he said, as much to it as to the man before him. "Those reflections ... they're not a good place, not something anyone can survive." Shifting, grasping, wrong. They threatened to engulf his sight once more, aware of them as he was.

"Hm. The Dominus has survived many lethal afflictions over the years. But I will accept your expertise on this matter," he said. "If you will not accede to becoming the new ruler, I would request something else of you, if you would allow it."

Stas said nothing, but the monk seemed to take it as permission to continue.

"Even in a situation as chaotic as this, rumors manage to flow. It is a human point of excellence, the seeking of information. When one asks what happened to the Dominus, many names surface: the Man in the Blue Mask. The Devil Himself. Libertas Incarnate. The Champion of the People. Some even acknowledge Stas the Gladiator, though it is a less known and less popular explanation, for obvious reasons. That you have been absent this past month only exacerbates the rumors. People do love a good mystery."

In a past life, Stas would have bristled that he was not being recognized for his deeds. In the here and now, he found he didn't care the slightest. "Get to the point.".

"The uncertainty is useful for me in crafting the narrative that would be most beneficial to the city. As you are not interested in stepping into the title, I would ask that you instead step away from it entirely: disappear from the story so that it may best be molded unhindered."

The words hung in the air. Stas traced the painted eye of his mask. A stabbing pain from the dagger jolted him from his consideration.

"No," he forced himself to say. "I will not die for your convenience."

"I would not ask you to," the monk said. "Rather, I would ask you to leave this world."

"The Gate is destroyed."

"Indeed, for good and ill. But it is not the only method of travel. The Dominus came before it existed. A select few have been pulled before, when it was important to escape notice. Returning you to the world of your birth is possible, with aid from the other side. I am willing to arrange it for you, should you accept."

Stas hadn't even known to consider it, going back to the provinces, that world he had so happily escaped. That dull, boring, empty village that was so different from here.

As if sensing his thoughts, the Mad Monk continued. "You should know that your birth world is much bigger than the tiny corner the Dominus commanded. Many would happily welcome you with open arms, knowing what you have done."

A world ... a new one or old one to explore. A new one to fail and disappoint. Did Stas have any reason to believe it would be any better?

"Alternatively, my previous offer is still open. If you wish to join me in making the best of this dying world, I would be more than happy to have you."

Again, a voice much like Enjolras cajoled him, extolling the good he could do here. This time, though, the dagger at his side stayed quiet.

In truth, he had no reason to believe the other world would be any worse. Here the dagger hummed. The blade's certainty solidified his own.

"Send me away, then. There is nothing for me in this miserable world."

* * *

When Stas opened his eyes, he was greeted by piercing blue skies and gentle slopes of verdant grass. A soft, white cloud lazily drifted overhead. On a neighboring hill, a flock of sheep leisurely grazed, unbothered by visible enclosure. The soft cry of birdsong, so long missing, chattered in his ear.

Beside him, his dagger marveled at the dandelions scattered in the grass. They waved in the soft breeze.

Stas inhaled deeply. The air felt clean, full, vibrant. The warmth of the sun was kind against his skin. The weight of the world had vanished from his shoulders. His muscles groaned in relief.

For the first time in ages, his stomach felt clear. The ever present nausea of the last year was nowhere to be found.

Stas unlatched his mask, and let the cool wind dance across his bare face. The mask fell from his grip.

He fell back to the ground, to the soft, dew-coated grass of the hill. His dagger trilled, lying beside him, beside the mask.

And, with a smile on his face, Stas fell into a restful slumber.

Made in the USA
Las Vegas, NV
01 October 2023

78391585R00206